# A Cup of
# Silver Linings

# A Cup of Silver Linings

*A Novel*

## Karen Hawkins

**THORNDIKE PRESS**
A part of Gale, a Cengage Company

Copyright © 2021 by Karen Hawkins.
Dove Pond #2.
Thorndike Press, a part of Gale, a Cengage Company.

**LIBRARY OF CONGRESS CIP DATA ON FILE.
CATALOGUING IN PUBLICATION FOR THIS BOOK
IS AVAILABLE FROM THE LIBRARY OF CONGRESS.**

ISBN-13: 978-1-4328-9134-3 (hardcover alk. paper)

Published in 2021 by arrangement with Gallery Books, a Division of Simon & Schuster, Inc.

Printed in Mexico
Print Number: 01        Print Year: 2022

To my sister Robin,
who left us far too early.
Every now and then, I read your old
emails, and they still make me laugh.

And to everyone who has lost
a sister, brother, mother, father,
spouse, child, or friend:
If I could, I'd give each and every one of
you a comfy lap blanket, a cup of hot
chocolate, and a great big hug.

# CHAPTER 1
## ELLEN

Standing beside her daughter's open grave, Ellen Foster dug her fingernails into her palms as the annoying sound of a kazoo wafted through the wintry, pine-scented air.

A kazoo.

At a funeral.

Worse, the kazoo wasn't playing anything remotely appropriate, like "The Lord Is My Shepherd" or "Amazing Grace," but instead ABBA's "Dancing Queen."

Ellen tried to ignore the other mourners who were silently lip-synching the song as they swayed to the music. Safely hidden behind her large sunglasses, she closed her aching eyes for a long moment. It was all so tasteless. But then, everything Julie had planned for her own funeral was, so far, bizarre and uniquely tasteless. *Julie would have loved it. She was always good at irking me. Frightfully so.*

Ellen pressed her lips firmly together,

7

holding back both a torrent of tears and the deep desire to shout a curse. She'd never uttered a curse in her entire life. Not once. But right now, it was all she could do to keep it inside. She was discovering that grief was a devious beast, a bitter mixture of loss and regret that ripped its way through her heart not once but over and over again, leaving her exposed and furious.

Two elderly women wearing *Game of Thrones* T-shirts under their open coats stepped up to Julie's shiny black casket, which had been painted with outrageous red glitter flames along each side and signed with Julie's familiar swooshing signature. With military precision, the women unfolded a huge dragon flag and draped it over the casket, nodding at the preacher as they rejoined the other mourners.

The purple dragon flag fluttered in the chilly January breeze, one heavily lashed eye seemingly locked on Ellen. The kazoo began playing once more, the lilting notes of "Macarena" drifting into the air.

Ellen cast a baleful gaze at the sky. *That's not funny, Julie. Not even a little.*

The echo of Julie's hearty, unchecked laugh rang through Ellen's mind, so immediate and clear that for one glorious second, hope flared and she instinctively looked around, searching the small crowd for her daughter. The almost-instant realization that the laugh was just a memory was followed by bone-crushing disappointment. *I'll never hear that laugh again.*

Chest aching, Ellen silently sucked in a deep, shaky breath. *I don't have time for this. I should be thinking about how I'm going to help Kristen. My granddaughter deserves a happy life, and I'm going to make sure she gets one.*

To accomplish Project K, as Ellen had labeled it in her Louis Vuitton Noir Epi leather agenda just this morning, she had to accomplish three Action Items. *Focus on the Action Items,* she told herself as the preacher started tapping his toe to the kazoo's hum. *Kristen is all that matters.*

Ellen closed her eyes and ignored everything going on around her.

*Item One: Make it through the funeral without crying.*

So far, so good, mainly thanks to the heavy cover provided by her sunglasses. All she had to do was fight her way through the next fifteen or so minutes, and she could move on.

*Item Two: Fix up Julie's house and put it on the market.*

That would be a big one, as, from what

Ellen could tell, Julie's creaky old Queen Anne–style house hadn't been updated since the '70s. Worse, now that Julie had lived in it for the past ten years, every closet and corner was piled high with kitsch. *All of it has to go.*

That the house wasn't in the best of shape and was stuffed with useless craft-quality items wasn't a surprise. It was just one example in a long line of examples of Julie's refusal to grow up. Not only had she become an artist rather than get a real job, but she'd also deliberately had a child without the benefit of either a father or a steady income. *Poor Kristen. The opportunities she's missed — I can't bear to think about it.*

Fortunately for her granddaughter, Ellen was ready and able to handle things from here on out, and the money made from the house sale would go straight into a college fund.

*Which leaves Item Three: Get Kristen out of this backward town and to my home in Raleigh where she can begin living a normal, orderly life.* Of all the Action Items, that one would be the trickiest. Ellen slanted a glance to her side where Kristen stood, loudly puffing out "Macarena" on her neon-green kazoo. Ellen tried not to gaze too long at the teenager's purple-streaked hair or the small diamond that twinkled in her nose.

*Don't stare.* Ellen jerked her gaze away from Kristen, away from the dragon flag–draped casket, and instead focused on the trees in the distance. Ellen had to proceed carefully where her granddaughter was concerned, as they barely knew one another thanks to Julie and her stubbornness. But with some time and effort, Ellen was convinced she and Kristen would grow closer and finally have the relationship they should have had all along.

Kristen tilted her kazoo to a jauntier angle and finished "Macarena" to a boisterous round of applause.

Ellen bit back the urge to snap out, *This is supposed to be a funeral!* Although it would be almost impossible to tell by how these supposed mourners were dressed. Behind the safety of her dark sunglasses, she eyed the residents of Dove Pond, who wore a wide range of mismatched, garishly colored clothes, just as the handwritten funeral invitation had requested.

She flinched at the memory of that invitation. When she'd found it in her mailbox just three days ago, she'd thought it a horrible joke. Julie's flowing script had adorned bright construction paper, breezily inviting her mother to "the funeral of all funerals,

11

date TBA." The invitation had requested that everyone wear bright colors, as Julie didn't wish to leave the earth in a parade of dull black or gray. She'd also added that she wanted no weeping, as dying wasn't really so hard "once one got over the surprise of it."

It had been ten years since Ellen had heard from her daughter, who'd stormed out of Ellen's world the same way she'd entered — screaming and red-faced, refusing to be held or told what to do. After their last argument, Julie had cut her mother from her and Kristen's lives. Ellen had been horrified when Julie had refused to allow her to even see her granddaughter, saying she didn't want Kristen's mind "polluted" by Ellen's "stuffy views."

In those first few months, Ellen had reached out repeatedly, desperate to see her granddaughter, but her calls had gone unanswered. As the silent weeks expanded to even more silent months, Ellen had decided to give Julie some space, thinking her daughter would come around more quickly if she didn't feel pressured. After that, Ellen had only called on birthdays and holidays . . . . calls that had gone to voice mail so often that — as time wore on — she'd eventually stopped even that.

Which was why Ellen hadn't taken the invitation to her daughter's future funeral seriously. Ellen had never understood Julie's sense of humor, so she'd just assumed it was some sort of cruel joke and had tossed the invitation into the closest trash can.

But then, the very next day, Kristen had called, crying. In between Kristen's hiccupping sobs and broken words, Ellen had learned that Julie had died after a two-year fight with breast cancer.

The invitation was real, and Julie was gone.

Stunned, Ellen had numbly assured her granddaughter she'd be there as soon as possible and hung up. Time had slammed to a halt and for some reason, Ellen had found herself staring down at her feet. She'd been wearing a pair of blue Manolo Blahnik Decebalo pumps with gold trim, adorned with large crystal brooches. If she closed her eyes now, she could still see her long, narrow feet in those shoes while tears she didn't even know she was crying fell onto the blue velvet, shimmering in the late-afternoon sun, brighter than the sparkling brooches.

She'd since thrown the shoes away because she couldn't look at them without remembering what had happened next.

She'd let out a moan like a wounded tiger and had dropped to her knees, desperately digging through the trash, looking for the invitation. When her fingers had closed over the discarded paper, her tears had turned into sobs, her pain tinged a bitter blue from the impersonal tone of the invitation. The truth hurt — that even while dying, Julie hadn't bothered to reach out to her mother.

Ellen had sat on the floor surrounded by trash as she hugged the ridiculous piece of construction paper, weeping for the daughter she'd lost and for the relationship she'd always hoped for, but now knew she would never have.

Eventually Ellen had run out of tears. So she'd done as she always had whenever she faced a problem: she'd picked herself up, dried her tears, closed the door on her too-raw emotions, and made a list of things that needed to be done. She'd taken time off work and packed for her trip, pausing now and then to add to her to-do list. As she did so, her sadness and fury grew. Once again Julie had withheld something precious from Ellen, her right to say goodbye to her one and only child. Ellen had been left standing on an emotional precipice, alone and empty.

A cool breeze rippled the dragon flag, and Ellen tugged her black wool coat tighter, catching Kristen's questioning gaze. Ellen realized her expression must be fury-tight, so she forced her mouth to curve into what she hoped was a comforting smile.

Kristen didn't look convinced. She turned her attention back to the preacher, the diamond stud in her nose sparkling in the late-afternoon sun. It was painfully obvious that Julie had allowed her daughter all the excesses she'd craved as a child, and Ellen shuddered to think what damage had already been done.

As if she could hear her grandmother's thoughts, Kristen hunched her shoulders against the breeze, causing her red-and-purple kimono to flap around her knees. Earlier today, as they'd gotten ready to attend the service, Ellen had balked at the sight of Kristen wearing the garment, but the teenager had flatly refused to change, saying she and her mother had picked out the kimono during Julie's final week.

*Final week.* Ellen's throat tightened. She hoped and prayed Julie hadn't suffered. *Please, no. Julie, why didn't you call me? I would have come. I would have helped.*

Fresh tears burned Ellen's eyes, and she furiously blinked them away behind her sunglasses. She would not cry. *Would. Not.*

The reverend, a round man who looked

sweaty even on a chilly January afternoon, smiled at Kristen before he launched into his opening. "My friends, we are not here to mourn the loss of resident artist and beloved town member Julie Foster but rather to celebrate the beauty she added to our lives by sharing her artwork, her smile, her life, and her lovely daughter, Kristen. Julie was a warm person. A generous person. A vibrant person. We will all miss her dearly." He faltered a bit as his gaze brushed by Ellen.

Ellen wondered what Julie had told people about their contentious relationship but decided it was best she didn't know. Still, she couldn't help noticing the uncertain glances cast her way, both curious and faintly disapproving. Had Julie complained about her, or were they upset Ellen wasn't weeping like a broken doll? They didn't know her if they expected a public display. When she wept, it was in private, away from prying, judgmental eyes.

Ellen's restless gaze swept over the residents of Dove Pond. She recognized a few of them from the five years she and Julie had lived here after the divorce. During the day, while Julie was in school, Ellen had been fighting her way to the top of an architectural firm in Asheville, where she'd overseen a number of complex commercial rehab projects. In those days, getting Julie to the bus stop on time had been a struggle, and Ellen could still see her daughter dashing out of the house, her thick blond hair uncombed, her book bag half open, her socks mismatched as she ran to meet the school bus, which was usually honking urgently from the street. That was Julie in a nutshell. She'd rushed through life underprepared and thoughtless, causing her organized and orderly mother decades of worry and concern. And now, for all of Julie's troublesome and rebellious ways, she was gone.

*Forever.*

Ellen's stomach ached as if someone had punched her. This was not how things were supposed to end. She and Julie were supposed to overcome their issues. They were supposed to become close — friends, even — working together to make Kristen's life better.

Ellen's eyes filled with tears yet again, so she took a deep breath and focused on the reverend, who had just asked Ava Dove to come forward and read. Ellen watched the young blond woman make her way from the crowd, a small book in her hands. Ellen disliked the Dove sisters almost as much as

17

she disliked this funeral. The entire town admired the Doves, and some even believed the seven sisters possessed "special" abilities, which was beyond ridiculous. During the drive over, Ellen had been horrified to hear Kristen say how much she loved working for Ava Dove. From some of the things Kristen had said over the past few days, it was obvious she believed the specialty teas Ava made from the flowers and herbs she grew in her greenhouses could cure a number of ills, including arthritis, heart palpitations, and even broken hearts. Ellen had had to fight to keep her lip from curling in disdain.

The Dove Family Nonsense, as Ellen thought of it, was exactly the sort of fairy tale–ish, new age baloney Julie had loved and had apparently fed to an impressionable Kristen. To accomplish Action Item Three, Ellen would have to disentangle her granddaughter from the town, which meant dissolving her close relationship with Ava Dove. That wouldn't be an easy task, as Kristen worked almost every day after school with Ava, who was planning on opening a tearoom this coming spring. Kristen positively glowed when she talked about it.

Ellen narrowly eyed Ava where she stood beside the preacher, ready to speak. She wore horribly inappropriate purple coveralls under a mustard-yellow Carhartt coat with a bright patch on one front pocket that read AVA DOVE'S LANDSCAPING AND GOURMET SPECIALTY TEAS.

*Ridiculous. Am I the only person who understands the proper attire for a funeral?*

Ava cleared her throat. "Julie and I became close this past year during her illness, and I consider her and Kristen family." Ava's pale gray-green gaze found Kristen's, and they smiled at each other, sending a twinge of jealousy through Ellen.

"Julie asked me to share a passage from her favorite book." Ava opened the book, removed a bright pink Post-it, and began reading. " 'Kama is the enjoyment of appropriate objects by the five senses of hearing, feeling, seeing, tasting, and smelling, assisted by the mind together with the soul.' "

Of course Julie would have some sort of ridiculous Far Eastern babble read at her funeral.

Kristen whispered, "Recognize the book?"

Ellen shook her head.

Kristen smirked. "It's the *Kama Sutra.*"

Ellen wondered if a person could burst into flames with mortification. If it had been physically possible, she was certain she

19

would have already done so long before now.

An odd noise came from Kristen. Ellen cut her granddaughter a sharp look and caught the teen attempting to smother a laugh, looking so much like her mother that Ellen's heart stuttered a beat. In that grin was a streak of pure rebellion, the same streak that had pushed Julie to run away from home at the tender age of seventeen, beginning the worst years of Ellen's life. And now, there it was, on Kristen's face. For the first time since Ellen had arrived in Dove Pond, a sliver of fear pierced her soul. *Please, God, don't let us go down the same road Julie and I traveled. I can't lose Kristen, too. I can't. I just can't.*

From across the grave, Ava continued reading, " '. . . without becoming the slave of his passions, will obtain success in everything he may do.' " She closed the book, a misty smile quivering. "So true."

Everyone nodded, wiping their eyes and sniffling.

Aware of Kristen's critical gaze, Ellen forced herself to murmur, "Wonderful." *Wonderful that it's over.*

Ava handed the book to her sister Sarah, who'd quietly come to stand beside her. Although Sarah was five years younger, she looked enough like Ava to be her twin. The younger Dove sister wore a flowing, multi-colored maxi dress under a long blue coat, which clashed with her bright orange sneakers.

People in this strange little town thought Sarah was a "book charmer," which would be laughable if it wasn't so pathetic. They thought she could talk to books and — more ridiculous yet — books could talk back, telling her which people they'd like to visit. Ellen supposed such a skill, *if* it existed, would be useful to Sarah, who was the town librarian. *All the Doves think they're so special. Well, they're not. They're strange, that's what they are. Every one of them.*

She wondered briefly where the other Dove sisters and their mother were. Perhaps, tired of the strangeness of this tiny town, they'd moved away. *Which would be completely understandable.*

Sarah patted the book and favored the group of mourners with a far-too-cheerful smile. "Julie asked me to set this book aside at the library in case any of you would like to check it out."

"So kind," the preacher said. "Thank you for that reading, Ava. And, Sarah, thank you for making the book available. After that lovely excerpt, I'm sure a lot of us will be checking out the *Kama Sutra.*" He beamed

21

around the group. "I met with Julie and Kristen as they planned this service, and I was impressed with their determination to bring joy today rather than having 'the usual weep-fest,' as Julie called it. She wanted all of us to leave today filled with hope and love. In keeping with that wish, before you head out, please take the time to hug your neighbor." He smiled. "God bless you. See you all Sunday."

*Hugs? With this group? No, thank you.* Ellen turned toward Kristen but found her hugging her friend Missy.

"Mrs. Foster?"

She instantly recognized Ava Dove's voice and, stifling a sigh, reluctantly turned to face the young woman.

Ava stood beside Mrs. Jolean Hamilton, known throughout town as "Aunt Jo." Ellen remembered the round, cane-carrying, artificially black-haired, ebony-skinned old woman well, as she had a startling tendency to say whatever was on her mind. At Aunt Jo's side sat a fat, wheezy bulldog, who was tentatively sniffing in Ellen's direction.

Ellen ignored the animal and offered a polite smile to Aunt Jo and Ava. "How nice of you both to come and say hello. Kristen said she didn't know what she or her mother would have done without you two these past few weeks." When Ellen had arrived at Julie's, she'd been relieved to find Ava staying with Kristen. Ellen now knew that Ava and Aunt Jo had taken turns cooking and cleaning and generally looking after things when Julie had grown too weak to get out of bed.

Ellen's jaw ached. *That should have been me.* But it hadn't been and, between waves of disappointment, she couldn't help but feel a deep, genuine gratitude. "I owe you more than I can say."

Ava's smile trembled, but she held on to it. "I'm going to miss Julie."

"The whole town will." Aunt Jo cocked an eyebrow at Ellen, a challenge in her clear brown eyes. "You haven't been in Dove Pond for quite a while. I daresay most of the people here today are strangers to you."

"I remember the Doves, of course," Ellen replied smoothly. "And I remember you, Mrs. Hamilton."

"I remember you too," Aunt Jo said. "You and Julie used to yell at each other in your front yard just about every morning."

Ellen's face heated. "We had a contentious relationship, but she was my daughter and I loved her."

Aunt Jo clicked her tongue. "Sweet Betsy, I wasn't criticizing you. Children are our greatest joys and our greatest pains in the ass, too. Mrs. Foster — Ellen, isn't it?"

Ellen nodded.

"Ha! I did remember it. You look as if you could use one of those hugs the preacher ordered."

*What? Oh no.* "That's very kind of you, but it's not necessary. I was just about to tell Kristen we should le—"

"We all need a hug now and then." Aunt Jo handed her cane to Ava and rolled up the sleeves of her bright pink windbreaker.

Ellen took a step back. She rarely hugged people, even those she was close to. She'd already put up with so much today and —

"Grandma."

Ellen found Kristen at her elbow, her face set in stubborn lines, her friend Missy standing behind her wearing a similarly disapproving expression.

*Fine.* Ellen pasted on a smile, one she was sure looked as if it had been cut from cardboard, turned back to Aunt Jo, and bestowed an air kiss on the elderly woman's round cheek. *There. That should do it.*

She was just straightening when Aunt Jo slipped her arms around Ellen and gave her a massive, enveloping hug. Despite being shorter by at least six inches, Aunt Jo lifted Ellen to her toes, sending one of her high

24

heels tumbling off. It rolled across the grass, stopping perilously close to the open grave.

Gasping for air, Ellen was planted back on her feet and released. Her remaining heel sunk into the soft grass, and as she stepped back, trying to regain her balance, she almost tripped over Aunt Jo's bulldog. Startled, the dog barked, hopping around and threatening to wrap them both in his orange-and-purple-striped leash.

Staggering back upright, Ellen caught Kristen trying to hide a grin.

"You almost stepped on Moon Pie," Aunt Jo admonished. "You should be more careful. He's more fragile than he looks."

Face hot, and too upset to speak, Ellen left the small group and went to collect her shoe.

"Welcome to Dove Pond, Grandma!" Kristen called after her as both she and Missy stifled giggles.

Jaw tight, Ellen slipped her shoe back in place. She took her time, calming herself with the thought that in just a few minutes, with the exception of Kristen, Ellen would be shut of this place and these people. *I cannot wait.* Calmed, she forced herself to return to the small group, ignoring the dog that was still barking loudly.

"Moon Pie, shush!" Aunt Jo said to the

animal. "I've already told you twice that it isn't polite to bark at a funeral."

Moon Pie, panting, dropped to his haunches and sat politely as if all he'd needed was a reminder of that earlier talk.

Kristen beamed at the dog. "Who's a good boy? You are!"

The dog's tail wagged so hard its butt wagged with it.

Glad to no longer be the center of attention, Ellen murmured, "Such a good boy."

Ava eyed Ellen with surprise. "You like dogs?"

"I love dogs like Moon Pie." Which was true. She loved any dog she didn't have to clean up after.

Ava looked relieved. "That's good. You're about to inherit four of them."

Ellen's smile froze in place. "I beg your pardon?"

Aunt Jo shot a hard look at Kristen. "You didn't tell your grandma about your wolf pack."

Kristen grinned. "It slipped my mind."

"What wolf pack?" Ellen asked, trying not to let her irritation show.

"Kristen's doggos," Missy explained. "They've been staying at my house for the past two weeks since Ms. Julie was so sick."

"How's Chuffy's hair?" Kristen asked.

"Still falling out even though we've been bathing him in that smelly stuff you sent over."

"Forget Chuffy," Aunt Jo said. "It's that black-and-white one that's a menace. He's so full of gas that it's a wonder he doesn't propel himself out a window."

Missy giggled. "Mom says if we could bottle it, we could sell it as bug spray at the Spring Fling."

"Can you bring them back tonight?" Kristen asked. "I miss them. I'm sure Grandma will be tickled to have company while I'm at school, too." She sent a sly, challenging look Ellen's way. "Won't you, Grandma?"

Fortunately for Ellen, the years she'd spent working for the largest architectural firm in Raleigh, which was filled with demanding clients and bossy men, had taught her not to rise to obvious bait. "I can't wait to meet them. I'd pick them up myself, but I'd hate to get dog hair in my new Lexus."

Clearly disappointed in Ellen's calm reaction, Kristen said in a less excited tone, "Missy has a truck. She can bring them home." Kristen turned back to her friend and they were soon lost in conversation.

"I'd best get to going," Aunt Jo announced. "I have a roast in my Crock-Pot. It was good to see you again, Ellen." The older lady retrieved her cane from Ava and then called to her dog. "Ready, Moon Pie?" Yawning, the dog followed her as she headed toward the parking lot.

Ava turned to Ellen. "Listen, if you need anything, Sarah and I are just a few houses down. Julie was —" The words caught in her throat, and she had to swallow hard to continue. "Julie was special."

The bruised expression on Ava's face was familiar to Ellen. She saw it every time she looked in a mirror. *Julie had friends here. Real friends.* Ava's obvious emotion eased Ellen's irritation. Perhaps, with a little work, she could turn Ava into an ally of sorts. *I could use more of those.* "Kristen says she's been working for you after school, getting your tearoom ready. It's helped her to stay busy."

"I don't know what I'd do without her. I was hoping to open in February, but now —" Ava grimaced. "I'm behind schedule. It'll be mid-March at the earliest."

"Most of my work involves rehabbing older buildings, so I know the trials and tribulations. I'd like to stop by sometime and see what you're doing. How about Monday?"

"That would be nice." Ava's smile was steadier now. "I'll fix you a cup of tea."

Ellen kindly returned the smile. "I'd love that." Feeling a little less alone, Ellen gave the dragon flag–draped coffin one final look and then turned to collect Kristen.

Item One was officially completed. On to Item Two. If everything went as planned, she and Kristen would soon be done with Dove Pond.

# CHAPTER 2
## AVA

On Monday morning, Ava Dove stood in
her unfinished tearoom and stifled a yawn.
For over four long, interminable months,
she hadn't slept for more than three hours a
night. It wasn't because she was worried
about opening her tearoom, even though
she was way behind schedule. Nor was it
because of the death of her friend Julie
Foster, although Ava missed her more every
day. The reason Ava couldn't sleep was
because she had a secret.

It wasn't a small, unassuming secret
either, one that affected her and no one else.
Her secret, a horrible mistake she'd made
long ago, threatened the happiness of those
she loved the most. And so, desperate to
keep it hidden, she'd long ago trapped the
ornery thing in a shoebox, duct-taped it
closed, and then shoved it under her bed.
She'd told herself that when the time came,
she'd confess, set the secret free, and make

things right.

But somehow that time never came. For months and months, she'd researched dusty tomes and ancient manuscripts and had spent hours upon hours performing experiment after experiment, but her efforts had all failed. As much as she hated to admit it, she couldn't undo her mistake. Worse, as the years progressed, the secret had gotten stronger and was now fighting to break out of its prison. Long after dark, night after night, it banged against the bottom of her old wrought-iron bed until the idea of sleep was nothing more than a hollow hope.

The tape holding the shoebox closed was beginning to fray, the box itself starting to tear. She'd tried re-taping it, but each morning, the new tape would be on the floor, wadded in an angry knot, the old tape stretched and exhausted. She knew deep in her heart that one day soon the secret would rip through the duct tape, and her world would fall apart.

Ava rubbed her tired eyes, trying to wipe away her anguished thoughts. "I don't have time for this," she muttered to herself, ignoring the panic that fluttered in her stomach. She knew from long experience that obsessing over her problems wouldn't help. She inhaled a deep breath, taking in the smell of freshly cut wood and new varnish, and then eyed the stacks of boxes and paint supplies that sat against the opposite wall. A neat pile of unassembled wrought-iron tables and chairs was dwarfed by boxes of supplies waiting for shelves that hadn't yet been installed. There was more painting to be done, a floor that needed to be repaired and refinished, windows that needed to be reglazed, and more. *So much to do, so little time.*

Stifling an exhausted yawn, she located the watering can she'd stashed behind the long mahogany bar that had just been installed, filled the can with water, and carried it to the row of plants she'd brought from her greenhouses. A healthy line of bamboo palms and dragon trees sat along the front window, basking in the late-morning sun. On a cart sat small decorative pots of mother-in-law's tongue, which were destined to be centerpieces for the tables. Ava loved green things and they loved her. She never felt more at peace than when she was surrounded by her plants. And right now, she greedily gulped their peacefulness the way a parched man would gulp a glass of sweet tea.

The door swung open, and her sister Sarah came in, staggering under a load of boxes. "Help!"

"Oh no!" Ava set the watering can down and hurried to take some of the boxes off the stack. She carried them to the bar and slid them onto the shiny surface.

Sarah placed her boxes next to Ava's. "That's the last time I go to the post office for you." Sarah rubbed her arms. "What's in there? Rocks?"

Ava peered at the boxes. "The four smaller ones are the wooden stir sticks, but those larger ones are wrought-iron trivets for the teapots."

Still rubbing her arms, Sarah walked to the center of the room, her bright yellow coat flaring as she turned, her gaze moving around the room. "Oh, Ava, it's going to be beautiful."

Ava agreed. She'd bought the narrow late-nineteenth-century redbrick building on a whim. The bottom level used to hold a florist's shop, while the upstairs had been divided into small offices and one too-tiny apartment. The businesses had folded long ago during an economic downturn, and the vacant building put on the market, the price dropping as the years passed. Last year, Ava had recognized the building for the bargain it had become and had snapped it up.

Not only was the building solid and

perfectly located in the center of Main Street, but it was blessed with a ton of striking, unique architectural details from its earliest years, all carefully preserved by the previous owner. The front of the old florist's shop had a gorgeous cast-iron bow window where Ava planned to display her teas, and the entire building was floored in beautifully worn wide oak planks. Best of all, the ceiling was lined with original pressed tin ceiling tiles.

Ava loved it all. Even now, as exhausted as she was from yet another near sleepless night, she couldn't help but feel proud. "I hope it's done in time. I have to open in March. I can't afford to wait any longer."

"It will be ready." Sarah smiled and came to slip her arm around Ava's shoulders. "Your tearoom is going to be amazing."

That was Sarah. Of all the people Ava knew — and between her tearoom and landscaping company, she knew just about everyone here in Dove Pond — her sister was the most positive person she'd ever met. Sarah had always been that way, even when she'd been a tiny thing.

Sarah hugged Ava. "It's going to be fine. Better than fine. Just look at this." Sarah went to the mahogany bar and ran her hand over the shining surface. "Dylan did a great job."

Dylan Fraser was a local contractor who lived in Dove Pond but worked mostly in Asheville. Ava had been doing his landscaping for years, and he'd cut the price of her reno in return for a discount on his yard. "That bar adds a lot of drama to the room. I love it." She cut her sister an amused look. "And to think that when you saw it at that auction house in Atlanta, you thought it was too big for this room."

"I was wrong," Sarah admitted. "Like most librarians, I can look at a pile of books and instantly know how much shelf space they'll take, but I can't seem to do that with plain old furniture. I —" A delicate bell chimed, and she pulled out her phone. "It's Kat. She wants the new Mariah Stewart book."

Kat Carter was a local real estate agent and one of Ava's best friends. "She's been going on and on about it."

"It came this morning, and I already have a waiting list, although Kat's first." Sarah dropped her phone back into her pocket and sighed. "There's another book that has been bound and determined to visit her, one about the history of turpentine."

"What does turpentine have to do with Kat?"

"I have no idea, but the book was insistent. I'd better get to the library before Kat." Sarah headed for the door, pausing when she got there. "I'll come back after work. Kristen should be here by then. Between the three of us, I bet we can get some of those tables assembled."

"Thanks, Sarah. That'll help a lot."

"You're welcome. Now stop looking so worried. You'll get it done in time, and everyone in Dove Pond will flock here the second you're open. You got this." With a bright smile, Sarah left.

The door softly closed behind her. Alone again, Ava rubbed her temples, where a faint ache was growing. Rubbing didn't help, so she decided to ignore the ache and instead retrieved her watering can. She watered the dragon trees, pausing to trail her fingers over the glossy, sword-shaped leaves. The plants hummed happily under her touch, easing her tiredness and making her smile. There were times she found her Dove gift a grave responsibility. But more often than not, it was soothing in ways she couldn't explain.

She was glad her connection with plants was useful, something bigger than merely making everyone's yards look like exotic gardens. Years ago, when Ava had just turned sixteen and was already landscaping her neighbors' yards for extra money, eleven-year-old Sarah had knocked on Ava's door in the middle of the night, saying she couldn't sleep because there was a book in the attic calling Ava's name. Clutching a cheap flashlight that only put out a dim, yellowish beam, they'd climbed the rickety stairs into the dark, dusty attic, past broken lamps, musty boxes of ancient pictures, forgotten Christmas decorations, and incomplete sets of old china to a large trunk that sat at the very back. They'd had to fight the rusted latch but finally managed to coax it open.

Sarah had pushed aside a mound of tattered velvet curtains and produced an old journal labeled TEAS AND ELIXIRS. She'd shushed the book and then held it toward Ava. "This is yours."

Smelling faintly of old vanilla, mint, and other herbs Ava didn't recognize, the notebook had been the property of their great-great-great-aunt Mildred Dove, a known hermit who had written up scores of herbal tea recipes and scribbled copious notes in the margins using such ill-spelled phrases as "Efecctive digestivo" and "Harvest during summer soltise or no gud." The notes rather than the recipes had intrigued Ava, who had studied the book relentlessly. One day, after hearing Momma murmur yet again how tired she was, Ava decided to make a tea Aunt Mildred had claimed "helped ease the tired."

It had taken Ava three days to concoct the brew. She'd prepared the herbs and plants, meticulously following the recipe and notes to create a delicate tea made from magnolia bark, dried ginger and cloves, and two dandelion petals she'd placed on a china plate and left out for one full night under a half-moon. To Ava's surprise, the plants had joined in, ideas of their usefulness flickering through her mind every time she'd touched a leaf or a flower.

No one had been happier than Ava when, after drinking a cup, Momma had slept better than she had in a long time.

Making that first tea — and seeing it work — had lit a fire in Ava's youthful heart. She could do more than tend yards; she could help others. All she had to do was listen to the plants and follow Aunt Mildred's recipes and notes. At first, Ava just made her teas for people she knew. But as time passed, just as with her landscaping business, more and more people came to Ava, asking for her help. Soon, she was making a brew for just about every family in town.

Ava stashed the watering can back in its place behind the bar, her gaze falling on her colorful planner, a gift from Julie. It looked as if it belonged to a sixteen-year-old, not a successful businesswoman, and even came with smiley stickers, which had particularly thrilled Julie.

Ava put her hand flat on the planner, the plastic cover cool under her palm, and wished yet again that she'd gotten to know Julie sooner. During those last few weeks, Ava had admitted as much to Julie, who'd merely shrugged and said she wasn't an easy woman to get to know. That was true; Julie's moods were swift and unfathomable. Ava had found out almost too late that her new friend had been so, so worth the effort.

With a heavy sigh, Ava turned away and picked up a blue tarp. She'd just unfolded it when someone rapped on the door.

Who on earth would knock? She never locked it. Stifling her irritation, she called out, "It's open!"

Ellen Foster breezed in, carrying a large, bulky package wrapped in brown paper.

Ava suddenly remembered that Ellen had mentioned at the funeral that she might stop by this morning. *I forgot, darn it.* Ava forced a smile. "Good morning."

"Good morning." Dressed in a pair of cream slacks and a flowy gray cashmere top under a navy wool coat, her paleness offset with deftly applied makeup, Ellen looked as if she should be on her way to a posh lunch in Manhattan rather than an unfinished tearoom. Ava was instantly aware of her own scrubbed face, ponytail, paint-stained coveralls, and work boots.

"This is yours." Ellen placed the package on the bar and then removed her coat and hung it over her arm, her gaze sweeping past Ava. "So this is the tearoom Kristen keeps talking about." Ellen walked slowly around the room, her gaze lingering on the unfinished walls and discolored wood floor. She paused to point to the floor. "Original wide-cut planks. That's fortunate."

"They need some work. I was thinking of whitewashing the floor and stenciling it with the names of the teas."

"I wouldn't. Even with a high-gloss polyurethane, your baristas will spend all their time trying to keep it clean. I'd stain it a deep color, something to complement the brick."

Ava sighed. Dylan had said the same thing. "You're probably right. I love whitewashed wood, but I guess it's not practical for a floor."

"If you ask me, *that* is where you should put whitewashed wood." Ellen nodded to the wall behind the bar. "I'd use reclaimed barn wood, as it has an interesting texture. A lighter stain would make the bar more of a focal point too."

That was a good idea. A really good one. "I could stencil the types of teas there."

"You could. It would make a nice contrast, especially if you put shelves here and there stained to match this dark mahogany." Ellen ran her pale hand along the bar. "A beautiful piece. Edwardian, I would think?"

"That's what I was told." Ava folded the tarp, placed it back on the floor, and went to join Ellen. "I'm going to follow your advice about the wall. That would be lovely."

Ellen's expression softened, a faint smile touching her mouth. "I've overseen a number of renovations of older buildings much like this one. My firm has a crack team of designers and over the years, I've learned a few things from them."

"A lot of things, from the sound of it." Ava pulled the package closer. Across the paper, scrawled in Julie's familiar loopy handwriting, were the words "The Ripening, for Ava Dove's new tearoom. Good luck!"

Ava's chest tightened. *Oh, Julie. Thank you.*

When Ellen and her daughter, Julie, had lived in Dove Pond years ago, Ava hadn't known either of them well. Ellen tended to keep to herself, and Julie — though friendly — was much older than Ava. They'd gone to different churches, too. Eventually, Ellen and Julie had moved away, and Ava had rarely thought about them until Julie returned ten years ago, this time with her six-year-old daughter, Kristen.

At first, no one knew how to take Julie, who was so moody, she seemed like two people in one. Most days, she'd breeze into town and talk everyone's ear off, but those were followed by days or even weeks when she'd hunker down in her house, only coming to town when necessary, scowling and muttering to herself while refusing to speak to anyone else. Later on, when Kristen was older, it wasn't unusual to see the young girl running the household errands whenever her mother was in one of her "solitary moods," as they came to be known.

Ava now knew that Julie had bipolar II or, as she called it, "bipolar lite." When Ava had begun visiting Julie during her last months, Julie had opened up about her condition, describing herself as a "too" sort of person — too loud, too assertive, too happy, too much. But then, at other times, her mood was too heavy to hold, like an overfilled sponge.

Not that it mattered. Over the years, the people of Dove Pond had accepted Julie as one of their own, enjoying her brighter days and leaving her alone when she wished it. They admired her art, too. Almost everyone had a few paintings they'd purchased from her earlier days when she used to have a booth at the summer farmer's market. And everyone had been sad when she'd started to lose her battle with breast cancer. Worried, Ava had asked Kristen if there was anything she could do, and Kristen had reluctantly admitted that her mom was having trouble sleeping because of the pain.

At the time, Ava didn't know Julie well, but one look at the older woman's face and it was obvious that there was more to her sleeplessness than pain. The truth was, Julie was afraid of going to sleep, worrying each time that she might not wake up, and she was desperate to prolong her time with Kristen.

It had taken Ava four days to make the tea, and when she'd returned, she'd brought a canister with a label that read FOR JULIE FOSTER TO ADD ENERGY AND EASE. STEEP FOR FIVE MINUTES IN BOILING WATER. ADD

SUGAR. AND PLEASE, EAT MORE CHOCO-
LATE.

The tea had allowed Julie to sleep because it had eased her anxiety so that she could savor her remaining days with her daughter. Kristen had been grateful, but it had been the relief in Julie's face that had made Ava return every day after that. She'd said she was coming to monitor the tea's effectiveness, but the reality was much simpler. If there was one thing Ava had learned from her connection with plants, it was that life's ebb wasn't always as peaceful as one might hope. Like some plants, some people fought to stay alive with every atom of their being. Julie was dying, but she couldn't accept it, and whenever her gaze rested on Kristen, it was obvious why.

In her daily visits, Ava finally got to know Julie and quickly grew to love the creative mind behind the paintings that had made "J Foster" a huge success. Ava also got to know the big heart that burst with energy for days at a time only to be pinched into a painful knot as Julie's moods swung down.

Ava lifted a finger and traced her name where Julie had written it across the brown paper. *I miss you.* Ava wistfully blinked back tears and, aware Ellen was watching, carefully untaped the package. As Ava peeled away the paper, four two-foot-by-two-foot paintings were revealed. She spread them across the counter and took in the muted gold, minty green, lavender, soft blue, misty gray backgrounds. The series was of a couple, a blond woman and a mysterious auburn-haired man. Their faces were never visible, but the paintings conveyed an instant feeling of intimacy and breathtaking, burgeoning love. The scenes were beautiful and quietly dramatic.

"Oh my," Ellen whispered.

Ava looked up to find Ellen a few feet away, her gaze locked on the paintings. Ava could feel Ellen's deep grief fighting for release behind her taut expression.

To give her some privacy, Ava turned back to the paintings. "Julie was so talented. I have one of her paintings at my house. It's of a little girl walking across a sunlit field. I'm pretty sure it's Kristen, because they have the same hair color, but I can't be sure, as Julie never painted faces."

Ellen turned away, saying over her shoulder, "She was talented."

The words were clipped, and Ava could tell Ellen was still struggling for control. "Julie was an amazing artist. She had quite a large following, too."

Ellen nodded, suddenly intent on studying the antique bow window, which kept her face turned away. After a long moment, she managed to say in a voice that quivered only a little, "I met with the attorney this morning. Julie was doing well. Very well, in fact."

Ava could hear the surprise in Ellen's voice. "You didn't know."

Ellen returned to the bar, absently rubbing her hip. "Julie and I hadn't spoken in ten years."

*Oh wow.* Ava tried to remember what Julie had said about her mother and realized that she'd never mentioned her at all. "I see. Ten years is a long time." Ava picked up two mugs from where they rested on a tray behind the bar. When the tearoom eventually opened, she'd serve the tea in china cups, but sturdy mugs were better suited for a work zone. "I believe I said something about tea the other day. Would you like some?"

A flicker of surprise warmed Ellen's expression. "Yes, thank you."

Ava went to the sink, filled a teakettle, and pulled out a few canisters, placing them on the bar in front of Ellen. "Chamomile? Willow bark and raspberry? Honey lemon?"

"Which do you suggest?"

"Willow bark and raspberry will help your

hip. Willow bark is an excellent natural pain-killer."

Ellen's smile disappeared. "I don't need a painkiller."

Ava let her gaze drop to where Ellen's hand still rested on her hip.

Ellen flushed and dropped her hand back to her side. After a long, stilted moment, she asked, "Is it safe?"

Ava had to smile. "Originally aspirin was made from the white willow, so yes, it's safe." She pushed the other canisters to one side. "I think I'll join you. I've had a slight headache all day, and the willow bark will help." She filled the mugs with hot water, found two infusers, and returned to the bar. She added leaves to the infusers, clicked them closed, and then dropped them into the gently steaming mugs. She slid one across the bar to Ellen. "Let it steep for five minutes." She set a small saucer between them so they could remove the infusers without dripping tea across the bar.

Ellen peered into her mug with polite curiosity. "I saw a canister of your tea in Julie's cupboard."

"I've been meaning to come by and pick that up. I made it just for Julie. My teas are made specifically for each client, so they don't work for anyone else."

A flicker of disbelief crossed Ellen's face, although she didn't say anything.

The people of Dove Pond had come to rely on Ava's teas, but every once in a while, someone from the outside world would give her just such a look.

She mentally shrugged. She didn't owe anyone an explanation, not about this, anyway. She saw Ellen eyeing her mug of tea with renewed suspicion and said with a touch of impatience, "That isn't a specialty tea. It's from my diffusion line, which is for everyone. You can get that same tea at just about every coffeehouse in Asheville."

Ellen bent and cautiously sniffed the tea. "It smells delicious."

Ava pulled her mug closer, her gaze falling back on the paintings, her thoughts returning to Julie. "When did she start painting? I always meant to ask her, but the subject never came up."

"I bought her a set of paints when she was in third grade. Little did I know what I was starting. By the time she reached high school, she was painting for hours each day, much to the detriment of her grades." Ellen gave a self-conscious laugh. "She was good, but I didn't think she — or anyone else, really — could make a living from it. I guess she proved me wrong."

48

"Julie said she had to eat a lot of ramen early on. It took her years to get to the caviar stage."

"Yes, well, I believed artists ate ramen their entire lives. I knew she was talented. I just didn't think talent was enough."

"She made it work. Art galleries from around the country were trying to get her to do shows. Once she started selling well, she refused those requests. She said she got more attention by being a hermit."

"That was astute of her. I have to say, she left Kristen quite well cared for. I expected —" A flicker of pain crossed Ellen's face. "It doesn't matter what I expected. I was wrong."

Ava wasn't sure what to say to that. "Sarah and I were going to make a lasagna for you all, but we figured you were already sinking under the amount of food being left at your house. But if you get low, let me know."

"Please, no more lasagnas! It's very kind, but I've never seen so many casserole dishes. I'll never remember who brought what pan."

Ava had to laugh. "I still have a red casserole pan at my house from when Momma died. I never could figure out who it belonged to, so it's mine now."

"Oh dear. I didn't know your mother had

passed away. I didn't know her well. When I lived here all those years ago, she was busy raising all of you, and our paths rarely crossed."

"We were a handful, which is something I never appreciated until I had to raise Sarah."

Ellen's eyebrows rose. "*You* raised Sarah? How old were you when your mother died?"

"Nineteen. Sarah was fourteen. She and I were close, plus I was going to college just down the road, so it made sense that of all my sisters, I would be the one to move back home."

"You were too young to take that on."

"Probably," Ava admitted. "Life doesn't always give you choices, does it?"

"No, it doesn't." Ellen eyed her curiously. "Where are your other sisters? I only saw Sarah at the funeral."

"Cara's in New York City. After she got her degree in programming, she moved out there and developed the Make-Magic app."

"The high-end matchmaking app? I've heard of that."

"She was named one of the Thirty Tech Geniuses to Watch this year. Tay is an English professor at Harvard specializing in ancient manuscripts. She can speak and read nine languages. Ella's a pastry chef and just opened her own patisserie in Paris."

"Fancy! She was the plump one, wasn't she?"

"And the one with the most boyfriends. Men love Ella. They always have." Ava slid a bowl of sugar cubes and a bottle of honey in front of Ellen. "Alex and Madison both live in Raleigh. Madison's a doctor, and Alex is a veterinarian." There was a lot more Ava could say about that, but she held her tongue. Madison and Alex lived only a few houses apart but hadn't spoken in years. Ava and Sarah weren't sure of the details; all they knew was that the argument had been over a man.

"So only you and Sarah are left here in Dove Pond."

Ava made a face. "A fact Sarah laments almost every day. She's determined to get them all back home."

Ellen removed the infuser from her mug and placed it on the saucer and then took a cautious sip. She blinked, as if surprised. "It's quite good."

"I thought you'd like it." Ava fixed her own tea. "The raspberry blends nicely, doesn't it? I hope the willow will help your hip."

Ellen smiled politely. "It's quite tasty, and that's all that matters. Will you have this on the menu?"

"Oh yes. The diffusion line has forty-seven teas in it."

"Forty-seven?" Ellen looked impressed. "I only know of a few types of tea. Earl Grey, green tea, English breakfast, chamomile, jasmine . . . and now willow and raspberry."

"There are hundreds, but I'm just going to offer the most common. By the way, Kristen's favorite is dandelion, but Julie loved peppermint."

Ellen's face softened. "Julie always loved peppermint. When she was little, she'd steal all the candy canes off the Christmas tree and hide them under her pillow. I tried to get her to stop so there'd be a few left for Christmas morning, but she never listened."

Ava smiled wistfully. "She didn't like rules."

"She hated them." Ellen sipped her tea, seeming far more at ease.

"How are you and Kristen holding up?"

Ellen lowered her mug and sighed. "I worry about Kristen. She's been very quiet."

"She's quiet sometimes. She's also smart, capable, super polite — I couldn't ask for a better employee. She's helped at my greenhouses for two summers now, and she's great with people she knows, although she's a bit shy when it comes to talking to new customers."

"I guess I fall into the 'new customer' category." Ellen put her mug back on the bar. "So far, our conversations have consisted of one-syllable answers and chilly silences."

Ava winced. That didn't sound like Kristen at all. "Julie's death hit Kristen really hard. I'm sure she'll adjust in time."

"It's more than that. She knows I expect her to move back to Raleigh with me, and I can tell she hates the thought."

Oh dear. That wasn't good at all. Ava tried to pick her words carefully. "Kristen hoped she would be able to stay in Dove Pond at least long enough to finish high school."

Ellen shook her head. "I can't spend a year and a half here. I have a new project coming up in April and I have to be there to oversee it. I've tried to talk to her about it, but she shuts me down every time I mention it."

"Teenagers are tough. May I give you a suggestion?"

"About Kristen?"

"About teenagers in general. If she's giving you the silent treatment, she's telling you something, whether you understand what it is or not."

"She's being childish." Ellen picked up her tea and took another sip. "I suppose that's no surprise, though. It's obvious from her purple hair and that horrible nose piercing that Julie left her daughter to fend for herself. Kristen may not like having a real parent, but that's what she has now. And the sooner she understands that, the better for us both."

Ava put her mug down. "Have you seen Kristen's grades?"

"I have an appointment with the school counselor tomorrow. I'm sure Kristen will need some tutoring to catch her up before she moves to another school."

"She's at the head of her class."

Ellen's mouth opened and then closed, her gaze searching Ava's face as if half expecting Ava to say she was joking. When Ava merely raised her eyebrows, the older woman's mouth pinched into a frown. "Kristen never mentioned that."

"She has straight A's. She hasn't missed so much as a single day of classes, even with her mother being sick. She works here most afternoons, too. She's responsible and very mature for her age."

Surprise flickered across Ellen's narrow face. "That's good to know. But it doesn't change the fact that piercings and purple hair are the sort of decisions that can make life much more difficult. You know how people judge."

"The way you did." The words slipped out before Ava could stop them.

Ellen flushed and set her mug down so firmly that it thunked. "I thought you might help me convince Kristen to listen to reason, but I can see that was a misplaced hope. I —"

The door swung open, and Erma Tingle entered wearing a red puffer coat, her usually perfectly coiffed gray hair in disarray. Short and square, with deep brown skin, Erma was an active member of the Dove Pond Improvement Committee and was known for her no-nonsense attitude. She also had a tendency to wear her hikers every day despite the fact that she owned the Peek-A-Boo Boutique, a surprisingly fashionable shop just down the street.

She scanned the room, brightening when she saw Ava. "Thank God you're here!" Erma hurried up and placed a tea canister on the bar directly in front of Ava. "This tea is messed up."

In all the years Ava had made her teas, no one had ever declared any of them "messed up." She picked up the canister. "What's wrong with it?"

"It's poison," Erma said firmly. "That's what is wrong with it. Pure poison!"

Ellen's finely plucked eyebrows arched, her gaze sharpening.

Ava bristled. *Great. Of course this had to happen in front of Ellen.* Refusing to look her way, Ava opened the canister and sniffed gently. The scent of lavender, peppermint, chamomile, a hint of coriander, and a half dozen other herbs wafted up out of the tin. As she always did for this recipe, she'd mixed the soil around the base of a lavender plant with a teaspoon of dried oregano and a drop of white vinegar that had been exposed to a waning moon for two days.

Ava replaced the lid. "This is the same tea I've made you for the past four years."

"No, it's not. It's cursed, I tell you!" Erma eyed the canister as if it contained a coiled snake.

"What happened?"

"It made me fall asleep the way it's supposed to, but I wasn't *all* the way asleep." Erma leaned closer, her eyes wide. "Ava, I spoke to my Uncle Jeb, the one who passed away a month ago!"

Ellen made a noise that sounded like a cross between a snort and a laugh. When Ava and Erma looked her way, Ellen glanced at her watch. "Goodness, look at the time. I just realized I'm missing an appointment. Ava, thank you for showing me your tearoom, but I really must go."

"Of course. I can put your tea in a to-go cup if you'd li—"

"No, no. I've had more than enough, thank you." Ellen headed out, putting on her coat as she went. "I'm sure I'll see you around. Good luck with your tearoom!" The door swung shut behind her.

Relieved Ellen was gone, Ava turned back to Erma. "About the tea . . . maybe you just had a dream."

"No. It wasn't a dream. It was him, Ava. And he was as mad as a wet hen."

"About what?"

"That I gave his antique cupboard to his ex, my Aunt Susan. He yelled so much that I was sure Christine would wake up, but she never missed a snore." Christine DeVault, who owned Antique Alley, which was just a few doors down from the tearoom, was Erma's longtime partner. The two lived over the antique store in a delightful apartment with large windows that overlooked Main Street.

"Ava, it was horrible!" Erma shuddered. "Uncle Jeb wrote in his will that he wanted one of his nieces — either me or one of my two sisters — to have that cupboard, but it's huge and Lord, is it ugly. I don't know who made it, but it had big ol' birds on each corner with their beaks open and their wings spread like they were getting ready to attack. The whole thing looked as if it belonged in a bad horror movie. So when Susan asked for it while we were sitting around after the funeral, we were more than happy to give it to her. She deserved something for staying married to that old coot as long as she did."

"How do you know it wasn't a dream?"

Erma gripped Ava's arm and leaned closer. "Before he faded away, Uncle Jeb said there was a secret drawer in the bottom right panel of that cupboard and that there was a treasure in it, one he wanted me and my sisters to have. So the second the sun came up, I called Aunt Susan and asked her to look for that drawer. And Ava" — Erma's eyes widened — "she found it!"

Ava's heart sunk.

"Inside that drawer were three like-new 1843 Seated Liberty dollars, one for each of us girls. Those coins can go for ten thousand dollars or more apiece. It was a treasure, just like Uncle Jeb said."

Ava's stomach churned. *Did my tea do that?* She wanted to argue but didn't know where to start. Her gift had come with precious little instruction. Momma used to tell Ava and her sisters, *"Trial and error will*

58

*tell you what you need to know. Just be sure there's more trial and less error, and never, ever hurt anyone."*

Ava rubbed her temples and wished for the hundredth time that she wasn't so tired. "This is — geez." She dropped her hands back to her sides. "Erma, I don't know what happened to your tea, but I'll figure it out and make you another batch."

"No!" Erma's frightened gaze locked on the canister. "I don't need more tea." As she spoke, she backed toward the door. "But I appreciate the offer. I really do."

"No, wait!" Ava followed her. "Erma, let me fix this. I'll figure out what went wrong and make sure it never, ever happens again."

Erma paused at the door. "Never?"

"Never. Maybe I got the wrong amount of something by mistake or — or maybe the canister wasn't prepared right, or . . ." Ava gave a helpless shrug. "It could have been a number of things."

Erma eyed the tea with an uneasy expression. "Maybe it got too hot in your truck."

Ava managed a wan smile. "It's possible. Whatever it is, I'll figure it out. And I'll make you another, free of charge, of course."

"Well . . . I would miss having my nightly cup of tea," Erma admitted. "I never sleep well without it. Plus, it's not like Uncle Jeb hurt me or anything. He just yelled."

"And told you about the treasure," Ava added, hoping that made things better.

Erma brightened. "That's true. To be honest, I was more surprised than scared. I guess I'll take a fresh batch of tea, but only after you figure out what went wrong." Her expression softened. "I'm sorry if I ruined your morning. I was just weirded out by the whole thing. But you'll fix it. I know you will."

Ava could only hope that was true.

Erma glanced at the clock that hung over the kitchen door. "I'd better get back to my store. Thanks, Ava." With an encouraging smile, she left.

Ava stared at the door, her head throbbing even more. She'd faced delay after delay with her tearoom opening, she'd lost her new friend and was deeply worried about Kristen's issues with her grandmother, and now this — one of her teas had misfired, something that had never happened before.

But even worse, hovering over her like an ominous cloud only she could see, was a growing sense of panic that the secret she had locked away in a frayed shoebox under her bed would soon escape. Life could get no worse.

# CHAPTER 3
## KRISTEN

Kristen dropped her backpack onto the long green bench by the front door and tugged off her coat. She listened for the familiar tap-tap-tap of dog nails on the wood floor but was met with silence. *The dogs must be in the backyard. Figures.*

Grandma Ellen didn't like dogs. From what Kristen could tell, her grandmother didn't like much of anything she'd seen in this house. *Which is stupid. This house is the best. I love it here.* The thought of leaving it behind made Kristen's stomach ache like she'd eaten a bad burrito. *I don't want to move. Ever.*

A door opened somewhere in the house, and she could hear Grandma Ellen talking on the phone about deadlines and permits. From the number of phone calls she got, it was obvious she was pretty important to her office.

*I wish she'd go back to Raleigh. They can*

*have her.* Kristen sunk onto the bench and slouched against the wall as she shoved her hands inside the front pocket of her hoodie. Her fingers curled around her kazoo, the metal growing warm under her fingers. She used to like coming home, especially on Fridays, like today, when the freedom of a weekend was within reach. *I used to like a lot of things, but that was before Mom —*

Her throat tightened. She couldn't even think it. Kristen released the kazoo and swiped at her burning eyes. In the distance, her grandmother's voice grew sharper and more annoying.

Kristen hated everything about her life right now. The way her teachers and friends talked to her as if afraid she might break, the pity on people's faces, the way the smallest thing made her so angry she wanted to scream. But more than anything else, she hated that Grandma Ellen was here, in the house that used to feel like home, pretending everything was fine when they both knew it wasn't.

Kristen took a deep breath, fighting the urge to burst into tears. She and Mom had been closer than most mothers and daughters, handling their world the best way they could. For years Kristen had watched her mother travel between what she called light and dark days. On light days, no one was more fun. No one. Mom was creative and bright, and she laughed at everything. She'd sometimes wake Kristen up in the middle of the night, talking a mile a minute, elated about a breakthrough she'd had with a painting. Chatting loudly, she'd make ice cream sundaes for them both while they talked about life and love and, well, everything — or rather, Mom would talk and Kristen would listen and laugh, because no one was as fascinating as Mom when she was feeling light.

But the dark days always followed the light. Mom, listless and silent, would go to bed and stay there, sometimes for days, curled up in a ball, staring out the window, unable to care for herself or Kristen.

Over the years, Kristen found ways to deal with the dark days. She and Mom were a team, so when Mom couldn't do things, Kristen did. She did the laundry, fixed meals, and got herself to school. Even before she could drive, she'd do the shopping, riding her bike three blocks to the Piggly Wiggly and returning home with her backpack full of ravioli and ramen noodles. Kristen was proud of her independence, and she liked helping Mom too. They were a team, she and Mom.

Around the time Kristen turned fourteen, Mom finally found a good mix of meds that eased her dark days so they were at least bearable, but by then, their pattern was set. When Mom didn't feel her best, Kristen stepped in. It wasn't the way other families did things, but that was fine because, as Mom always said, everyone danced to the beat of their own drum.

Well, except Grandma Ellen. Kristen couldn't imagine her probably-ironed-her-jeans grandmother dancing, not even a little.

Impatiently shoving a loose strand of hair behind her ear, Kristen looked down the hallway to the mural Mom had painted for her. Years ago, when the new Wonder Woman movie had come out, Mom had bought them opening-night tickets. Oh, how they'd loved that movie. It was wild to see a woman — a whole island of women! — who were total badasses. After the movie, they'd started reading all the Wonder Woman comic books, watched the older movies, and even sat through the corny but fun TV series. Kristen had wanted to be Wonder Woman so badly that she'd started staging pretend fights with the couch cushions, using a pool noodle as a sword. If Mom was having a good day and had the energy for it, sometimes she would join in.

One day, after an epic pool noodle/sword fight, Mom had had the idea of painting a mural of Wonder Woman kicking a brown-shirted bad guy in the face. To Kristen's delight, Mom had replaced Wonder Woman's face with Kristen's and had called the mural *Wonder Kristen Saves the World (Again)*.

After that, whenever Kristen was curled up on the lumpy violet couch in the living room doing her homework, she would look into the hallway at the mural and imagine she really was kicking evil in the face. For a moment, she'd feel powerful and unstoppable. It had been months since she'd felt either way.

Her gaze moved from the mural to the stairs. When Mom was alive, as soon as Kristen got home, she'd let the dogs out, make a snack for two, and take the tray upstairs to Mom's room. There they'd talk about Kristen's day at school, about Kristen's work with Ava, and everything else.

But Mom was gone now, and here sat Kristen, alone. *Forever.*

Her chest tightened until it felt as if someone were sitting on it, but it was nothing compared to the hollowness that now echoed in her very soul. That was the hardest part, the loneliness. Even when she was sitting with her friends or walking through the crowded halls of her high school, she felt deeply alone. She didn't know why, but she did. It just was, and now that feeling was a part of Kristen.

Suddenly restless, she got up and went into the living room. But everywhere she looked, she saw bits and pieces of Mom. Paintings, figurines, sketchbooks, and cups of colored pencils were scattered around the room like a trail of breadcrumbs.

"You're home early." Grandma Ellen stood in the opposite doorway, her phone in one hand.

Kristen shrugged. "Ava had something to take care of at the greenhouses."

"Ah. I didn't even realize you were here. I've been on a conference call with the office all afternoon."

Grandma Ellen was dressed in blue slacks and a shimmery cream-colored shirt, her hair in a neat bun at the back of her neck. She looked as if she were in a commercial for an expensive brand of old women's makeup rather than standing in Kristen's and Mom's messy house.

Not that there was anything wrong with a messy house. Mom used to say that dust bunnies were the spirit animals of creatives.

Grandma Ellen smiled in her too-stiff,

too-cautious way, as if she expected Kristen to suddenly sprout wings and a tail and fly through the air like a bat. "How was school today?"

"Fine." She walked past Grandma and went to the kitchen. Mom had rarely mentioned her mother, so Kristen didn't know much about her grandma except that she was an architect and was "super judgy," as Mom had put it. Kristen had been six when Grandma and Mom had had their big falling-out, which had led to Mom and Kristen moving here to Dove Pond. Kristen barely remembered the time before their move, and over the years, her memories of her grandmother had scattered and faded until there were few left.

"There are so many paintings in this house." Grandma Ellen had followed Kristen into the kitchen and now stood beside a series of small paintings Mom had made of the park downtown. "Your mother was prolific, wasn't she?"

"It's who she was." Kristen opened the back door and stood to one side so the dogs could crowd inside, their tails wagging so hard it looked as if they were dancing. She patted them all, cooing over them and smiling as they wandered off to their various perches on the living room couches and chairs.

"Your poor furniture," Grandma Ellen murmured.

Kristen ignored her. Grandma Ellen could dislike the dogs all she wanted, but Kristen loved her doggos and wasn't about to part with them — not a one.

She realized her hands had curled into fists and she stuffed them back into the front pocket of her hoodie before her grandmother noticed. Geez, but she was so *mad*. It was as if every bit of her boiled with fury, and she was exhausted from fighting the urge to explode.

Her anger was childish, but she couldn't seem to snuff it out. It simmered through her off and on throughout the day, growing as the hours ticked past. Worse, she wanted other people to be angry, too, especially her uptight, critical grandmother. Slanting a look at her now, Kristen said, "You never said what you thought of Mom's funeral. Pretty cool, wasn't it?"

Grandma Ellen's smile froze in place. "I'm sure it was exactly what your mother wanted."

"Yes, but what did you think of it?" Kristen waited, savoring the uncomfortable expression on Grandma Ellen's thin face. It had been painfully obvious to everyone at the funeral that Grandma had hated everything, but it was equally obvious she was also trying extremely hard not to upset Kristen. *She wants me to agree to go to Raleigh without a fuss. That's not going to happen. I won't go. I just won't.*

True to form, Grandma Ellen said in a bland, neutral voice, "It was different."

"And?" Kristen said in a challenging tone.

Grandma Ellen's gaze moved over Kristen's face and then narrowed as if she knew what was going on. "It was original, just like your mother. She could never stand to be thought of as normal."

*That's because, unlike you, she knew "normal" doesn't exist.* It said a lot that Grandma Ellen had ignored the instructions from the invitation. Everyone else in Dove Pond had dressed in bright colors, which had left Grandma Ellen looking like a thin black crow perched in a row of songbirds.

Turning away, Kristen opened the fridge and poured herself a glass of chocolate milk, wondering if that was what Mom had had in mind all along.

"Well!" Grandma Ellen said brightly. "I'm glad you got to come home early today."

Kristen wasn't glad of that at all. She was worried about Ava, who'd been acting weird this whole week, too quiet and inside her head a lot. *What's going on with her? She's super on edge.* It was upsetting to see her like that, and Kristen, who didn't want to add to Ava's stress, was left even more alone than usual. *Absolutely fricking everything in my life sucks right now.*

Grandma Ellen slid into a chair on the other side of the counter. "The tearoom is going to be beautiful once it's done. I was quite impressed with what I saw when I stopped by Monday."

Come to think of it, that was about the same time Ava had started acting so distracted. Kristen eyed her grandmother narrowly. "What did you two talk about when you were there?"

Grandma Ellen shrugged. "The tearoom, some decorating possibilities, the new bar she'd just installed . . . that sort of thing. And you, of course. She had a lot of good things to say about you."

Kristen took a quick drink of her milk, hoping to hide her suddenly hot cheeks. She was glad to hear that. If she had an older sister, she'd want one just like Ava.

"We didn't have time to talk about much because some woman came in — I can't remember her name — and complained that her tea hadn't helped in the way she'd been promised." Grandma Ellen absently traced the edge of the counter with her finger. "I suppose it's not surprising some people feel cheated. Ava promises a lot more than is possible."

"Ava's teas work," Kristen said fiercely. "I've seen them."

"Oh?" It was said politely, calmly, but it was painfully clear what that "oh" meant.

Too angry to speak, Kristen turned back to the fridge and poured more chocolate milk into her glass. The old woman was the queen of criticizing people without saying anything negative. Every remark was a thinly veiled suggestion that if Kristen or Mom had really tried, they could have done better. That must be what Mom had meant when she said her mother was judgy.

Everything about Grandma was tightly controlled — her hair, her clothes, her expressions, her job — all of it. Kristen tried to picture her grandmother with a smudge on her cheek, her silver hair uncombed, a paintbrush forgotten over one ear, which was Mom's usual day-to-day look, but it was impossible.

Grandma Ellen folded her hands in front of her and put on her best fake smile. "Since you're home now and we have some extra time, we should talk."

And there it was — the conversation Kristen had been avoiding since the day of the funeral, saying she had homework or pretending to be tired and heading off to bed at ridiculously early hours, but her excuses were running out. *I'm not ready for this argument.*

And she knew it was going to be just that — an argument. She picked up her glass of chocolate milk and walked past Grandma Ellen to the dining room.

Grandma Ellen followed, and Kristen could feel her grandmother's critical gaze moving over the hodgepodge of colorful furniture Mom had collected. Every chair around the large, rustic farm table was painted a different color, the seats covered in decoupage pictures of various movie stars, including Mom's favorites, Cary Grant and Woody Harrelson. She'd done the work over two nights, never sleeping and barely eating. That was how Mom had done things. When the work "spoke" to her, she was in a frenzy to get it done before the idea and her energy slipped away.

"Come and sit." Grandma Ellen perched on Cary Grant and patted the seat next to hers. "We need to make some plans."

Kristen eyed the chair. It was one of her favorites — who didn't love Ben Stiller? —

but she decided against it. If they were going to have this conversation, then she wanted — no, *needed* — some space between them.

So instead Kristen walked to the other side of the table and sat on Audrey Hepburn. For good measure, she threw her feet onto Orlando Bloom's chin.

A flash of disapproval crossed Grandma Ellen's face, but it lasted only a second. Still, that tiny flicker of disapproval felt like a win to Kristen, which only proved how sad her life was right now.

Grandma Ellen put her elbows on the table and clasped her hands together, her collection of gold and diamond rings glittering in the warm light. "You know I can't stay here in Dove Pond. I've mentioned before that I have a big project coming up and I have to be on-site, especially during the beginning phases. I was lucky I could come here right now, but I have to be back in the office by the first week in April, which means" — Grandma Ellen's smile became more fixed — "that you need to move to Raleigh by then."

Kristen jammed her hands into her front pocket and clutched the kazoo. "I don't want to move. My friends are here."

Sympathy flickered over Grandma Ellen's

73

face, softening the hard lines. "I know," she said simply. "This isn't going to be easy for you. But it's what's best for us both. The schools in Raleigh are —"

"I don't need another school. This one is fine." More than fine. Dove Pond High School was where she felt safe and at home. She loved her teachers, even the strict ones, and wouldn't trade them for the world.

Grandma sighed. "You and I both know there are better schools. A student with your abilities could do much better with a more rigorous academic program that —"

"What do you know about my school's academic program?" Kristen interrupted.

"Whatever it is, I'm sure it's no match for the private schools in Raleigh. There are over two dozen of them, and I'm sure we can find one that will guarantee you entry into the best colleges out there. Some of them have such good reputations that Harvard and Yale and MIT send recruiters to their college fairs. Can you say that about Dove Pond High?"

Kristen didn't answer.

Grandma Ellen nodded as if she'd just won the argument. "Once we sell the house —"

"No! And stop saying 'we.' This is all you, and you know it."

Grandma Ellen's lips thinned. "Kristen, I know this isn't easy, but it's what must happen. There are no other options."

Each word burned through Kristen's soul like acid, and she stood, her chair scooting noisily across the floor. "What are you going to do? Are you going to *make* me go to Raleigh? Tie me up and throw me in the back of your Lexus?"

At her raised voice, Floofy, Dangus, and Luffy raised their heads from where they sprawled on the couch in the living room, watching through the open doorway. Even little Chuffy, his gaze wary, wagged his tail hesitantly as if he wished he could help. *At least the dogs are on my side.* Right now, it felt as if they were the only ones.

Grandma Ellen's mouth had hardened into a fine line. "We can talk about this without yelling."

"*You're* not the one losing her only home! My friends are here. My job with Ava is here. My school, and my town, and everything I know and love is here. Everything except Mom." Kristen's voice cracked, but she ignored it, pulling herself together enough to say loudly, "I don't want to sell the house and I sure as hell don't want to move to Raleigh."

Instead of getting angry, Grandma Ellen

75

merely looked disappointed. "Oh, Kristen."

There it was again, that judgy tone, which Kristen was beginning to hate almost as much as she hated the thought of moving.

But it was more than that. The less angry Grandma was, the more angry Kristen became. Not once since the funeral had Grandma showed any emotion about Mom's death. The old woman hadn't wept or gotten mad or suffered from any of the millions of emotions Kristen was drowning in. If felt as if she were the only person on earth who was really and genuinely sorry Mom was gone. The only one who cared what happened to the house Mom had loved, and the things Mom had collected. For all her polite words, it was obvious Grandma Ellen couldn't care less.

"Kristen, we need to get the house ready to sell so —"

"Don't say another word. Just don't. This isn't just a house; it's my home and it's all I have left of Mom. I don't want anything painted or fixed up or changed in any way. I love it the way it is."

"I'm not saying there's anything wrong with this house. I'm sure, with a little cleaning and sorting, it could be just lovely. But if we want top dollar for it, then we have to update —"

"No! Have you heard anything I've said? I don't want to sell it!"

Grandma Ellen frowned. "If I could do this any other way, I would. You can't stay here alone, and it makes no sense to leave this house empty. And don't suggest we rent it out, because I'm too busy to deal with that all the way from Raleigh."

"I don't want to rent it! I don't want anyone to live here but me. I'm not moving to Raleigh. Not now, not in two months, not ever."

"Kristen, don't —" Grandma Ellen caught herself. She took a deep breath and straightened her shoulders. "I told myself I wouldn't let this turn into an argument, because it won't solve anything. I know this is hard. I'm just trying to do what's best for us both."

"You don't know what's best for me. That was Mom's job and now it's mine."

"I wish your mother had left us a letter to explain what she wanted, but —" Grandma Ellen gave a short laugh. "That wouldn't have been like her, would it? Responsibility gave her hives."

Kristen realized she was holding the kazoo so tightly it was a wonder it hadn't bent. She relaxed her grip, the metal warm under her fingers. "Mom was responsible. She took good care of me."

Grandma Ellen's thin eyebrows rose as her gaze flickered to Kristen's purple hair and nose piercing. "Well, what matters now is that we do what's best for you." She hesitated and then added, "I realize that moving is never easy, but you'll have two whole months to say goodbye to your friends. As you know, this house is going to need some work before we put it on the market. The floors need refinishing, the kitchen and bathrooms need updating, the stairway has loose boards, and that wretched mural in the front hallway needs —"

"I love that mural!"

"Then your mother should have painted it on a canvas and not on a wall." Grandma sighed, looking suddenly tired. "We don't have time to argue. I need to line up repairmen and painters and . . . Seriously, we'll be lucky to have half of it done before I have to be back at work. And it all has to be done before we list it —"

"You're not selling Mom's house, I'm not going to Raleigh, and that's that!" A tear rolled down Kristen's cheek. Embarrassed, she swiped it away, her face hot.

Grandma Ellen's expression softened. "Sweetheart, we don't have a choice. I can't stay here, and you can't live alone, which means —"

"I could live alone if I wanted. I could have myself declared independent."

Grandma Ellen froze in place. Her hands, which had been loosely clasped on the table in front of her, were now tightly woven together. "You could," she said slowly, her gaze never wavering. "But you'd have no money, so you'd eventually lose the house. There's a mortgage to be paid, plus electricity and water and taxes."

"Mom left me money."

"I'm the executor of the will and your guardian. I wouldn't release a penny to you under those circumstances."

They stared at each other, Kristen's fury now focused on Mom. *Why did you leave Grandma in charge? You had to know she'd try to take me away from here.*

But there was no answer. Kristen was alone.

Her eyes burned as her gaze slid past Grandma Ellen to the mural in the hallway. And somewhere deep in Kristen's head, she heard Mom say, "You're Wonder Kristen. You'll win over evil no matter how hard the fight." *Oh, Mom. I wish that were true. But I can't win this one.*

That was the problem with superhero mythology. Unless you had real, honest-to-

God powers, you were just plain old Diana Prince, whose only skill was gathering crucial information on the sly. Sadly, Kristen couldn't think of any information that could help her right now.

Still, there was no benefit in letting her enemy know how deeply determined she was to stay in Dove Pond. *Maybe I should be Diana Prince for a while and pretend I'm growing used to the idea of moving. That would keep Grandma Ellen off my back while I look for a way out of this mess.*

"Kristen, surely we can find some middle ground here. A way to make this process more palatable to you." Grandma Ellen leaned forward, her hands still neatly folded together, looking like a TV lawyer about to state the case-winning premise. "Would it help if I involved you in the process more?"

*No. Not even a little.* But all Kristen said was "How?"

Grandma Ellen's tight expression eased. "How about I make a list of the updates that need to be made, and we go over them together? If you see something on the list you absolutely hate seeing changed, then we'll cross that off."

*Be Diana Prince*, Kristen told herself. "You'd do that?"

"I would. It might lower the overall profit,

but —" Grandma Ellen shrugged. "I'm willing to compromise. I hope you are too."

*Ha!* But instead of scoffing out loud, Kristen said, "We can try it, I guess."

Grandma Ellen brightened. "There! Progress. And maybe, sometime over the next few weeks, we can spend a weekend at my home in Raleigh. I think you'll love the city once you've gotten to know it a little. But right now, we can work on the list of updates. I've already started one. I'll get it, and we can —"

"Maybe tomorrow. I'm starving, plus I have an essay due Monday and I haven't really started."

Grandma Ellen's smile dimmed a little, but after a moment, she shrugged. "Sure. Just promise we'll do it within the next day or so. And Kristen, difficult decisions don't get easier with time. It's best to attack them early and with confidence."

As if Kristen didn't know that. "Sure." There. That was easily said. All of it had been, to be honest. And she'd won a few days for herself in the process. A few days to plan her next steps. A few days without Grandma Ellen hounding her for "a talk." Although thankful for the reprieve, Kristen felt an overwhelming need to do something comforting. Something normal.

She picked up her glass of chocolate milk and headed for the kitchen. "I'm going to make chicken parm."

Once there, she set her glass in the sink, opened the refrigerator, and leaned in as if examining the contents, although she knew exactly what was in there. The cool air calmed her hot cheeks, and she took a steadying breath before she pulled out a package of chicken.

When she turned around, Grandma Ellen was standing on the other side of the counter, her expression softer and far less guarded than it had been in a week.

*She thinks she's won. Wonder Kristen: score one.* "Chicken parm is one of my favorite meals." Kristen put the package on the counter beside the refrigerator. "We have plenty of chicken, and I bought breadcrumbs when I was at the store yesterday."

"I noticed you'd gone to the store. If you'd let me know what you wanted, I could have gone while you were in school."

"I like grocery shopping. I did it most of the time, especially when Mom didn't feel like it." Kristen grabbed a carton of eggs and the milk and then shoved the fridge door closed with her hip. "I did all the cooking and laundry, too. I also vacuumed and dusted."

"And what did your mother do?"

"She created."

Grandma Ellen frowned. "She should have been taking care of you."

Kristen gestured to herself. "Do I look untaken care of?"

Her grandmother's gaze flickered from Kristen's hoodie to her purple hair. But after a pause, Grandma Ellen said in a cool, no-nonsense tone, "Of course not."

It was obvious that wasn't what she thought. Kristen knew she wasn't like most of the kids her age. She had responsibilities her classmates never thought about, which was why she had very little in common with them. They thought she was weird, and she thought them shallow and stupid.

She hadn't made friends — not good ones, anyway — until high school, when she'd met Missy Robinson and Josh Perez. Missy's mother was an LPN who worked in family homes with people suffering from dementia, strokes, that sort of thing, so she was gone most nights. And since Missy's father was the local postmaster, he was gone most mornings, which left Missy with the chores and the task of getting herself to school.

Of course Josh had it worse than either

her or Missy. He came from a large family and both of his parents worked long hours, which left him in charge of his little sisters, making them dinner and getting them to bed. He was a good cook, though, and both Kristen and Missy agreed that their best recipes had come from him.

What was really funny was that at school, the three of them were considered rebels, and their refusal to look and act like everyone else had cemented that reputation. Once they'd found one another, they didn't mind either the reputation or the teasing that accompanied it. It was hysterical to be thought rebellious when they were anything but.

Kristen opened the package of chicken. "I like cooking. Besides, Mom needed time and space to work."

"She was quite good."

"She wasn't just good," Kristen said sharply. She cracked two eggs into a bowl and tossed the shells into the trash. "She was brilliant. That's what the New York Times said, anyway."

That caught Grandma Ellen's attention. "The Times?"

"Yeah. And the Chicago Trib said she was 'a mad, female Renoir.' She loved that." So had Kristen. Having a famous mom was cool.

Kristen's throat suddenly tightened. *Had, not have.* Her heart was constantly clinging to the idea that Mom was just in the other room, while her brain kept coldly pointing out that Mom was now nowhere. Nowhere at all. Her eyes burned, and she turned back to the cabinets, pulling out a pan, a box of spaghetti, and a jar of sauce.

As Kristen worked, Grandma Ellen sat quietly, lost in her own thoughts. She finally roused herself to say, "You should see the kitchen in my house. Julie used to love it. She said it made her feel like Julia Child."

"I've seen it."

An odd expression flickered across Grandma Ellen's face. "Julie kept pictures of it?"

There was so much hope in that question that Kristen hated to admit the truth. "I saw it in a magazine at the doctor's office while I was waiting for Mom."

Although Grandma Ellen's face never changed, Kristen felt the invisible disappointment.

Grandma nodded as if she wasn't surprised. "My home has been featured in *Architectural Digest* twice now. Since you've seen it, you know the kitchen is especially nice. I have a part-time chef, too, who could teach you to cook new dishes, if you'd like."

A chef? *Please, no.* "Your house looked huge. How many people can eat in that dining room?"

"Thirty. I usually eat in the kitchen, though. To be honest, it gets a bit lonely now and then."

A faint quaver crackled along Ellen's words, surprising Kristen. Unsure what to say, she turned away and filled the pan with water before setting it on the stove.

"When you move to Raleigh," Grandma added, "you'll enjoy —"

"Do you like mushrooms?" Kristen opened the refrigerator door again. "I usually add mushrooms and spinach to the sauce just to get more vegetables in there." There was no answer, so she glanced over her shoulder.

Grandma Ellen's gaze locked with hers. Kristen held up the package of mushrooms. "Yes? Or no?" There was a long silence, and Kristen could feel her grandmother's frustration.

But after a moment, Grandma shrugged. "Sure. I love mushrooms. And spinach, too."

It was a tiny capitulation, but it felt like a big win. *Score two, Wonder Kristen.* For the first time today, a genuine smile touched

Kristen's mouth. "At least we can agree on that."

Grandma Ellen's gaze softened ever so slightly. "That's a start, isn't it?"

"Yes, it is." Kristen turned back to the stove, feeling a little lighter. "What other houses have you rehabbed? They have to have been bigger than this one."

"Some of them were, although the project I'm the proudest of wasn't much larger than this. It was an old Victorian located in downtown Asheville." Grandma continued to share the details of the rehab she'd overseen, her enthusiasm softening her voice until it was actually pleasant to hear.

Kristen asked a question now and then to make it seem as if she was listening, but her mind raced over her next steps. Whatever she had to do, she would find a way to stay in Dove Pond. It might take a miracle, but she was Wonder Kristen, and she'd figure it out.

Somewhere in the distance, over the soothing sound of water boiling and Grandma's long tale about the Victorian house she'd brought back to glory, Kristen could almost hear Mom whisper, "Always."

# CHAPTER 4
## SARAH

Monday afternoon, scanner in hand, Sarah Dove reached for the next book waiting to be checked back into the library system. The second her hand brushed the cover, scenes from the book flashed through her mind, vivid and immediate. The book was a young-adult work called *Children of Blood and Bone,* a riveting, magical sort of tale that had been beloved by every middle schooler who'd read it.

At the end of the flash of scenes came a crystal-clear image, that of young Daisy Wheeler. *She must read me,* said the book.

"I'll ask her." Sarah scanned the book and then made sure it had been logged into the computer correctly. "But I have to warn you; she's gotten picky about what she'll try, so I can't promise anything."

*She will like me.* When Sarah didn't answer, the book added in a cajoling tone, *A lot.*

"I'll ask her when she comes in tomorrow for Children's Hour." Over the past two-plus years, Daisy had become the unofficial queen of Children's Hour. The feisty eleven-year-old was a natural entertainer, and the number of children coming to her weekly reading was almost more than could fit into the library's largest conference room.

Sarah put a Post-it with Daisy's name on the cover. The book rustled impatiently, so she smiled and gave it a comforting pat. "I'll do my best. I promise." That seemed to re-assure the book, as it settled down and didn't speak again while she went back to work, checking in the other books.

Since the day she'd turned seven, Sarah had been able to talk to books. Even better, they talked back. They told her their stories and shared their worries and hopes, and once in a while would tell her who in their small town needed to read them. That made her job as town librarian easy as pie.

Of course, with great gifts came great responsibilities. Momma had pounded that fact into her daughters' heads from the time they were children. She had insisted Sarah and her sisters only use their gifts for good, which wasn't always as easy as one might think. Right now, poor Ava was stressed out because, through no fault of her own, one of her teas had gone wonky. For the past week, Ava had pored over her notes and various ancient herbal books, looking for a solution. This morning, Sarah had come downstairs, rubbing sleep from her eyes and longing for some coffee, and had found her sister exactly where she'd been the night before, sitting at the dining room table, surrounded by piles of books and papers. It was obvious that Erma Tingle's misbehaving tea was weighing on Ava something fierce.

That was no surprise, as Ava was a bit of a perfectionist. Not only was she worried about her reputation, but she also believed the family's good name rested on her shoulders. The people of Dove Pond knew that when the Dove family had seven daughters, as they did now, good things happened. Centuries ago, in 1702, the Dove family had stood on the crest of Black Mountain and looked down into the green valley below at a sapphire pond and declared themselves "finally home." Since then, there had been dozens, if not hundreds, of times the family had brought good fortune to their town.

In 1744, when window glass was a precious commodity, Agnes Dove, the oldest of seven sisters, had used alchemy to make glass for the homes being built in their growing town. Fourteen houses from that era still stood in Dove Pond, and none of their windows had ever had so much as one pane crack. In fact, when a fire had gutted the old Hendersen house in 1978 after sixteen-year-old Robbie Hendersen fell asleep smoking a forbidden cigarette, the only thing left in the ashes had been the windows, which looked as if they were brand-new.

And in 1933, at the height of the Depression, when everyone was struggling just to put food on the table, the town had been delighted to discover that whenever eight-year-old Clarissa Dove, the third of seven Dove sisters, played her violin on her front porch, her family's cows and chickens produced ten times what they normally did. Not only did they produce more, but the milk was extra creamy and most of the eggs had double yolks. Naturally, being a Dove, Clarissa had shared her gift with her neighbors, playing her violin for any Dove Pond farmer who asked. Soon all the farms in their small town were producing more than enough milk and eggs to keep their little town fed.

There were dozens of stories like that about the Dove sisters. Still, as Momma Dove always pointed out, no matter how many stories there were, or how many good things the Doves brought to their hometown, there would always be those who didn't believe. Momma had warned her daughters about the dangers of letting others place doubts in their minds about their own abilities. They alone knew the limits of their gifts.

Of course, like all life lessons mommas handed down to their daughters, some took and some didn't. No matter how much Sarah wished it otherwise, she still cared what other people thought. And so, too, did Ava. Sarah wasn't surprised her sister was taking the failure of one of her teas so personally. No one had a bigger heart.

Sarah had just reached for the next stack of returns when someone thunked a book onto the desk in front of her.

She looked up to find Kat Carter standing on the other side of the desk, her face flushed. Tall and brunette, Kat was a real estate agent who specialized in commercial properties. Her mother, a notoriously sexy flirt, was currently preparing for her fifth — or was it sixth? — marriage. Sarah couldn't keep up, and neither could anyone else in town. According to local lore, Kat and her mother had what was called the Carter gift. Wealthy men fell madly, crazily in love with them, although, at least with Kat's mother, it didn't seem to last. As if to defy tradition, Kat had had the same beau since high school, although she'd been steadfastly refusing to marry him for over twenty years now.

Kat shoved the book across the desk. "Why on earth would I need a book on the history of turpentine?"

"I don't know. It said you should read it, so I sent it your way."

An impatient look crossed Kat's face. "I don't need it. It was boring as heck, too."

The book on the desk hissed, *She skimmed. Ask her what oleoresin is.*

Sarah frowned at the book. "I'm not going to give her a pop quiz just because you say she skimmed."

Kat gasped and then glared at the book.

Sarah crossed her arms and leaned back in her chair, which creaked loudly in the quiet of the library. "You didn't read it, did you?"

Kat threw up her hands. "Fine! I skimmed. It's not my fault. *The History of Turpentine* isn't exactly a riveting read." She slanted a cautious look at the book. "Not that you didn't try. I just —" She grimaced. "Oh God, I'm talking to a book."

Sarah smiled and placed the book on the

return cart. "You'll regret you didn't read it."

Kat eyed the book with a sour expression. "Did it tell you why I need to read it?"

"They never do."

"Can you ask?"

Sarah sighed and picked up the book once more. "Well?"

*She'll find out when the time is right,* the book replied grumpily.

Sarah repeated the book's answer to Kat and then added, "I'd read it if I were you, but it's your decision."

"I don't even know why I asked," Kat said in a petulant tone. She stared at the book uneasily, finally saying, "No. I'm not going to read it. It's about turpentine. Do people even use that stuff these days?"

*Yesssss,* hissed the book angrily.

Sarah ignored it, tucking it back out of sight behind a pile of other books. "I'm glad you stopped in," she said to Kat. "How are things in the commercial real estate world?"

Kat's irked expression eased. "Great. Better than great, in fact. Remember the old Seed and Feed on SR 20? I'm showing it to a guy who's thinking about opening a Farmers' Depot."

"Oh wow. I've heard those were nice."

"Everything a farmer needs. That's what

the ads say about those places. It's a huge deal and . . ." Kat waved her hand. "But never mind that. I had another reason for stopping by." She frowned, worry plain on her face. "Is Ava okay? I've never seen her so distracted. I'm worried about her."

"Me too," Sarah admitted. "She didn't say three words at lunch today. She's behind on the tearoom, and that messed-up tea is bothering her, too."

"Which one?"

Sarah blinked. *Which one?* "I thought only Erma Tingle's tea had messed up."

"Two more were returned this morning." Kat frowned. "Ava didn't tell you?"

"She didn't say a word. That explains why she barely touched her meal, though."

"I've never seen her like this. She's absent-minded, quiet, and just . . ." Kat impatiently raked a hand through her dark hair. "I didn't want to say anything, because she's already upset, but people are starting to talk."

Sarah's shoulders sunk. "What did you hear?"

"An hour ago, I stopped by the Moonlight Café to pick up some coffee, and Marian Freely was telling everyone at the counter how Ava's teas were all messed up."

Sarah winced at the mention of the gossip-hungry waitress at the Moonlight. "Oh no."

"Marian said that until she knows it's safe, she's going to stop drinking the tea Ava made to calm her psoriasis."

"How many people heard Marian say that?"

"Everyone in the café. She was talking loud enough that I heard every word she said and I was sitting on the other side of the dining room."

"This just keeps getting worse and worse."

Kat agreed. "Does Ava have any idea what's gone wrong?"

"No. Which other two teas were messed up? I assume you heard names."

Kat looked around to make sure no one was close by, and then leaned closer. "Ava made Jon Ferguson a tea a few weeks ago to help him be more romantic with his lady."

"Romantic? He and Ellen have been going out forever. I'd think he'd have already figured that out."

"Ellen has been telling him her love language is affirmations. She wanted him to write her notes and poems and stuff like that."

"Jon? Write a poem?"

"Exactly. So he asked Ava to make him a tea to help him be more creative in expressing himself."

That sounded simple enough. Sarah had seen Ava's teas do much, much more. "And?"

"He tried her tea a few days ago, and it didn't make him more creative at all. Instead, the tea made him blurt out his feelings. And he couldn't stop." Kat leaned closer, her eyes wide. "Sarah, he talked for *two* days *and* nights."

"Noooo!"

"Oh yes. He talked so much he lost his voice. Ellen finally drove him to Doc Bolton, who had to give the poor guy a muscle relaxer just so he could shut up."

"Poor Jon! And poor Ava too." Sarah thought of how pale her sister had been at lunch. *It wasn't just tiredness. She is worried to death.* "What other tea was messed up?"

"Just before lunch today, Jessica Long brought back her tea. Ava's been making Jess the same tea for years now to help her deal with her anxiety, and it's always worked perfectly. She only drinks a cup when she's stressed out, so Jess hadn't had any from the new batch until this past Saturday."

"And?"

"When she got out of the shower, Jess found herself staring at her own reflection in her bathroom mirror and she couldn't stop. She ended up stuck there, unable to move for hours. Fortunately, her mom keeps pretty close tabs on her and knew something was wrong when her phone kept going to voice mail. When Jess didn't answer her door, Mrs. Long climbed in through the kitchen window and saw what was happening. She had to throw a blanket over Jess's head just to get her away from her mirror."

"That's . . . I don't even know what to say. Are Jon and Jess okay now?"

"Sort of. Jon is staying away from Ellen for now. His voice isn't quite back to normal, but it's better. Plus, now that he hasn't had Ava's tea for a few days, the impulse to tell Ellen his feelings has lessened. Jess felt fine after she stopped looking in the mirror. She even went on to work, although once she got there, she was near useless because she couldn't stop staring at her reflection in the coffeepot. They finally sent her home. She's probably there now. But, like Jon, since it's been a few days since she had the tea, she's getting better as time passes."

"Sheesh. Ava's never had anything like this happen before. Kat, what are we going to do? Ava's reputation will be in shambles. *All* our reputations will be in shambles."

"We just have to hope that Ava can fix whatever is wrong with her teas. And the sooner the better."

Sarah thought about Ava's exhausted expression at lunch. "I've got to talk to her. She said she was heading up to her greenhouses for the afternoon. Now I know why." Sarah stood and reached for her phone. "I'll text Grace and see if she can work the desk for an hour or so while I go see Ava." Grace Wheeler was the new mayor of Dove Pond and was both Sarah's best friend and next-door neighbor.

"Grace can do that? Just come and work here in the library?"

"She's the mayor. She can do anything she wants."

Kat had to smile. "I wouldn't tell her that. She's bossy enough as it is."

"I won't." Sarah texted Grace, and the answer came back almost instantly. "She's on her way."

Five minutes later, Sarah and Kat were hurrying up the sidewalk to Kat's white Audi roadster, which was parked in front of Paw Printz.

As they neared it, the door to the pet store swung open.

Kat stopped and spun to face Sarah. "Don't look."

Sarah came to an abrupt halt, confused. "What —"

"Just don't look," Kat hissed.

"Don't look at wha—"

Town sheriff Blake McIntyre sauntered out of the pet store and across the street, a bag of cat food tucked under one arm.

Sarah's breath caught in her throat, and her knees grew wobbly.

Kat said firmly, "Look. Away."

But it was too late. Sarah was already looking. And whenever she looked at Blake, she reacted.

Most of the time, Sarah considered herself a mature, capable, independent woman. Although Ava paid most of their housing costs, Sarah had her own job, paid her own bills, and drove her doublecab pickup truck like a boss. She'd been doing all of that since she graduated high school, too. But there was one thing that made her fall apart at the seams. He was six foot one, with light-brown hair and green eyes, and looked downright edible in his sheriff's uniform.

And right now, he was walking toward his office, striding along without a care in the world while she watched him, aching to say something brilliant, or fascinating, or —

"For the love of heaven!" Kat slipped her arm through Sarah's and dragged her the final steps to the Audi. "Come on!"

Sarah knew she should look away from Blake. Back in high school, she and Blake had had a strange on-again, off-again relationship. Although, technically, their relationship had never been fully "on." Instead, she'd liked him when he hadn't liked her and then vice versa. They'd done that strange back-and-forth for several years until, in high school, The Incident had happened.

Just thinking about it now made Sarah slightly sick to her stomach. For her own mental health, she should forget about The Incident and Blake and never think of either of them again. She knew that, but the second she saw him, her mind went into overdrive, and she couldn't seem to remember anything except how desperately she wanted him to like her.

Kat unlocked her car and practically shoved Sarah into the seat. Then Kat reached into the back seat, grabbed a ball cap, and slapped it on Sarah's head.

The brim obscured Sarah's vision, and Blake was mercifully out of sight.

Sarah put her hands over her hot face and moaned. "Why, oh why do I do that?"

"I have no idea." Kat shot Sarah an exasperated look. "But you need to figure it out. I've never seen anyone so determined to make a fool of themselves around a man."

"I can't help it. He's just there, and then I

start thinking, or maybe I stop thinking — Sheesh, I don't know, but it's been like this since I was fourteen."

Kat started her car and pulled out of her parking spot. "Maybe one of your books will tell you what's going on."

"I've asked and none of them know." Sarah slid down in her seat and tugged her ball cap lower, glad they were driving in the opposite direction, away from Blake. She didn't have time for this nonsense; she needed to focus on helping Ava. That was what was really important. "I wish Momma was still here. She always knew how to find answers, no matter what problems we had."

Kat turned the car onto Maple Street. "I'm just glad none of Ava's teas seem to have caused permanent damage."

"Ava makes them super weak, so they'll only work for a short time. She says people should be able to decide from day to day how they want to feel."

"She's as smart as your momma. I'd hate to think what would have happened if her teas didn't wear off. Erma, Jon, and Jess would be royally screwed."

Sarah agreed. They drove on in silence for a few moments and soon Kat turned the car down the long street that led to Ava's green-houses. *Hang on, Ava,* thought Sarah.

*We'll be there soon. We'll figure out what's going on with your teas and find an answer. I promise.*

# CHAPTER 5
## AVA

Ava stepped out of her greenhouse and walked past the half whiskey barrels that lined the parking lot. During the spring and summer months, big trucks arrived to pick up flats of herbs and flowers for various grocery and garden stores. Then, the dirt-filled barrels would be filled with a colorful array of flowers and would provide a much-needed protective barrier — more than one was cracked from being hit by an inattentive driver. But for now, the barrels stood silent and colorless, which matched her mood perfectly. She reached into her truck bed and fished out an empty box, then started back to the greenhouse.

Her steps slowed as she got closer. Things were going so, so wrong. After a nearly sleepless week searching for an answer to Erma's misfiring tea, and haunted by the mad thumping of the box under her bed, this morning Ava had discovered that two more of her teas had gone crazy.

*Two more. Oh God.*

Her head aching, she closed her eyes and took a deep breath. She'd had lunch with Sarah and had tried to keep her worries to herself. There was no sense in worrying her sister. Once lunch was over, Ava had immediately come here, to the greenhouses, where she and Sofia Rodriguez-Kaine, her greenhouse manager, had pored over the tea-making records, looking for clues.

What they'd discovered had given Ava a faint glimmer of hope — all three messed-up teas had been made at the exact same time. Even better, they were the only teas she'd made that night. The next step was to look at the common ingredients, but she'd had to leave that to Sofia, as Ava had been interrupted all afternoon by people calling to cancel their specialty tea orders. Ava had managed to talk most of them into waiting while she investigated the situation, but a few people had refused to be so patient. Her chest tightened. *I have to figure this out. I have to.*

She set the box by the door, too distressed to go back inside just yet. Sofia was there now with Kristen, moving all the plants Ava had used to make the wonky teas to one place so they could examine them. *Thank goodness for Sofia. I don't know what I'd do without her.*

When Sofia and her son, Noah, had first moved to Dove Pond, they'd rented the small farmhouse that sat at the bottom of the hill in front of the greenhouses. While living there, Noah had made friends with their next-door neighbor, Jake Kaine, a brilliant if odd game developer. One thing had led to another, and over time Jake and Sofia had started dating. They'd recently married, which meant that Ava's farmhouse was once again empty.

She wondered if Rick Donovan, whom she'd promoted from crew chief to manager of her landscaping business, might be interested in the rental. He was currently commuting from Bryson, which was quite a distance, so the little house might be just the thing for him. She made a mental note to ask him the next time she spoke to him.

Her shoulders tight, Ava stretched her arms over her head. She really should be inside helping Sofia and Kristen. And yet she lingered where she was, enjoying the afternoon sun as it dispelled the usual January chill. A row of Zéphirine Drouhin roses, thornless climbers she'd planted along a trellis that stood along the walkway to the supply shed, sat flowerless in the late-

January sun. The climbers had all been put to bed months ago, but come summer they'd bloom with pink, deliciously fragrant roses. She stooped beside one now and ran a finger over a branch. Instantly, her mind was filled with the tranquility of the healthy plant's deep slumber, which soothed her own troubled thoughts.

Her gaze moved from the branch to her hands, which always seemed faintly green, as if her skin had been stained from touching plants so often. She had discovered her gift on her seventh birthday, as all her sisters had. In the Dove household, the birthday girl always got her favorite meal, and at the time, Ava's happened to be hot dogs and baked beans. While waiting for her mother to finish the birthday feast, Ava had pushed Sarah in a stroller up and down their long driveway, a delightfully big and rambling if somewhat decrepit Queen Anne–style house. After their father's death, the house had grown more ramshackle each year and was now surrounded by thick overgrowth, the shrubbery out of control.

That day, the tenacious Floribunda rosebush at the corner of the front walk kept getting tangled around the stroller's wheels. At first, Ava had tried to steer out of the way, but the rosebush seemed determined to capture them as they passed. The fourth time it happened, Ava had gotten irritated, and without thinking, she'd snapped, "Stop that!"

For a startled moment she and the plant had stared at each other; then, after a stilted minute, the plant had rustled as if offering an apology. Slowly, leaf by leaf, it had curled back from the stroller and out of the way. The next time Ava walked past the bush, there was plenty of room for Sarah's stroller.

After that day, Ava would walk around the yard, trailing her fingertips over every leaf, every petal, every fresh bud. Plants didn't talk to her the way books talked to Sarah, as plants didn't use words so much as feelings. But Ava became an expert in reading those feelings. She started tending to the plants in their yard, knowing when they needed more water or sun, when they longed for shade, or just wanted some company. Later, she would grow flowers, shrubs, and herbs in the chipped pots she found in the old shed behind the house and then replant them in their yard until their house stood in the center of a lush, beguiling, fragrant garden.

The neighbors, enchanted by Ava's results, had hired her to work in their yards, too. Growing busier by the year, Ava had started her own landscaping business at the young age of sixteen. She'd been wildly successful, later branching into her specialty gourmet teas, which had done well, too. And soon, the Pink Magnolia Tearoom would be up and running, yet another notch in her business belt.

Or it would be another notch, if her misbehaving teas didn't derail her whole plan.

Ava collected the empty box she'd left beside the door. Before she'd faced this tea emergency, her biggest worry had been the secret she'd been keeping under her bed. Now she wasn't sure which she dreaded more. Either one could be disastrous.

Her shoulders aching under the weight of her thoughts, she had just swung the door open when a car pulled into the parking lot, the tires crunching on the gravel. She turned to see Sarah getting out of Kat's Audi.

Sarah hurried forward while Kat climbed out of the driver's seat. "Oh, Ava, I heard about the other two teas. Have you figured anything out?"

Ava looked past Sarah at Kat. "Chatty thing, aren't you?"

Kat closed her car door, looking sheepish. "If she hadn't heard it from me, she'd have found out from someone else. People in town have started talking."

"I know. I've had some cancellations."

Kat winced. "Oh no."

"We're here to help," Sarah announced, as if that made all the difference in the world.

Ava supposed a few more hands wouldn't hurt. "Come on in. Sofia, Kristen, and I have been —"

A familiar red pickup pulled into the lot and parked beside Kat's Audi. Dylan Fraser jumped out, flashing them an infectious smile. He was tall, Dylan was, close to six foot three. His hair was a deep auburn brown, an unusual color that was made all the more noticeable by how much it contrasted with his red beard. "I brought you all a visitor," he announced as he went to open his passenger door.

Aunt Jo swung her feet out, her cane in one hand, her huge purse in the other. Dylan helped her out of the truck and then followed her to where Ava, Sarah, and Kat stood. Aunt Jo's flowered dress and red wool coat were a stark contrast to Dylan's flannel, jeans, and work boots.

"Aunt Jo, what are you doing here? Did I forget your tea?" Ava rubbed her forehead, trying to remember her deliveries from yesterday. "I thought I dropped it off, but maybe I —"

"I've got it right here." Aunt Jo reached into her purse and pulled out her tea canister. "I brought it so you could test it."

"Test it?"

"To make sure it's not poison or anything."

Ava's face heated.

Dylan turned to Aunt Jo. "You've been using Ava's teas for years. I don't know how many times you've told me that your arthritis practically disappeared when you started taking that tea at bedtime."

"What do you know about tea? You don't even like it." Aunt Jo's bright brown gaze turned to Ava. "Is it true what they're saying about your teas? That they've been poisoned?"

"No, no! It's just . . ." Ava took a breath. "There was something wrong with three teas I made on a particular day. Just those three, and no more."

Sarah brightened. "They were all made on the same day?"

Ava nodded. "So far it doesn't seem any others were affected."

"That's a relief," Kat said.

"It is if I can figure out what went wrong." Aunt Jo put her canister back into her purse. "I guess I'll just hang on to this then. I was afraid I'd have to reuse my old tea leaves until you sorted things out. They would work, but the tea would be weak."

"You keep your old tea leaves?" Kat asked curiously.

"I mix them with potting soil. My petunias love them."

Sarah's attention was still on Ava. "You look a lot more hopeful this afternoon than you did at lunch."

"I make teas in groups that use similar ingredients. These three teas had four in common: lavender, peppermint, ginger, and dandelion root. Something had to have happened to one of the plants I used. Sofia and Kristen are pulling all of them out right now so we can look for fungal infections, thrips, scales — something that might affect a plant's health."

"We can help," Kat said.

"I'll come too," Aunt Jo announced. "Dylan, you might have to wait."

"I need to get back to the tearoom." He smiled at Ava. "I got a call that your cabinets are ready."

"They're early!" Ava exclaimed, ridiculously grateful for some good news.

"Surprised me too. I was on my way to pick them up when Aunt Jo called and asked for a ride. If I work a little extra, I should be able to get most of them installed today."

"By all means, go get them. I'll take Aunt Jo home later."

"We'll have to pick up Moon Pie from his spa day," Aunt Jo said. "He's at Paw Printz getting his hair done."

Ava smiled. "No problem. It's near my tearoom. Dylan, thanks for offering to work late. I feel bad about that."

He shrugged. "Your opening is coming up. I figured I'd better hop on this while I'm free. Will you be coming by?" His warm hazel gaze seemed hopeful.

"After I drop off Aunt Jo, sure." Ava appreciated Dylan's commitment to her tearoom. She couldn't have asked for a better contractor. "I want to see these cabinets in place. The kitchen will finally look kitchen-y."

"Yes, it will. I'll see you later, then." Still smiling, he headed for his truck.

They watched him pull out of the parking lot.

"Mm-hmm." Aunt Jo pursed her lips. "I knew it. That boy has a thing for you."

Kat nodded. "I was just thinking the same thing."

"Seemed like it to me too," Sarah added.

"You guys are crazy," Ava said. "Just because a guy is nice doesn't mean he 'has a thing' for you."

"I don't know," Sarah said. "He offered to work late."

Kat gave a nod. "Without any prompting, too."

"Sounds like love to me," Aunt Jo announced. "Come on, Kat. Let's go find Sofia. She's supposed to give me the recipe for that dish she made for Sunday supper at the church." The older woman went inside and Kat, grinning, followed.

"Ridiculous," Ava muttered as she moved the empty box to her other hip and started to follow them.

Sarah grabbed Ava's arm and stopped her. "Ridiculous or not, he's a nice guy."

"I don't have time for nice guys, or bad ones, either. I've got this mess with the teas, and the tearoom, and the b—" She caught herself just in time, adding lamely, "And other things, too."

"Once we get this tea mystery solved, you'll have more time. Ava, don't look so worried. It's all going to work out. I know it."

Despite the circumstances, Sarah's smile made Ava smile in return.

That was Sarah for you. Her inherent optimism brought hope and happiness to those she loved. Ava still remembered when, three days after her fifth birthday, their mother had brought Sarah home from the hospital. Their father had died only a few months before, and times had been dark. But then Momma had brought home Sarah, who with her toothless grin and belly-deep chuckle had brought them all back to life.

When Ava first held her baby sister, she'd been speechless with delight. Sarah had been tiny and doll-like, and she'd gurgled with happiness as if just as pleased to meet Ava as Ava was to meet her. Since Ava had just celebrated her birthday, she'd believed with all her five-year-old heart that the baby was her own special birthday present.

After Sarah's birth, Momma was often tired, and since her older sisters rolled their eyes and complained when asked to babysit, playing with and caring for Sarah became Ava's expected chore, one she enthusiastically accepted, and one she took on full-time fourteen years later when Momma died.

Ava smiled at her sister now. "I wish I believed in me as much as you do."

"You make it easy," Sarah said simply. "Now, come on. We'd better get in there. Aunt Jo isn't what I'd call patient." She grinned and then went inside, leaving Ava standing at the threshold.

Ava closed her eyes. *I don't deserve that. I should —*

"Ava?" Aunt Jo called from the green-house. "Are you gonna help or not?"

Ava sighed and went inside.

Kat, Aunt Jo, and Sarah were standing to one side of a long, shiny metal worktable that held a neat row of ginger and pep-permint plants. Kristen was at another table, examining a row of lavender plants.

"Where's Sofia?" Ava set the empty box on the table near Aunt Jo.

"Here!" Sofia came in carrying a flat of dandelions and placed it near the lavender. She was a small, slender woman with thick brown hair and sparkling brown eyes. "This is the last one."

"All right, then." Ava turned to her friends. "Divide the plants up between you. We have to examine them one at a time. Every leaf, every stem."

Sofia gave Sarah, Kat, and Aunt Jo a quick lesson on what to look for, and soon they were all working.

Kat pulled a plant closer so she could see it better. "You didn't mention looking for aphids or anything like that. Should we keep an eye out for those, too?"

"I doubt you'll find aphids," Sofia said,

not looking up from where she was examining a leaf. "We use organic, natural pesticides like lemon oil and basil. Still, if you see anything unexpected, let us know."

Kat nodded and went back to work.

Not seeing anything amiss with the plant she'd been examining, Ava moved to a new one. Right now, the three canisters of messed-up teas were safely locked in a cabinet in the tearoom's kitchen. As soon as she figured out what had gone amiss, she'd get rid of them. She'd kept them just in case she needed to have them analyzed by a lab. *Which I'll do if we don't find anything today.*

They continued to examine the plants. A half hour later, Ava pulled a dandelion plant closer, trailing her fingers over each leaf, flower, and stalk. They all hummed with health, not a leaf out of place. *What could it be? I don't —*

"My gosh."

She turned around to find Sarah staring at a peppermint plant.

"Look at this." Sarah pulled the pot to the edge of the metal table.

Everyone moved closer. The side facing Ava looked normal enough, the leaves green and healthy. Sarah turned the plant, and Ava's eyebrows rose. The other side of the plant was a wilted, brown-spotted mess.

117

"Oh dear."

"What caused that?" Aunt Jo asked. "A blight of some kind?"

"I've never seen a blight like that." Sofia peered at the leaves. "It looks as if it's been burned, but only in spots."

Ava reached out and ran her fingers over the closest leaves. Instantly, a tingle rose through her fingers to her arm and then her heart — a deep darkness that ripped her breath away and left her gasping.

She yanked her hand free and stepped back, waving her burning fingers in the air. "Ow, ow, ow!"

Aunt Jo's eyes were as round as saucers. "Lord, but I thought you were going to pass out."

"Are you okay?" Sarah demanded. "You went white."

"I'm fine," Ava said shortly. But she wasn't fine. Not even a little. Her hands were shaking, her head ached even more than it had before, and her stomach was faintly sick. In all her years of working with plants, she'd never felt such a strong reaction. She looked at the poor thing. *Dear God, what happened to you?*

Sarah touched the damaged leaves. "Sofia's right; these look burned. You're sure there was no fire?"

Ava shook her head. "Are any of the other plants this way? We should check them all."

Everyone hurried to look.

After a few minutes, Sofia set the last pot of dandelions down. "Nothing here."

"None of the ginger has those spots," Kat announced.

"The rest of the peppermint looks fine too," Sarah said.

Sofia looked at Kristen. "How about the lavender?"

The teen blinked. "I didn't look. I was — But I'll check them now." She spun on her heel and hurried to the lavender plants and looked through them. "They're fine."

"It's settled, then," Aunt Jo announced. "This is the plant that messed up your teas."

"It's not enough to know which plant caused the problem." Ava eyed the wilted, blackened leaves. "If we don't figure out what harmed this plant, we can't keep it from happening again."

Sarah sighed and touched the leaves closest to her. A few fell off, drifting to the countertop. "You might as well destroy this one. You can't use it in your teas anymore, and —"

*"No!"*

Everyone turned to where Kristen stood. She flushed. "Please don't hurt it." She

119

looked ready to burst into tears. "Mom loved peppermint. I used to take her sprigs of it. She'd put them under her pillow so she could wake up to the smell." Kristen's lips quivered as she spoke.

*Oh dear. I've been so wrapped up in the tea mystery that I forgot how raw Kristen's feelings are right now.* "That was very kind of you. But don't worry; I'm not going to destroy this plant."

"You promise?"

"Of course. I'm going to take it to my house and make it healthy again. It may take a while, though." Ava held her breath and gently removed a crumbled leaf, fighting the wave of despair that rippled through her at that simple touch. "I just wish I knew what happened to the poor thing."

"Can't it tell you?" Aunt Jo asked.

"They don't communicate like that."

Aunt Jo glanced at Sarah and asked hopefully, "Have any books asked to visit your sister? Maybe one of them knows something helpful."

Sarah shook her head. "I walked through the gardening section twice today, but nope. They were all quiet."

Ava rubbed her hand on her jeans, trying to ease the burning sensation. "I don't understand this at all. This plant . . . it felt

120

as if she had been through something horrible. I just don't know what —"

"I know what happened to her," Kristen said.

Sarah and Ava exchanged surprised glances while the others stared at the teenager. Ava finally found her voice. "Kristen? Did you . . . did you do something to this plant?"

"I might have. But I didn't mean to. I was . . . I didn't know . . ." Kristen swiped a tear from her cheek. "The night Mom died, I needed to get away from the house. I didn't want to see them put her in the ambulance with a sheet over her, so I came here. I took one of the peppermint plants, it must have been this one, and I — I was just going to hug it, but I was crying and . . . I guess it was bad for the plant."

"You wept over it," Ava said slowly. Which explained the wrenching emotion she'd felt when she'd touched the leaves. The plant must have absorbed Kristen's grief along with her tears. *I've never seen anything like this.*

"How did you get in?" Sarah asked.

"She has a key," Sofia said. "She sometimes stops by to do the watering and pH testing when I'm busy."

Kristen nodded miserably, another tear

rolling down and joining the others, her face streaked with wetness.

"Oh, sweetheart." Aunt Jo picked up her huge purse from where she'd set it on a low shelf and dug out a packet of tissues.

"Thank you," Kristen said in a choked voice.

"That's quite all right. Keep the whole pack. I have ten more in my purse, and they're just getting in the way. I almost couldn't find my sandwich at lunch."

Kristen swiped at her eyes. "Ava, I'm so sorry. I didn't mean any harm. I just —" Another tear leaked out, and she wiped at it with her crumpled tissue. "Ugh! I hate that I keep crying."

"Don't," Ava said. "That's just normal."

"Nothing feels normal right now. I'm so over it." Kristen's gaze moved back to the plant, and she walked closer to it, reaching out to touch one of the wilted leaves. "I didn't mean to hurt it."

"Of course you didn't." Ava watched Kristen, remembering her own grief when Momma died. "Do you come here often?"

The teenager shot Ava a sad, guilty look. "Once in a while, when I can't stand being in the house anymore. I rarely stay long. Well, except that night. I came here and took this plant, and we sat on the couch in the office and waited until —" She winced. "I waited until I thought it was safe to go home. Ava, I promise I didn't know my tears would hurt the leaves. They didn't look any different when I left. But I should have told you I'd been here. I didn't think it would matter. When I heard that some of your teas were acting up, I didn't even think about that night."

"I wouldn't have thought about it, either." Ava went to Kristen and gave the girl a hug. "But now we know, don't we?"

"I'm so sorry."

"Pah! Stop worrying about it." Ava smiled and kissed Kristen's cheek before releasing her. "I'm just glad that the mystery has been solved." She turned to Sofia. "What day did I make those teas?"

Sofia picked up the clipboard and flipped through some pages. "Two days after Julie's death. I collected the leaves you needed and left them on the table for you. So they must have come from that particular plant."

Ava nodded, a slow roll of relief easing the tightness in her chest. *It won't happen again. That's all that matters.* "I'll be taking this plant home with me."

Kristen still looked worried. "The teas didn't hurt anyone, did they? I mean —"

"No, no! No one was hurt. The teas acted

up in silly ways, plus I never make them full strength, so they wear off." That was one mistake she'd made early, early on. *Never again.*

Kristen wrung her hands. "I won't come back to the greenhouses without permission again. I —"

"Kristen, stop. You're always welcome here. If you want some space or privacy, you have the keys, so use them. Or, if you want, come to our house. Sarah and I would love to have you any time you need a little break."

"You could visit me, too," Kat added. "Mom would love more visitors."

"Kristen would be happier at my house." Aunt Jo cupped her mouth and said in a stage whisper, "I always have cake, *and* I have Moon Pie. He loves a visitor."

"Thank you." The sadness on Kristen's face softened. She looked around the conservatory. "It's peaceful here, though, and sometimes I just want to be alone."

Ava looked at the plant that had soaked in Kristen's grief and suffered with her. She put her arm around Kristen once more. "The plant will recover."

Kristen looked hopeful. "Really?"

"Yes. And so will you. It'll just take some extra care and some time."

"I'm embarrassed I cried that much." Kristen gave an awkward grimace as she hugged Ava back. "It was an ugly cry, too."

"Tears are angel breaths," Aunt Jo said. "You were just giving your mom a proper send-off. She would have approved, too."

Ava had to agree. "If there was one thing Julie was an expert at, it was emotion. She understood it deeply. Probably because she had a bit more than the rest of us."

Kristen nodded. "I used to wonder what it would be like to be inside her head."

Sarah smiled. "Your mother used to come to the library all the time. When she was on the upswing, she'd check out happy books, hopeful books, books about love and friendship and happiness — mostly romances."

Kristen's gaze locked on Sarah. "And when she was on the downswing?"

"Books about struggles and the people who overcame them. She found hope in those stories. She never once checked out a negative book, even when she didn't feel well."

Kristen smiled. It wasn't a big smile, but a tiny, almost hopeful smile, one that might, if given the chance, grow into something bigger. "Mom was different, but I loved that about her." Kristen's voice thickened. "I loved everything about her."

Ava thought she knew what would help the plant, but she had no idea how to help Kristen. Experience, and a certain book Sarah had given her long ago, had taught Ava that grief wasn't eased from the outside in, but from the inside out.

Kristen sniffed and pulled out her tissue pack, mumbling, "Sorry."

Aunt Jo chuckled. "Lord love you, child. Tears are a testament to the strength of a person's memory. I hope y'all weep for *months* when I decide to float up the golden ladder."

Sarah pretended to be shocked. "Months?"

"Well, two days, anyway."

"Tell you what. I'll make it three if you'll bake me some of your cinnamon scones."

Aunt Jo pretended to consider this. "That's three whole days of weeping? And lots of sighs, too?"

Sarah's eyes narrowed. "How many scones?"

"A dozen. But you have to weep in public." Aunt Jo leaned closer to Kristen. "It's nice to be publicly acknowledged."

"Deal." Sarah held out her hand.

Aunt Jo shook it. "I do love to bake. Kristen, I can drop a batch of scones off for you and your grandmother, too, if you'd like."

"I'd love that, but I'm not sure about Grandma Ellen. She doesn't eat a lot of carbs."

"Unnatural creature!" Aunt Jo declared, making Kristen laugh.

Ava picked up the sagging plant. "Kristen, would you mind putting this in my truck? It should be safe on the passenger-side floorboard."

Sofia added, "And when you're done with that, would you mind heading to the shed and putting those new pots on the correct shelves? I haven't had time to do it today."

"Sure." Looking relieved to be busy, Kristen picked up the plant and carefully carried it out of the greenhouse.

Ava watched her go, glad they'd been able to get Kristen to smile, at least for a moment. Grief was tricky. It came and went like the surf, knocking a person off their feet when they least expected it. It would take a thousand little smiles before Kristen's grief-stricken heart healed enough to give her the stability to fight off those waves by herself, but time would see to that.

Ava eyed the spot where the plant had been and picked up a browned, curled-up leaf that had dropped. It crumbled under her touch, and she felt that sweep of anguish yet again. "I can see how grief affected the plant, but I'm not entirely sure how it changed the purpose of those three teas."

"We should consider the effects one at a time," Kat suggested. "The tea you gave Jon, the one that infuses romance into tired relationships, made him speak nonstop. What does grief have to do with that?"

Ava didn't know.

Sofia shook her head slowly. "That's the question, isn't it?"

They all stared at the empty spot where the plant had been.

Sarah fiddled with her braid, absently running the ends through her fingers. "Some people want to be around other people when they're sad. Maybe grief makes them all want to talk to someone?"

Ava pursed her lips. "I don't think that's it. Jon felt like he had to express his feelings, but Erma's uncle had something specific to tell her, while Jessica didn't talk at all and just kept staring at her own reflection."

"That's true," Kat said, scrunching her nose. "I don't see what those three cases have in common with grief."

There had to be something. Ava frowned, trying to think of an answer. The silence lengthened, and Ava, unable to think of a single thing, had just opened her mouth to suggest they all go home and ruminate on the puzzle for a few days, when Aunt Jo snorted.

"I know what it is," she announced. "If there's one thing I've learned over my lifetime, it's that grief can be brutally honest. When you're young, you think you'll live forever, so it's easy to pretend things are okay when they're not. It's when you know without question that you have no more time that you're forced to face the truth."

"What truth?" Sarah asked.

Aunt Jo shrugged. "Whatever truth you've been avoiding. Grief can cause people to blurt out their most brutal truths. That's why there are so many arguments at funerals. And there was Jon, blurting out his feelings nonstop."

"So the grief in the plant made Jon more honest," Ava said thoughtfully. It was possible.

"Ah. I can see that," Sofia said. "Jon is friends with my husband, so I see him and Ellen often. It drove Ellen bonkers he wasn't comfortable talking about his feelings because she's the opposite. It was obvious, though, that he was crazy about her, but just couldn't put it into words. Maybe all the feelings he'd bottled up just poured out and kept pouring out."

"Brutal truth," Aunt Jo said, nodding.

"What about the tea that was supposed to ease Jessica's anxiety?" Kat asked.

"That one's tougher," Ava said. "What does anxiety have to do with truth?"

"I know all about anxiety," Sofia said. "My son has Asperger's, so worrying is second nature for me. I've found that if I don't have a reason for feeling anxious, I'll start looking for one." She winced. "That's silly, but anxiety does that. In those instances, it would make sense if I looked in the mirror to remind myself of who I really am. That I'm Noah's mother and that we're both okay, and that while I may make a few mistakes, I'm doing the best I can."

"Another brutal truth," Aunt Jo announced. "Jessica is fine; she just doesn't *feel* fine. That's a big difference."

"You do great with Noah," Ava said to Sofia.

She sent Ava a grateful smile. "Thank you. I try. That's all I can do."

Aunt Jo rubbed her hands together. "Look at us, solving mysteries like Sherlock Holmes! Ava, what exactly did Erma's tea do?"

"It was supposed to help her sleep," Ava answered. "That part worked, but while she was sleeping, her dead uncle visited her and yelled at her for giving something to his ex-wife that he'd wanted Erma and her sisters to have. Now that I think about it, that's a brutal truth all by itself."

"Well, there you have it, then." Aunt Jo beamed at them. "Three teas and three brutal truths. Problem solved!"

"Apparently so." Ava let out a deep sigh, grateful all over again for her friends.

Aunt Jo picked up her purse. "Well, children, now that you're on your way to salvation, I'd better go. Poor Moon Pie will wonder where I am. Plus, I have to get ready for the deacon's meeting. If I'm not there, Evelyn Fabrizio will vote out the annual bake sale. She's a devil in a blue dress, that one, and I don't trust her as far as I can throw her, although she doesn't weigh much, so I could probably throw her a long way."

"She's a pain," Sarah agreed. "I'm surprised Preacher Thomas named her a deacon."

"I wasn't," Aunt Jo said. "Keep your friends close and your enemies closer."

Ava had to laugh. "Good advice, always. Aunt Jo, I'll take you home after we rescue Moon Pie from his spa day. I need to get that plant to the house, and then I want to stop by the tearoom to see the new cabinets."

"Don't forget you owe me scones," Sarah said.

"You'll get them." Aunt Jo made her way to the door, saying as she went, "Scones or no, after I'm gone, if you all don't mourn me loud enough, I'll haunt each and every one of you. And I won't need one of Ava's grief teas to do it, neither." Grinning, Aunt Jo waved and left, the door closing smartly behind her.

"I guess we've been told," Ava said to the others. Laughing, she followed Aunt Jo into the parking lot. One problem was solved, and for that Ava was grateful. Now all she had to do was finish her tearoom and find the strength to face the secret that was banging away under her bed. *Two out of three problems left. It's a start.*

And yet, even as Ava drove Aunt Jo home, somewhere in the distance, she could hear the wild thumping of the box under her bed. The time was coming. Everything she'd worked so hard to hide would be out in the open for everyone to see. And that was one brutal truth she wasn't ready, willing, or able to face.

Not yet.

# CHAPTER 6
## KRISTEN

A week later, Kristen sat down at one of the two wrought-iron café tables that had been assembled for the tearoom, taking a break after three long hours of unpacking merchandise. "I'm so tired I could sleep to next Christmas."

Missy, who'd just arrived, sent her a sympathetic look. "Still not sleeping?" She slid a cup of hot chocolate to Kristen, the words MOONLIGHT CAFÉ printed on the paper cup.

"Not a wink. I keep thinking about stuff." What she really kept thinking about was Mom and the poor plant Kristen had accidentally ruined, but she didn't feel like explaining all of that to Missy.

Kristen took the hot chocolate and removed the lid, steam curling up. "Grandma Ellen's not sleeping well either. I hear her walking around at all hours of the night."

"I'm surprised your wolf pack doesn't

complain about that."

"They're used to her now. Well, except Chuffy. He doesn't like strangers in the house, and Grandma Ellen hasn't exactly tried to charm him." Kristen blew on the hot chocolate and took a sip. She waited for the deliciousness to slip over her tongue, but nothing happened. Somehow missing Mom had affected Kristen's taste buds until food had the flavor of sawdust.

Aware of Missy's expectant gaze, Kristen forced a smile. "Sooo good." She was getting good at fake-smiling, even with her friends, which made her feel like a poser.

"It's the best." Missy's gaze swept around the tearoom. "I can't wait for this place to open. It's already lit and it's not even done yet."

A burst of pride warmed Kristen. "It's been a lot of work," she admitted. "But totally worth it."

A few years ago, when Mom had suggested Kristen ask Ava for a job at her greenhouses during the summer months, Kristen had dragged her feet. She knew the Dove sisters, of course. Everyone did. But it had seemed awkward to ask one of them for a job. Mom had persisted, though, and Kristen had eventually screwed up the nerve to ask. To her surprise, Ava had hired her on the spot.

"How is life with the Frosty One?" Missy asked.

Kristen sighed, her breath rippling across her hot chocolate. "The Frosty One is pretending she has no choice but to fix up my house and sell it, and I'm pretending I don't care if she does and forces me to move to her ice castle in Raleigh."

"Still being super nice to her?"

"As sweet as pie. It's working, too, at least for now. She's not bringing up the move quite as often, so I have some time to come up with a way out of this mess." Kristen looked at her cup of hot chocolate. "Of course, I've had more than a week and I haven't thought of a single thing."

Missy lowered her cup of hot chocolate, looking concerned. "Can she really sell your house out from under you like that?"

"She's the executor of the estate, and I'm a minor, so yes. Right now, she's holding off on talking about the actual sale and instead just talks about how much I'll like Raleigh, the schools there, her big house, yada yada. And in return, I act as if I'm interested."

"That's some passive-aggressive stuff right there."

Kristen shrugged, a little hurt Missy thought that. Kristen wasn't being passive-aggressive; she was being Diana Prince–level strategic. But Kristen didn't have the energy to explain herself, not even to her friend.

Mom had said that after she died, Kristen would feel alone at times. What Mom hadn't mentioned was how bleak and empty that feeling would be. How it would seep through her body and weigh her down like she was trying to swim upstream while wearing a coat stuffed with bricks. That there would be moments when she would feel as if she couldn't breathe, as if her heart might drop out of its place and —

Missy grasped Kristen's wrist. "Don't look like that."

Her face hot, Kristen gently freed her wrist, picked up her cup, and took another sip. "I'm fine. I really am. I just need to —"

The door swung open, and Josh stuck his head in. He brightened on seeing the two of them and came inside. "There you are! I looked for you all at the Moonlight." He unwound his scarf as he walked to their table, and Kristen could tell from the way it had been neatly knotted around his throat that his mother had put it on him as he left the house.

Kristen loved his family. Josh's mom, Juana, was a waitress at the truck stop off Highway 26 that crossed Sam's Gap near the Tennessee border. She was funny and sharp and ran her household with an iron fist, while her husband, a large man with an even bigger smile who owned his own auto parts store, made sure Josh and his sisters jumped whenever Momma Juana said to.

Josh dropped into a chair next to Missy, his gaze falling on their cups of hot chocolate. "You guys went to the Moonlight." There was a definite note of disappointment in his voice.

"No, *I* went to the Moonlight," Missy said primly. "I would have gotten you something, too, but you never answer your texts, so . . ." She shrugged.

Josh pulled out his old, beaten-up iPhone. Kristen didn't think she'd ever seen it when the screen wasn't cracked.

He scowled. "I don't have any messages from you."

"Sure you do. Look. . . ." Missy had leaned over, ready to prove him wrong. "Huh. They're not there. I sent you four." She reached into her purse and pulled out her brand-new monster of a phone, which shone in a sparkling pink case. "See?" She showed him the texts she'd sent. "You need a new phone."

"Tell me about it," Josh grumbled as he stuffed his phone back into his pocket. "I'm only making $115.14 a week working for my dad at his auto parts store, and I have to pay for my own gas and insurance out of that." He slumped in his chair and said sourly, "I'll be thirty before I can afford a new phone. Heck, I can't even afford hot chocolate."

Kristen slid her cup to his side of the table. "You can have the rest of mine." She couldn't taste it anyway.

"I'm not taking your hot chocolate. I was just kidding about not being able to afford it. It's the new phone I can't afford."

"Take it." She got up. "I've got to get back to work."

"I guess that means we should go," Missy said, looking disappointed.

"You all can stay. I'm just unpacking boxes."

Josh picked up the hot chocolate and looked around the room. "Where's Ava?"

Kristen went to a row of boxes resting against a wall. "She's at the post office trying to trace a shipment that never arrived." She carried a box to a table near her friends, opened it, and began to unpack a number of small, vintage china plates. They were beautiful, all different sizes and colors.

Missy leaned forward. "I like those."

"Me too. Ava wanted every teacup and

saucer to be different, so she bought boxes of them from an antique store in New York City that was closing."

Missy eyed the plates with envy. "That's a neat idea. When I have my own apartment, I'm going to do the same thing."

Josh rolled his eyes. "You and your imaginary apartment."

"Kristen will be my roommate and she is not imaginary. We're going to Appy State together and are going to join the same sorority. Aren't we, Kristen?"

Kristen didn't want to join a sorority, but she decided not to go Godzilla on Missy's Tokyo. "Sure. Why not."

"Ohhh!" Missy pointed to the plate Kristen had just unwrapped. "I love that one."

The delicate eggshell-white saucer had an array of beautiful blue and purple flowers hand-painted along one edge. *Mom will love these. I should show her —*

A sweeping pain rippled through her. *Oh God. How could I forget?*

It wasn't the first time, either. Just this morning, in a hurry to leave for school, she'd glanced through the open door of her mom's bedroom and said, "See you later!" She'd done it out of habit, but no answering smile had met her. Instead, Kristen had found herself standing in the doorway, staring at an empty bed, her heart breaking all over again.

"Kristen?"

Both Missy and Josh were looking at her, their expressions a mixture of embarrassment and sympathy, neither of which she wanted.

She ducked her head and collected the plates she'd already unwrapped. "I need to take these to the kitchen." Clutching the plates, she hurried from the room.

Once in the kitchen she let out her breath and set the plates on the stainless-steel counter, angry at her lack of control. It was so embarrassing to break down in front of her friends like that. It seemed weak and needy. "Life is so damn unfair!" For some reason, cursing out loud gave her a tiny release. Grateful even for that, she rinsed the plates and then looked for a dish towel. Seeing none, she went to the storage cabinet, pulled her keys from her pocket, and undid the lock.

As she tugged a new dish towel out of the package, she accidentally knocked over a tea canister that had been sitting behind it. "Oof." She returned it to an upright position, absently noting that the label had been partially torn off, only the words TO INDUCE SLEEP still visible. *That must be Erma Tin-*

*gle's messed-up tea. I wonder why Ava's keeping it?*

Shrugging, Kristen locked the door, returned her keys to her pocket, and went back to the sink. There, she soaked the dish towel in cold water, wrung it out, and held it over her burning eyelids. The coolness helped her eyes, but did nothing for her aching chest. She gritted her teeth, refusing to give in to the tears that threatened. *Oh, Mom. I don't know if I can do this. This is so much harder than we thought it would be.*

In the months after Mom had gotten sick, she'd begun what she'd dubbed "Life After." Life After was short for Life After Mom Is Gone. Just like everything she did, Mom had been overly enthusiastic, even making matching T-shirts with a logo she'd sketched of the two of them, arms around each other, facing a beautiful sunset.

Kristen had hated wearing that stupid shirt, but after Mom died, she'd kept it under her pillow. Every night, exhausted and unable to sleep, she wept into the soft folds of the shirt.

Kristen removed the wet dish towel from her eyes, rinsed it again, and hung it over the edge of the sink. Life After was a fail. None of the things Mom had thought would help had lessened Kristen's grief even a little

— not the scrapbook filled with memories, the shadow box of what they thought the afterlife might look like, the discussions about grief and depression, the recipe book of comfort food that consisted mainly of mac and cheese and bacon dishes, or the cards and videos Mom had made to mark the landmark events in Kristen's future that she would miss.

"This will help," Mom would say as she tucked another thing into the nearly full box.

*As if anything could.* Nothing could erase the fact that Kristen was alone. So alone that her bones felt empty and hollow.

She realized she was clenching her jaw so tightly her entire face ached from it. She'd had six whole months to prepare for Mom's death. Six months and three days from the time Mom had sat her down and told her the treatment for her breast cancer wasn't working and all that was left was "stretching" time.

But time didn't stretch. The more Mom had tried to hold on to it, the faster it had slipped away.

"Kristen?" Missy called from the front room, sounding worried.

"Just a sec!" Kristen winced when her voice cracked. She knew what she'd see when she went back into the tearoom: the furtive looks of sympathy and pity, as if they thought she might melt away right in front of them.

She couldn't blame them, though. Emotions tangled inside of her, knotted so tightly that she could barely function, her anger bubbling inside like a volcano just waiting to blow. If she hadn't had her friends and her job, she would have been well and truly lost.

*But I do have this job. And I do have friends. And Ava is there if I need her, too.* Kristen pressed her fingertips over her hot, swollen eyes. *I can do this. I just have to keep busy and find a way to convince Grandma Ellen to let me stay in Dove Pond. That's it. Just those two things. Nothing else matters.*

She took a long, slow, shuddering breath and then schooled her expression into what she hoped was a fairly normal one. Squaring her shoulders, she returned to the main room. Just as she came around the corner, she heard Missy say, "*You* ask her. I'm not going to. I'm —"

"Ask me what?" Kristen's voice cracked with impatience. Embarrassed at how demanding she sounded, she went back to the crate and pulled out another stack of dishes.

Missy sent Josh a hard look. "Nothing.

Josh is just being insensitive."

"How am I being insensitive?" He turned to Kristen. "I was just saying that we should ask what you're going to do now. There's nothing wrong with that, is there?"

"No." She was grateful for his honesty. "I was telling Missy before you came in that I could use some help trying to figure out a way to keep Grandma Ellen from making me move to Raleigh."

"Sure," Josh said, as if it would be the easiest thing in the world.

Missy rolled her eyes but didn't argue.

Kristen unwrapped a plate, this one a delicate yellow with a silver edge. She didn't have control over a lot of things right now, so being able to keep Grandma and her demands at bay had been a particularly sweet victory, but it was only a temporary one. "I'm not going to move to Raleigh, no matter what Grandma says."

"Can't your grandma move here?" Josh asked.

"She has a job. She's pretty important, if the number of phone calls she gets is any indication." Kristen thought about her grandmother's house on the glossy pages of *Architectural Digest*. It was beautiful, decorated in shades of white and cream and gray, as chilly as her grandmother's too-polite smile. It was funny how opposite Mom's house was from her mother's. *Polar opposites.*

"If you don't want to move, then you shouldn't have to," Josh said in a firm tone. He stared at his hot chocolate cup as if looking for an answer there, his brow furrowed. "Hmm. I wonder if . . ."

Missy waited, her eyebrows raising. Finally, she snapped out, "Josh, spit it out! Can't you see how shook Kristen is?"

He flushed. "I was just wondering if she could come live with one of us." He looked at Kristen. "My parents love you. Mom says you're her *otra niña.*"

Kristen sighed wistfully. "I wish I could, but Grandma Ellen would never agree to it. She doesn't know your parents."

"She doesn't know mine, either," Missy said regretfully.

"Can't you go to court and ask to be . . ." He frowned. "I don't know what it's called, but I know it can be done."

"Emancipated." Kristen pulled another plate from the box and unwrapped it. "I called the lawyer who represents the estate and asked."

"What did he say?" Missy asked.

"Unless Grandma gives her permission, I still couldn't access the money Mom left me. Not until I'm twenty-five, anyway."

"*Twenty-five?*" Missy had stiffened with outrage.

Kristen nodded. "Until then, the money is under the Frosty One's control."

Missy scowled. "Why did your mom do that?"

"I have no idea."

They were silent a moment, all thinking, when Missy said, "Then do it without the money. You've already got a house. What more do you need?"

"Food." Josh started counting on his fingers. "Gas, insurance, electricity, water, cable, clothes —"

Missy punched his arm.

"Ow!"

"Can't you think of something positive to say?"

"Not about this, I can't!"

Kristen put another plate on the stack. "He's right. There's still a mortgage on the house, too. It's a lot of money, a lot more than I make here."

Missy's face fell. "I guess a second job wouldn't be enough then, either."

"No, and I can't risk my grades. I've got calculus and chemistry next year." Kristen was on track to be the class valedictorian and she couldn't give that up. She hadn't told either Missy or Josh about it, as neither of them cared about grades the way she did, but she and Mom had been excited about it.

Josh rubbed his chin. "I can't believe your mom didn't realize this would happen."

"She wasn't the best at planning." Kristen put the empty box on the floor and came to sit with them, sliding back into her chair. "I'm surprised she had a will and set up a trust. Grandma Ellen was shocked by that." Mom had been haphazard about everything in her life. Kristen couldn't count the times the electricity had been shut off; not because Mom didn't have the money, but because she'd simply forgotten to pay it. Two years ago, tired of cold showers, Kristen had set up online payments and had kept an eye on it since.

But somehow, for all of Mom's inability to pay attention to the details of life, with the exception of whom she'd chosen as Kristen's guardian, she had been meticulous when it had come to her death.

Josh sighed. "I hate to say this, but it sounds like your only option is to win over the Frosty One."

"That won't happen."

Missy's jaw set in a stubborn line. "You can't leave us. We're all going to junior prom together, and who will eat lunch with us every day?"

"I'm lucky Grandma Ellen didn't pack my stuff and toss it in her car the second the funeral was over," Kristen said somberly. She didn't know what she'd have done then. "She's not very patient. I can tell that already."

Suddenly restless, Kristen stood and returned to the wall of boxes, where she picked up a small but heavy box of silverware. She set it on the table beside the stacks of plates and opened it. Inside was an assortment of silver teaspoons, the handles flowered or engraved, each one as different as the plates. She started sorting them into stacks of ten.

Josh put an elbow on the table and rested his chin in his palm. "It's too bad your dad isn't around. He could —"

"Josh!" Missy sent him a warning glance.

"What? It's true. If Kristen's dad lived in Dove P— *Ow*!" He bent down and rubbed his shin. "Why did you kick me?"

"Because sometimes you don't think before you talk!" Missy's face was red. "She doesn't know who her dad is. She's told us that before."

"Sorry," Josh mumbled as he sent a self-conscious look at Kristen.

She shrugged, still counting out the silver-ware. "I don't mind. Besides, my dad lives here; I've just never met him."

Neither Missy nor Josh said anything.

Kristen started a new stack of ten spoons.

The silence lingered.

And lingered.

She looked up to see what they were do-ing.

Both of them were staring at her, their mouths agape.

*"You know who your dad is?"* Missy asked.

"I didn't say that. I said he lives here in Dove Pond. Or he did four years ago."

Josh slapped his hands on the table. "That's it, then! Kristen, your dad is the answer. You just have to find him and convince him to let you live with him until you graduate."

Kristen froze, her gaze locked on Josh. The idea was so beautifully simple. So perfect and simple that it just might work. She put down the spoon she was holding and said in a wondering voice, "I need to find my dad."

"Right away," Missy said eagerly. "Where in Dove Pond does he live?"

"I don't know." Kristen left the spoons and went back to the table to sit with her friends. "I know he lives in town but that's it."

Missy's smile faded. "That's it? You don't have a name or a picture or anything else?" When Kristen shook her head, Missy leaned back in her seat, looking stunned.

Josh held up his hands like he was trying to stop traffic. "Wait, wait, wait. How does that even happen?"

"Mom never talked about him. When I was twelve, I decided I wanted to know who he was, so I asked."

Missy blinked. "You hadn't asked before that? Not once?"

"A few times, but not seriously. It upset Mom, so I stopped. Besides, I was happy. Mom was happy. I probably wouldn't have asked again, but then there was that father-daughter dance in middle school. Remember that, Missy?"

"It was only the lamest evening of my life. Humiliating. My dad did the funky chicken right there in front of God and everyone." She shuddered.

"Yeah, well, everyone went to that dance except me and Ashley Morgan. Ashley's dad was in jail at the time — bad checks, I think — but I wanted to go, so I asked Mom about my dad."

"And?"

"She didn't want to tell me at first, said it was complicated and we didn't need another person in our lives, but I begged and begged. After a while, she gave in. She said he was here, in town, and that he'd always been close by."

Missy's eyes couldn't get any bigger. "I bet you were shocked."

"I was. *But* she also admitted that he didn't know about me and would be surprised to meet me."

Josh winced. "Ouch!"

"I know, right? Not the best circumstances to get an invitation to a father-daughter dance. But I really, really wanted to go. So Mom and I got in the car, and we headed to town. And on the way, I changed my mind."

"Why?" Missy asked, bewildered.

"I got cold feet, I guess. I'm not really sure. Mom was so relieved, though. I could see it in her eyes. She took me to the store instead, and we bought ice cream and cake and had our own dance." Kristen laughed a little, thinking about that night. "I never asked her about it again. As I got older, I liked that I only had one parent to deal with. Mom and I were fine alone; we didn't need anyone else."

"So you never met him," Missy said.

151

"Which means you still don't know who he is. Whew!" Josh blew out his breath. "Your mom never told you anything else about him?"

"Nope. She never mentioned him except that one time. All I know is that he lives in Dove Pond. I guess he grew up here, too. Most people who live here did."

"They had to have been classmates." Missy grabbed her backpack from the floor and pulled out a notebook and sparkly pen, her eyes bright with excitement. "Let's figure out what we know and what we need to find out."

"He lives in Dove Pond," Josh said. "And he's alive. Or he was — when was that?"

"Four years ago."

"Four years ago," he repeated.

They were quiet a moment.

Josh slumped in his seat. "That's not a lot to go on."

"True," Missy said. "*But* we know just about everyone who lives here, which will help. We can find him. I know we can."

Hope warmed Kristen's heart. Maybe she could find her dad. And maybe, just maybe, he would let her live with him until she graduated high school. Kristen shook her head wonderingly. "I don't know why I didn't think of this before."

"Because you've spent your whole life not thinking about him." Josh tossed his empty hot chocolate cup toward the large trash can at the end of the counter. It hit the rim and, after bouncing on the opposite edge, disappeared inside. "You need him now."

Missy tapped her pen on her notebook, the tap-tap-tap impatient and demanding. "Your mom was young when she had you, so it's a pretty good guess she and your dad knew each other from school."

"Probably." Kristen watched Missy write it down. "I wonder . . ."

"Yes?" Missy looked up eagerly.

"Mom has a trunk at the foot of her bed filled with stuff from her high school days. Every once in a while, she'd go through it and talk about the parties and football games and some of the stuff she and her friends did. She kept everything. There are music programs, old yearbooks, a few pressed petals from corsages, all sorts of stuff."

"Any letters?"

"Maybe. I didn't really pay attention."

"You need to go through that trunk," Missy said firmly. "Look through every single piece of paper, every picture, every note — all of it. I bet there are love letters or . . . or a signature in one of those yearbooks — *something* that will give us a clue."

"You're right." Kristen thought for a moment, then grimaced. "There's one problem. Grandma Ellen. Neither of us are sleeping well right now, and she's always at the house during the day."

Josh shrugged. "So she sees you going through the trunk. Just tell her you were missing your mom or something."

"She would ask questions. She's already suspicious."

"Of what?" Josh asked.

"She thinks I'll run away. That's what Mom did when she was seventeen. They didn't see each other for years."

Missy's eyes rounded. "Your mom was a runaway?"

Kristen nodded. "She slayed it, too. Never got caught. She bought a fake ID and Social Security card and got a job bartending at a golf club on Hilton Head Island. She said she made a killing."

"Wow," Josh said, looking impressed. "Your mom was such a badass."

"I know, right? But that's why Grandma Ellen is keeping such close tabs on me. If I'm so much as ten minutes late getting home, she blows up my phone. And when I'm there, she follows me around, trying to connect."

"Ugh!" Missy wrinkled her nose. "I'd hate that."

"Me too," Josh agreed.

"It sucks. But that's why I can't let her see me going through Mom's things. If Grandma Ellen figures out I'm looking for my dad, she'll demand we leave for Raleigh immediately. I know she would."

"She'd either do that or try to find him first," Missy said.

Josh frowned. "Why?"

"To buy him off so he won't let Kristen live with him. She may even convince him to deny he's her dad altogether."

Looking stunned, Josh asked Kristen, "Would your grandma do that?"

"She might." To be honest, Kristen wasn't sure how Grandma Ellen would react, but it would be safer not to know. "I need to get her out of the house so I can go through that trunk. . . . Maybe I could get Ava to invite her out for dinner or something." Kristen thought about it and then sighed. "No, she'd expect me to go with her."

"I know!" Missy said. "Hide all the Pepto in the house and pretend you're sick. Then, while she's at the drugstore, you can —"

"You guys are making this way too complicated," Josh said. "Just wait until she's asleep."

"She's not sleeping well, Josh. I already said that," Kristen said impatiently.

"So she's only sleeping a half hour here and there. How long do you need? Ten minutes? Fifteen? It's one trunk, not an entire room."

He had a point. It wouldn't take long. But Kristen knew from experience that her own sleepless nights were punctuated by short dozes, most of them painfully light, so that the smallest noise jerked her awake. *If only I had some sleeping pills or —*

Kristen stood, almost knocking over her chair. "Wait right here!" She hurried into the kitchen, where she quickly unlocked the cabinet again.

There, sitting off to one side near the back of the cabinet, was the tea canister. She grabbed it and pried off the lid. A faint, pleasant aroma lifted to meet her, and she was glad to see that the small canister was still fairly full. She put the lid back on, dug in her back pocket, pulled out a worn twenty-dollar bill, and set it where the canister had been. She relocked the cabinet and then hurried back to Missy and Josh. "Here." She set the canister on the table and slid into her seat.

Missy leaned over to read the torn label. "Where did you get this?"

"Ava had it in the cabinet. Don't worry — I'm not stealing it. I left a twenty to cover it."

Josh touched the label. "Ava made this for someone."

"I think it's Erma Tingle's old tea."

Missy's eyes widened. "The one that made her have bad dreams?"

Josh frowned. "I heard it made her sleep-walk."

"Whatever it did," Kristen said impatiently, "she did it in her sleep. Look, all I need is twenty minutes or so to go through Mom's chest. Plus, Ava said the teas didn't hurt anyone. And while this tea isn't perfect, it should give me the time I need."

Missy nodded enthusiastically, but Josh still looked concerned, so Kristen added, "It's not poison, Josh. I saw Ms. Tingle this morning, and she's perfectly fine." Kristen pulled the canister closer. "I'm going to give Grandma Ellen this tea tonight."

Josh sat back in his seat. "Without telling her? Wouldn't that be illegal or something?"

Gee, Josh was making this hard. "Fine! I'll tell her. I'll say, 'Here. Try this tea. It'll help you sleep. It's better than chamomile.' Which is all true. I'm not a liar. Ava's teas

157

"always deliver."

"Oh. I guess if you tell her, then it's okay."

"I just wonder . . ." Missy shot Kristen an apologetic look. "My mom says Ava's teas are made specifically for one person. They don't work the same on everyone."

"Good God! If it doesn't work, then it doesn't work." Kristen gave them a pointed stare. "I thought you two were going to help me, not complicate things."

"We're helping," Josh said, flushing. "I was just worried because I'd heard Ava had had problems with some of her teas."

"Only a few," Missy said dismissively. "My mom says there's no way a Dove tea would ever fail the way people have been saying. Jealousy is an awful thing."

"I trust Ava and her teas," Kristen said. "She had an issue with one little plant, but she's not using it anymore, so —" She shrugged. She still felt guilty about what had happened to that poor plant, although Ava said it was already looking healthier, which was a relief.

Josh sighed. "All right, then." He shot her a concerned look. "Just be careful."

He sounded and looked so much like his father that Kristen smiled as she pulled the canister closer. "I'll make sure Grandma Ellen's fast asleep before I search Mom's trunk. I'll do it toni—"

The door swung open and Ava walked in carrying a large plastic bin filled with extension cords. "Hello, kiddos."

"Hi, Ava!" Kristen slid the tea toward Missy, who quickly tucked it into her backpack.

"Hi, Ms. Ava!" Missy put her notebook and pen away, then tugged on her coat. "Josh and I were just leaving. We brought Kristen some hot chocolate."

"How nice of you. How are you doing, Josh? I haven't seen you in a while."

Josh stood, looking his usual awkward self. "I'm fine. I've got to go, though. Mom's at the library checking out that *Camel Sutures* book you read at Kristen's mom's funeral."

Missy giggled. "It's *Kama Sutra.*"

"Your mother is checking it out, is she?" Ava murmured. "Interesting." She exchanged a droll look with Kristen.

Kristen loved that Ava treated her like a grown-up. So few people did. Guilt pinched her at the thought of the tea she'd just taken, although it was old and partially used. *No one will miss it, and I paid for it, too.* Feeling better, she waved at Missy and Josh. "See you later."

"See you." Josh opened the door for Missy.

"Bye, guys!" Missy waved and left, Josh

following her out.

Kristen watched her two friends through the bow window as they walked down the sidewalk, both of them talking excitedly. She turned to Ava. "I unpacked the plates and was working on the spoons."

"Good! I —"

The door opened, and Dylan came in wearing a Carhartt jacket over a flannel shirt, a box tucked under one arm. Kristen liked Dylan. He'd worked his carpenter's magic on the tearoom and had done it all while looking like a more mature, bearded Liam Hemsworth. It was too bad Missy had already left; she thought he was a complete snack.

Ava eyed the box he carried. "Please tell me that's the new spigot for the sink."

"Stainless steel and hard to break, just as you requested."

"Great. We'll need the hard-to-break part." Ava walked past him to look at the teaspoons Kristen had stacked on the table. "These are even prettier than I'd hoped." She picked up one and then another, holding them to the light.

Dylan set his box down and followed Ava to the table. "Let me see those spoons." He pretended to examine them closely. "Dainty, aren't they?" His gaze fell on the tea plates.

"Whoa. This is some *Downton Abbey*–level stuff."

Ava impatiently reclaimed the spoons he held. "They're both dainty and expensive. So please don't drop anything."

Kristen watched them, trying to imagine a man looking at Mom the way Dylan looked at Ava, but just couldn't. Mom had never dated, not once, saying she had Kristen and that was enough. But could there be another reason Mom had never dated? *Was it possible she was still in love with my dad? Oh wow. And maybe he still loves her.* If that was true, then there was someone in town hurting the same way Kristen hurt. The thought filled her with a fresh determination to find him.

Ava waved Dylan away. "Get on to the kitchen where you belong. I need a spigot I can count on. The one that's in there leaks."

Dylan gave a heavy sigh. "That's all I am to you, isn't it? Just a handsome, brazen contractor who can fix anything, anywhere."

"The clock's ticking, Fraser. We don't have a lot of time before opening day, as you well know."

"Right. Got it. Get to work and stop talking." He picked up his box and headed toward the kitchen. "Don't mind me," he called over his shoulder. "I'll just guess where to put this spigot since no one is coming to tell me. Maybe I'll install it over the stove. That would work, wouldn't it?" His voice drifted out of the kitchen.

Ava ignored him and turned back to Kristen. "Look at all these empty boxes. You did a lot today."

"It's good to keep busy."

"It's also good to have fun. Want to head out early?"

"Would you mind?" If Kristen hurried, she might be able to catch up with Missy and Josh, and they could work out yet more details of their plan.

"Not at all. See you tomorrow."

"Thanks." Kristen grabbed her coat from where it hung over the back of one of the stools by the counter.

"And, Kristen?"

She stopped and turned around.

"If you need anything, let me know. Okay?"

Kristen smiled. Ava had already helped her; she just didn't know it. "Will do. Thanks. See you tomorrow."

And with that, she slipped out of the tearoom and went to look for her friends. Maybe, just maybe, she'd found the solution to her biggest problem.

# CHAPTER 7
## ELLEN

"What are you doing?"

Ellen lowered the painting she was carrying so she could see over the top.

Kristen, wearing a powder-pink ski jacket and a pair of patterned purple yoga pants, stood just inside the front door, her backpack hanging from one shoulder.

"I'm moving this painting, which isn't easy because it's huge, and I —" The painting was almost jerked out of her hands.

Kristen carried it past Ellen and into the living room.

Ellen followed, irritated all the way to her toes. She'd had a horrible day. Once again, she'd slept only a few hours, which had left her mind a mass of fog and indecision. She'd had far too many meetings today, and on top of that, she'd just found out that all three of her favorite contractors were booked through the rest of the year, so she'd have to find a substitute for her big fall project.

But that wasn't even the worst of it. While pacing around the house during a particularly boring conference call, trying desperately to stay awake, she'd found herself standing in the doorway of Julie's studio. In the weeks since Ellen had arrived, she'd avoided two rooms — the studio and Julie's bedroom. And yet there Ellen stood.

The studio was filled with Julie's things. A half-done painting sat on an easel near a window. Books were scattered around the room, open and half read. A fluffy lap blanket was pooled on the floor beside a chair. Two pairs of shoes were piled beside the door where they'd been hastily kicked off. It looked as if Julie had just that second left.

Ellen's throat had tightened, and she'd pressed her hand to it, trying to dislodge the feelings that had threatened to overwhelm her. It had taken every bit of strength she'd possessed to gather herself and continue the phone call.

Kristen placed the painting in a corner of the living room, handling the canvas as if it were glass.

A twinge of remorse made Ellen say, "I brought it down here from your mom's studio so I could catalogue it. The light's better in here."

Kristen's eyebrows rose, her disbelief obvious. "There are skylights in Mom's studio. The light is *always* better in there."

Ellen sighed. "Fine. To be honest, I can't stay in Julie's studio. It feels . . ." The words knotted, and she had to take a breath to untangle them. "I've been avoiding that room, but somehow I ended up in there today and I —" She just shook her head.

Kristen's expression softened. "I haven't been in there yet." She sent Ellen a surprisingly understanding look and hitched her backpack a little higher. "Are the dogs still outside?"

Ellen nodded, touched by Kristen's sympathy. "It was warm today. They didn't want to come back in after lunch."

"I wish you wouldn't leave them outside all day, I —" Kristen clamped her lips over the rest of her sentence. "Never mind. I'll let them in." With that, she disappeared into the kitchen.

Ellen heard the thunk of Kristen's backpack as it landed on a chair, followed by the creak of the back door. That was followed by the rumble of the dog herd being welcomed indoors. *Lovely. That's just what this place needs, a stampede of hairy beasts.*

Ellen sighed and started to head for the kitchen, but her footsteps slowed before she reached the doorway. She'd thought she and Kristen had reached a new understanding. Things were definitely better. They weren't arguing and had actually had some not-so-chilly-and-almost-normal discussions. But every time Ellen tried to talk about the future, Kristen still closed up, and Ellen, instantly missing the small connection she was forming with her granddaughter, would do the most unthinkable, most un-Ellen thing in the world — she'd capitulate and let the subject drop.

It was beyond frustrating. But time was passing, and she only had seven weeks before her new project was scheduled to begin. Seven weeks to clean out the house, schedule necessary repairs, and have the main rooms repainted. *Meanwhile, Kristen still gets upset when I move a single painting.*

Ellen grimaced and then, smoothing her face into a smile, went into the kitchen, where Kristen sat on the floor, hugging her dogs. *Just be calm and positive. Don't over-react, no matter what she says. She's going through a lot.*

Ellen slipped her hands into the pockets of her cardigan. "The dogs are glad to see you." *And so am I.* She wondered what would happen if she said it aloud. Would Kristen send her that disgusted "you're kidding me" look? Or would it make her smile?

Kristen gave Chuffy one last kiss on his forehead and then stood, dusting her jeans.

And just like that, the moment to say something meaningful passed. Ellen was left with the taste of defeat on her tongue. *Why do I find it so hard to say what I feel? God knows I wish I'd said more to Julie.*

Feeling lost, she cleared her throat, trying to dislodge the lump that seemed to be growing. "You're home early."

Kristen went to the counter and pulled out a plastic jug of dog treats. She said, "Sit!," and the dogs obediently plopped their butts on the wood floor. They waited quietly, but intently, while she gave each one a treat.

Ellen had to admit that the dogs were well behaved, although they shed far too much for her liking. She also wished they wouldn't climb all over the furniture. But that was an argument for another day. "Is everything okay at work?"

"Yeah. Dylan got there just as I left. He's installing the spigot. But you should see the cabinets." Excitement warmed Kristen's voice. "The whole kitchen looks great."

Ellen felt a twinge of jealousy. Kristen's

voice was never that lively when she talked to her. That Kristen loved her job made Ellen miss working from her office too. Until these past few weeks, she hadn't realized how much she depended on the camaraderie of the jobsite, the feeling of accomplishment, and the utter joy of being in control of at least one thing in her life.

Kristen closed up the dog treats and then went to the sink to wash her hands. "Have you eaten?"

"Not yet."

"Me neither. I figured I'd make something light."

"Let me do that." Ellen started forward. "How about a —"

"No." Kristen offered a quick smile. "I'm used to taking care of myself. Remember?"

*Which is so wrong. But you don't know that, so . . .* Ellen reluctantly returned the smile. "I was going to offer to make you a sandwich, not a casserole."

"I've got this." Kristen opened the refrigerator door and stared at the contents.

"Fine." Ellen slipped onto a stool behind the counter. "You know, I don't think I ate lunch. I can't remember." She grimaced. "Food doesn't have the appeal it once did."

"Missy brought me hot chocolate, and I couldn't even taste it." Kristen started opening drawers in the fridge.

"It's bad when you can't taste chocolate." Ellen watched as Kristen pulled out an assortment of wrapped cheeses. "Listen, about that painting. I didn't mean to get on your nerves moving stuff around, but we really need to take inventory of what's in the house so we can —"

"How about a cheese tray?" Kristen dropped the packets of cheese on the counter.

Recognizing the sheer exhaustion on Kristen's face and the circles under her hazel eyes, Ellen put away her thoughts about inventories and such. *She needs more time. We both do.* "A cheese tray would be lovely."

"I picked up some Brie yesterday, and we already have cheddar, Parmesan, Gouda, and goat cheese. Plus, there are two kinds of crackers and some walnuts. I even have a little honey."

Ellen was surprised Kristen knew that most cheese trays came with honey or a jam of some sort. "Perfect."

Kristen began unwrapping the cheeses. "Mom used to say I should have become a *maître fromager.*"

"Ooh-la-la," Ellen said, smiling. "Your accent is excellent."

"It should be. I took two years of French.

Mr. Roth said I was a natural." Kristen shot her a curious look. "Do you speak French?"

"*Très bien, en fait.* I go to France for a week or so every summer."

Interest flickered across Kristen's face, so Ellen added, "We could go this spring, once you're out of school. I know a lovely hotel off the Champs-Élysées."

Kristen looked as if she wanted to agree, but caution caught her just in time. Instead, she shrugged. "Maybe."

Ellen forced herself to be satisfied with that noncommittal answer, although she added "can speak French" to the list of pleasant discoveries she'd made about her granddaughter. It was a growing and impressive list. In the last two and a half weeks, she had learned that Kristen was a hard worker who could balance work and school with seeming ease, a conscientious dog mom to her pack of wildlings, a talented cook, and a responsible teenager who completed her chores without being reminded. To her surprise, Ellen had had to go to the grocery store only one time since she'd arrived, and that was only because she'd forgotten to write "soy milk" on the grocery list Kristen kept on the fridge.

She couldn't have been more different from Julie as a teen, which was a relief in many ways and a mystery in others.

Kristen opened a drawer and pulled out a small, round slab of slate and set it on the counter. "This," she announced, "is the cheese tray. Mom got it for me last Christmas. She bought it from a craftsman who had a booth at the Apple Festival. It comes with chalk so you can write the name of the cheese beside it, although I never do that. I don't want chalk near my cheese."

Ellen leaned over to look at it, nodding thoughtfully, as if she were an expert. "Very chic."

Kristen smiled, and Ellen's chest tightened. It was the first nonpained smile she'd seen, and it was so much like Julie's it hurt.

The teenager added wedges of the softer cheeses to the tray, cut the harder cheeses into slices, then pulled out two small ramekins and filled one with honey and the other with walnuts.

Watching Kristen was almost soothing, and when she finished, the tray really did look as if it could have been served at a high-end restaurant. "That's beautiful." Ellen couldn't stop a small yawn from slipping out as she spoke. "Sorry. I haven't been sleeping well."

"That reminds me. I brought you a present."

"You did?" Ellen couldn't keep the surprise from her voice.

Kristen wiped her hands on a dish towel and went to where her book bag sat on a chair at the kitchen table. She reached in and pulled out a canister. "For you." She set it on the counter near Ellen and then started rewrapping the uneaten cheese. "It's some of Ava's specialty tea. It'll help you sleep."

Ellen pushed the canister away. "Thanks, but no thanks. I was with Ava when Erma Tingle came in, and I'm not a Dove family fan, the way some of the people in this town are." Ellen caught the flash of anger on Kristen's face and could have kicked herself. "Not that Ava and her sister aren't nice. It's just that I don't believe in the Dove magic."

"Have you ever had chamomile tea?"

Ellen sighed. "Yes, but this —"

"— is the exact same thing. It's an herbal tea. As for Erma's tea, Ava figured out what went wrong with it. It was a plant that had — I guess you could say it got sick. She's not using it to make teas now, so . . ." Kristen shrugged as if that solved that.

*Be careful what you say here,* Ellen warned herself. "I'm not big on herbal remedies in general, although yes, I've used a chamomile tea to help me sleep. I don't know that it worked, though." That much was true.

And yet, even as she spoke, Ellen's gaze wandered back to the canister. She desperately needed to sleep. Her body ached from the lack of it, but every time she lay down, unwanted thoughts came crashing in until in desperation she'd get back up, throw on some clothes, and go to work. Still, as tired as she was, she wasn't yet desperate enough to use an Ava Dove tea. "Thank you for thinking of me, but I'm okay. I really am."

"You're not sleeping." Kristen pushed the canister closer to Ellen. "I heard you up last night, and it was really late." Her dark gaze rested on Ellen's face as if assessing the circles under her eyes.

Of course Kristen had heard her, Ellen thought with a grimace. Julie's house creaked as much as it leaked. "I'm sorry if I woke you. I was trying to keep quiet, but I accidentally bumped into the gold statue at the bottom of the stairs."

"Did it break?" There was an instant note of worry in Kristen's voice.

"No, no. It was fine." Ellen paused a pointed moment and then added, "So was I."

A reluctant smile touched Kristen's mouth. "Sorry." She slid the cheese tray across the counter. "You should try the Brie.

It's delicious."

"Brie is always delicious." Ellen was rewarded with a smile that wasn't just polite, but warm, too. She'd been right to not press the inventory issue right now. *We need to get to know each other first. Then we can sort out our differences.*

She wondered if that would have helped where Julie was concerned, but Julie was gone and with her the answers to hundreds — no, thousands — of questions.

As they ate, Kristen talked about her latest math test while Ellen's tired mind absently drifted to the painting that hung nearby. A small, plump, blond child stood watching a sunrise, a bedraggled teddy bear hanging from one hand. Ellen was just beginning to understand Julie's success as an artist. She captured those few, precious moments of life that were important, memorable even —

"You like that one."

Ellen realized Kristen had been watching her. "I'm sorry. I should have been listening."

Kristen shrugged. "I was talking about math class. It wasn't important." She nodded toward the picture and repeated, "You like that one."

"Yes," Ellen replied simply. "Is that you?"

"Me and Toddy, my old teddy bear."

"I thought it might be. Do you remember who bought you Toddy the teddy?"

Kristen's eyebrows rose, surprise flickering through her hazel eyes. "You?"

Ellen nodded. "For your fourth birthday." She looked back at the picture. "Your mother's use of color is striking." Ellen's eyes ached, and she closed them, trying to ease the dryness.

Kristen laughed softly. "If you fall asleep on that stool, you'll slip off and hit your head."

Ellen laughed and opened her eyes. "I promise I won't fall." She fixed herself another cracker and dipped a walnut in honey, too. "The sweetness of the honey really complements the saltiness of the cheeses."

"Mom learned that trick when she was bartending. She said a lot of the snacks were salty so people would drink more."

"She never told me much about that job, just that she enjoyed it. She said she made some good friends there."

"She loved working there."

Ellen could see Kristen and Julie sitting here, at this counter, eating cheese and talking and laughing. She saw it so clearly that it was as if she'd been here, hovering at a distance. *God, listen to me. I'm exhausted.*

Her gaze returned to the tea canister. The last thing she wanted to do was try a Dove tea, but it would make Kristen happy. And who knew, maybe it would help. One cup couldn't hurt. "I think I will try some of that tea."

Kristen looked relieved, which touched Ellen deeply. *She's starting to care for me. We might make this work after all.*

Ellen cast around for a topic of conversation that wouldn't set off any alarms and make this moment disappear. "So . . . which painting was your mom's favorite?"

Kristen nodded toward the arched opening to the living room. "The one you were carrying earlier. The one of the dogs."

Of all the paintings in the house, that was Ellen's least favorite. She looked at it now and tried to see it with new eyes. "You may think I'm kidding, but Floofy had that exact expression when I caught him drinking the milk out of your cereal bowl this morning."

"I thought I put my bowl in the sink."

"You had," Ellen said drily.

Kristen's chuckle brightened the room like a burst of sunshine on a gray day, so welcome that Ellen had to swallow back a surprisingly strong surge of emotion. She didn't know this child well, but oh, how she longed to.

"Floofy makes the weirdest faces. Mom used to laugh at him all the time." Kristen looked through the archway at the dogs lying on their various perches in the living room. "They're good dogs, and now they're all —" She clamped her mouth over the rest of her sentence, her humor disappearing as quickly as it had appeared.

*All I have left.* Ellen heard the words so plainly that it was as if Kristen had said them aloud. Ellen didn't want the dogs at her home in Raleigh, but perhaps, just perhaps, if it cheered up Kristen, a compromise could be reached. *The things we do for love.*

"Oh! I almost forgot." Kristen opened a cupboard and pulled out two wineglasses and set them beside her cheese tray.

"Wine? You're too young for —"

"No. Sparkling cider." Kristen pulled a jug from the fridge and filled the glasses. "Mom couldn't drink, but we liked the ambiance of these glasses." She slid a glass toward Ellen.

"Julie couldn't drink? Why not? Was there a problem?" *Oh God. Was she an alcoholic?*

Kristen had already turned to put the cider back in the fridge, but now she stopped and looked back at Ellen. "She couldn't drink because of her bipolar meds."

Ellen opened her mouth, but no sound came out.

Kristen's eyes widened. "You didn't know."

Ellen shook her head. "I hadn't spoken to her in a while, though."

"It wasn't a recent diagnosis." Kristen closed the refrigerator door, folded her arms, and leaned on the counter, her gaze soft with concern. "Right after she ran away, a counselor in a homeless shelter recognized her symptoms and got her some help."

Ellen gripped the edge of the countertop. Julie had known about her diagnosis for years and hadn't once mentioned it. *Oh God. Yet another thing she didn't tell me. What else did she hide from me?*

"Mom should have told you she had bipolar two."

"I wish she had. I would have —" Ellen pressed her lips over the rest of her sentence. "It doesn't matter now, I guess. I'm not even sure what bipolar two is."

"It's a softer version. Mom called it 'bipolar lite.' "

"I see. What are the symptoms? She was moody, but she was always moody. Teenagers argue and overdo this and underdo that."

"The symptoms don't always show up until late teens or early twenties. Mom said she didn't experience full-fledged symptoms until after she ran away."

"She told you about running away, about her illness and diagnosis. She didn't keep any secrets from you, just from me." Which Ellen would never understand. *I wanted to help her. I told her that, too, but she would have none of it. None of me.* "I suppose she told you about our fights, too."

"She told me everything. Probably even some things she shouldn't have."

"I wish she'd trusted me more. Her diagnosis explains a lot. I always thought she was just being difficult. . . ." Ellen bit her lip, guilt flooding her. *Oh God, I blamed her.*

Kristen's hand closed over Ellen's. "Don't look like that. Mom would tell you she was a handful as a teenager. She told me that hundreds of times."

"When she ran away, I looked for her, and when I couldn't find her, I worried so much. And now I find out she was battling this — and I didn't even know about it. I can't imagine how hard that must have been."

"Mom never did anything the easy way." Kristen released Ellen's hand and pushed her glass of apple cider closer. "She called

179

her six years as a runaway her Big Adventure. It was hard at first, but she was smart and she figured things out."

"You said she was in a homeless shelter?"

"One of several. She wasn't homeless for long, though."

Ellen's stomach felt sick. *She was only seventeen. Oh, Julie, why didn't you stay with me? We would have figured it out eventually, you and I.*

Kristen took a thoughtful sip of her cider. "Mom took care of her condition as well as she could. She went to her therapist, never missed her meds, did what she could to offset her downswings. She was vigilant."

Ellen didn't know what to say, what to think. "When she finally came back home, she already had you. She never said a word about what she'd been through, and I was so happy to have her there and excited to meet you that I was afraid to ask too many questions." Ellen's eyes burned, so dry they hurt. Her tears had already been spent, and she couldn't wring out another. "God, what an idiot I was."

"How could you know?"

"I should have asked or — or done something. Julie and I . . . we couldn't connect. I don't know why. When she came back with you, we tried to figure things out, but we

180

could never get over the barriers between us. I kept trying to help her, and she kept trying to do everything on her own. And things got more and more tense. Eventually, she got tired of the arguments, took you, and left. And then I —" Her voice caught. *I lost both of you.*

Kristen sighed. "I love my mom, I always will, but she wasn't great at relationships. I know she wished it were otherwise, but it was hard for her to make friends. She and Ava didn't get close until Mom was sick."

Ellen took a careful sip of cider. "I never understood Julie. We were so different, opposites in almost every way. A lot of it was my fault. I had no patience with her. No patience with anyone, really. Her dad left us when she was little, and we never heard from him again."

"What a loser."

"He wasn't a strong person and I — to be honest, I think I overwhelmed him. Like Julie, I wasn't very good at relationships either. I was too hard on both of them. I see that now. I felt she was my responsibility, mine alone, and I wanted her to be successful *so* badly that I pushed her, and eventually —" Ellen pressed her lips together.

"She didn't have the same definition of success."

"That was part of the problem, although some of it was just her stubbornness. And mine." Ellen winced. "Sadly, we had that in common. Maybe her illness kept her from —"

"Hold on. She didn't think of being bipolar as an illness. It was just part of who she was. It helped her in some ways and hurt in others, just like any personality trait. Look at me; I obsess over things and get tangled up in doing one thing over and over. But it also means when I get something done, it's done right. Mom wouldn't have been able to create all she did if she hadn't been so in touch with her own emotions. It let her see the world in a really unique way, and that made her who she was."

Ellen looked around the house, trying to see it through new eyes, Kristen's eyes. And what she saw surprised her. Among the clutter and cacophony of color were splashes of Julie's vibrance. "She used it."

"And made a lot of money, too."

Ellen gave a dry laugh. "Very true, I suppose. I just wish she'd told me what was going on."

"She didn't tell many people." Kristen put a piece of cheese on a cracker. "She only told Ava during those last few months."

That drew Ellen's gaze back to the tea.

She dusted her fingers on her napkin and picked up the canister. "I guess I'll make myself some tea." She smiled at Kristen and was surprised by a flash of — was it regret? No wonder; they'd been talking about a lot of heavy topics. "It was very kind of you to bring me this. I've got to get more sleep."

Kristen started cleaning up. "It'll help."

Ellen opened the canister and sniffed it carefully, catching the scent of ginger and peppermint and other herbs, too. "It smells delicious. How about you? I've seen the light under your door late at night, too. Maybe you should have a cup with me."

"No, I'm good." Kristen glanced at the clock over the kitchen door and made a face. "I've got to get to work. I have a paper due tomorrow and I've only written half of it."

"Leave the rest of the dishes. I'll finish cleaning up since you 'cooked.' It's only fair."

Kristen smiled. "Thank you." She headed for the door.

"Wait a second." Ellen slid off her stool and pulled out a small plate. She added some crackers and cheese and handed it to Kristen. "So you can snack while you study."

Kristen took the plate, her face pink. "Thank you. You're going to eat the rest, right? We both need to do better in the self-care department."

Ellen had to fight the urge to give the child a hug. *Don't move too quickly. You'll ruin what progress you've made this evening.* So instead of a hug, she held up her hand as if making a pledge. "I'll eat every last one."

"And the tea?"

Ellen laughed. "I'll make a cup right before bedtime. I promise."

Kristen nodded and, balancing the plate, she picked up her book bag. "Come on, doggos," she called. The dogs jumped up, wagging their tails as, in a line, they followed her upstairs, leaving Ellen in the kitchen with the canister of tea.

# CHAPTER 8
## ELLEN

Ellen awoke with a start, sitting bolt upright as if she'd just surfaced from deep underwater. Gasping for air, she looked around her, alarmed when she didn't recognize anything. It wasn't until she caught sight of a painting on the wall which featured Luffy sitting on a dock at a lake that Ellen remembered everything — the invitation, the funeral, her conversation with Kristen, the shared cheese tray, and finally, a comforting cup of Ava Dove's specialty tea.

Still groggy, Ellen fell back against her pillows and fumbled for the clock beside the empty teacup on her nightstand. The red dots spelled out 3:33. So much for Ava Dove's "make you sleep" tea. *It tasted good, I'll give her that, and I did fall asleep almost as soon as I hit the pillow, which was nice for a change. But now here I am, wide awake and it's not even —*

"For the love of heaven! At least you went

to sleep right away; that's better than you've done since my funeral."

Ellen froze, blinking in the dark. She knew that voice. She'd raised it.

"Well?" Julie continued, more impatiently now. "Let's get this show on the road. I can't stay all night. I've time limits."

That couldn't have been Julie's voice. It just couldn't.

And yet . . .

*This is a dream. I'm still asleep.* Ellen would prove it, too. She sat up, sliding her legs out from under the heavy blankets. It was still dark, although there was an odd blue glow in the room. *It's nothing. A street-light too close to the window.*

It seemed brighter behind her, so she looked over her shoulder.

*"Ack!"* She leapt from the bed, grabbing the blanket and holding it in front of her like a shield.

Julie sat in one of the fat reading chairs beside the window, her blue eyes shimmering mischievously. "Hi, Mom."

"No. You . . . how . . . where . . . how come . . . I—"

Julie laughed her larger-than-life laugh. Ellen closed her eyes and soaked in the sound, reveling in it. *I've missed that laugh.*

"Come sit with me."

Ellen opened her eyes. Julie sat smiling, the faint blue glow surrounding her. She wore the clothes she'd been buried in: green-and-yellow-plaid flannel pajama pants emblazoned with a Green Bay Packers logo, a worn-out-looking T-shirt with the words MOTHER OF DRAGONS across the chest, a purple silk kimono embroidered with white and orange lotuses, and a pair of ridiculously large bunny slippers.

Ellen let go of one corner of the blanket and pressed a shaking hand to her cheek. "I'm dreaming."

"Oh, for the love of —" Julie stood and made a flourishing gesture. "Behold, the ghost!"

"I don't believe in ghosts."

Julie snorted. "You can see and hear me, so . . . If it walks like a duck and quacks like a duck, then it's a —"

"No. You're dead. Or were. I mean, *are.*" This was so weird. And it hurt like the dickens to see Julie and know she wasn't really there. Ellen closed her eyes and whispered, "Please let me wake up."

There was a deep silence.

Ellen waited, holding her breath.

Finally, she cracked open one eye.

"Boo!" Julie laughed, the infectious sound

roiling around the room as if trying to break free.

"That's not funny."

Julie's grin was every bit as big as Ellen's growing irritation. "It's sort of funny." She sat back down and waved a hand. "You'll laugh later, after the shock has worn off."

"I will not. You're dead, Julie."

"I know. But I'm also here, so . . ." Julie shrugged.

"This isn't a joke! Not to me, anyway!" Ellen had to swallow before she could continue. "Kristen and I are alone and trying to find a way to move on, which has been so, so hard. And there you are, laughing like nothing happened and I —" Ellen's voice broke.

"Whoa!" Julie's smile had faded. "I didn't mean to upset you, but — look, I didn't expect to be here either. I'm supposed to be" — she waved her hand — "other places."

"What other places?"

"I don't know, just not here. But since I am" — she shrugged — "we might as well make use of it."

Ellen stared at her daughter, torn between irritation at Julie's casual attitude and a deep yearning to believe this moment was really happening.

*It's a dream,* Ellen told herself desperately. *Just because you want it to be real doesn't mean it is.*

Still, for a dream, everything was shockingly clear. She could see every detail of Julie's thick purple-dyed hair, every stitch in the lotuses on the kimono, every sparkle in those blue, blue eyes. "This is bizarre."

"Tell me about it. One minute I'm watching Kristen sleep and the next I'm sitting with you. What's weirder, you can see me. I didn't expect that." She gestured toward the blanket. "You can drop that if you want. I've seen your pajamas before."

Realizing she was still holding the blanket in front of her, Ellen folded it and placed it back on the bed, then reached for her robe.

Julie rolled her eyes. "Yes, please wear a robe. Us ghosts can't see you if you put on a robe."

Ellen felt more protected wearing a robe, so she ignored Julie's taunt. The tie neatly knotted, she slid her feet into her slippers, which were lined up at the end of her bed.

Julie watched her with a faintly annoyed expression. "You don't need to dress up. This isn't a formal event."

Ellen took a step toward Julie. "What this is, is weird."

"True." Julie tilted her head to one side, a

189

thoughtful expression crossing her face. "I wonder why we're here?"

"I'm dreaming. That's all I know."

"Yes, but I don't dream, and I'm here too. There's a reason we're talking. If there's one thing I've learned about the afterlife, it's that nothing happens without a reason."

"The afterlife? Then —"

"There is one? Yes. Not what I'd imagined it would be, but then, I didn't really have expectations. Not big ones." Julie's brow creased. "Which brings me back to my original question: Why are we here, in this room, together?"

Ellen had no idea. This was a dream, no question, but she still yearned to make it last as long as possible. Julie was *right there,* and even if it wasn't real, it was as close to Julie as Ellen would ever be again.

*I must be careful not to wake up or this — Julie — will be gone.* Moving slowly, Ellen sat in the chair opposite her daughter, perching uneasily on the edge of the seat.

Julie watched every move. "Are you okay?"

"I don't want to jar myself awake."

"Oh. That's actually pretty smart." Julie eyed her curiously. "You always were clever."

"So were you."

Julie raised her eyebrows. "Wow. That's — I never thought I'd hear you say that."

190

Ellen frowned. "Why wouldn't I? I gave you credit when you did things well."

"Mmm. No. You gave me credit when I did things the way you thought they should be done."

That was utter nonsense. Ellen opened her mouth to argue but then thought better of it. *Why ruin a perfectly good dream?* "How are things" — she waved a hand — "wherever you are?"

"Not bad." Julie pulled her feet up into her seat and wrapped her arms around her knees. She looked ridiculously young, and Ellen noticed that even in the afterlife, her daughter had scorned the need for a hairbrush.

Julie started to raise her hand to her hair but then caught herself and sighed. "Please. I *like* my hair this way."

*She can read my thoughts.*

Julie grinned, a touch of scamp in her expression. "Yes. Yes, I can. But I like hearing your voice." Her smile faded, and her gaze searched Ellen's face. "How's Kristen?"

"She's sad. Exhausted. And upset, too. But that's to be expected. She's still going to school and working at Ava's tearoom, too, *although*," Ellen added, "I worry about that. She's really busy between classes and

191

her job. I wonder if she shouldn't just focus on her grades."

"How are her grades? Have they slipped?"

"From what her teachers have told me, she's maintaining them, but she's far too busy. She should be home more."

"Kristen needs the challenge of a demanding schedule. Trust me, I've seen her when she has too much free time. She frets and worries — she needs to stay busy."

"Children also need downtime. You did, when you were that age."

"My daughter isn't like me. She wants everything to be perfect. It's where her impulses, her character, lead her. So she worries. A lot. Too much, in fact."

Ellen was silent a moment, digesting this information. "Her counselor at the school did call her an overachiever."

"Kristen's test scores are off the charts. She was tested for the gifted program in middle school, and the counselor said they'd never seen anything like it."

A trill of pride lit Ellen's heart. "That's good to know. I'm just not sure about her job. The Doves are . . . well, they're different. Maybe if she worked somewhere else —"

"Mom, stop it!" Julie's smile was long gone. "There's nothing wrong with the

Doves. And Kristen's job has been the saving of her. Working for Ava forced Kristen out of her shell. Before she started working there, she was painfully shy. She kept to herself, and not just at home, but at school, too. She only has two friends — just two. Now she knows almost everyone in town. When she walks down the street, people speak to her, and she waves and smiles back." Julie's expression softened. "Her job has given her confidence. She needed that."

Maybe. Ellen thought about the pamphlets she'd brought with her of the private schools she'd thought would welcome Kristen. They were filled with colorful pictures of happy, healthy, cheerful students, none of whom had purple hair or nose studs. "Kristen could get the same thing from an academically rigorous, culturally enriching school. If she'd just —"

"Mom, no. Kristen is getting all the cultural enriching she needs right here in Dove Pond."

Ellen couldn't have disagreed more. While she was sure there were some good things to be said about living in a small, backwoods place like Dove Pond, nothing could match the carefully constructed benefits offered by a premier private school.

Julie rolled her eyes. "Bullshit."

Ellen's jaw tightened. "Stop reading my mind!"

A half hour ago, she'd wanted nothing more than to talk to her daughter. But now . . . she struggled to calm her thoughts. *If I'm going to dream about Julie, I might as well make it better than real life. Fewer arguments. Less anger. More understanding. More connecting.* For a horrible minute, Ellen remembered the last argument she and Julie had had, the terrible things they'd both said, their anger striking each other like flint against a stone. *I don't want that again. Never again.*

"Mom." Julie's expression had softened. "That's what I want too. And I'm just as worried about Kristen as you are. She's really, really sad."

Ellen nodded. "She's not sleeping well."

"I know." Julie's expression was somber. "I come to see her all the time. I know she's suffering. I can feel it."

"She's going to hurt, Julie. She's going to grieve."

Julie's bright blue light visibly dimmed. "I hate that."

"So do I."

They were quiet a minute, commiserating on their one common heartache.

Julie sighed. "I miss her. It's hard to know

194

your daughter is alive and going through her life, but you aren't there and won't ever be, even when she needs you."

Ellen raised her eyebrows and said drily, "I can't imagine what that's like."

Julie looked at her with surprise. After a moment, her mouth formed an O. "I guess I did do that to you when I ran away, didn't I?"

Ellen nodded.

"I never realized how you must have felt, how worried you must have been. It just never dawned on me." Julie winced. "I'm sorry."

The words, so simple, hung in the room between them.

Ellen pressed her lips together to stop them from trembling. When she could, she said, "Thank you."

Julie's eyes glistened with tears. "I wish I had time to explain what I was going through, but we need to talk about Kristen. I don't know how long I'll be here."

"Dreams don't last forever," Ellen agreed, saddened by the thought. Suddenly chilly, she tugged her robe closer. "What can I do to help Kristen? Just tell me, and I'll do it."

Julie's gaze rested on Ellen's face. "You like her."

"I love her."

"Of course you do," Julie said, instantly impatient. "She's your granddaughter. But you also *like* her. When you add that to love, it's special."

"She's a good person. And kind too."

Julie nodded, tucking a strand of her unruly hair behind one ear.

Ellen noticed the stains on Julie's fingers. "Your hands . . . what's that?"

"It's paint." Julie held up her hands and eyed them as if she were admiring a recent nail job. "When you die, you get to carry reminders of who you once were."

Ellen wondered what reminder she'd have. Perhaps a handheld laser distance meter would shine out of one ear. *Lovely.*

Julie snorted. "I'd pay good money to see that. Or I would if I had money. They don't use it here, so . . ."

"Where is 'here'?"

"If you're asking if I'm in heaven or hell, I'm not telling." Julie's grin broadened. "But let's just say I'm glad to be here."

"With you, that could mean either place."

Julie's laugh rang out once more. "So it could."

Ellen had to laugh, too. It had been so long since she'd done so, that her laugh sounded almost rusty. "I wish I could hug you."

A flash of regret crossed Julie's face. "I wish you could, too, but there are rules." She winced. "Too many, if you ask me."

Ellen smiled. "They have rules, eh? That must chafe."

"I'm used to it. I lived with you, didn't I?" The twinkle in Julie's eyes took the sting from her words, and for a moment, they smiled at each other.

"Oh, Julie. You seem the same as ever. A little pale, but good."

" 'A little pale,' she says. I'm dead, Mom. That's more than 'a little pale.' "

"Fine. You're —" The word stuck in Ellen's throat, her humor fleeing as suddenly as it had arrived. Tears burned behind her eyes.

Julie leaned forward, her eyebrows lifting. "You're crying."

"Of course I'm crying; you *died.*" The words came out sharp, almost angry. *No. Stop it. That wasn't her fault.*

Julie said softly, "I miss you too."

The tears did fall then. Ellen had to use the edge of her robe to dab them away. "I'm sorry. I can't seem to stop. . . ." Why was she explaining herself? *It's just a dream.* "I don't know why I'm even talking to you. You're not here. I shouldn't have had all that cheese before bed. I won't do it again.

Or maybe it was that silly tea. I should have never drunk a tea made by a Dove. It tasted okay, good even, but —"

"Mom, you're wasting our time," Julie said sharply. She straightened in her chair, her bunny-slippered feet now resting on the floor. "I just wish you understood Kristen. I —" Julie stopped, her eyes widening. "That's it. That's why I'm here. I'm supposed to help you with Kristen."

"That's ridiculous. You're not even —" *Alive.* The word stuck in Ellen's throat like a huge rock. She hated saying it out loud, even in a dream. Hated saying it with a passion so deep it burned. After a short struggle, she said, "You're gone."

"I'm right here. And I think I'm supposed to help you and Kristen become a family. Mom, there's something you should know. Kristen is not going to Raleigh with you."

"Of course she is. We haven't set the details, but we've been talking about it. And she doesn't get as angry as she used to when I mention it, which is good. We've come a long way this past week."

Julie rolled her eyes. "Mom, think! What would you have thought if I suddenly agreed with you about something I hated?"

"You? I'd think you were lying to me so you could —" Ellen frowned. "Kristen

198

wouldn't do that."

"Wouldn't she? I know my own daughter. And I know you, too. You aren't very good at listening to other people. But you're very good at hearing what you want to hear."

"I listen just fine. You just never told me anything. That's why our relationship was so strained. You refused to let me *be* your mother. You could have asked for my help with anything, and I would have moved heaven and earth to make it happen."

"I didn't need any help, so . . ." Julie shrugged.

"Didn't you? Kristen told me about your diagnosis, which you *never* mentioned to me, not once. You should have told me."

"Why?"

"*Why?* Because I was right there. I could have —"

"Whoa, whoa. It was mine to handle, not yours. Plus, if I had told you, you would have swept in and taken over. Even when you didn't know I was bipolar, you acted as if I couldn't do anything correctly." Julie tucked a tangled strand of hair behind her ear. "You don't even think I can comb my hair right."

"You don't comb it at all."

"I comb my hair all the time. See?" Julie raked her fingers through her hair, brushing it back from her face. "See?"

"That's not combing."

"It is to me. And it's fine. But not to you. It's your way, or it's wrong. I *hated* that. So when I found out I was bipolar, I decided to handle it myself. And I did. I didn't come home until I had it under control. I couldn't fight both you *and* being bipolar."

"Julie, I —" Ellen threw her hands up. "This is ridiculous. You know I would have helped. I don't need to keep saying it. Whatever happened, I'm just glad you finally came home. I only wished you'd stayed and given us another chance."

"I came back because I wanted you to meet Kristen, but you did what you always do. You charged in, criticized everything, and acted as if I couldn't raise my own child. So I packed up and came here, which I never regretted." Julie leaned back in her seat, a resigned expression on her face. "I'm not saying I'm perfect or that it was easy. It took a while before I got my meds lined up right. But I did it. And Kristen helped."

Julie's gaze moved from Ellen to the window. Outside, the tree limbs were illuminated by Julie's blue light, and beyond them, the night sky gleamed a dark velvet. "I'm so glad we moved here. Dove Pond is special."

Ellen sighed. "Dove Pond is special to you, maybe."

"There it is. *That's* what I'm talking about. *That's* why Kristen isn't being honest about her intentions right now. She hates arguing even more than I do." Julie put her hands on her knees and leaned forward. "Listen carefully, Mom. Kristen isn't going to Raleigh with you."

The sincerity in Julie's voice hit Ellen hard. *I thought Kristen was beginning to see things my way. But . . . is she?* Now that Ellen thought about it, Kristen hadn't exactly agreed to move to Raleigh. And yes, she was stonewalling Ellen's attempts to nail down the details of the move. *But surely she'll come around when . . . When what?*

*Oh dear. Julie is right.*

"Finally!"

Ellen stood.

"Where are you going?"

"I'm going to have a talk with Kristen."

"Right now? She's asleep."

*And I'm dreaming.* Ellen sighed and sat back down.

"Mom, she's hurting. She's lonely and scared, and she needs you right now. But she also needs you to stop pushing her so hard. She wants to stay in Dove Pond."

"She'll have to trust that I know what's best."

"Trust is earned. You used to tell me that. What have you done to earn Kristen's?"

Ellen opened her mouth, then slowly closed it. "It's only been a few weeks. I haven't had time to really get to know her."

"So slow down. Get to know her. Let her get to know you. But I'm warning you; she's not going to go quietly. She has enough of me in her to keep that from happening."

Ellen's chest ached. "She's going to run away."

Julie chuckled, her eyes twinkling. "Lord, no. She'd never do that."

"How do you know?"

"She's not the type. She won't run away, but she'll find a way to stay here, and she'll do it with or without your permission."

Ellen had thought her heart couldn't hurt any more after Julie's death, but she was beginning to realize she'd been wrong. She'd really believed she and Kristen had grown closer, but Julie's words made too much sense. *I'm being played. That's all there is to it.*

Julie watched her, sadness in her eyes. "I love you. And I know you love me and Kristen, too. But you have trouble accepting people for who and what they are. You're always trying to make them better."

"Isn't that what parents are supposed to do?"

"They're supposed to love you, Mom. No matter what."

Ellen could feel her lips quivering. "I did."

Smiling softly, Julie crossed her arms and rested them on top of her knees. "I know that now."

Ellen fought to regain control against a staggering flood of raw emotions. "I have to ask you this. Why did you put Kristen under my care? You surprised both of us with that decision."

Julie tilted her head to one side, her gaze lively. "You haven't figured that out yet?"

"I assumed it was because you knew she'd be safe with me and would have a good life. But now you're questioning my decisions, so there must be another reason."

"There is. You and Kristen . . ." Julie's words faded as the blue light around her flickered.

"What's wrong?" Ellen asked, alarmed.

"My time is almost up. I've got to go soon. Kristen will be safe with you, but you have to be careful. Don't hold her to the same sort of perfection matrix you did me." Julie leaned forward earnestly. "Let Kristen be who she is. Listen to . . . Stop making . . .

203

for her."

"She's sixteen."

"And smarter than you or I will ever be. Trust her . . . knows what's best for her."

"Wait!" Alarmed, Ellen scooted forward in her seat. "Who knows what's best for her?"

The bluish glow around Julie began to pulse steadily. "You're waking up."

Ellen started. *"No!"* She stood. "I don't want to wake up! This isn't real, I know that, but I —"

"Mom, it's real. Listen. . . ." Julie leaned closer, her lips moving but her voice flickering in and out. "Kristen and I had an agreement. I promised her I'd always . . . and in return she'd . . . And it worked, too. I . . ." Julie faded and then slowly came back into sight. "There's more to it. You need to find it."

"Find what?"

"The red cube. It'll . . . what Kristen wants and needs." Julie faded with each pulse, her voice flickering in and out. "You must . . . and then read it . . . -self."

Ellen took a hasty step forward. "Red cube?"

"In the . . . behind . . ."

Julie was almost gone.

"Julie! Where do I find it? What will it do?"

But it was too late. The blue light faded, and Julie disappeared with it.

The light flickered to black.

And Ellen was alone in the dark.

She stood staring at the spot where Julie had disappeared, unsure what to do or say.

How long Ellen stood there, she didn't know, but when she finally moved, her legs and back were stiff. She made her way to her bed. *That didn't happen. It's a dream.*

And yet . . . and *yet* . . . "No," she announced, the sound of her voice shockingly loud in the quiet. "I'm just dreaming. I know how to handle Kristen. I definitely don't need Julie to tell me what to do."

Irritated at herself for being so foolish as to believe in something as fanciful and ridiculous as a ghost, Ellen took off her robe, slid off her slippers, and crawled back under the covers. "I'm still asleep," she told herself as she settled deeper into the bed. Her voice sounded sleepy, even to her.

She closed her eyes and, as she tried to reason away the things Julie had told her in the dream, slipped into a deep, blissfully dreamless sleep.

# CHAPTER 9
## AVA

A cold February wind whipped Ava's hair across her eyes. She tucked the loose strands behind her ear, shivering as she pulled her knit cap farther down and hurried across the street to the Moonlight Café. Most Wednesdays, she, Sarah, Kat, Grace, and Zoe met here for lunch. But because of Ava's schedule over the past few weeks, she'd had to skip a couple. But not today. She'd missed this time with her friends.

The sky was dark, the threat of sleet heavy in the air. Her temples ached with the change in the weather, throbbing as if to the beat of a distant drum. She'd had so many headaches lately. *I should talk to Doc Bolton about that the next time I see him. Meanwhile, I need some coffee.*

She stepped inside the café and stopped to breathe in the rich scent of the day's specials, shepherd's pie and a bison burger with bacon aioli. Her stomach growling, she tugged off her cap and coat and hung them on a peg beside the door. She loved the Moonlight Café. Run first by Don Stewart, and now his daughter, Jules, the café kept the grill going even in the worst of weather.

Ava wiped her feet on the doormat, soaking in the comforting sight of the red-checked tablecloths and mason jar tea mugs and the soothing sounds of low laughter and the clink of dishes. The Moonlight felt like home and eased her headache.

Gray-haired, buzz-cut Joe Kavanaugh sat in his usual seat at the counter, nursing a cup of coffee. Rumor had it that the fifty-something bachelor who owned the Bait Me sports shop was having a secret relationship with Jules, the owner of the Moonlight. Ava couldn't think of a single reason for the two of them to hide their relationship, so she didn't believe that particular rumor, but still . . . he was here frequently. Pretty much every day. Joe saw her and lifted a hand in greeting before he went back to his cup of coffee and sandwich.

"Ava!" Eric Callahan called from where he and his brother, Nick, sat near the window. "See you at the tearoom at two?"

Ava gave him a thumbs-up as she looked past him and caught sight of Sarah standing beside their usual booth, waving wildly. Ava headed in the direction of her sister and their friends. She'd only taken a few steps when a voice stopped her.

"Well, well, well, if it isn't Trouble heading over to meet More Trouble."

Ava turned to see Dylan standing behind her. She smiled. "Aren't you supposed to be working on my tearoom?"

He held up a brown paper bag printed with the Moonlight Café logo. "Can't a man pick up a meal while he's waiting for paint to dry?"

"I guess that's fair."

"Thank you, boss," he said meekly, although the gleam in his hazel eyes was anything but.

Despite her headache, she grinned. "You're quite welcome. By the way, I left you a note on the tearoom door. Eric Callahan is stopping by around two. If I'm not back when he gets there, can you let him into the upstairs area? He's going to take a look around and give me a quote on turning that upstairs space into two rentable apartments."

Dylan's smile, so bright in his red beard, disappeared instantly. "You're hiring my competition to complete your building?"

"You told me to."

"When?"

"When you first started work on the tearoom, you said you were booked through next year and wouldn't have time for more."

He sighed. "I did say that, didn't I. I guess I should have clarified."

"Clarified it how?"

"By saying that if you really wanted it done, I would find the time." He raked a hand through his hair, looking both vexed and amused. "I guess I'm just feeling a little proprietary."

She could understand that; she felt the same way about the tea-room. Dylan had put a lot of hours into her place, and his craftsmanship was evident on every wall, floor, and shiny surface. "If you want to give me a quote on the second story, too, then please do. I'll need more than one anyway, and — Oh. Kat's waving. I've got to go."

He looked disappointed but shrugged. "Sure. Catch you later."

She waved and left, threading her way between tables to the booth.

"It's about time," Grace declared from where she sat flipping through the pages of a thick folder. No one in Dove Pond worked harder than Grace, the town mayor. She was a huge upgrade from the last guy, who only wanted to fish. Grace, meanwhile, was constantly working to improve their small

209

town, and her ideas and programs had already made a huge difference.

Sarah scooted over to make room for Ava. "You look tired."

"I have a headache, that's all." She slid into her seat and made a face. "This weather front isn't being kind to my sinuses."

Kat slid an iced tea in front of Ava. "We ordered for you. If I'd known you had a headache, I would have gotten you a coffee."

"This is fine," Ava said, taking a grateful drink. Caffeine was caffeine, after all.

"We saw you come in," Kat said. "We were beginning to wonder if you were going to join us. It looked as if you were going to have lunch with Team Construction instead."

"By Team Construction, she means Dylan," Sarah explained.

"I think Ava got that," Zoe said in a dry voice. Zoe was the vice president of First People's Bank and dressed the way Ava had always wanted to, but knew better than to try. She had neither the glamorous persona nor the svelte figure to carry off fashion the way Zoe did. Today she wore a stunningly simple red wool dress, a silk scarf draped around her elegant neck, and thick silver hoop earrings that shimmered against her dark skin. All of which made Ava feel utterly dowdy in her flannel shirt, jeans, and work boots.

Zoe eyed Ava over her cappuccino. "I'm jealous. Not a single construction hunk called out to me when I entered, and I'm wearing a push-up bra."

Ava laughed and sent her friends a sweeping look. "You're all jealous. I kind of like that."

Kat grinned. "Possibly." But she wasn't, and she and Ava knew it. Kat had her own guy, Mark Maclean. He lived in Charlotte but came to town frequently, usually to try to pester Kat into marrying him, which he'd been doing almost every year since high school. Personally, Ava thought Kat was afraid of marriage, and no wonder, looking at the number of times Kat's mother had been married.

"Well, *I* was jealous," Grace said.

"Better not let Trav hear that," Sarah said.

"Trav and I have an understanding. Looking is healthy, touching is a solid no."

Zoe laughed and said, "Ignore them all. Ava, you had one of the best-looking men in town hanging on your every word. If any of us had been in that position, we'd have forgotten the rest of us, too. Besides, it's less than a week until Valentine's Day, so it's smart to give off a romantic glow to attract beaus."

"Zoe, you make me sound like a lightning bug! I'm not celebrating Valentine's Day this year. I'm working all day Monday, so there will be no 'romantic glow' for me."

"Will Dylan be there?" Grace asked, her gaze sharp.

"Yeah, but he'll be working in the kitchen while I work in the dining area, so —"

"Will you talk?" Kat asked.

"And laugh about stuff?" Sarah added.

"I guess, but —"

"Then it counts," Zoe said firmly. "You're glowing and you don't even know it."

Grace, Kat, and Sarah nodded.

"Look, Dylan isn't — we're not —" Ava's headache wouldn't let her think straight enough to argue. She looked around the café, searching for the waitress. "Where's Marian?"

"She'll be around soon," Sarah said. "We ordered you a BLT, light on the mayo."

"Thank you." Ava leaned back, resting her aching head against the back of the booth. It didn't help, so she rubbed her temples.

"What you need is some Tylenol." Kat pulled her purse from under the table and dug out a packet. "Mom keeps these in a candy dish on her desk. She's always prepared for the worst."

Ava took the Tylenol, hoping it would work quickly.

Zoe waited until Ava had put her tea glass back on the table before she asked, "What's brought you up for air? No one in town has seen you out in weeks."

"I'm sure you all heard about the wonky-tea incident."

Grace nodded. "Kat and Sarah mentioned it. Sarah said you'd figured out what went wrong. Are you sure those three teas were the only ones affected?"

"Positive. They were the only three made at that time, and we discovered the sick peppermint plant before I used it again."

"One less thing," Sarah said cheerfully. "Now all you have to do is open the tearoom, and all your problems will be solved."

Ava had to fight the urge to scowl at her sister's understatement of the year. Her headache thudded sickly, making her eyes water. What was it with this headache? She'd never had one that pounded against her temples in quite this way.

"Stressing?" Kat said with sympathy.

"Yeah. I don't know why. I mean, everything is going well, except —" Ava gestured. "The tearoom and stuff." To be honest, it was the *stuff* that was bothering her the most.

For the last week, the taped-up box had been even noisier than usual, banging for hours at a time. Unsatisfied with waking her up in the middle of the night, now it wouldn't let her fall asleep to begin with.

But most unsettling of all was what had happened when she'd woken up this morning at 4 a.m. She'd found the battered shoebox sitting near her door, two long strands of duct tape trailing off one corner. *If Sarah had seen that —*

No. Ava couldn't think about that. Not now.

Not ever.

Grace pulled her water glass closer, her engagement ring sparkling against the mason jar. Now that the election was over, new mayor Grace, with the help of her niece Daisy, was planning a big June wedding to her fiancé, Trav Parker. Ava liked Grace but found Trav intimidating, even though he and Sarah had been friends since elementary school. He was a smoldering, never-smiling sort of guy, and Ava preferred . . . well, she didn't know what she preferred, but it wasn't the too-serious type.

Ava looked up and caught Sarah's concerned gaze.

"Are you okay?"

Ava managed a laugh. "I'm fine. I've just been thinking a lot about what happened with that poor peppermint plant."

"What did happen?" Grace asked, flicking a curious glance Ava's way. "Sarah never gave us any details."

"One of my peppermint plants was infused with grief."

Zoe squinted at Ava. "Did you say 'grief'?"

"What do you mean 'infused'?" Grace asked.

Ava rubbed her temple. "Someone wept over one of my peppermint plants, and it soaked up their sorrow."

Zoe's thin eyebrows rose. "Plants can *feel*?"

"Plants have always felt things, much more than people realize."

Grace nodded thoughtfully. "I read an article the other day that scientists have proven that stressed plants emit high-frequency noises, sort of like screams, when they or a nearby plant need water."

Zoe cast a shocked glance at the tiny pink-and-green succulent that decorated the table. "Are you serious?"

"Look it up," Ava said. "Plants move on their own, too. Heliotropic flowers turn their faces toward the sun. Sunflowers will even level their leaves so they get the full impact."

"The sunflowers you planted beside my garage do that," Kat said, wonder in her voice.

"Plants are not hard, cold objects. I used some leaves from that peppermint plant to make a few teas and, well, there you have it. It changed the purpose of those teas. Apparently grief can force us to face unpleasant truths."

Grace and Zoe exchanged a look.

Ava stifled a sigh and explained. "When a person dies, we stand around at their funeral and remind one another about the good things we knew about that person, but grief is a lot more honest." Ava thought about when her mother died. "When you love someone, you remember every single bit of them, good and bad, happy and sad. All the wonderful traits and unpleasant truths can cause both bitter regrets and empty wishes for things that can never be."

"You guys are making me miss Mama G." Grace's eyes shone brightly.

Zoe freed a napkin from the holder sitting on the table beside the ketchup and handed it to Grace, who gratefully took it.

About three years ago, Grace had moved to Dove Pond with Daisy and her adoptive mother, Mama G. Mama G, who was born

216

and raised in Dove Pond before moving away, had been loved by everyone. Sadly, when she returned to town, she was already suffering from the beginning stages of Alzheimer's. She'd passed away in her sleep two years ago, and they all missed her and her wisdom.

Sarah put her hand over Grace's. "We can talk about something else."

"No, no. It's okay." She turned to Ava. "Back to your peppermint plant. Who infused it with grief? It sounds like —"

"BLT, double tomato, heavy on the mayo." The Moonlight's redheaded waitress, Marian Freely, settled a large tray on an empty nearby table.

She knew all their orders, and they busied themselves passing plates to one another.

Ava looked at her BLT and wished she felt hungrier. The headache was lessening a little, though, so that was something.

"So," Grace said, salting the tomato on her BLT. "Who griefed up your peppermint plant?"

"Kristen Foster."

"Poor kid," Zoe said. "She's had it rough these last few weeks."

Kat put ketchup on her fries. "She's a good one, but I'm not sure how I feel about her grandmother."

"Correct me if I'm wrong," Zoe said, "but Ellen Foster doesn't seem like the warm, cookie-making grandma we were all promised in the movies."

"She's stiff," Ava agreed. "I think her heart is in the right place, although I'm worried about Kristen. She's been distracted lately."

Grace's face softened. "It takes a special person to be there for someone else's child, even if they're a relative. When I asked Mama G how I could help Daisy understand death, you know what she said?"

Ava, who knew this would be counseling gold, leaned forward. "Yes?"

"Talk to her."

Everyone stared at Grace, who took another sip of coffee.

Sarah's shoulders dropped. "That's it?"

"It sounds simple, but it's not. Ava, talk to Kristen, encourage her to talk to you, and *never* pretend things are better than they are." Grace put her coffee cup down. "She'll act as if she doesn't want to talk, but just knowing you're there and willing to listen — that's some good stuff right there."

*That's at least doable.* "I'll do what I can. I hate to admit it, but I've avoided mentioning Julie when Kristen is around. I don't want to make things harder for her."

"Big mistake," Grace said.

"I didn't want to rush things. I figured Kristen would talk about her mom when she was ready."

"That's what everyone thinks. That means no one is talking to her about her mother, which can feel isolating."

"I never thought of that." Ava would bet everyone in Dove Pond was tiptoeing around the topic.

Grace smiled. "One of the good things about Kristen is that she has friends — close ones, from the looks of things."

"Missy and Josh are great," Ava said. "Although I doubt they understand fully what she's going through."

Sarah agreed. "She needs an adult in her life. I wish I had more confidence in Ellen, but I don't get the impression she and Kristen mesh."

"I doubt Ellen meshes with many people," Kat said. "That woman reminds me way too much of Mrs. McIntyre."

Grace grimaced at the mention of Blake's mother. "She's ice-cold, that one. I see her at some of the community forums and I've yet to see her smile."

"I feel sorry for them both," Sarah said. "They don't seem very comfortable with themselves. I —" She gulped and went pale.

Ava followed her sister's gaze. Blake McIntyre had walked in, the dull gleam of his badge evident even from where they sat.

Sarah dropped her fork on her plate and eyed the door as if judging how fast she'd have to sprint to make an escape.

Ava watched, her heart sinking. "Sarah, just ignore him. He's —"

"I can't!" Sarah pressed her hands to her flushed cheeks. "I need to, but I can't."

Grace sighed. "He won't bite you. He's a really nice guy."

"I know that! He just — Oh! He's looking this way. I —" Sarah stood, half in the booth and half out. "I need to go."

"Please sit down." Ava's headache roared back to life.

"You haven't finished your lunch," Zoe pointed out.

"Stay there," Grace ordered. "Just ignore him. He can't —"

"I'll see you all later." Sarah grabbed her coat and hurried for the door, one hand tangling in a sleeve as she speed-walked away, her face as red as her scarf.

Blake said something to Sarah as she passed, and she shot him a panicked look, then hurried on, one arm still caught in her sleeve.

He stopped, watching her struggle with

her coat as she went out the door. Still fighting the inside-out sleeve, she dashed past the front window in the rain, her head down, her coat only halfway on.

Ava watched, her heart aching with each frantic step her sister took.

Blake watched until she was out of sight, then made his way to the counter.

"Ay-yi-yi." Zoe broke the silence. "Those two." She shook her head. "Do you think they know they're in love with each other?"

"They know." Ava put her fork down and pressed her fingertips to her head, which was pounding worse than it ever had. *I hate seeing Sarah so upset. If only I could fix it. I have to do something about this. I can't stand to see her suffer. My —*

CRACK! Outside, thunder rumbled, and rain sluiced down even harder.

Ava rubbed her temples and murmured, "This is killing me."

Zoe was still staring at the door Sarah had disappeared through. "I don't get it. Sarah's so upbeat and positive in every other area of her life except Blake."

"She can barely talk to him." Grace looked perplexed. "Sarah's not shy, either. She can talk to anyone else without hesitation, even strangers. But him? She can't even breathe when he's nearby. I've never seen anything like it."

Kat picked up another French fry. "It's weird, almost like she's —"

"I've got to go." Ava pushed her plate away and stood. "I need to get back to the tearoom."

Kat looked surprised. "You barely touched your lunch."

"My head is killing me. Plus I'm supposed to deliver some teas later this afternoon and I haven't labeled them."

Zoe dipped a spinach leaf in her vinaigrette dressing. "You have a lot on your plate right now."

"Too much," Kat said.

"I can handle it. Once the tearoom is up and running, everything will be simpler. Grace, thanks for the advice about Kristen. I'll try it."

"Let me know if it helps."

"Will do. Bye, you all. See you around." Ava headed to the door, her feet unconsciously moving to the throbbing beat in her head. She collected her coat, careful not to look toward Blake as she went, although she could feel his questioning gaze.

Without waiting, she put her head down and hurried out into the rain after Sarah, the cool air welcome on her hot cheeks.

# CHAPTER 10
## KRISTEN

Kristen parked her Camry in the driveway and slumped down in her seat, staring at her house. The chilly afternoon drizzle pattered on the car roof as she watched her grandmother through the living room window. Grandma Ellen was cleaning bookshelves, handling the duster with the fierce concentration of a professional cleaner.

Since the night Grandma Ellen had used Ava's tea, something had changed. She now watched Kristen with obvious suspicion, and more than once, she'd showed up at the tearoom as if checking to see if Kristen was where she said she was. *Did she figure out what I was doing? That I gave her that tea so she'd sleep while I searched through Mom's things?*

*God, I hope not.*

Kristen dropped her head against the headrest. *I've made things worse. I should just run away like Mom did.* But sadly, the genetics gods hadn't seen fit to gift Kristen with her mom's bravery. Kristen wasn't the sort to throw caution to the wind. She was a homebody and loved the familiar so much so that Mom used to tease her about it, calling her Cozy Home Bear.

Sighing, Kristen looked at her home and tried to imagine living somewhere else, but couldn't. From the first time she'd seen the rambling, faded mint-green house, Kristen had loved it. Everything about it felt like home — the creaky floors, the wavy glass in the huge windows, the heavy brass doorknobs. Mom had made their place even more homey by filling it with her paintings, especially the Wonder Kristen mural in the front hallway. *I wish Grandma Ellen understood that.*

Grimacing with frustration, Kristen crossed her arms over the steering wheel and looked up at the window over the front porch. Mom's studio was dark, the curtains drawn, as empty as the rest of the house. Kristen's chest tightened, so she closed her eyes, took a long breath through her nose, and hummed. *"Release your pain and irritation into the world,"* Mom would say. *"Let it go. Don't let it fester in your heart."*

It didn't help. It never helped.

Inside the house, Grandma Ellen set aside

the duster only to reappear with a hand vacuum. She attacked a chair near the window as if she were trying to vanquish a pack of demons. *I bet the dogs are hiding under the dining room table. That's where I'd be, too.*

Kristen dropped her arms from the steering wheel and slid her hand into her pocket, her fingers closing over the kazoo. She still kept it close. Sometimes, when no one was around, she'd play "Dancing Queen" over and over.

She sighed and leaned back against the headrest once more. *Oh, Mom, this is hard. Harder than I ever imagined.* Her eyes grew blurry, and she angrily swiped at them. In a box in Kristen's closet at this very minute, jumbled with scrapbooks and photos and other memorabilia, was a thumb drive containing dozens of videos of Mom. There was a clip about learning new things, a few about having children, a half dozen on the importance of balance — in all, Mom had made more than forty videos for Kristen to watch as she grew up. Mom had wanted her to wait as each topic came up in her life, but right now, Kristen couldn't even watch the two Mom had recorded about death. Every time she tried, she'd cry too hard to hear or see it. And not a soft, weepy cry, but the deep, bellyaching, ugly cry that people usually did when they were alone and no one could hear or see. The same thing happened whenever Kristen tried to look at the picture albums she and Mom had made or when she went to burn the good-memories candles Mom had left. Kristen couldn't do any of it.

Worse, she didn't want to.

What she wanted was her mom back.

A loud rumble announced the arrival of a truck with a bad exhaust pipe as it pulled into the driveway behind her. Kristen wiped her sleeve over her eyes one last time and then adjusted her rearview mirror and watched as Missy hopped out.

Kristen waved, and Missy dashed to the car, her head ducked against the cold drizzle.

Missy opened the passenger door and plopped into the seat, the car rocking as she closed the door. "Geez, it's cold!"

"At least it's not snowing."

"Snow is better than this mess. I *hate* icy drizzle." Missy's curly brown hair surrounded her round face like a halo, water droplets sparkling on the ringlets. "What are you doing out here?"

"I didn't want to go inside."

"Don't blame you." Missy watched

Grandma Ellen, who was looking out the window, no doubt drawn there by the sound of Missy's broken exhaust pipe. "She doesn't look happy."

"She's been acting weird the past few days."

Missy's eyes widened. "You think she knows you drugged her?"

Kristen flushed. "I didn't drug her! I told her the tea would make her sleep, which it did. She told me the next morning she'd slept most of the night, too, so it worked just fine." Kristen shrugged, her gaze moving back to the front window. "I don't know why, but she's been really quiet lately, and I've caught her watching me as if she thinks I robbed a bank or something."

"Weird. It's also sort of weird to sit in your car in the driveway, unless, of course, you're making out with a guy. Are you okay?"

Kristen sent Missy a hard side glance.

Missy threw her hands up. "Right. That was a ridiculous thing to say. Of course you aren't okay. I just meant —"

"Don't be stupid." Kristen shrugged, although she felt more like gritting her teeth. "I'm tired, that's all."

Missy nodded sympathetically. "I'm glad I'm here, then, but can you turn on your heater? I'm cold. That rain was like ice water."

Kristen slid her key back into the ignition, and the car jolted to life. Since she'd just parked, warm air instantly streamed into the car.

Missy cupped her hands over the nearest vent. "That's so much better, I — Good Lord, is your grandma *vacuuming* the curtains?"

"Dove Pond is too dusty for her."

"Huh. My mom just takes them down and throws them in the wash. Works every time."

Kristen couldn't remember her mom ever washing the curtains. They probably needed vacuuming *and* washing. "That's what she's been doing. She cleans, vacuums, and watches me as if she thinks I might explode or something."

"Impressive." Missy rubbed her hands together, her gaze suddenly a little sharper. "So . . . since I'm here . . . Did you get it done? You said you took a bunch of stuff out of your mom's trunk and had to go through it. You've had plenty of time now."

"I finished late last night. I made of list of suspects." Kristen reached behind her seat and grabbed her book bag. She pulled it to her lap, slipped out a creased piece of notebook paper, and then returned the backpack to the floorboard. "It took me a while to go through all of Mom's stuff, or I would have finished sooner."

Missy looked eagerly at the paper. "How many?"

"Three." She handed the paper to Missy.

"That's all?" There was no disguising the disappointment in Missy's voice.

"The fewer the better."

"I guess so. I just thought it would be more fun if there were a bunch." She started to unfold the paper, but then she glanced at Kristen and paused. "Know what we need before we look at this? A latte."

"I can't go now. Grandma Ellen's already seen me."

"No problem." Missy pulled out her phone. Her thumbs flew over the screen.

"What are you doing?"

"Ordering caramel lattes with two — no, let's make that three — extra pumps. Or I am if Josh's phone cooperates. That thing is complete trash and — ah. There he is. He said no problem. He was sitting in the Moonlight when I drove past on my way here, so he won't be long."

A three-pump latte while sitting in her car with her friends in the rain. Life wasn't so bad, Kristen decided. *Mom would approve.*

Missy dropped her phone into the cup

holder. "I told him we were here in the car, so he won't go to the door."

Inside the house, Grandma Ellen waved, gesturing for them to come in.

Kristen pointed at Missy and waved to say no, thank you.

Grandma Ellen gave a tight smile and then disappeared from sight.

Missy watched the exchange with interest. "I'm glad the tea worked. Pity your grandma is still passive-aggressiving you to death."

"More aggressive than passive now. This morning during breakfast, she announced about eight times that she couldn't take off much more time from work."

Missy rolled her eyes. "Josh is right; it's surprising she hasn't been more forceful. Personally, I think she's afraid you'll run off the way your mom did."

Kristen stared at the window Grandma Ellen had just left. "If she thinks I'm runaway material, then she doesn't know me well."

"She doesn't know you at all. I wouldn't tell her she's wrong about that, though. It's in your favor to keep her afraid you might bolt. I — Oh! There's our lattes."

A battered van had pulled up on the street. Josh hopped out, carrying a tray of three drinks. He hurried toward them, his hood pulled up to protect him from the rain. He slid into the back seat and closed the door. "The windows are so fogged up, I wasn't sure who was in here."

"Latte me!" Missy reached into the back seat.

Grinning, Josh handed out the drinks. He took one sip and then said, "Well? How many dad candidates are there?"

"Three." Kristen took the lid off her latte and blew on it.

"That's all?"

"That's what I said too," Missy said. "I was hoping there'd be at least a dozen."

"Three is plenty." Kristen held her coffee cup in both hands, soaking in the warmth.

Josh took a noisy sip. "So what's the plan?"

"We ask, we find, and Kristen is rescued," Missy declared. "Simple." Kristen wasn't convinced it would be that easy. "If you ask me, that list has two too many maybe-dads." When Josh had first come up with this idea, Kristen had loved it. She'd even been excited. But over the past few days, doubts had begun to worm their way into her thoughts. Other than that one time long ago, she'd never wanted to know her father. And having to look for him like this, already needing something from him, made it even worse.

"Do we know any of these guys?" Josh asked.

"Sort of," Kristen said.

Missy put her coffee down and picked up the folded paper. "Shall I?"

"Might as well. I just hope one of them is my dad. We're just guessing, you know. There was a lot of stuff in that trunk, but not one piece of paper that read, 'Kristen's father is . . .'"

"That would have been nice," Missy admitted. "How did you decide these guys might be the ones?"

"I found an unfinished letter stuck between the pages of an old book. That led me to Mom's yearbooks."

Mom had written to a friend of hers where she'd airily claimed, *I find it funny that, for the future father of my baby, I chose the guy who wrote such a corny poem in my yearbook. I guess it really does pay to know how to rhyme.*

That had been the one and only clue. After reading that, Kristen had gone through Mom's yearbooks one at a time, looking for poems, and had found these three.

Missy had unfolded the paper. "Jack Lind," she announced, then frowned. "I thought you said we knew all of them?"

232

"We've seen him around," Kristen said. "He owns the new property management company in that office over by Doc Bolton's. He lives in Asheville but has a house here, too."

Josh asked, "Does he drive a black Audi?"

"He has a black car. I guess it's an Audi."

"Oh, I know that guy," Missy said. "I've seen him driving through town. Nice car, good job, great hair. So far, so good." She read the next name. "Nate Stevens. Everyone knows him."

Kristen nodded. "He's got the only hardware store in town."

Josh took another noisy sip of coffee. "My mom says he's a dead ringer for that guy in *Outlander*."

"Jamie Fraser," Missy said dreamily. "They do look a lot alike." Josh and Kristen looked at Missy, who said in a defensive tone, "What? My mom watches it, not me."

Kristen didn't believe that for a minute. "I know Mr. Stevens, but not well."

"Dad and I go to his store all the time," Josh said. "Mr. Stevens seems cool. I like him."

"He's cute, that's all I know," Missy said. "I bet all of these guys are fine. Your mother was an artist, so she'd be attracted to good-looking guys." She returned to the list. "And number three is . . . ." Her eyes widened, and she stared at Kristen. "Are you serious?"

*If only I weren't.* "That one's going to be tricky."

"Who is it?" Josh leaned over the seat, trying to see the paper over Missy's shoulder.

She turned it so he couldn't, her gaze still on Kristen. "If he figures out what we're doing, he'll tell your grandmother."

Kristen nodded miserably.

"Big yikes." Missy didn't look happy, but she tried to lighten the moment by saying, "Still, he's not bad-looking for an older guy. Your mom had great taste."

"Missy, stop. I don't care what he looks like. I just need him to be cool enough to let me stay here in Dove Pond, even if Grandma Ellen makes a fuss."

"Who is number three?" Josh asked impatiently.

Missy sighed. "Blake McIntyre."

"The *sheriff?* Oh wow. That's awkward."

"Tell me about it," Kristen muttered. "We should save him for last. If one of these other guys is my dad, then we'd just be wasting our time trying to talk to him anyway."

"No kidding." Missy refolded the paper and handed it to Kristen, who tucked it into her shirt pocket. "So those are our targets."

"What do we do now?" Josh asked.

That was the big question, wasn't it? "I don't know," Kristen admitted. "I guess we'll have to talk to them. But before I ask a guy if he's my father, we should at least make sure the timeline works out."

"Right." Missy's brow furrowed. "We need to count back from your birthday, which means your mom would have been dating this guy . . ."

Kristen had a lot of patience, but she knew better than to expect Missy to do math without a calculator. "August or September 2004. Or somewhere around there."

"So right off the bat, you need to find out which of these guys was dating your mom during those months."

"Wow." Josh grinned over the top of his coffee cup. "This is awesome. I feel like we're in a movie."

"Yeah, a horror movie," Kristen said.

"No, no," Missy protested. "This is one of those epic movies from the Hallmark channel. We're going to find your dad and you're going to stay here in Dove Pond and live happily ever after, and when that happens, we'll film a montage of ourselves sipping coffee and laughing and dancing at junior prom, and . . . and . . . doing all sorts of things."

"If that's how it ends up. It's just . . ." Kristen put her latte down, her chest suddenly tight. "Missy, what if my dad doesn't want to know me?"

A stunned silence met her words.

"Of course he'll want to know you," Missy scoffed. "Why wouldn't he? If I had a long-lost daughter, I'd want to know her. I'd want her to be just like you, too. Except younger, of course."

Josh added, "It's not like you're going to be a burden. You have your own house and car and money. You really just need him to get your grandma off your back."

"Exactly." Missy sent Josh a grateful glance that made him beam. "What dad wouldn't want to find out he had a daughter under circumstances like that? Heck, I wouldn't mind finding out I had an unknown daughter if that was the way things were. She could take me out to dinner once in a while and maybe buy me a new purse. I'd let her do that."

Kristen wished she could be as certain as they were that their desperate plan would succeed. Right now, all she felt was sad, lost, and anxious. She picked up her latte and tried to tell herself that things would work out. They had to.

"Oh look!" Missy leaned forward so she could see out Kristen's side window. "There's Sarah Dove."

Three doors down, a pickup truck had pulled up to the Dove house, which was painted a delicate mauve. Sarah climbed out of the truck dressed in an orange flowered raincoat and matching boots, her blond hair pulled to one side in a loose ponytail. She popped open a bright yellow umbrella and pulled out a stack of books from where they rested in the back seat.

Missy watched, seemingly mesmerized. "Mom says Sarah always takes books home with her, not to read but to visit."

"She's got to be a huge reader, though," Josh said. "I mean, if books talked to me, I'd read more of them."

Missy glanced at Kristen. "Has Sarah ever brought you a book?"

"Once when I was ten years old," Kristen said wistfully. "I wish she would bring me more."

"She once brought me a book on coin collecting, and two days later I found a wheat penny. A real one."

"Those aren't worth that much," Josh said.

"They're *rare*. I — Look! She's coming this way."

Sarah's umbrella bobbed as she hurried down the sidewalk, her orange boots splashing whenever she hit a puddle. She came up to the car and bent over to smile at them.

Kristen opened her window, glad the umbrella kept the rain out. "I'm so glad I saw you all out here." Sarah handed not one but four books to Kristen.

Missy leaned forward eagerly.

Kristen blinked. "All of these are for me?"

"The top three are. They said you weren't sleeping, so . . ." Sarah patted the stack.

Kristen looked at them. Terry Brooks's Sword of Shannara trilogy. She'd read them a few years ago and had loved them.

"They won't help you sleep, but now you'll have some company." Sarah tapped the top book. "They're very excited to be reread. For a book, there is no higher honor."

Well, that was something. To be honest, it was bone-achingly lonely at night when Grandma Ellen was in bed and the world was echo-silent. Kristen eyed the colorful cover, and her heart warmed a little. Rereading a favorite book was like coming home, something she hadn't felt in a while. "It'll be nice to have something else to think about." Sarah nodded as if she'd expected Kristen to say that. "Books are warriors. If you let them, they'll fight off boredom, pain, fear, even loneliness." She bent a little lower so she could see Missy. "The bottom one is for you."

"Oh, thank you, thank you!" Missy eagerly reached for the book, but her smile disappeared the second she freed it from the pile. "This is a physics book."

"You have a test or something, I think?" Sarah wasn't really asking. It was obvious she already knew the answer. "From what the book said, you're not doing great in that class and could use a little extra help."

Missy's face turned bright red, and her shoulders drooped. "Thank you," she said in a chastened tone.

Josh leaned forward. "Anything for me?"

"Not this time," Sarah said. "But I'll keep an ear out." Disappointed, he nodded.

"I'd better get home and start supper. Ava will be home soon and —" Sarah's brows lowered, and she turned to look over her shoulder. "Do you hear that?"

Kristen and Missy exchanged a look. "Hear what?" Kristen asked. "That thumping." Sarah tilted her head to one side, her gray-green eyes narrowed. "It's been going on for about a week now. I'll hear it, and then it'll go away, and I — Oh." She waved her hand, her smile back. "It's gone now.

Someone must be playing their music too loud, which is so annoying I —" She caught Kristen's gaze, and her smile slipped. "You didn't hear it, did you."

Kristen and Missy both shook their heads.

"It's just me, then." Sarah gave an uncertain laugh. "Maybe my hearing is better than I thought. Whatever it is, I'd better go start supper. I've been trying to help Ava out by making sure there's something on the table when she gets home."

"She's been working hard," Kristen agreed. "How's the peppermint plant doing?" She was still a little embarrassed about that whole incident.

"Much better. It's only a little wilted now, so it's coming along." That was something, Kristen supposed. "I hope it heals."

"It will. It will just take time." Sarah flashed a comforting smile. "Enjoy the books." Her umbrella held close, she headed home.

Kristen closed the window before the rain fell on the books in her lap.

Missy dropped her book onto the floorboard, where it landed with a thud. "Of all the books she could give me, she picks a stupid physics book. What the heck."

"You've got to pass that class if you want to graduate," Josh said. "Maybe that book

240

explains things better than the textbook, which sucks. If my dad couldn't explain that stuff to me, I'd be failing too."

Missy flushed. "I'm not failing!"

"Sorry! I just thought —"

"Don't think. It's annoying."

He sighed and started collecting his things. "I've got to get home. I guess we'll start with Nate Stevens first thing tomorrow after school. Right?"

*Tomorrow? That's so soon!* Kristen's chest tightened even more. "I can't do it tomorrow. Ava's expecting a shipment of table linens and she can't be there to sign for them, so I said I would. I work Friday evening and most of the weekend, too. Ava's really determined to get the tearoom back on track." Kristen was making excuses and she knew it, but she wasn't ready for this. She needed some time to think things through.

Josh looked disappointed. "What about Monday, then? We can stop by the hardware store after school."

"Isn't that Valentine's Day?"

He shrugged. "So? None of us are dating anyone. I don't know about Mr. Stevens, but he works as much as Ava does. I bet he'll be there."

They looked expectantly at Kristen.

She couldn't think of an excuse, so she said glumly, "I guess that will work. We just need to be sure I'm home on time. The Frosty One is acting suspicious."

"No problem," Missy said, gathering her things.

"Monday afternoon it is." Josh climbed out of the car. "See you guys later."

"I'd better go, too." Missy stuffed the physics book into her book bag. "To be honest, I forgot about that stupid test. Maybe this book will help." She paused before she got out of the car. "Kristen . . . about the dad search. This is a good start."

"I just hope it works. I don't know what I'll do if it doesn't."

"It's a great plan. In a few days, you'll know who your father is and you won't be fighting your grandmother alone. That'll make everything better." One corner of Missy's mouth lifted in a half smile. "Besides, if Mr. Stevens is your father, you could qualify for the family discount at the hardware store."

"A dream come true," Kristen said drily.

Missy grinned. "Just trying to find the positive. See you tomorrow." She hopped out and bolted through the rain. Soon Missy's truck noisily chugged out of the driveway.

Kristen grabbed her backpack from the back seat. She unzipped it and slid in the books Sarah had given her. She had just closed the bag when she remembered the list. She pulled it out of her pocket and looked at it again. The names seemed to dance in front of her. *I don't know any of them. Not really.*

She looked back at the house. Inside, she could see Grandma Ellen walking through the living room. She paused by the couch, her expression softening. To Kristen's surprise, Grandma reached down and pulled a blanket over Luffy, who was sleeping soundly in his favorite corner.

Wow. When Grandma first came to Dove Pond, she'd hated the dogs. But now . . . *Maybe things can change. Maybe, instead of looking for a dad I've never met and who doesn't even know about me, I should spend time with Grandma and get to know her.*

But no. That wouldn't change Grandma Ellen's mind about moving away. If Kristen wanted to stay here with her friends and in her house, she had no choice but to find her dad.

Sighing, Kristen stuffed the list back in her pocket, grabbed her backpack, and headed through the rain toward the wide porch. As her feet splashed through the puddles, she whispered to herself, "Please, please, please let this work."

# Chapter 11
## Ellen

Friday morning, as soon as Kristen left for school, Ellen drove to Main Street and parked her Lexus in front of Ava's tearoom. Outside, a new brass sign that read THE PINK MAGNOLIA TEAROOM hung over the door. Ellen rather liked the lettering, which fit the antique vibe of the place.

She went inside, where she was met by the familiar whine of a sander. Dylan stood on a ladder behind the bar, smoothing down a rough corner on the reclaimed barn wood that was now fastened to the wall. Buckets of white stain sat on a tarp by the wall, ready for when he finished.

*Well, well, well. Ava Dove took my advice.* Ellen wasn't sure why that surprised her, but it did. She remained near the door, watching Dylan work and admiring his competent handling of the old wood. Everyone loved reclaimed wood. The texture was gorgeous, the scarring adding interest, the environmental benefit obvious, yet few people realized how much prep work it took to do it right.

Ellen waited for him to finish the board before she yelled over the noise, "Pardon me!"

Dylan turned and, seeing her, released the trigger. "Sorry. I didn't hear you."

"Of course. Is Ava here?"

"She stepped out, but she'll be back soon. Do you want to leave a message or —"

"No, thank you. I'll wait."

"Sure." He gave her a polite nod and went back to work, the noise loud as it bounced against the tin ceiling tiles.

Ellen's gaze moved down the long bar, rested briefly on the wrought-iron tables and chairs, and ended up on the paintings Julie had made for Ava. They were hung, four in a row, right above the creamer station, fitting so perfectly they could have been designed for the space.

It had been a wearying few days. Although she'd tried, Ellen hadn't been able to forget that odd dream. She knew it wasn't real and yet she'd found herself searching the house for the red cube Julie had mentioned. Ellen had pretended to be on a cleaning spree so Kristen wouldn't think she had completely lost her mind. Of course, the whole thing had been an utter waste of time. She hadn't found anything even resembling a red cube although she'd searched just about every corner, cabinet, and closet of the house.

"I didn't find it because it doesn't exist," she muttered to herself, a little embarrassed she'd even looked for it.

Sheesh, she had to get out of Dove Pond. *All I have to do is complete Project K and I'll be home in time for —*

"Ellen?" Ava said over the noise. She stood by the door, bundled up in her overly large Carhartt coat, a paper sack in one hand. She looked pale and tired, which was odd, considering how early it was.

"Good morning." Ellen had to yell to be heard.

Dylan glanced over his shoulder and, seeing them both, turned off the sander and climbed down the ladder.

"Don't stop on our account," Ellen told him.

"I didn't." He put the sander on the floor by the ladder and dusted off his shirt. "I quit because Ava brought me breakfast."

Ava handed him the paper bag. "I lost a bet," she told Ellen. "Never wager on a horse named Going To Win."

"Sage advice." Dylan opened the bag and pulled out a wrapped breakfast sandwich.

As he did so, he glanced at Ellen. "Did you get in touch with the Callahan brothers?"

Ava's eyebrows went up.

Ellen explained, "I ran into Dylan at the bank yesterday and asked if he knew any painters, and he recommended the Callahans." She turned back to Dylan. "Eric came out last night and gave me a quote. He and Nick had a job that just canceled, so they are free for a few days. In fact, if he can get the paint, they're starting later this morning."

"They're good guys, both of them, and super careful. Glad you could work it out. Now, if you'll pardon me, I'm going to head into the kitchen to eat this delicious egg sandwich I won because I'm smart and I know things." With a wave, he left.

Smiling, Ava shrugged out of her coat and hung it on a peg.

"Your tearoom is shaping up nicely. Are you back on schedule?"

"Getting closer." Ava went behind the counter and grabbed a watering can. She filled it at the sink and then started watering the plants along the front window. Ellen watched her, deciding that Ava looked like one of the tomboys Norman Rockwell liked to paint, what with her coveralls and long-sleeved red T-shirt, her blond hair in a messy braid over one shoulder.

Ellen briefly wondered what Ava would look like in decent clothes, but then she shrugged the thought aside. She had far more important things to talk about than Ava's lack of fashion sense. "I came to see you this morning because I have a question."

Ava looked up, surprise in her gray-green eyes. "What's that?"

"It's about your teas. When I first came to your little shop here, you mentioned you made regular herbal teas. I believe you called those your diffusion line?"

"Right. I sell them to local boutiques and coffeehouses."

"So those are 'normal' teas, then — green, Earl Grey, black, chamomile, honey lavender, lemon and ginger, and so on."

Ava smiled politely, obviously curious as to what Ellen was getting at.

"But then you also make 'specialty teas.' " Ellen air-quoted the term. "From what Kristen and others have told me, you believe those teas can do things that are . . . rather odd."

"Why are you asking about this?"

"I was wondering how they work. If they're even real."

Ava's smile had disappeared. "Ask the

people who've used them."

"That's a rather safe answer. If you tell someone something they want to hear, they're very likely to believe it."

Ava's jaw tightened. "I'm not a charlatan, if that's what you're saying."

"Of course not," Ellen said shortly. "I just — Look, Kristen made me a cup of tea saying it would help me sleep. It was one of yours."

"It was probably chamomile. I've been encouraging her to use the diffusion teas so she'll know them well enough to make recommendations when we open."

"It didn't taste like any chamomile tea I've ever had."

"So . . . it *didn't* work? Is that why you're here?"

"No, I slept. But I —" She met Ava's gray-green gaze and the words "spoke to Julie" stuck in Ellen's throat.

It sounded so ridiculous.

*For the love of God, why am I even here? It was just a dream.* She couldn't — wouldn't — make a fool of herself in front of Ava, or anyone else, for that matter. *What's wrong with me?*

But she knew the answer. Just like all the pathetic people who drank their Ava Dove teas, she wanted a miracle. She *wanted* the dream to be real.

Embarrassed, Ellen waved her hand. "It's nothing. The tea worked, although it wasn't a particularly restful sleep."

"Steep it a little longer. Chamomile has been used for centuries; its name comes from a Greek word meaning 'ground apples.' It was used in ancient Egypt, too."

It was obvious Ava loved her teas. *Someone has to.* Ellen regretted coming. There were no magical teas. No magical doors to the other world where a sad, lonely mother could speak to her only child, if only for a few moments. She knew that and yet she couldn't stop the painful burn of disappointment that rippled through her.

She collected herself and backed away toward the door. "Thank you for the information. I just wanted to be sure I hadn't gotten one of your 'specialty teas' by mistake." Before Ava could comment, Ellen nodded toward the wall behind the bar. "I like the wall. It — the whole place, really — is looking wonderful."

Ava's smile returned. "We're getting there. The soft opening is only a month away, though, and I still have a lot to do."

"I'll let you get back to it, then. Good luck hitting your deadline, although it looks like you're going to do it." With a final wave, Ellen hurried outside, the chilly air a welcome relief as she went to her car. *That answered that.* She hadn't taken some sort of Ava Dove peyote-and-mushroom-or-whatever-she-uses tea after all. *It was just chamomile. Now I can forget that stupid dream and move forward with Project K and get that monstrously creaky house ready to sell.*

Ellen headed home, more determined than ever to press ahead. She'd lost days of precious house rehab time waiting for Kristen to accept the move to Raleigh.

They couldn't wait any longer. She pulled into the driveway, pleased to see a white truck sitting by the walkway with the words THE CALLAHAN BROTHERS: CARPENTERS, PAINTERS, GENERAL FIXERS scrawled on the side. Eric and Nick were there, unloading ladders, drop cloths, paint buckets, and brushes.

Ellen parked her car and joined them. "You're early."

Eric grinned. "Are you complaining or bragging on us?"

"Definitely bragging." She pulled out her front door key and led the way.

The dogs crowded forward to greet them, wagging their tails and begging for pats. As quickly as she could, Ellen took them to the backyard and then hurried back to the foyer where the men were setting up.

Eric looked around the front hallway. "There's a lot of wood trim."

"I like that about older houses," Nick said. "I — Whoa!" He was standing in front of Julie's mural, obviously admiring the cartoony work. "Did Julie do this?"

"She did. I hate having it painted over, but it'll be the first thing people see when they walk inside, so . . ." She sighed and turned away. There were dozens of paintings by Julie in the house, more than enough to serve as a reminder of her too-short life. "Please start here in the front hall and then paint the downstairs bathroom. When you're ready to work in the living room, the furniture will need to be moved and covered."

"We can handle that." Nick went to look at the living room. "Cream in the hall and gray in here, right?" At her nod, he put his hand on the heavy wood trim of the wide doorway between the front hall and the living room. "This is original. You don't want us to paint it, do you?"

"Heavens no. Leave the trim alone. Once you all are done, I'll clean it. It really is beautiful wood."

"You don't see wood trim like this anymore." Eric picked up his bucket. "I guess that's all we need to know."

"I'll be in the dining room, packing away some figurines my daughter was collecting. Let me know if you need anything else."

The men went to work, and so did Ellen. Hours later, she put her hands on her lower back and stretched as she looked at the growing stack of boxes. She'd gone through the house this morning and collected every figurine she could find. There weren't just dozens, but hundreds. As of now, unless Kristen wanted some, they were all slated for Goodwill. "Julie, you were such a clutter queen," Ellen muttered as she placed a wrapped wizard carrying a lightning bolt into a waiting box.

Out in the hallway, the painters talked as they worked, swapping stories and laughing often. It was nice to hear voices during the day, and it made her realize how lonely she'd found her time here to be. When lunchtime came, she offered to fix the men sandwiches. When they discovered she was an architect, the three of them spent an hour sharing tales of the homes they'd worked on and the mistakes they'd seen homeowners make. Afterward, still chuckling, they all went back to work.

A few hours later, Ellen eyed the boxes along the wall, pleased to note that the pile was growing by the hour. The smell of fresh paint lingered in the house, and for the first time since she'd arrived, Ellen felt as if she was making some progress. The only blip on her success meter was Kristen.

Ellen's gaze narrowed as she absently wrapped a nearly naked fairy in the sports section of the latest edition of the *Dove Pond Register.* In that ridiculous dream, Julie had been convinced that although Kristen would never run away, she wasn't going to Raleigh quietly. *Maybe I had that dream because my instincts were trying to tell me something. That I should be wary of the way Kristen has —*

A shout from the hallway made Ellen turn.

"What are you doing?" Kristen's voice came from the entryway. "Stop it! Stop it right now! That's my mother's painting, you —"

"Kristen?" Ellen set the fairy onto a table and hurried to the front hallway. She arrived just in time to see her granddaughter grab Nick's paintbrush. "What are you doing?"

Kristen spun on Ellen. "*You* did this!"

Shocked at such naked anger, Ellen took a step back. "I hired painters, just as I said I would. We talked about this. Many times, in fact. We have to freshen up the house before we put it on the —"

"Get out!" Kristen spun back to Nick. "You too! You had no right to touch that mural! My *mother* painted it!"

Nick held up his hands. "Sorry! We were just doing what we were paid to do."

Eric had come around the corner. His eyes widened on seeing the threatening way Kristen was holding the paintbrush. "Hey! Easy there."

"This is *my* house. Both of you need to leave. And if you don't, I'll . . . I'll . . . I'll call the sheriff!"

"Whoa!" Eric said. "Take it easy! We haven't done anything wrong. Ms. Foster invited us here."

"Kristen." Ellen stepped forward, embarrassed for herself and her granddaughter. "Stop this instant. These gentlemen are here on my —"

"And you!" Kristen spun back to Ellen, the paintbrush pointed straight at her. "You didn't have my permission to do this! You know you didn't."

"I'm the executor of the will and your guardian. I have every right to see to it that things are handled properly. I tried to talk to you about this, but you kept putting me off. Over and over and over."

Kristen, her face a deep red, held the

paintbrush tighter, her fingers white on the handle.

Ellen had seen Kristen upset before, but never like this. "I'm sorry about the mural, but there are dozens of other paintings in this house. We'll pick out your favorites and take them with us to Raleigh. This one painting isn't going to matter —"

"It matters to me!" The teenager's warm hazel eyes shimmered with tears.

"We'd better go." Eric nodded to Nick, who immediately began to gather his things. "Ms. Foster, just let us know when you're ready for us to come back."

*"Never,"* Kristen snapped.

Ellen ignored her and said firmly, "Thank you. I'll call you later today."

Nick put the lid on his paint can and then picked up the drop cloth he'd already rolled up. He held out his hand for his paintbrush, eyeing Kristen cautiously.

There was a tense moment when Ellen wondered if Kristen might throw it, but after a threatening moment, she handed it to him with a scowl.

"Thanks," Nick said. He and his brother quickly mumbled, "See you later," and then the door closed behind them.

Kristen spun on Ellen. "How could you?"

"I don't have a choice. April will be here

before you know it, and there are things that must be done. I told you repeatedly that we needed to start on the updates. If you don't like the color choices, there's still time to change them. I'll call —"

"I don't care about the color! I care about the mural! Mom —" Kristen's face crumpled, tears filling her eyes, her hands shaking as she tried to shove her hair from her face.

Deeply alarmed, Ellen put her hand on Kristen's arm, flinching when the girl yanked herself free and took a step back.

"I *hate* you!" Kristen pushed past Ellen and went to let the dogs inside. They crowded around her. She sunk to the floor beside them, put her arms around the largest dog, buried her face in his neck, and wept. The other animals, sensing Kristen's mood, quietly lay down nearby, watching her with dark, worried eyes.

The sound of Kristen's sobs tore at Ellen's heart. She didn't know what to say or do, so she stayed where she was, struggling to find words that could help them both. "Kristen . . . I'm sorry. I didn't realize you'd be this upset."

She waited, but Kristen didn't speak, just stayed where she was, her face against the dog's neck.

Ellen sighed. "I'm trying to get you top dollar for this creaky, leaky old house, and that mural of Wonder Woman is in the worst place. It's the first thing people will see when they come in, so I —"

"Stop!" Kristen lifted her head and looked at Ellen with a tear-streaked face. "That's not a picture of Wonder Woman. It's a picture of me."

"That's . . . that's you?" Ellen's stomach sunk.

"Mom used to call me Wonder Kristen." Kristen let go of the dog and wiped her eyes with her sleeve, looking achingly young and uncertain.

Ellen handed Kristen the box of tissues that sat on the buffet.

Kristen pulled out a handful and blew her nose. "When I started middle school, I didn't have friends the way I do now, and" — she shrugged — "I don't know why, but things were just hard. Then the movie came out, and Mom and I went and . . ." Kristen's voice quavered. "She painted that picture for me. She said that when I grew up, I could be just like Wonder Woman and fight the world's evil. Every morning, before I'd go to school, I'd see that mural, and it reminded me that maybe, if I tried really, really hard, I'd grow up to be something special."

*Oh dear.* Ellen's gaze moved from Kristen to the mural that was barely visible now through a thin coat of primer. *That face is Kristen's. I can see the resemblance now. How did I miss that?* "I'm so sorry. I didn't know. Why didn't you tell me about this before?"

"I *told* you I loved that mural."

Had she? Ellen had a sudden, crystal-clear memory of Julie saying, *"You aren't very good at listening to other people."*

Ellen's stomach clenched, her chest tight with guilt. Julie was right. Ellen hadn't listened. And if she was being completely honest, she knew why — it was easier and more efficient to do what needed to be done without slowing down to convince someone to agree with her. It was a shortcut that worked wonders on a job site, but in real life it sometimes meant other people and their opinions got shoved aside. *Oh God, when did I get to be so selfish?*

She'd done this to Kristen. Tears dampened Ellen's eyes. "I should have spoken with you, but . . . look, I'll . . . I'll have someone come and fix it. Maybe we can clean it off now, before the primer dries." She went to the hallway. "I had some rags around here I used to wipe mud from the dog's feet, and I — Here they are!" She scooped up a rag from a bucket under the bench. "See?" She hurried to the mural and scrubbed at the primer. The paint was dry in places and sticky in others. She pressed harder, hoping against all reason that she could clean it up.

"Stop it!" Kristen said from where she now stood in the doorway. "You're just making it worse."

Ellen looked at the mural. Where she'd wiped away the partially dry primer, she had also lifted some of the paint beneath it, smearing the white until it was streaked pink and blue and green.

"You can't fix this. Only Mom could, and she's gone."

Ellen's throat tightened. "Surely there's some way —"

"You ruined it." Kristen's voice was quiet and tired. "Just the way you've ruined everything."

"No, no. We just need —"

"Don't." Kristen walked past Ellen toward front door, grabbing her book bag from the bench.

Ellen followed, feeling as small as an ant. "Don't go! I never meant —"

"No." Kristen pulled her keys from her pocket as she walked out the door.

Ellen followed her onto the porch. "Where are you going?"

"Away." Kristen headed down the steps toward her car, every step stiff and hard.

Ellen followed, her heart aching. This exact same scene had played out twenty-odd years ago, but with a different teenager. Ellen's feet felt heavy as she went, her gaze locked on Kristen. *I can't let her run away. I'll never find her.* "Please! We'll —"

The car door slammed, and the Camry's engine roared to life. With an abrupt crunch, Kristen threw the car into reverse and sped out of the driveway, the wheels screeching on the asphalt as if she were fighting for a place at a NASCAR race.

And then she was gone, taillights disappearing from sight as Ellen was left standing at the end of the sidewalk, alone.

It wasn't until moments later that she realized her eyes were leaking the same hot, useless tears she'd wept all those years ago when Julie had run away. *Oh God, what have I done?*

# CHAPTER 12
## KRISTEN

"What are you going to do?" Missy asked over her cup of hot chocolate.

Kristen sunk lower in her seat. "I have no idea." They sat in a big booth at the Moonlight Café, hot chocolates already on the table, a plate of chicken nachos on the way. It was just after four, so they were the only people in the entire place, which made the café, with its red-checked tablecloths and country kitsch wall decor, seem cozy. Or it would have if Kristen hadn't still been stinging from her argument with her grandmother. "I can't believe she did that."

"Me neither." Missy sent her a sympathetic look.

Kristen aimlessly turned her mug in a circle. After storming out of her house, she'd called Ava and asked if she could have the rest of the day off, saying she needed some extra time to study. Kristen had felt bad lying, but she hadn't had the energy to explain herself. Ava hadn't seemed to mind, though, which was good. "I'm glad you could come out for an early dinner."

"I told my parents you needed to talk." Missy scowled. "Your grandmother is a witch. Your mom spent weeks on that mural."

Kristen remembered Mom sitting cross-legged on the floor, putting the finishing touches on Wonder Kristen's boots, laughing about having to make them larger so they'd be true to life and match Kristen's larger-than-usual feet. *I miss her laugh.*

A wave of sadness hit Kristen. She picked up her hot chocolate. Leaning her elbows on the table, she held her mug in front of her as if waiting for it to cool, hoping Missy hadn't noticed how her lips trembled.

One glance at Missy told Kristen she'd wasted her time.

Missy's gaze had darkened, her mouth pressed in a straight line. "I could smack that woman! More than once, too."

Kristen took a slow sip, the warmth softening the tightness of her emotions enough for her to speak again. "I've never been so mad. I completely forgot I was playing it low-key to keep her out of my business."

"Does she suspect we're trying to find your dad?"

"Not yet. I hope we find him soon, though. I need —"

"Hi!" Josh slid into the seat beside Missy. He eyed their hot chocolates with envy. "Sorry I'm late. I had to wait for Dad to get home, and then he told me I had to empty the recycling. That took forever. I'm just glad it's his early day off so I didn't have to babysit."

"We ordered nachos," Kristen told him.

He brightened but then dropped his gaze. "That's okay. I ate at home. I'll just get a hot chocolate."

She knew Josh's parents were struggling financially. For the first time since she'd had her argument with her grandmother, a tiny bit of Kristen's anger faded. She'd lost Mom and things were upside down at home, but she wasn't the only one struggling. Mom used to say, *"It is well to give when asked but it is better to give unasked, through understanding."* Kristen was pretty sure Mom had read that in a book somewhere, but she liked it anyway.

She told Josh, "We ordered an extra-large, so there's plenty for you."

"With extra jalapeños," Missy added. "You might as well eat some. Kristen and I can never finish an extra-large."

Josh looked happier already. "If you guys

aren't going to eat all of it, I guess I could help. Did you ask for extra sour cream?"

He looked so hopeful that Kristen had to smile. "Of course we did."

Josh rubbed his hands together. "I love nachos. If I could eat just one thing for the rest of my life, it would be —"

"Enough about the nachos!" Missy said impatiently. "Kristen has A Situation."

"Oh?" He looked at Kristen. "What did she do now?"

Kristen opened her mouth to answer, but Missy was quicker. "She snuck painters into the house while Kristen was in school and had them ruin Kristen's mural."

Josh looked so horrified that Kristen's heart eased yet more.

It was funny, but his genuine outrage stilled some of hers. "She didn't sneak painters in. She just hired them. And to be fair, she didn't realize Mom had made me Wonder Woman. I doubt Grandma Ellen ever really looked at that mural. It's not her style."

Missy set her hot chocolate down with an indignant thunk. "How could she not recognize you?"

"I don't know, but she was surprised. Really surprised."

Josh rubbed his chin. "Maybe you should

have told her."

"I'd already told her how much I loved the mural. I thought that was enough."

"It should have been," Missy said stoutly. "She had no right. That's *your* house."

It didn't feel like Kristen's house. It hadn't felt like hers since the day Mom died. "I don't know what I'm going to do. I'm too mad to go home right now."

"Stay at my house tonight," Missy offered. "My mom asks about you all the time, so I know she'd love to see you."

"I didn't bring any clothes."

"You can wear those jeans again, and I'll give you one of my sweatshirts. We're about the same size."

Josh turned a skeptical look at Missy, his gaze measuring her plump figure and then Kristen's rail-thin one, but he wisely didn't say anything.

The nachos came, and Missy kept them laughing as she talked about an argument she'd had with her science teacher about an assignment she'd sworn she'd turned in but really hadn't. When Missy set her mind to it, she could be very persuasive, and she'd finally managed to convince Mr. Vickers that maybe — just maybe — he had lost it and needed to give her an opportunity to do the assignment over.

"So now you have homework," Josh pointed out.

"That's better than a zero." Missy pushed the half-finished plate of nachos toward Josh. "Finish those up. I don't know about Kristen, but I can't eat another bite."

Kristen had barely eaten anything, but she shook her head when Josh looked her way. "I'm stuffed."

Josh pulled the plate in front of him and loaded a chip with chili and jalapeños. "I guess we need to start the daddy search pronto."

Missy cut him a hard look. "Kristen has had a rough day already."

Kristen agreed. She felt as wrung out as a dishrag.

Josh piled a final jalapeño on his chip. "If her grandma's already having the house painted, then Kristen's almost out of time. My mom said that once that house hits the market, it'll get snapped up. It's on a great street."

Missy almost choked on her hot chocolate. "Even if it does sell fast, there are still papers to sign and bank stuff to do, right? That takes months, doesn't it?"

"I have no idea," Kristen said. It didn't matter, either. A few days ago, Grandma had casually mentioned that once the house was ready for listing, there would be no reason to stay in Dove Pond. She'd just hand the keys over to a real estate agent, and that would be that.

Kristen looked at her empty mug, the restaurant quiet except for the crunch of chips as Josh cleaned the plate. *I've got to figure this out. What would Wonder Kristen do?*

And just like that, she knew. "Josh is right."

Missy blinked. "About what?"

"The dad search. We don't have time to mess around, so we have to ramp this thing up. In fact, we should start right now." Kristen shoved her mug away, stood, and collected her stuff.

"Where are you going?" Missy asked.

"To the hardware store," Kristen said. "I was going to do this Monday after work, but we can't wait."

Missy scooted out of the booth and pulled on her coat and scarf. "Hurry up, Josh."

Josh crammed a nacho into his mouth and then said around it, "Want to walk? It's just a few blocks away."

"I'd rather drive," Kristen said. "In case we want to leave fast."

"Always have an escape plan," Missy said with approval.

Josh ate the final nacho, then wiped his hands on his napkin. "Let's go!"

Ten minutes later, they were standing in the parking lot, leaning against Kristen's Camry as they stared at the hardware store.

Kristen rammed her hands into her coat pockets, her fingers closing around her kazoo. Through the wide plate-glass window, she could see Nate Stevens stacking large bags of dog food into a big display near the front of the store. He looked calm, comfortable even. *Just wait until I talk to him. There's no better way to ruin a perfectly good day than to be confronted by a kid you didn't know you had. If, that is, I am his kid.*

Her stomach suddenly ached, and she turned to Missy and Josh. "How do I start this? 'Hi, guess what? I'm your daughter. Maybe.' " Her breath puffed out as she spoke, punctuating each word.

Josh squinted from her to Mr. Stevens and then back. "That could work," he said cautiously.

"I wouldn't hint," Missy said breezily, as if she'd done this before. She whipped a huge pair of sunglasses out of her purse and slid them on. "Just come right out and ask him if he dated your mother during the crucial months. No sense in making things complicated."

270

"I can't just march in there and ask him that." Kristen pulled her scarf a little closer. "He'd know what I was getting at the second I asked."

"So? He's going to figure it out eventually. I wouldn't waste time with small talk."

"Not even 'hello'?"

Missy considered this. "I guess you have to say hello," she conceded. "That's only polite. But I'd dive in right after that."

"So, 'Hello. Did you screw my mother in 2004, and did you use protection?'"

"Something like that."

God, this was going to be so hard.

Josh sent Kristen a sympathetic look. "It wouldn't hurt to start out with a little small talk and then ease into it."

Kristen hunched her shoulders against the wind. "Right. After hello, I should say something normal, and then jump into the harder stuff." She pursed her lips. "I could ask him what he thinks of this cold snap. Old people talk about the weather a lot."

"That's a safe topic." Josh nodded wisely. "Very safe."

"Good Lord, you two." Missy slid her sunglasses to the top of her head, her voice dripping with irritation. "If you want to drag it out, then by all means, mention the weather and maybe chat him up about the coming election. Heck, you can even tell him how much you love a good hot chocolate too."

"That's too much," Josh said. "I think Kristen should start with the weather and then move into a more direct line of questioning. I wouldn't bring up the election or —"

"I was *joking*, Josh!" Missy looked as if she wanted to kick him in the shins.

"Oh. Sorry."

Missy turned back to Kristen. "Say hi. Mention the weather, if you must. Then ask him the important question."

"Just throw it out there?"

"Throw it like a grenade." Missy dropped her sunglasses back into place. "See where it lands."

"Missy, come on," Josh said. "This isn't going to be easy on either Kristen or Mr. Stevens. If she marches in there like a demanding brat, even if Mr. Stevens suspects he *is* her dad, he might deny it just to get rid of her. That would be —"

"Shut up, Josh!" Missy snapped. "This is hard enough without you going straight to the worst-case scenario!"

But it was too late. Kristen was already imagining Mr. Stevens, red-faced and furious, yelling at her to leave and never come back. She'd met him a bunch of times, and he'd always been super nice, but this was a totally different situation. *Oh God, what if Mr. Stevens just denies it? What if he is my dad and he lies to get me to leave him alone?* To her surprise, the thought sparked a flood of anger so sudden and hot that raw energy pumped through her. For the first time in her life, she *needed* her dad, and not for a stupid father-daughter dance, either. This was life, it was serious and important, and if this man was her father, then she refused to be denied.

Her anger must have showed, because both Josh and Missy pulled back a little, their eyes wide. Their shocked reaction made Kristen's anger fizzle out as quickly as it had arrived, leaving her deflated like a popped balloon.

"Are you okay?" Missy asked.

"I'm fine," Kristen mumbled. "I don't know if I can do this."

"You can. I know you can." Missy took Kristen by the arms and gave her a little shake. "Do you want to stay in Dove Pond?"

"Yes."

"Then get in there and start chatting that man up." Missy gave Kristen a final shake for good measure, then released her. "Go on. Get it over with. You'll never know until you talk to him."

Kristen fought the urge to get back in her car and drive home as fast as she could. But Missy was right. If Kristen wanted to keep her home and stay in Dove Pond, she had to do this.

Taking a deep breath, she ducked her head and walked toward the door.

She was two steps away when she slowed to a stop. *Oh my God, I have to ask this guy if he slept with my mother. I can't do that. I just can't.*

She turned on her heel and returned to Missy and Josh. "I can't." Kristen crossed her arms, hunching into her coat. "This is so hard."

"You're thinking about it too much," Missy said.

"Maybe," Kristen admitted. "All I know is that I can't march up to a guy and ask, 'In 2004, did you sleep with my mother and forget to use a condom?' It would embarrass us both."

"She has a point," Josh said.

Kristen added, "I wouldn't blame him if he was insulted by the whole thing. I'd be mad if someone asked me something like that, especially out in public."

Missy sighed. "Fine. So what do we do?"

Kristen tucked a strand of hair behind her

ear, feeling more uncertain by the moment. "I don't know how to move a conversation with a man I barely know from 'Hello' to 'Did you sleep with my mom?' to 'Let me live with you.' That's a lot."

"It's complicated, I'll give you that. And you're not super quick in social situations, either." Missy thought about it a moment. "What you need is a script. Then you'd know exactly what to say."

"That could help," Kristen said.

"Let's make one up. Josh, take notes."

He looked down at his empty hands. "With what?"

"Your phone! I — Oh. Right. Your phone sucks."

"I don't need notes," Kristen said impatiently. "It's not like I can stand there and read from a piece of paper, anyway. That would be stupid."

"We'll keep it simple, then," Missy said. "Number one, say hello."

"Okay."

"Number two, do your weather thing, which is lame, but it is what it is."

Kristen nodded.

"And then, number three, slide in a question about him going to Dove Pond High School and what it must have been like back then."

"That's good," Josh said approvingly. "Old people love to talk about the past."

"Okay. This sounds good so far." Kristen looked at Missy. "And after that?"

"Last, ask if he knew your mother back then. And by 'know,' you mean in the biblical sense."

Kristen's face grew hot. "Missy! I can't say that!"

"You don't have to. Just wink when you say 'know.' He'll get it."

Josh winced. "That's sort of rude, Missy."

"Fine. Do you have a better idea?"

"Yeah, I do. What Kristen needs is a cover."

Missy frowned. "A what?"

"A cover. Like a spy. Total double-o-seven stuff." When Missy's frown didn't change, he impatiently turned to Kristen. "Think about how spies get information. They go in undercover, on the down low, and pretend they're a wealthy businessman in town or a foreign power looking to buy a nuke or something like that. Once everyone believes the spy's cover, that he's there for those reasons, then he can start collecting information."

Kristen didn't think she'd ever heard a stupider idea. "I can't pretend I'm from out of town. Mr. Stevens knows me. Heck, everyone knows me. I've lived here since I was six and —"

"No! You don't understand. I meant you —" Josh took a deep breath. "You don't have to pretend to be anyone else. You need a *local* cover, something that will give you a *reason* to talk to Mr. Stevens about his past. Something legit. Something that won't set off any alarms. *That's* a cover."

"Ohhhh," Missy said. "A cover."

"Fine," Kristen said. "I need a cover. What reason could I possibly have for asking Mr. Stevens questions about his youth?" Inside the store, Mr. Stevens had started putting new dog treats into a nearby rack. Kristen watched him, trying to picture him with her mother. She could see what her mom must have found so attractive. He was tall and auburn-haired and had one of those half smiles that made you smile back whether you meant to or not. He was swole, too. *Good genetics. That would be a plus.* Kristen knew very little else about him, though. The entire extent of their relationship so far had consisted of "Can I help you find anything?" and "Do you want the receipt in the bag?"

Josh suddenly gave a quick hop. "I've got it! We'll tell him we're from the yearbook."

Kristen and Missy stared at him, waiting, but he just grinned as if he'd solved all their problems.

Missy sighed. "And?" she prompted.

"We'll tell Mr. Stevens we're working for the yearbook and we want to feature him in a new alumni section. We can ask him all sorts of personal questions then. We can ask where he's lived, what sports he played, who he dated and when — all of it!"

"That's true," Missy said slowly. "Josh, that's brilliant. We can use this same cover on all three suspects, too."

"Exactly. Plus, we can do it together instead of Kristen having to go in there alone."

*Thank you, thank you, thank you.* "I love this."

"It could be fun." Missy rubbed her hands together, warming to the idea. "Josh, you can pretend to take pictures with your phone. Mr. Stevens won't know it doesn't work. I'll take a notebook and act like I'm keeping notes. That leaves Kristen to do the 'interview.'"

Kristen wished Missy would do the talking, but since Kristen was the one looking for her father, she supposed it was only fair she had the hardest job.

Missy went to the car and pulled her notebook and pen from her backpack. She slid the pen behind her ear, tucked the notebook under her arm, and bumped the door closed with her hip. "There. Let's go!"

Together, they went into the hardware store. Missy called out to Mr. Stevens the second they walked inside.

A half hour later, the door whooshed closed behind them, and they walked to Kristen's car, moving faster the closer they got. When they reached it, Missy whirled around to face Kristen and Josh, her face alight with excitement. "Oh my God, that was *intense.*"

Kristen shuddered. "I'm so glad we figured out a cover first."

Josh glanced back at Mr. Stevens, who was fixing a sign over a display of rock salt. "I don't think he suspected anything."

"No, but sadly, it was a complete waste of time." Missy cast a sympathetic look at Kristen. "He's not your dad. He never saw your mom after high school."

"Nope." Kristen was sure that later on, when she could breathe, she would be sorry she hadn't found her father in this first round. But right now, she felt nothing but pure, unalloyed relief. The entire time Mr. Stevens regaled them with stories about his time at Dove Pond High School, she'd heard her mother's voice in the background, warning Kristen about the complications bringing her father into her life could cause them both.

A car pulled into the parking lot behind them.

"Uh-oh," Missy muttered.

Kristen turned to see the Dove Pond police car sitting a few spaces down, Sheriff McIntyre doing something on the computer bolted to his center console.

"Don't look!" Missy hissed. "He'll think it's suspicious."

Josh, who'd been looking at the police car, too, sent Missy a startled look. "Suspicious how? We're just standing here."

"When have we ever hung out at the hardware store?"

"Never, I guess. Still, I don't see why he'd care."

"He wouldn't, but we don't want him to think we're acting weird. He's candidate three, remember? We don't want him to know we're — Oh! He's getting out!"

Kristen fished her keys from her coat pocket. She'd just pointed the fob at her car, ready to punch the unlock button, when a shadow fell across them.

"Nice day for a trip to the hardware store, isn't it?"

Kristen and Missy exchanged wide-eyed looks before they plastered identical smiles on their faces and turned toward the sheriff.

"Hi, Sheriff McIntyre," Missy said brightly. "Chasing any criminals today?"

Josh gave an uneasy laugh, which made the sheriff turn his cool green gaze in his direction.

Kristen hoped against hope that they were acting normal, at least a little.

"What's so funny there, Perez?" the sheriff asked.

Josh flushed. "Nothing. I mean . . . everyone knows there aren't any criminals here in Dove Pond. Not real ones."

"You might be surprised." The sheriff's gaze narrowed. "You kids seem nervous. Everything okay?"

Missy slid her sunglasses back in place. "Technically, we're not kids, or I'm not. I'll be eighteen in a few months." Missy loved that she was older than the rest of them, which was funny because it was only because she'd failed third grade years ago and had to go twice.

The sheriff nodded thoughtfully. "Which means that under the right circumstances, you could be jailed for murder. No more juvie for you." He eyed first Josh and then Kristen. "What are you all doing here?"

"Nothing," Missy and Kristen said at the same time, each of them sending a frantic glare at the other.

Josh shifted from one foot to the other. "I guess we might as well tell the sheriff the truth."

*What?* Kristen and Missy turned startled looks his way.

"We were just interviewing Mr. Stevens for an alumni section in the yearbook."

*Oh, thank God.* Kristen let out a relieved sigh.

The sheriff flicked her a hard glance before he said to Josh, "The yearbook, hmm?"

"Yes!" Missy dove in. "We're only focusing on successful graduates, of course, like Mr. Stevens, you, and a few other people. It's nothing huge, just a cute little addition."

The sheriff didn't appear impressed. "I'm sure you can find far more successful people than me."

"You have a really interesting job," Josh said. "We'd interview you right now, but we just finished our interview with Mr. Stevens and, uh . . . we need to go through the notes and . . . and make sure we have good photos, too."

"Right." The sheriff's gaze moved over each of them, resting the longest on Kristen. "Whatever you all are doing, be careful. You don't want to get in trouble. I'd hate to have to call someone's parents." He gave them a cool nod and went on inside the hardware store.

Her heart thudding wildly, Kristen unlocked the car, and they all climbed in, sighing in relief when the doors closed.

"Oh my God!" Kristen covered her cheeks with her hands. "He was so suspicious!"

Although flushed, Missy pretended she hadn't been in the least worried. "He probably thinks we're up to a prank of some sort. He'd never suspect our real reason."

Kristen guessed that was true. Suddenly, she wanted nothing more than to be home, in her own room, surrounded by her own things and her dogs. She started the car. "Come on. I'll drop you guys off at your cars."

Missy looked disappointed. "I thought you were spending the night with me."

"If we're going to start the dad search now, I've got to do what I can to keep Grandma Ellen from suspecting anything." *I guess I'm back to being Wonder Kristen, at least for now.*

"If you go home right now and act like nothing is wrong, she'll know something's up for sure. You were pretty mad when you last saw her."

"Don't worry, I'll let her know I'm still

mad. She'll expect that, but she'll also be glad I'm home."

"That's a good strategy." Josh leaned forward between the seats. "We should meet up tomorrow and work on our cover. Pulling that over on Mr. Stevens was one thing. Doing it to Sheriff McIntyre is going to be a lot harder. That man was born suspicious."

Kristen couldn't agree more. "He'll ask us more questions than we ask him. I work at the tearoom until six. We can meet after that, if you all want to. I'll just tell Grandma I'm working late."

"We could use the practice," Missy said brightly. "We should come up with a standard list of questions, too."

Kristen murmured in agreement and then dropped off Missy and Josh at their cars, the two of them chatting excitedly, planning and plotting as if they really were in a spy movie.

But Kristen knew this wasn't a movie. It was real.

And if she continued on this path, she might one day soon meet her dad.

Her friends might be excited, but she felt nothing but a growing sense of dread. And with that dread came anger, not just at Grandma Ellen, who had pushed her in this direction, but at Mom, too. Right now, every adult in Kristen's life seemed determined to ruin it. Her hands tightened on the steering wheel. She wouldn't let that happen. Wonder Kristen was brave, and she would find a way to stay in Dove Pond with her friends, even if it meant she had to do something wild, something daring. *That's what superheroes do — the unexpected and the impossible.*

And right now, Kristen had no choice but to do both.

"It's looking better. What did you do to it?"

Ava looked up from where she was kneeling beside the peppermint plant she'd brought home from the greenhouse and smiled at Sarah. "I repotted it to give the roots more room. To be honest, I think the sun has helped it more than anything."

"It's getting healthier by the day." Sarah tied her scarf around her neck, the brilliant stripes no more colorful than her flowered leggings and bright red tunic top. "This room always did get the most sun. That's why Momma loved it so much."

The breakfast room was one of Ava's favorite rooms, too, and for that very reason. It was located in the bottom floor of the turret just off the entryway. That was the beauty of a large, rambling Queen Anne–style home — they had more windows than walls. This particular room was octagonal in shape, with heavy wood trim, five large windows, a set of ornate pocket doors, and a fireplace with a black iron grate set against peacock-blue and green tiles.

Momma had loved every corner, nook, and cranny of this old house, although with seven daughters, she'd had neither the time nor the money to keep it up. As big as it was — nine bedrooms and three and a half bathrooms — the house had never felt too large to Ava, even after all her sisters except Sarah had moved away, one at a time, on their way to either college or new jobs. She and Sarah still hoped their sisters would eventually move back home, although so far, none of them had.

Ava slid the peppermint plant back in line with the other plants and set the watering can to one side. "I can't believe you're already dressed. You never get up this early." Outside, the morning sun was just now gleaming bright enough to light the house.

"Do you know what today is?" Sarah asked, giving an excited little hop.

"It's Monday. No, wait, it's Valentine's Day, isn't it?"

"Yes, it's Monday, and yes it's Valentine's Day, but those don't matter. Today is the day I get to order new books." Sarah's smile could get no wider. "If I spend wisely, I can get three dozen!"

"I'm surprised you're not already at work."

"I know, right?" Sarah tilted her head to one side, her smile fading as her gaze moved over Ava's face. "You look so tired. Did you sleep at all?"

No. She hadn't. Last night, every time she'd closed her eyes, the stupid box had thumped up a storm. It had gone on for hours, too. Even now, she could hear it upstairs, thumping an angry beat that matched the headache already forming behind her eyes. *Bam. Bam. Bam.* It was remorseless.

When the secret had first started its banging and thumping, she'd been terrified that Sarah, who slept just down the hallway, would hear it. But she never had. Apparently only Ava could hear the box's demanding fury. *Thank God.* She pressed her fingers to her temple, which throbbed in sync with the box.

"Another headache?" Sarah asked.

Ava nodded. "I just need some hot tea." Gallons of it, to judge by the heaviness of her eyes. She walked past Sarah and headed to the kitchen, where she'd spent most of her money over the years. She'd gone a little crazy with granite countertops, Viking appliances, and other ridiculously expensive gadgets, but she and Sarah loved it, so it was worthwhile.

She filled a kettle with water and put it on the stove. Then she opened a nearby cabinet and pulled out a canister of rooibos and ginger tea, one of her newer blends.

Sarah walked to the counter, watching her with a concerned look.

Ava waved her away. "Go order your books. I'm fine."

Sarah propped her elbows on the counter. "You always have trouble sleeping. It's been going on forever."

"It's just how I am. The best thing I can do is just keep on keeping on."

"But these headaches. Ava, I'm worried. Have you seen Doc Bolton?"

Ava almost smiled to think of Doc's expression if she told him she was being kept awake by a box under her bed holding a secret she'd locked away. "I don't need to talk to the doc."

Sarah sighed. "I wish you would."

"And I wish you'd stop worrying about me and go buy your books. I'm heading to work in a few minutes myself, where I plan on staying so busy that I completely forget about my nagging headache."

The kettle whistled, and Ava made her tea, stirring in a little honey as a boost. As soon as she got the tearoom up and running, she'd focus on the secret. *Again.* Over the years, she'd tried just about everything to make it stop, but nothing had worked. But there had to be something she could do.

"Can't you make a tea to help you sleep?"

"Sarah!" Ava laughed. "Will you go to work already? Those books won't buy themselves."

"I just hate that you're hurting." Sarah drummed her fingers on the granite counter. "I wish I knew a — Oh! Maybe Aunt Mildred's recipe book could help."

Ava paused, her teacup halfway to her mouth. It had been years since Sarah had mentioned that book. Ava blew on her tea, the earthy scent rising to greet her. "I hadn't thought about that book in forever. But I'll check."

Upstairs, the box settled into an even louder, even more demanding beat than usual. Ava's headache quickened to match it. *Stupid box. Stop that!*

Sarah nodded absently, tapping her fingers on the counter as she thought. "I'll walk through the science section of the library today and see if any of the medical books have an answer."

Ava put her tea down. "Sarah, stop worrying. There's no need to —" Her gaze locked on her tea. Small circles appeared on the dark tea, spiraling out in perfect harmony with the thumping upstairs.

*No.*

Slowly, Ava's gaze moved from her cup to Sarah's fingers, where they drummed in a steady row, perfectly matching the rhythm of the box.

Ava's heart dropped. *Oh my God. She can hear it.*

Sarah frowned, her fingers stilling. "What's wrong?"

"You . . . you can hear that?"

"Hear what?" She looked confused.

"There's a —" Ava couldn't breathe. Should she tell her? Would that make it worse? Better? *No! Don't say anything. I can figure this out and make it go away. I just need more time.* Ava forced a shrug. "I just thought I heard something. Must have been a bird." She turned around and pulled an insulated cup from a cupboard and poured her tea inside. "I'd better get to work. You coming?"

"Sure." Sarah went to collect her things. "Want to ride together?"

"I wish we could, but I have to go to the greenhouses this afternoon. And I — You know, I left my key to the tearoom upstairs.

291

Why don't you head on out? I'll see you at lunch."

"Okay. See you then." With a wave and a final, concerned look, Sarah left.

Ava waited until she heard Sarah's truck pull out of the driveway before she went up the stairs to her room. She only made it three steps down the hallway before she saw it.

There, right outside the doorway of her bedroom, sitting on the floor for the world to see, was the box.

Her stomach grew ill. In all the years she'd fought to keep the box secret, it had never before made it out of her bedroom. Not once. And yet there it sat, thumping so angrily she could feel it through the floor under her feet. Two long duct tape tendrils lay behind it, almost like a pair of tails. One corner, crushed from being slammed on the floor, now had the beginning of a frightening rip.

It was getting stronger. And Ava was getting weaker.

Fear threatened to overwhelm her, and she had to take deep, even breaths before she could move. Slowly, she went down the hall and picked up the box. It vibrated in her hands, the broken and fuzzy cardboard burning her fingers. Swallowing a curse, she carried the box into her room, dropped it beside her bed, and shoved it under with her foot. Then, feeling as if she were being chased, she left, closing the door firmly behind her.

By the time she got to work, her headache was blazing, her stomach slightly ill. Her hands trembled so badly, she had trouble unlocking the door.

Once inside, she sunk into a chair, her mind racing in circles. She had to do something. She had to. She'd hidden the secret for far too long. If she couldn't find a way to defuse it, she'd have to admit her mistake to everyone. Even Sarah.

Ava moaned and closed her eyes, pressing her cold fingers to her eyelids. Maybe that would be for the best. *She'll hate me. They'll* all *hate me.* And Ava wouldn't blame them.

She heard the back door open and close, and Dylan came in through the kitchen. Whistling a tune, he put his toolbox down and shrugged out of his coat. He headed for the coatrack but stopped on seeing her sitting alone. "Ava! I didn't know you were here."

"I came in early."

He frowned. "Are you okay?"

"Sinus headache. That's all." She stood and slid the chair back under the table.

He watched, his gaze dark with concern. "You get a lot of headaches."

"Sometimes. It's just this weather." She managed a smile.

"Can I do anything to help? Run to the Moonlight and get you some coffee?"

She shook her head.

He watched her a moment longer, then crossed the room, pulled out a chair, and sat down. He slid another chair so that it faced his and patted the seat. "Sit."

"I have too much to do —"

"Ava." He patted the chair again, his hazel gaze locked on her face. "Please."

Reluctantly, she sat back down.

He rested his elbows on his knees and leaned forward, watching her. "You're upset. To be honest, it seems you've been upset about something for the past few months."

*Years. It's been years.* She managed a shaky laugh. "You have no idea. I —" Tears threatened, and suddenly, it was all too much. The secret, the torn box, her hopes for her tearoom, her worries about Sarah and Kristen — all of it was more than Ava could handle. She pressed her palms over her eyes, trying to stop the tears.

"Ava, what's happened?"

"Nothing." Her voice quavered pitifully, and she hated it. A tear leaked out and ran down her cheek.

His warm hand came to rest on her knee. "Whatever it is, you're not facing it alone. I'm right here."

That was more than she could ask for. She dropped her hands from her eyes. "Thank you." She pulled a napkin from the holder on the table and wiped away her tears. "Have you ever done something you regretted so much that you'd give anything — *anything* — to take it back?"

He looked surprised, his gaze searching, but then he gave a rueful laugh. "Of course I have. I'm pretty sure we all have."

"Yeah, but this . . . I need to fix this one, and I — I can't. I've tried, but I don't know how."

"I don't suppose you can tell me a little more? Maybe then I might think of a way to help."

She shook her head. "No. I can't tell anyone." Her gaze dropped to where his hand clasped her knee. His calloused fingers bore traces of the wood stain he'd used on the shelves he was making for the tearoom. One of his thumbs was bruised, the nail black at the base, while a deep red scratch ran across his wrist. It was beautiful, this rough, scarred, calloused hand. And strong, too.

"You're too hard on yourself, Dove." He squeezed her knee and then released it. "I don't know what you did, or think you did, but I know you. I've worked alongside you for months now. I've seen you make your teas for almost everyone in this town. I know the plants whisper their secrets or whatever it is they do, but, Ava, a lot of it's you. You help so many people. And you do it every day, without hesitation. Whatever's happened, I know you didn't hurt anyone on purpose. You would never do that. And I think everyone in this town knows that."

His words, spoken so simply, so softly, washed over her broken heart like rain on a parched patch of earth. To her surprise, a sob broke from her lips as fresh tears leaked from her eyes. God, how she hoped he was right.

He pulled more napkins out of the holder and handed them to her, watching as she dried her eyes.

She sniffed. "I hate crying."

"Sweetheart, I don't think any of us like it."

She laughed and wadded up the damp napkins. "Probably not. Thank you for what you said. I wish things were that simple. But this thing . . ." She took a shuddering breath. "I made a horrible mistake. And I hurt someone. They just don't know it yet."

"You're sure you can't fix it?"

She shook her head. "I tried to find a way. I tried for years. But . . . I can't."

He nodded slowly. "Well. If that's the case, then I guess you don't fix it. You'll have to fess up, ask for forgiveness, and move on."

That wasn't the answer she wanted, but Ava supposed it was the best she'd get. "I know. I just hate letting people down."

"That's both a virtue and a burden."

"I guess so. I have to do it, though. I have to find the right words."

He reached over and put his hand over hers and gave it a squeeze. "You will."

She nodded, still miserable. It would be nice to stay here, sharing her burdens and weeping like a bucket with a hole in it, but she had things to do. *Keep busy. It doesn't help to just think about this. I know that.* She pulled her hand from under his and forced a smile. "Thanks for listening, but we'd better get back to work."

He looked as if he might say something more, but whatever he saw on her face made him rethink it. "Okay, then. I'm heading over to the Moonlight to pick up some breakfast. Can I bring you something?"

She hesitated.

"Come on, Dove." Dylan laughed as he

spoke. "It's Valentine's Day. At least let me get you an egg sandwich." He threw his hands up. "I know! It's probably the most romantic gift you've ever gotten, better than a diamond."

"They are excellent egg sandwiches," she said somberly, fighting a reluctant smile. "They're tastier than a diamond." Feeling a little better, she thanked Dylan and watched him leave. He really was a nice guy.

She went to the restroom and washed her face, wincing when she saw her reflection in the mirror. The rings under her eyes were starting to look permanent. "Great," she muttered, drying her face with a paper towel and then heading back into the main room. She went behind the bar, pulled out a box of her diffusion line teas, and started stacking them on one of the new shelves.

Dylan returned with their breakfast, and they spent the next half hour talking. She was glad he didn't mention her earlier meltdown, as she was far more comfortable talking about the new vents he'd just installed in the kitchen.

After breakfast, they set to work. Ava stayed as busy as she could, although she kept remembering how Sarah's fingers had tapped to the box's thumps. She didn't know what that meant, but it wasn't good.

None of it was good.

Lunchtime came, and Sarah stopped by with the always-elegant Zoe, bringing sandwiches and salads. Ava ate, but she had to fight to keep up with their conversation, lamenting the fact that it was Valentine's Day and neither had plans, as they were too picky to date anyone from town. They then started talking about the former mayor, Mr. Moore, who, after Grace won his seat in the town election, had gone on to become a successful fishing guide and had even started his own YouTube channel.

Sarah's phone chimed. "Oops! I promised Grace I'd bring her that Alice Hoffman book, *Magic Lessons,* but I left it at home." Sarah stood and put on her coat.

"What's it doing at your house?" Zoe asked.

Sarah scrunched up her nose, looking both sorry and not sorry. "I might have read it last night. That's why I'm sleepy today. That and I seem to have borrowed Ava's headache." She turned to Ava. "Your head still hurting?"

"It's better," Ava lied.

"Good. Do you need anything from the house?"

"No, I —" The image of the box lying in the middle of the hallway flared in front of

299

her. *Oh God. What if it's in the hallway when Sarah goes home?* But no, Ava had closed her bedroom door and —

"Ava?"

Both Sarah and Zoe were staring at her, looking worried. "Sorry. I just remembered a tea I need to make later this afternoon. I don't need anything from the house, thanks."

"Okay. I'll just run home and grab it, then. I've got to hurry, though. I need to be back at the library by one."

Ava followed Sarah to the door. "If you want, I can run and grab the book for you. I don't mind."

"No, no. You stay here and get this place finished. Besides, I know right where I left it. I brought it downstairs this morning, but I set it on the bookshelf by the door while I was putting on my coat."

*At least she won't be going upstairs.* That was a relief, and yet, Ava still worried. "Are you sure you don't want me to go —"

"Ava! No!" Sarah sent her a confused, half-amused look. "I'm old enough to go to the house by myself, thank you."

Ava threw her hands up. "Sorry! That's not what I meant."

"Yeah, well, I've got to go. See you all later." Zipping up her coat, Sarah hurried outside, the door closing behind her.

Zoe closed the lid on her salad. "That was weird."

"What was weird?" Ava couldn't keep the defensive note from her voice.

"You not wanting Sarah to go to your house by herself. What's going on? Is she hot on the trail of a hidden birthday present?"

"Something like that," Ava said. "I just —"

The door swung open.

Aunt Jo came inside, Moon Pie following. Today Aunt Jo wore a bright red suit with a pink-and-purple-flowered shirt, her gold-topped cane matching her earrings. As if in solidarity with Aunt Jo's brightness, the little bulldog wore a bedraggled yellow ribbon with hot-pink rosettes. "Good afternoon!"

Zoe bent to pat Moon Pie, who'd made a beeline for the young banker while Aunt Jo stood leaning on her cane, taking in the tearoom. "Moon Pie and I came to see how things are shaping up. Everyone is talking about how nice it looks." Aunt Jo made her way to the middle of the room. "They are right. You, Miss Ava, have a winner here."

"We're getting there." Ava pulled out a chair for Aunt Jo. "Come and sit."

Aunt Jo limped over and lowered herself

into the chair. "Just the right height. Some chairs are too tall, like the ones at the Moonlight. My feet don't even touch the floor." She stuck her legs out in front of her and crossed them at the ankle. Moon Pie, having enjoyed his pats, came to her side and dropped to the floor, stretching out so his stomach was on the smooth, cool wood.

"It'll be nice to have a place to get a cup of hot tea and a piece of pie. Nothing against the Moonlight — you know what a fan I am of their stroganoff — but it'll be nice to have somewhere a little less diner-ish." She hung her cane on the chair next to her. "Moon Pie, think we can convince Miss Ava to make us some of that hot chocolate we heard Kristen Foster bragging on?"

Ava was more than glad to have something to do. "I'll be happy to. I need to practice all the drinks on the menu, and I expect the hot chocolate will be highly requested in the winter. Kristen and I have been experimenting, and I think we've finally got the recipe just right." Ava ignored the throbbing at her temples and went to work. "What are you up to today, Aunt Jo? You look festive."

"Moon Pie needed some treats, so I had the sheriff bring me to town so I could shop. I'm to call him when I'm ready to go home."

"I like your suit," Zoe said.

"Thank you. You know me, I can't stand being the worst-dressed woman in any situation, even at Paw Printz."

Ava smiled. "Momma always said you'd be the best-dressed person at her funeral, and she was right."

"I still have that purple frock. I may whip it out for the Baptist Cake Walk as a distracting factor."

Zoe shot Aunt Jo a curious look. "Distracting? For a cake walk?"

"It shows my cleavage, and I guarantee it'll distract certain gentlemen who can't keep their eyes in their sockets to save their souls. It won't help me beat Myrtle Clinch, though. She is a mean one when it comes to sweets. She'd shiv her own aunt to get her hands on a chocolate cake."

Ava steamed some milk and added it to the hot chocolate, then put a healthy dash of whipped cream on top. "Sprinkles?"

"Extra, please."

"You got it." Ava brought the hot chocolate to Aunt Jo's table.

The door opened again, and Kat poked her head inside. When she saw the group at the table, she joined them. "I knew you'd all be here! Hi, Aunt Jo, Zoe." She gave Ava a cool nod. "Hi, Dove."

"Uh-oh," Zoe said, her gaze bright. "She called you Dove, Ava. You'd better be careful. Kat's never happy when she's calling you by your last name. That's a warning shot if I ever heard one."

Ava eyed her friend. "Are you mad at me?"

"You tell me." Kat crossed her arms. "I thought we were having breakfast this morning. I sat at the Moonlight for an hour, but you never showed."

"Tsk-tsk," Aunt Jo said. "Ava Dove, it's not like you to be so rude."

"She didn't answer her phone, either," Kat added, sinking into the empty seat beside Aunt Jo.

Ava looked around the room for her phone. "I guess I left it in my truck." *Along with my sanity. Sheesh. What a day.* "I'm so sorry. I completely forgot."

"Mmm-mmm." Aunt Jo took a noisy sip of her chocolate. "Lord, that's good! I almost had a 'gasm, right here in this chair."

Kat leaned closer to Aunt Jo. "Is that hot chocolate?" At Aunt Jo's nod, Kat said, "I want some."

"I'll make it," Ava said. "Consider it my apology in liquid form. Zoe, do you want some too?"

"No, thanks. I'll save it for a colder day."

Ava went to make Kat's hot chocolate.

Aunt Jo watched from over the top of her cup. "I don't want to scare no one, but I swear, things are going to hell in a hand-basket here in Dove Pond."

"What things?" Kat asked.

"I don't know yet, but Siegfried is back."

"I thought he'd run away," Zoe said. Siegfried was the town cat, a sleek black cat with green eyes who was — if Aunt Jo was to be believed — a prime mouser.

"I thought he had, too," Aunt Jo said. "Hadn't seen him in a month. But he's back and he's doing his thing again." Besides being the official town cat, Siegfried was also disturbingly good at predicting when something big was about to happen in Dove Pond.

"What's he doing?" Kat asked, taking the cup of hot chocolate Ava had just brought her.

"He sat in front of the library all day yesterday, tapping his paw on the ground."

"How odd!" Kat said.

"I saw him doing that," Zoe said. She pursed her lips and added thoughtfully, "I wonder what it means."

"Oddest cat ever." Aunt Jo pulled a napkin from a holder and delicately wiped her mouth. "He was tapping that paw like he was playing a drum."

*Tapping. Surely not . . .* Ava wet her dry lips. "Maybe he was trying to catch a bug."

"No. He had a beat going. Weirdest thing I ever saw. Sarah and I sat and watched him for a whole hour, and he never stopped." Aunt Jo took another sip of her hot chocolate. "That beat was sort of catchy, too. Before long, Sarah was tapping her toes right along with the cat. Looked as if she and Siegfried were in a band together. I don't think she even knew she was doing it."

Ava turned away and busied herself filling up the hot water urns, her hands faintly shaking. *It doesn't mean anything,* she told herself. *He's just a cat.* She should stop by the hardware store and get some more duct tape. *The box is tearing. Maybe if I —*

"So you all know what that means. Something is about to happen. There's a bite to the air today, too. A bitterness, like that of spoiled fruit about to drop." Aunt Jo looked out the front window, her gaze narrowing as if she were looking into the distance. "I don't know what it is, but it's there. I can taste it."

Ava's gaze followed Aunt Jo's. Sunlight poured into the tearoom, golden beams spilling across the café tables and chairs. Except for the pounding behind her temples, she didn't think she'd ever seen a more beautiful winter day. *Aunt Jo is just being dramatic.*

Kat shrugged. "Everything looks okay to me."

"Me too," Zoe said.

Aunt Jo's eyebrows rose. "You can't feel it? A sense of darkness, of doom? I woke up to it this morning." She looked down at Moon Pie, who whimpered in his sleep. "See? Even Moon Pie feels it."

Zoe sighed. "I can't feel a thing, but then I've never been very prescient. Wish I were, though. I'd have made a lot fewer mistakes and a lot more money."

Deeply unsettled, Ava picked up the canister of chocolate and had just slid it back on its shelf when a crack of thunder sounded.

Everyone jumped and turned startled gazes toward the window.

The sunlight still poured in, not a cloud visible in the blue sky.

"What was *that*?" Kat asked, sounding a little breathless.

*CRACK!* This time, there was an ominous rustling sound, a whoosh of wind and energy. Outside, the red awning over the door began to ripple as little whirls of wind danced up and down the street. Inside the tearoom, napkins fluttered out of their holder while Aunt Jo's skirt flapped against her legs.

Kat jumped to her feet, her eyes wide, her hot chocolate forgotten on the table. Zoe didn't move, seemingly frozen in place. Moon Pie, who'd scurried behind Aunt Jo, lifted his head and howled.

"That's unholy!" Aunt Jo grabbed her cane and pulled herself to her feet.

"Oh my gosh, look at that." Kat pointed to the street.

Ava came from behind the counter. A wild gust whipped down the street, yanking at the awnings, groaning as it swept past, as if it were alive and in deep, agonizing pain. Paper and brown leaves swirled into the air, shoved forward before the wind. The colorful awnings over the shop doors lifted like parachutes, frantically tugging at their ties. Branches, torn from shrubs and trees, tumbled past, one after the other.

And then . . . it stopped.

Silence filled the air and the littered street outside.

Aunt Jo moved closer to the window, Moon Pie following, the dog sniffing at the edge of the glass. "If that don't beat all. It's still as a mouse out there now."

Kat joined her. "What was that?"

308

Zoe peered over Kat's shoulder. "I guess it was one of those wind things. A derecho, I think it's called."

"There has to be a weather front of some sort for those to happen. I can't — Ava? Where are you going?"

Ava was already at the door. "Out."

"But your coat —"

The door closed behind Ava as she ran down the sidewalk to her truck. *Oh God, no. Not today. Pleasepleaseplease. I'm not ready for this. Not yet.*

She said the words over and over as she drove home, as she turned into the driveway and parked behind Sarah, as she hurried into the house, leaving the front door open behind her.

In the middle of the front hallway floor sat the old shoebox. Once a bright orange, now dull with age, it sat in a heap of ripped tape, gaping and empty.

Ava's heart dropped to the soles of her feet. *No, no, no!* She turned on her heel and walked through the foyer, her steps jerky and stiff.

She stopped in the kitchen doorway.

Sarah sat at the counter, Aunt Mildred's ancient recipe book in her hands. It was closed, but Ava knew from the paleness of Sarah's face that she already knew.

The book had told Sarah everything.

"Sarah —"

Sarah closed her eyes and looked away.

Ava gulped. "Please, Sarah. I know it sounds bad, but I was just trying to help." She pushed back a tendril of hair that had fallen from her scrunchie, aware her hands were shaking, her heart beating sickly in her chest. "I can explain —"

"No." Sarah's gaze was so filled with pain that Ava's throat tightened. "How could you do that to me?"

"I didn't mean to! I was stupid and young, and I didn't know what I was doing."

"You knew. And now I know. It wasn't real."

Ava took a step forward. "No, no. It's real."

"Not according to the book." Sarah ran her fingers over the faded cover, wincing as if it had whispered something ugly.

Ava was sure it had. Books loved Sarah, but Ava knew this particular book, which was old and cranky and rightfully furious at being locked away for so many years. The thing was bursting with rancid intent. "Sarah, I was stupid. I shouldn't have tried it, but I thought it might help. I —"

"*Help?*" Sarah gave a laugh that was so sharp even the book in her hands seemed to

310

shudder. "You tested one of your teas on me. Without telling me!"

"I wasn't testing anything. I mean, I'd never done that particular brew before, but — Look, you have to understand. Momma had died, and I was trying to take care of you. And you were so, so sad. I was worried about you, and I thought that if you fell in love and he fell in love with you, you'd be happy again."

Sarah's eyes blazed. "Oh my God, our mother had just died. Of course I was sad! So were you!"

"Yes, but —" Ava's tongue tripped over itself, and she stopped, struggling for a way to explain herself. "Sarah, you were sad for a long, long time. I thought falling in love a little might give you something positive to focus on."

Sarah's eyebrows shot up. "A *little*?"

Ava flushed. "The tea was way stronger than I expected. I was wrong. I know that. And I'm so, so, *so* sorry. When the tea didn't work the way I thought it would, I should have told you. But you were so miserable, and I thought I could fix this —" She shook her head. "I couldn't stand seeing you so sad. It was killing me."

"Momma told us to never, *ever* use our

abilities on each other, *or* without permission."

"I know, I know. I just . . . I thought it would be such a wonderful thing."

"Wonderful? I've spent my whole life thinking I loved Blake. And that at one time he'd loved me. But now I know it was all an empty joke. A prank you pulled on us both."

"It wasn't a prank!"

A tear slid down Sarah's cheek. "No wonder I can never talk to him. I was cursed."

"Not cursed! Just . . . it didn't work the way I thought it would. It made you crazy for him, too much so. Those old recipes, they're way too strong. I know that now, but I didn't then. I made some errors that —"

"Hello?" a male voice called from the front of the house.

Ava started. "You called Blake?"

"We're in here!" Sarah said loudly. She looked back at Ava. "I asked him to come here so you could tell him. I would do it myself, but you know better than anyone why I can't."

"Sarah, no! We can work together now and figure out how to fix this. We don't need to tell him anything that —" Ava swallowed the rest of her sentence as Blake came into

312

the room.

He wasn't wearing his uniform today but a pair of jeans, a soft Henley shirt showing from under his coat, which made him look younger than usual.

*Oh God. He's going to be so mad. I can't blame either of them.* Feeling sick, Ava pressed her hand to her mouth, aware that her lips were trembling as if she were cold.

He looked from Sarah to Ava and then back, concern on his face. "What's wrong?"

Her eyes wet, Sarah's gaze locked on Ava. "Tell him what you did."

"Sarah, I don't —"

"Tell. Him."

"Fine. Fine." Ava crossed her arms over her chest. "I did something I shouldn't have. It was a long time ago, but . . . it was a mistake."

His eyebrows rose, but he didn't speak.

Ava's whole body was trembling now. She hugged herself a little tighter. "When you were in high school, I gave you a tea that . . . did something to you."

His expression grew dark. "What the hell, Ava."

"It was stupid, I know." Ava rammed her hands into her pockets.

"What exactly did you do?"

"It's — Oh God. You need to understand

what I — we — were going through. A long time ago, when we were younger, Sarah found a book in the cellar written by our great-great-great-aunt. There were recipes in the book. For teas. They made people do and feel things, not bad things — well, sometimes bad, but I never used those."

Sarah muttered something under her breath. "Ava, just tell him!"

"Okay! After Mom died, I used a recipe from that book for a tea that would make people feel a certain way."

"She used it on us," Sarah said bitterly.

His gaze stayed locked on Ava. "What was this tea supposed to do?" he asked grimly.

Ava had to swallow twice before she could answer. "It was supposed to make people fall in love."

His mouth whitened.

Ava winced. "I'm sorry! Sarah was so sad after Momma died, and I thought maybe falling in love would help her move past that. I could see that you two were already interested in each other. So I made the tea and slipped it to both of you so you would . . ." Ava couldn't look at either of them. "I shouldn't have done it. It was wrong. But it's not as if you all weren't already thinking about it! You just kept missing each other. You were crazy for her when she was too young to care, then she was crazy for you after you'd moved on and had started dating someone else. Back and forth and back and forth. It was obvious to everyone you belonged together. So I just . . . gave it a push."

"A push?" Sarah gave a short laugh. "Aunt Mildred's teas don't push. They shove."

Blake's gaze had never left Ava's face. "Let me get this straight. You tricked me and Sarah into drinking a *love* potion?"

"It wasn't a love potion, not exactly. It's a tea. A brew that helps . . ." She grimaced. "Not that it matters."

"It explains so much," Sarah said. She looked at Blake. "Why I can't talk to you without feeling so much that I can't think and why I can never see you without —" Her face pinkened, and she looked down at the book, her lips thinned as she tried to hold in the torrent of words that threatened to spill out.

Seeing the agony on Sarah's face, Ava took a step toward her sister. "Sarah, don't look like that! Please don't. And, Blake, this — all of this, it's my fault. Not Sarah's. I just didn't know . . ." The words, tumbling and incoherent, locked themselves in her throat, and she was left speechless.

"You 'just didn't know.' " Blake gave an

odd, shaky laugh. "God, you Doves. You're something, aren't you? You always think you're the answer to the world's problems, but the truth is, you can't even fix your own." Blake eyed Ava. "When did you give us this tea?"

"The summer before Sarah's junior year."

He turned to Sarah. "That's when you suddenly realized I was alive."

Sarah, her face red, swiped at her tears and gave him a short nod. "After that, I couldn't speak to you without my tongue bumbling over itself. I kept losing track of what I wanted to say, or I'd just ramble on and on and — Oh God. I'm doing it now. I can't talk to you without wanting to share every thought, every hope, every —" She slapped her hand over her mouth and looked at him pleadingly, her eyelashes spiked with wetness.

Blake's face tightened. "Since Ava gave you that tea, you've thought you were in love with me, but you're not."

Sarah, who looked as miserable as Ava felt, nodded. She lowered her hand from her mouth. "I'm sure that's a relief to you, but —"

His laugh was harsh. "Good Lord, Sarah. You never got it, did you? You might have been enchanted, but I wasn't."

Ava frowned. "I gave you the same tea I gave Sarah. I watched you both drink it."

He cut her a hard glare, his tone as icy as his stare. "Unless you slipped me that magic tea when I was seven years old, then how I feel about your sister has nothing to do with you or your potions."

Sarah's eyes widened. "Seven?" The word was more a whisper than anything else.

"We had art class together. You remember that, don't you?"

Sarah nodded slowly.

Blake's lopsided smile was bitter. "This isn't how I'd planned on telling you. Heck, I hadn't planned on saying anything ever, to be honest."

"Why not?"

"You know why not." He clenched his jaw, suddenly looking as tired as Ava felt. "Sarah, you and I have danced this dance a million times. And it never works for us, although" — Ava felt the weight of his gaze — "now we know why."

"It was a mistake," Ava said desperately. "I know that now."

"So you've said, for all the good it does. Tell me, Ava, what would a love potion of yours do to a person who was already in love?"

Ava took a deep breath. Over the years,

while looking for a remedy, she'd spent thousands upon thousands of hours reading ancient, dusty tomes about potions, teas, and other herbal remedies. After a moment, she spread her hands wide. "I don't know."

"Now you do. It kills it, Ava. That's what it does. Not that it matters, as apparently Sarah never felt anything for me to begin with. Not anything real, anyway." Sarah made a protesting noise, but he didn't give her time to speak. "Meanwhile, I grew so exhausted by the song and dance that, to keep sane, I refused to be a part of it any longer."

"Don't blame Sarah," Ava said. "Please, Blake, this is all my fault. I just wish you'd told her how you'd felt. Then there would have never been any need for —"

"Tell her?" Blake turned to Sarah. "When we were in high school, how many times did I ask you out? A hundred? Two hundred?"

Her face pinkened. "In high school, yes, but later —"

"Later? After you'd rejected me so often that my buddies started calling me Blind Blake? And now . . . Sarah, I saw you at the Moonlight Café last night. I was eating alone. I waved at you, and you turned on your heel and ran away without even placing your order. That was *last night,* Sarah. You run away every time you see me, as if I have leprosy or —" He pressed his lips together and shook his head. "I'm tired of it. A few years ago, I decided we'd never be anything but acquaintances. Finding out about this now, I can see how right that decision was."

Sarah shook her head, tears rolling down her face. "No," she whispered.

Ava stepped forward. "Blake, *please.* This isn't Sarah's fault. Give her another chance. I'll stay out of it, I promise. I —"

"No. I'm done with you Doves. Now, if you'll excuse me, it's Valentine's Day, and I was about to go fishing with a friend. A female friend. Someone who might actually find the courage to speak to me without a magic tea. Goodbye, Sarah. And Ava? From here on out, keep your damn teas to yourself."

He stalked out, the front door slamming behind him.

Sarah crumpled against the counter, dropping her head onto her arms, her shoulders heaving as she sobbed.

Ava reached for her. "Sarah, I'm —"

The second Ava's hand touched her, Sarah jerked away. "Don't!" The word snapped with all the sharpness of an icy morning. Sarah stood, her wet eyes blazing. "You've done enough! I loved him! Or I thought I did, but —" A sob cut her off.

"Oh, Sarah, please. I was trying to *help.*"

"Like that makes it better? You're in the clear because you had good intentions? If they were so good, then why didn't you tell me what happened, instead of locking the book away? All this time we've lived together, you've had thousands of opportunities to say something. You've had years, Ava. *Years.* And yet . . ." Sarah's mouth thinned. "God, when I think of all the times I've talked to you about Blake, about my feelings and how hard it was for me, and there you were, you and your little secret, not saying a word. You just stood there and let me believe there was something wrong with me when . . ." Tears fell freely down Sarah's face, dropping onto her bright shirt. "I trusted you. I trusted you more than anyone I know. And now I feel like I don't even know you."

"Sarah, it was an . . . an accident. I just wanted to help you, and it didn't work. I'm so, so sorry. If you'll just let me try to make this right. Let me —"

"Make another tea that doesn't work the way you want it to? He *loved* me all those years, Ava. He. Loved. *Me.* And I drove him away because of what that stupid tea did to me. And now he's gone. Out with another woman, one he'll fall in love with while I'm still here, alone. I don't even know how I'll face him again. I could barely do it before, but now —" Her gray-green eyes shimmered with misery. "I've lost him."

She looked so broken, so wounded. Ava's heart ached as if it had been cut in two.

Sarah gulped back another sob. She swiped at her eyes with her sleeve and then turned and picked up the ancient book. "I'm leaving."

Ava nodded miserably. "You need some space. I understand. I'll —"

"It's not temporary, Ava. I'm moving out."

"Sarah, no. There's no need for —"

"Oh, yes, there is. There's every need. I need to get away from your secrets and your teas, but most of all, I need to get away from you. I'm never going to forgive you for this, Ava. Never."

Every word cut. She struggled to find the words that might make Sarah change her mind but knew deep in her heart they didn't exist. She watched helplessly as Sarah went upstairs and started packing, slamming drawers and stomping across her bedroom.

Just as Ava had feared, Sarah couldn't forgive her for her mistake.

And Ava couldn't blame her.

All too soon, Sarah came downstairs, a suitcase in one hand, the ancient book in her other. She didn't spare Ava so much as a glance as she went outside, and soon her truck roared to life and pulled out of the driveway.

Then Ava was alone, alone with an echoing silence filled with nothing but the sound of her own bitter, regretful sobs.

# CHAPTER 14
## SARAH

Sarah rested her head against the couch cushion and gently pressed an ice pack to her hot, swollen eyes. *How could Ava do that to me? And then hide it for so many y—*

"Here you go."

Sarah lowered the ice pack.

Grace, still dressed for work in her suit and heels, walked across her living room holding out a knee-length pajama shirt. "It's huge. You're going to love it."

Sarah set the ice pack aside and took the shirt. "I can't believe I forgot to pack pajamas." She hadn't brought socks, either, but that was tomorrow's problem.

"You left in a hurry. It happens." Grace went to the fireplace and used the brass poker to stir the crackling flames, sending out new warmth.

"Thank you for letting me stay here."

Grace, who'd immediately gone to the library on receiving Sarah's call, had taken one look at her tear-streaked face and announced that, as the mayor, she was allowed to close the library under "emergency circumstances." She'd then locked up the library and swept Sarah off to her house.

No one had ever had a better friend. Sarah managed a tremulous smile. "You're the best."

Grace flushed, obviously pleased. "Thank you. Back atcha." She put the poker down and came to sit on the couch next to Sarah. "Feeling any better?"

"The ice pack helped a lot. My eyes are so swollen they hurt."

"Crying can do that. When Mama G passed, I thought I'd never stop."

The fire crackled noisily as a log settled, the sound comforting. "It's so cozy here since you and Daisy moved in with Trav."

"He's been great. I didn't have to give up one stick of Mama G's furniture." Grace looked around the room. "Fortunately, he wasn't attached to any of his stuff except a few pieces that had belonged to his dad. We kept all of those, of course. You know how it is, living with another person — you have to make compromises."

"Until they lie to you and then hide it."

Grace's expression softened. "Why don't you put on that shirt and get comfy?"

Sarah held the pajama shirt at arm's length so she could see the graphic on the back. "Power Rangers?"

Grace said solemnly, "It's one of my most prized possessions."

"I bet. It looks super comfy." Sarah folded the shirt and put it beside the book she'd brought from the library with her.

The book seemed to take this as an invitation, because it immediately murmured, *You should read me. That would make you feel better.*

Sarah always brought books home from the library, but this one had been far more insistent than most. She eyed it now, THE FUNDAMENTALS OF BALLROOM DANCING written in script. Why, oh why, did she need to learn ballroom dancing? Was she destined to be in one of those classes where single ladies took turns dancing with each other while imagining the partners of their dreams? *Blake would never be caught dead at one of those.*

She winced. *I have to stop thinking about him. I have to.* Sarah picked up the sleep shirt and dropped it over the book. It murmured with irritation but took the hint and quieted down.

Grace settled deeper into the couch. She nodded to the book. "What's going on?"

Sarah grimaced. "It wanted to come with me, but it's chatty. Too chatty."

"What's it about?"

"Ballroom dancing."

"Oh! Thinking of taking a class?"

"No. Some books just get lonely and want to visit." From under the sleep shirt, the book murmured a protest. "This one wants to be read, though."

"I didn't know you could learn to dance from a book."

"I doubt anyone could." The book protested more loudly at that, so she reached for the sweater she'd taken off earlier and piled it on top of the shirt. "There," she told it. "Be quiet. I'll read you later." Before bed, on the off chance it might help her sleep. *As if.*

Grace shook her head. "You and your books."

"I'm glad to have them. They never lie to me." She didn't think books could lie. Even fiction, especially when well written, stayed true to its voice and purpose, no matter what happened between the pages.

Grace glanced at Sarah's phone, which was facedown on the coffee table. "I'm surprised Ava isn't calling you."

"I have it on silent. I can't talk to her." Mainly because Sarah didn't know exactly what to do with all the emotions that were tumbling through her, alternating between hurt and fury. She'd never been so crushed, so devastated. She wasn't sure whether it was because she'd lost Blake for good, or because she'd lost every last ounce of trust and respect for her own sister. *It's probably both.*

Grace sighed. "I wish you'd rethink moving out. I love having you next door. It's one of the best things about living here."

"I'll miss you guys too." Sarah would also miss her huge bedroom with its large windows, antique pink-flowered wallpaper, and the wrought-iron bed she'd had since she was a kid. She glanced at the window where she could see the edge of the huge wraparound porch. Her house was so close, and yet it felt far, far away. "I feel like my whole life has been ripped apart. There was no one I trusted more than Ava."

"She was wrong, but . . ." Grace's eyebrows drew down. "I know you want to move out, and I support you, whatever you do. But I think you should hold off on making any big decisions right now. You're angry, and with reason, but you grew up in that house. And you and Ava have always been so close. Maybe you'll find a way —"

"No. I can't live with her now. I just

can't." Sarah's chest had been aching ever since that evil book had whispered its ugly secret, but now an extra weight pressed against her. In ten short minutes, she'd lost her home, her sister, and the love of her life. *How could she do that to me? How could she keep a secret from me for all those years? All those times I told her how I felt about Blake and she just sat there! And then Blake —*

Sarah covered her face with both hands. "I've got to stop *thinking*! My mind just keeps hopping from horrible thought to horrible thought over and over and over, and it hurts like I'm touching a hot stove."

"You've had a shock. It's going to take some time to adjust."

Sarah dropped her hands to her lap. "Adjust? How do I adjust to the fact that my sister has been lying to me for years? And there I was, so stupidly unaware that I didn't even suspect it."

"Why would you suspect it? Ava loves you. We all know that. *You* know that."

Did she know that? Right now Sarah couldn't say. "She's lucky our mother isn't alive. She'd have rung a bell over Ava for what she did. Momma brought us up better than that."

Grace's eyebrows rose, and she said in a thoughtful tone, "Whew. What your momma must have gone through. Raising my niece is hard enough, and she can't do any of the things you all can." Grace tilted her head to one side, her expression serious. "When I first moved to Dove Pond, I didn't believe a word people said about you Doves. But then you always knew what book I needed to read, and I saw the good Ava's teas were doing for Mama G when nothing else worked. . . . I believe now. I really do."

Sarah sighed. "Not everyone does, but that's okay. Momma used to say it was their loss, not ours."

"You and Ava have always done so much good, but . . ." Grace grimaced. "What about this book she'd locked away? Is it possible it has another tonic that could rectify things?"

"I've already looked. Even if there was, I'd be afraid to use it. That book is . . ." Sarah had to fight a shiver. That book was unlike any book she'd ever seen. The pages were soaked with fury and hate.

After her fight with Ava, Sarah had taken the book to the library. The entire way there, it had suggested vile potions and evil curses so disturbing that Sarah had locked it in a heavy metal cabinet in the library archives, far enough away to silence its strident fury.

"If I thought it was safe to destroy it, I would."

Grace's eyes widened. "It's that bad?"

"It's worse. Every book carries the aura of its author. If the author is funny or emotional or just plain mean, then no matter the topic, a hint of that lingers within the pages. After being around that book, I'm glad I never knew my great-great-great-aunt Mildred. The book being locked away didn't help."

"It's a pity you never heard it calling out."

Sarah agreed. Ava must have used a heck of a good charm on that old shoebox. Sighing, Sarah looked out the window to where the wind tangled with the tree branches. This morning's sunshine was long gone, the world now covered in gray clouds. *Which is appropriate, given everything that's happened.*

She sighed restlessly. "I hate that Blake is involved in this mess."

"I'm not happy with him right now. He was rude to you. Sure, he can be mad at Ava if he wants, but you? That's not right."

"He was shocked."

"So were you. Instead of understanding what you were going through, he roared in, announced he was going on a date, of all things, and then stomped out. I'd have smacked him if it had been me."

Sarah gave a tired smile. "I can't blame him for being mad." She dropped her head back against the couch cushions. Every time she closed her eyes, she saw Blake's furious expression, which made her wince.

Grace said in a cautious tone, "Look, if you don't want talk about it, I understand, but what exactly is your history with Blake? You've said that something happened between the two of you in high school and that it ruined things, but you've never shared the details."

"It's complicated."

Grace gave her a wry smile. "That much I guessed."

Sarah sighed. "I've liked him for what seems like forever. At first, it was just one of those normal kid things, but always off-kilter. You know, I liked him, but he didn't like me. And then he'd like me, but I wouldn't like him. We could never get our timing right, but things were . . . interesting. Or they were until the year after Momma died; that's when The Incident happened." Sarah winced. "For a while, that was all this town talked about."

"Small-town problems."

Sarah nodded. "I'm glad you didn't live here then. I embarrassed myself so badly. Now I know it was because of Ava's tea, but at the time, I thought it was just me, and I was crazy for him. Sadly, like most high schoolers, I had no filter." Sarah thought about this. "I don't really have much of a filter now either."

Grace chuckled. "Which is why we all love you. But what exactly was The Incident?"

"Ugh. I hate even thinking about it." Sarah rubbed her face with both hands. "One day, wildly in love with Blake, I decided to act. And, Grace, I didn't just love him, I was obsessed. Now I know why, but it felt so real. What really sent me over the edge was when, to my wonder of wonders, he suddenly noticed me, too. I thought that, for once, we felt the same way at the same time. He started talking to me and smiling and . . ." She dropped her hands back to her lap. "I was over the moon. I was so sure we were meant to be together that I planned a very public display of our newfound love."

"Oh no."

"Oh yes. I just had to *show* him how much I loved him." She winced. "It was Homecoming Week, so on the water tower over the football field right before the big game, in huge four-foot-high letters, I painted SARAH LOVES BLAKE MCINTYRE. HOMECOMING DANCE?"

Grace covered her eyes. "Nooooo!"

"Yep."

Grace peeked out between her fingers. "Everyone teased him, didn't they?"

"Mercilessly."

Grace dropped her hands back to her lap. "Kids can be so cruel."

"His teammates, the cheerleaders, the other team, every single person there laughed and pointed. During halftime, someone even started a Blake-take-your-girl-to-Homecoming-she's-desperate chant. He was embarrassed, and so was I."

"Oh, Sarah, I'm so sorry."

"It was my own fault."

"No, it was Ava's. You were under the influence, remember?"

"I guess. All I know is that it was brutal. It really affected him, too. He was really, really good at football, but that game was his worst. He fumbled the ball left and right and read plays wrong. It was bad. But the worst part was at the end of the game."

"There's more? I'm afraid to ask."

"We lost, of course, and as the team headed off the field, someone yelled, 'Blake, are you going to ask Sarah to Homecoming?' and he stopped, looked directly at me, and said, 'When hell freezes over!'"

Grace let out her breath in a long whoosh.

"Wow. Sarah, I'm so, so sorry."

"Me too. I tried to apologize, but you know how I get around him. It was worse after that, too. And that's pretty much where I am today." Sarah shuddered. "It's been agony."

"And Ava knew it."

"She knew everything. She's hugged me while I cried, watched me struggle for years trying to talk to him, and knew how desperately I wanted to connect with him but couldn't. She used to tell me to be patient, that he wasn't worth it, and . . . oh God, all sorts of things that weren't true and —" Sarah's voice caught. "Not once did she tell me what she'd done."

"What she did was wrong. But, Sarah, surely there's still reason for hope. I've watched Blake try to talk to you hundreds of times since I moved here. He's done it as recently as Saturday. Surely that means something. He wouldn't keep trying if he didn't want the same things you do."

"He's done," Sarah said morosely. "He's washed his hands of the Doves. And I can't blame him." She sighed, picked up a pillow, and hugged it. "Grace, I like him so, *so* much. Too much. And now, because of Ava's stupid tea, I don't know if it's real or not." That was the hardest part, not being able to trust her own feelings.

The book under the sweater whispered, *Maybe if you learned to dance you'd —*

Sarah plopped her pillow on it.

Grace reached over and patted Sarah's knee. "Stop looking so glum. Things aren't as bad as they seem. I promise."

"I just don't know what to say to Ava. I'm so *angry* at her."

"Then don't say anything. Not for a while, at least. Let yourself heal. When you're ready, you'll know what to do."

Sarah hoped that was true.

A log dropped in the fire, sending out a few sparks. Grace watched as the flames settled. "I knew something was going on with Ava. She hasn't been herself for a while now."

"She hasn't been sleeping well for months. I just thought she was worried about the tearoom and the messed-up teas, but it was that secret, trying to break free."

Grace started to say something, but then hesitated. After a moment, she said, "What Ava said a few weeks ago about those messed-up teas was true, right? That she had eliminated the problem?"

"Yes," Sarah said, surprised at the flash of irritation Grace's question caused. "I was there when she figured out what happened.

The plant that caused it is at the house now."

Grace threw her hands up. "Sorry! But now that I know Ava's lied to you, of all people, then who wouldn't she lie to? If I was using a Dove tea right now and I heard about what happened between the two of you and how she hid it, added to the fact that she had some messed-up teas less than a month ago . . ." Grace shrugged. "I'll be honest, Sarah. Right now, I'd be afraid to use anything she made."

Oh dear. Sarah hadn't thought of that. "I hope other people don't think that way."

"Me too." Grace sighed. "Maybe I'm over-reacting. When Mama G was on the decline with her Alzheimer's, I don't know what we would have done without the tea Ava made for her. It was the only thing that helped."

"Well, I'm not going to tell anyone what happened between Ava and me. I'm sure you and Trav will keep it quiet too."

"Do you really think it's possible to keep something like this quiet here in Dove Pond? People are going to notice that you and Ava aren't living together and are no longer talking to each other. Plus, Blake's so furious, I don't think you can expect him to keep it to himself."

Geez, this was so much more complicated

than Sarah had realized. "I guess you're right. Everyone will be talking." She could almost picture it. Wincing, she rubbed her face with both hands, trying to free herself from her own imagination. "I shouldn't have called him when I found out what had happened."

"I'm surprised you did. What were you thinking?"

"I don't know. I guess I thought he had as much of a right to know as I did." Not that it had helped anything. *He was so angry. I hate that.*

Grace patted Sarah's knee. "You need a margarita."

"I might need more than one."

"I'll make a pitcher." Grace got up, and then slipped off her suit jacket and hung it neatly over a chair. "Don't move. I'll be right back." She disappeared into the kitchen.

Sarah rested her head against the over-stuffed cushions and looked out the window at the gray sky. As if sensing her mood, the sky rumbled with thunder.

She pulled one of Grace's decorative pillows into her lap and absently traced the embroidered surface. *How could Ava do that to me? And for all those years? How could she —*

"Stop it!" Sarah told herself and then buried her face in the pillow, closing her eyes against the grayness outside, wishing she could block her own thoughts as easily. *I have to stop asking myself questions I can't answer. It won't help anything.*

She was so confused right now. She owed Ava so much. *I was so grateful to her for being there when Momma died — I still am. I just don't understand why she didn't just tell me what happened —*

"Here we go!" Grace placed a tray holding two glasses, a small plate of salt, and a pitcher of margaritas on the coffee table in front of Sarah.

"That was quick."

"I had a mix, so it wasn't that complicated."

Sarah eyed the huge flowered pitcher. "That's like, what, a gallon pitcher?"

"At least. I got it from the Dollar Store. It's pretty, isn't it?"

"It's pretty huge."

"I'm sure we're up to the challenge." Grace turned each glass upside down and dipped the rim into the pitcher, then into the salt. She poured them each a drink, the ice tinkling noisily against the sides of the glasses.

Sarah took a sip and almost choked.

"That's a little strong, don't you think?"

"No." Grace sat back beside Sarah and took a sip. "It tastes perfect to me, but then, I'm not a lightweight like you."

Sarah had to smile. "I don't have your experience."

"It's a good thing I made so much, then, isn't it?" Grace took another drink. "Darn, but I'm a good margarita maker. Want to know my secret? Practice, practice, practice. That and pay for the good mix."

Sarah took another sip, enjoying the fresh tang of the margarita. It was cozy here at Grace's. The fire crackled, and the light from the living room lamps made golden circles over the side tables, brightening up the room darkened by the growing storm outside. A tiny bit of the hurt in Sarah's heart eased. It wasn't much, but it gave her hope, and she needed that right now. She caught Grace's concerned gaze and held up her glass. "This is the best margarita I've ever had."

"I have talents." Grace leaned back, her gaze still on Sarah's face. "But I wish I knew how to help you."

Sarah set her margarita on the coffee table. "I feel like I can't trust myself anymore. I couldn't tell Ava was lying, and I know her better than anyone else. How will

I know when other people are lying to me?"

Outside, rain came down in sheets, pattering against the window. Grace placed her drink on the table beside Sarah's. "I've told you about my sister, Hannah."

Sarah nodded. She'd never met Grace's sister, a longtime addict who'd died of an overdose just before Grace had moved to Dove Pond.

"The more Hannah fell into drugs, the more of a liar she became. She'd lie about what happened to her money, about why she was evicted from this place or that, about why she needed bail money, about why she needed to drop Daisy off and why she didn't come back to get her when she'd promised." Grace sighed. "She told so many lies, I can't remember them all. The first few times it happened, I felt just the way you do right now, that there was something wrong with me that I couldn't tell when she was lying. But once I accepted that was exactly what she was doing — lying just to get her way — I never fell for it again."

"You think I'll know if Ava lies to me again?"

"I do. You're immune from here on out. Every time she tells you anything, you'll wonder if it's true. And in wondering, you'll know."

"I hope so. I hate that. I don't want to wonder if she's telling the truth, but you're right, that's exactly what I'll do." Sarah's eyes burned once more. "She and I will never be the same, will we?"

"Not for a while," Grace agreed regretfully. "It's possible, though, if you and she do the right things, that you'll get back to normal. Maybe even better."

"Better? How?"

"It was taking a toll on her. We all saw it, but, like you, we thought she was just worried about the tearoom. Now it's plain as day she was feeling guilty. She didn't blithely lie to you and then merrily go about her business. She hated what she'd done. She just didn't have the strength to face disappointing you."

Sarah supposed that made sense. "Ava's a perfectionist. I guess that comes with a cost."

"Oh boy, does it." Grace reclaimed her glass. "Overachievers carry their own burdens."

Sarah dropped her gaze to her own margarita, absently admiring the reflection of the crackling fire in the curved glass. What Grace said explained a lot, but right now, Sarah couldn't think her way through it. All she could do was *feel.* She was so wrung out, so emotionally exhausted that all she wanted to do was climb into bed, pull the covers over her head, and never get back up.

A car pulled into the driveway, and Grace put her drink down. "There's Daisy. She went to Paw Printz after school to help Maggie Mayhew with her grooming appointments. Maggie said she'd drop Daisy off once they were done."

Grace got up and went to the door. As she opened it, the sound of the rain grew louder. She looked out and then yelled, "Daisy, your raincoat won't work if you don't put up the hood."

Daisy stomped across the front porch, and Sarah heard her say, "I didn't know it was raining that hard." Her hair plastered to her head, Daisy dropped her backpack on the floor, peeled off her raincoat, and flung it over the coatrack by the door, water splattering over the entryway.

"Daisy!" Grace said, giving her niece a flat look.

"Sorry," Daisy muttered.

"Take off those boots. I don't want the rug to get wet too."

Daisy wrinkled her nose but did as she was told. She was small for her age and had messy blond hair and blue eyes, which made her look just like Grace.

Daisy dropped her boots by the door, opened her backpack, and pulled out a book.

"How was school?" Grace asked.

"Okay, I guess." Daisy walked toward the kitchen, stopping when she saw Sarah curled up on the couch. "Hi."

"Hi." Sarah waved at Daisy. "I bet you're surprised to find me here."

"Mrs. Mayhew said you'd be here." Daisy wiped water from her forehead where it dripped from her hair. "She said you had a fight with Ava, who should be ashamed of herself."

*Oh dear. Grace was right; word is getting around fast.* Sarah forced a smile and nodded at the book under Daisy's arm. "Is that the book I gave you? *Children of Blood and Bones?*"

"This is my history book. Aunt Grace won't let me take library books to school, so it's upstairs under my pillow."

"When you finish the library book, let me know what you think."

"So far, it's really, *really* good. Sort of violent, but I like that."

"You would," Grace said drily. "By the way, it's bath day. Since you're already wet, why don't you hop in before dinner?"

Daisy scrunched up her nose. "Can't I wait until tomorrow?"

"Not if you want to eat the pizza I'm about to order."

Daisy rolled her eyes. "Fine. But I'm not washing my hair."

"Yes, you are. Sarah and I will be right here when you finish."

"Okay," Daisy said glumly, dragging her feet as she walked to the stairs.

"Hey, Daisy," Sarah called after her.

Daisy looked back over her shoulder.

"When I had to take a bath and didn't want to, I used to take every pot and pan in the kitchen into the tub with me and pretend to cook."

Daisy brightened and looked at Grace.

Grace eyed Sarah sourly. "Whose side are you on?"

"Fun's." Sarah took a sip of her margarita.

"Can I?" Daisy asked her aunt.

Grace was still looking at Sarah. "Do you promise to wash all the pots and pans she uses?"

Sarah held out her pinkie.

Grace sighed, but she hooked her pinkie with Sarah's and shook it. "Okay, Daisy. Just a few."

"YAY!" Daisy darted into the kitchen, and they soon heard banging and crashing as she went through the cupboards.

"Nothing that's glass," Grace yelled.

"Okay," came back a muffled reply.

Sarah was just taking another sip of her margarita when Daisy staggered by, carrying a ton of pots and pans and wooden spoons. Sarah watched the eleven-year-old navigate the stairs and disappear from sight. "Wow. That's impressive."

"If I could only get her to carry her laundry basket like that. She says it's too heavy and hurts her back."

"Ha!"

"I know, right?" Grace picked up her margarita glass once more. "Speaking of promises, I want one from you."

Sarah, just about to take another drink, lowered her glass. "Yes?"

"Stay here at least two weeks before you start looking for an apartment."

"Grace, thank you, but I —"

"Hear me out. You need a little time to think things through and decide what it is you really want to do."

"I'm not moving back in with Ava."

"I know. I wouldn't expect you to. But after what's happened, you need to heal before you make any decisions."

Sarah took another drink, surprised to note that her glass now held more ice than margarita. "Are you sure you don't mind me being here?"

"I love you being here. You already know how Daisy and Trav feel about it. You and Trav have been friends since elementary school, and you won Daisy over just now. She'll be your best friend for at least a week. You'll need another trick for the second week, but I'm sure you'll come up with something." Grace picked up the pitcher and refilled Sarah's glass.

"I guess it can't hurt to wait a while. But not too long."

"That's settled, then. There's just one more thing." Grace set the pitcher down, her clear brown gaze meeting Sarah's. "Blake. You need to talk to him."

Sarah lowered her glass. "I can't! You've seen what happens. Every time I try to talk to him, I . . . I . . . I freeze up like a . . . a . . . a . . . oh, heck, I don't even know what freezes up like I do! Or, worse, words just pile up and then I erupt like a word volcano."

"Sarah, that isn't you. It never was. And now you know that."

"But it doesn't change anything."

"Doesn't it? How will you know if you don't try?"

Sarah lifted her glass and took a nervous

gulp. Could she? *Should* she? "I don't know, Grace. Even if I could, he made it clear that he never wants to talk to me again. And what if things are exactly the same? What if I just freeze up and can't speak? And then he'll be mad and I'll be embarrassed —"

"Which is exactly where you are today, so . . ." Grace shrugged. "It can't get worse, can it?"

Sarah didn't know if that was true, but she was too tired to think of worse scenarios. "I suppose."

"Just think about it. Like I said, don't make any decisions right now. But, Sarah, if you don't at least try, then that evil tonic will have won. And I don't think it should." Grace stood, put her empty glass on the tray, and picked it up. "Come on. We'll finish this pitcher in the kitchen while I set the table. We'll order pizza once Daisy's out of the tub."

Sarah agreed, and with a sigh she stood and slowly followed Grace into the kitchen. She didn't want to talk to Blake or Ava or anyone else right now. But somewhere inside, a small part of her agreed that at some point, she had to talk to Blake again. Even if it was just to apologize for pulling him into a Dove family argument. *Why, oh why, did I call him?*

Her gaze drifted to the kitchen window where the rain slashed down. Through the hedge, she could just make out the porch of her own house.

She was going to have to face the fears Ava's tonic had caused. Face them and defeat them, if it could be done. Even more troubling, she was going to have to do it alone. She no longer had Ava by her side. Not now, nor would she ever.

Her heart heavy, Sarah turned away from the window and tried to rest her burning eyes.

# CHAPTER 15
## KRISTEN

Kristen put her book bag down just inside the tearoom door and hung up her jacket.

Ava looked up from where she was on the phone and gave a short, unsmiling wave, then turned back to the notepad in front of her. "Of course," Ava said to the caller. "I understand, but I —" She grimaced as the person on the other end of the phone interrupted her.

A week ago, Ava and her sister Sarah had had some sort of a fight. Kristen didn't know the exact details, as there were a myriad of stories racing around town, all of them different, but whatever happened, Ava seemed shaken.

Kristen nodded at Dylan, who was on a ladder in the back of the shop putting light bulbs in the new brass-and-crystal light fixtures.

His gaze slid from Kristen to Ava and back. Kristen could tell he was worried.

"I understand," Ava said to the person on the phone. "Of course not. I — Yes. I know. Goodbye." She hung up the phone and added another name to her list. When she finished, she threw the pen down and rubbed her hands together, as if they ached.

Aware of Kristen's gaze, Ava stuffed her hands into her pockets and forced a stiff smile. "Good afternoon. Would you mind filling the napkin holders on the tables?"

"Will do. I —"

The phone rang, and they all looked at it.

It rang again.

Ava started to move toward it, but hesitated. The phone rang again, sounding shriller with each ring.

She dropped her hand back to her side, a defeated expression on her face.

"I'll get it." Dylan climbed down from his ladder. "I'll tell them you're busy. You have a lot going on today and —"

Ava spun on her heel and disappeared into the kitchen. As the door swung shut behind her, the phone rang two more times and then stopped.

Kristen glanced at Dylan. "More cancellations."

He nodded morosely. "I've only been here an hour, and that's about the fifteenth one. Whatever happened between her and Sarah,

350

it's shattered Ava's reputation."

"Stupid people. Don't they remember all the good things she's done?" Kristen went to a small stack of boxes near the rows of tables and found the one marked NAPKINS in Ava's neat handwriting.

"They're dropping like flies. Four of them canceled their landscaping contracts, too, and one of them had been using Ava's service since she first started it."

Kristen went from table to table and filled the napkin holders. "The tearoom is scheduled to open next month. Ava should be focused on that. Instead she's dealing with . . ." Kristen glanced at the kitchen door. "It's not fair."

The phone rang again, and Kristen glared at it.

"I'll get it." Dylan wiped his hands on his jeans and strode to the phone. "Hello? Oh. Hi, Mrs. Meyer. This is Dylan Fraser. I —" He listened a moment. "No, Ava's not available right now. Should I —"

Kristen could hear Mrs. Meyer's high-pitched voice even from where she stood across the room.

Dylan's expression darkened. "No, I don't know what happened between Ava and Sarah. Whatever it was, I'm sure they'll work it out."

Mrs. Meyer apparently didn't agree, because as she spoke, Dylan grew redder and redder. Finally, he broke in. "That doesn't make sense! You just said you don't know what happened between them either, or who was at fault, but you're canceling your —"

Mrs. Meyer interrupted him. The second she paused for breath, he said shortly, "I'll let her know. Goodbye."

He slammed the phone back into place. "You're right. They're stupid idiots!" He scribbled Mrs. Meyer's name on the list, threw the pen down, then stalked back to his ladder. "Fools, the lot of them. Ava's worked her fingers to the bone for this town and now this." He moved the ladder to a new location and collected two more boxes of light bulbs. "She's too good for them. She always has been."

Kristen unwrapped a new package of napkins, the thin plastic loud in the quiet that followed. "I don't know what Ava's going to do."

"Yeah, well, I don't know what Mrs. Meyer's husband is going to do, either. He takes that tea to help with his arthritis. We go to the same church, and I've heard Mrs. Meyer brag about Ava's tea and how much it helps her poor Robert and how they don't know what they'd do without it." Dylan climbed up the ladder, slapped his screwdriver onto the top rung, and opened the box of light bulbs. "I'll wager my last dollar the Meyers will be back as soon as Robert's in pain. When the people of this town find themselves lying awake at night, hurting too much to sleep, they'll all be back."

Kristen pulled another napkin holder forward and started loading it. "Has Ava told you what happened? You two are close, so . . ." Kristen shrugged.

He unscrewed the light fixture and lowered the cover. "We're not as close as I'd like."

She shot him a startled look. She'd suspected he had a thing for Ava. What red-blooded guy wouldn't? But she was surprised to hear him admit it like that.

Now that Kristen thought about it, Dylan and Ava had a lot in common. They'd both grown up here and seemed destined to stay in Dove Pond forever. Kristen supposed Dylan was decent-looking for an older guy, if a little basic, although Missy would have argued vehemently about that.

Kristen opened another package of napkins. "So you like Ava."

His eyebrows knit as if he regretted sharing that little tidbit. After a minute, he shrugged. "We've been friends a long time." He retrieved his screwdriver and returned the glass-and-brass holder to its place. "Before you go getting any ideas, though, we're only friends."

He glanced at the kitchen door and then added in a regretful voice, "At least for now."

Kristen finished stocking the last napkin holder. They'd make a cute couple, Ava short and blond and Dylan tall, auburn-haired, and with a serious beard. "You should ask her out. It might cheer her up."

"What? No! I should wait for all this to blow over. She's too upset to think of anything else right now."

He looked uneasy, and Kristen thought she knew why. He was worried Ava would say no. Kristen couldn't fault him for that. It had been more than a week since she'd "interviewed" Nate Stevens to see if he might possibly be her dad, which had been a total waste of time, not to mention embarrassing. Since then, despite Josh and Missy's best efforts, Kristen had come up with dozens of excuses not to move on to the next possible "dad" on her short list.

Missy and Josh had grown frustrated with her inaction and were insistent that she interview their next target, Jack Lind, the property manager with the "sweet ride," as Josh called it. Kristen wasn't looking forward to it, but she had finally agreed it had to be done. *No one gets how bad this could turn out. What if he and Grandma Ellen like each other and work together against me? I'll be trapped then.* There were so many things that could go wrong.

Dylan finished tightening the last screw and descended the ladder. He sent Kristen a self-conscious look. "You'll keep all of that about Ava on the Q.T., right?"

"Sure." Kristen glanced at the closed kitchen door. "Did she tell you what happened between her and Sarah?"

"Some of it." He carried the empty bulb carton to a black garbage bag slumped beside the bar. As he stuffed the carton into the bag, he said, "It's complicated."

Kristen hated it when adults said that. It usually meant they didn't trust someone her age with important information. "Try me. I'm good at complex theory. Ask my chem teacher."

A reluctant smile touched his mouth. "It's not that I think you won't understand. It's just that it's not my story to tell. When Ava wants people to know what really happened, she'll tell them." He came to stand with Kristen at the long bar, his gaze moving to

355

the door Ava had disappeared behind. "All I know is that she's crushed. I haven't seen her this low since her mom died." Dylan's hazel gaze moved back to Kristen. "She wasn't much older than you when that happened, and she was left with Sarah to take care of, too."

Kristen tried to imagine being responsible for another person and couldn't. Just being responsible for herself felt like a lot. "It's hard losing your mom, no matter what age you are."

He nodded. "How are you and your grandma getting along? She seems like a tough one."

"You have no idea. She —"

The kitchen door swung open, and Ava returned. Her face was pink, as if she'd just scrubbed it, her eyes still shiny with tears.

Ava walked past them.

"You're leaving?" Dylan didn't try to hide his disappointment.

"I'm going to the greenhouses for a while, but I'll be back when —" The phone's loud trill made Ava wince, but she didn't look at it. "Let the calls go to voice mail." She pulled her coat off a peg by the door. "Kristen, we only got about half of the menu items into the point-of-sale program yesterday. Can you do the rest? The list is on the clipboard by the computer."

"Sure."

Ava put on her coat. "I'll see you all later."

Kristen followed Ava to the door. "When I get done, I'll organize the stockroom too. It's looking a little crazy in there right now."

Ava's gaze softened. "Thank you."

Pleased she'd taken a little of the edge off Ava's bad day, Kristen shrugged. "No problem. And hey, Ava?"

Ava paused, one hand on the knob. "Yes?"

"Things are going to work out."

Ava's smile was wobbly at best. "I hope so." She gave Kristen a hopeful wink and left.

Kristen watched the door softly close.

"Well done," Dylan said approvingly.

"Thanks." While Dylan went back to installing lights, Kristen found the clipboard and headed to the computer, trying to ignore the constantly ringing phone. She finished the point-of-sale inventory, then spent the rest of her scheduled time getting the stockroom into usable shape.

When she came back into the main room, Dylan was eyeing the pictures Mom had given Ava. "One of them was crooked." He stepped back and looked at them again. "Are they straight now?"

"I think so." She walked closer. "Mom was

a great painter."

"I always thought so. I didn't know her well, but she seemed like a good egg."

Kristen smiled. Mom would have laughed at that description. Kristen was pretty sure that would have prompted Mom to draw pictures of herself as an egg, complete with a roundish shape and short, flailing arms. She could almost see the drawings now. "How did you know my mom?"

"She was older than me, so we never went to school together, although I ran into her once just after I'd started college. Me and some buddies went on a golf weekend to Hilton Head." He laughed and shook his head ruefully. "We thought we were such ballers, going golfing. Anyway, when we stopped by the clubhouse, there was your mom, bartending. I was glad to see a familiar face. You don't run into many Dove Pond people out in the real world."

"She loved that job. She always said that if she hadn't been called to paint, she would have been a bartender instead."

"She was great at it. We must have talked two hours, just remembering this place and the people here. I think it was that conversation that made me realize I didn't want to live anywhere else."

Kristen cut him a curious glance. "You

guys didn't date or anything like that?"

"Nah. That was the only time we ran into each other until you all moved back to town. And then she didn't seem interested in even saying hello, which was fine." He shrugged. "Like I said, I didn't really know her."

"Sometimes she didn't like to talk. I —" A knock sounded on the front window, and Kristen looked over her shoulder to see Missy standing outside, her hands cupped around her eyes as she peered into the tearoom.

"I think that's for you," Dylan said drily.

Kristen waved at Missy. "I've got to go. You'll lock up?"

"Sure. I'll call Ava and let her know."

"Thanks, Dylan." Kristen headed for the door. "See you tomorrow." She slipped her coat on, grabbed her book bag, and left, the chilly late-February air making her shiver as she met up with Missy.

"Finally! I can't parallel park in that truck, so I had to use the lot by the courthouse." Missy hunkered down in her coat, hugging herself, the ends of her scarf dancing in the wind. "Are you ready?"

"Where's Josh?"

"He should be on his way." Missy clasped her bare hands together and blew on them. "Can we wait in your car? I'm freezing."

Kristen led the way, and Missy tossed her backpack onto the floorboard and climbed in the passenger side. As soon as her door closed, Missy turned to Kristen. "Well? Did she say anything?"

Kristen didn't ask who "she" was. Every day since the big blowup between Ava and Sarah, Missy had asked this same question. "She was really quiet, just like yesterday."

"She knows she's guilty," Missy said. "I would feel guilty, too, if I'd poisoned my sister just because I was in love with her man."

"Wait. Poison? And what man? You mean the sheriff?" At Missy's nod, Kristen demanded, "Who told you that?"

"My mom."

"She's wrong. I've seen Ava and the sheriff talk hundreds of times, and they're just friends. I'd bet my right arm on it. And Ava's never poisoned anyone. You know that."

Missy looked disappointed. "Maybe Mom heard it wrong. I can't believe Ava hasn't said anything."

"Why should she? Whatever happened, it was between her and Sarah. I can tell Ava's really hurt, though. People have been canceling their tea orders left and right. I'm worried about her, and so is Dylan."

"Mom says people are angry because Sarah's one of the nicest people in town."

"Ava's nice, too," Kristen protested. "And she's helped people just as often as Sarah. I don't know what my mom would have done without Ava's —"

The back door opened. Josh tossed his book bag onto the seat and slid in. "So? Did Ava say anything today?"

Kristen rolled her eyes.

Missy frowned at Josh over the back of her seat. "I just asked her that same thing."

"Oh. Sorry. I didn't know."

Kristen stifled a sigh. "Look, can we talk about why we're here? I'm looking for my dad, remember?"

"Sure." Josh scooted forward, resting his elbows between the two front seats. "About that. I sort of wonder if we should talk to Sheriff McIntyre today instead of Mr. Lind."

Kristen turned to glare at him. "Why would we do that?"

"On my way here, I saw Mr. Lind driving toward the highway. He spends a lot of time in Asheville, and that was the direction he was headed."

Great. That didn't leave her a lot of choices. "We should wait until he comes back. I don't want to interview the sheriff yet. Of all the dad candidates, he's the one most likely to figure things out and tell my grandma. It would be smarter to leave him until last."

"That's true," Missy said. "Plus, if he's involved in the Dove-sister dustup, the last thing he's going to want to do is talk to us. He's probably too busy with the investigation to even meet."

"What investigation?" Josh asked.

Missy shot a quick look at Kristen before she answered. "I heard that Ava tried to poison Sarah in order to keep her and Blake apart."

"That's not what happened," Josh said indignantly.

Kristen was glad at least one of her friends wasn't buying into town gossip. "See, Missy? Even Josh thinks that's wrong."

"It's stupid wrong," Josh said. "My sister's music teacher told my dad that what happened was that Ava stole an ancient book of spells from Sarah. It's super valuable because it belonged to one of their ancestors. Sarah was so mad she called Sheriff McIntyre to have Ava arrested, but he refused to —"

"Josh!" Kristen snapped. "That's not true either!"

"*Oh!*" Missy bounced in her seat, crossing

her arms over her chest. "Fine, Kristen! What did happen, then?"

"Whatever it was, it can't be Ava's fault. She'd never hurt anyone, especially Sarah."

"Well, something happened. Daisy said Sarah's been staying at her house all week."

"I don't know, but it wasn't either of those two things. Look . . ." Kristen pressed her fingers over her aching eyes. "I don't have the time or patience for this right now. I've got to find my dad, who doesn't even know I exist. And I've got to convince him to let me live with him, too." She dropped her hands to her lap. "Remember?"

There was a long silence, and then Missy said in a small voice, "Sorry."

"Me too," Josh said, equally chastened.

Kristen sent them both an exasperated look. "This town gossips too much. There are way too many stories, and they're all different except that in every one, Ava's the bad guy."

Missy bit her lip.

"It's been a tough week, and time is flying by. I've got to stop my grandmother before it's too late." Kristen sighed and leaned her head against the headrest. "In between packing everything that even looks like Mom into boxes, Grandma Ellen has been hovering around with this weirdly hopeful smile as if I'll suddenly decide I'd just *love* to live in Raleigh. Worse, I can tell she definitely suspects I'm up to something, too, because she's asking where I'm going more than usual. And I'm still not sleeping, which is stupid, because you'd think I'd be over that part by now. But the worst thing is that I just miss Mom so much that I can't . . ." She wiped away a tear that had leaked out, her voice trembling as she said, "Sorry. It's just a lot."

Missy, instantly contrite, leaned over the console and pulled Kristen into a comforting hug. "I'm so sorry! You're going through hell right now, and Josh and I are all caught up in town drama. We'll find your dad, and he'll make things better. I'm sure of it."

Kristen returned Missy's hug and then untangled herself. "Thanks, Missy. I hope you're right."

"We don't mean to make things worse," Josh added. "I was hoping your grandma would soften up and make amends after what she did to your mur—"

"Look!" Missy said fervently. "There's the sheriff now."

Sheriff McIntyre had just parked his squad car and was headed for his office, each step a slam on the pavement. As he stormed along, scowling, he appeared to be talking to himself, too.

"Uh-oh." Josh watched as the sheriff disappeared into his office. "My dad talks to himself just like that when he's mad. Has whole arguments sometimes."

Kristen slumped in her seat. *Great. Another obstacle.* "We can't talk to the sheriff if he's in a mood. We should wait for Mr. Lind to come back."

"We can't," Missy said. "Come on, Kristen. You've put this off long enough. We're here and we might as well get this over with." She pulled her notebook from her book bag and opened it to the questions they'd come up with over the past week. "If your grandmother is already packing your mom's things away, then we can't waste any more time."

Josh had grown quiet, but now he leaned between the seats and added, "I have to agree with Missy on this one. Your grandma isn't waiting, so neither can we."

Kristen thought of the ever-growing wall of boxes, and her stomach churned. "I hate this."

Missy's brown gaze softened. "Of course you do. You're the most cautious person I've ever known. You never take chances without thinking it through. Heck, if your mother hadn't dyed her hair purple, you wouldn't have done it, either."

That was true. Since she'd been a kid, she and Mom had dyed their hair the same color. When Mom had lost her hair to chemo, Kristen had wanted to shave her own, but Mom had refused and had instead gotten a ridiculously long, bright purple wig, which she'd worn until her own hair grew back. Then they'd matched once again. At least for a while.

Aware of her friends' concerned gazes, Kristen forced a shrug. "I guess we have no choice."

Josh sighed with obvious relief. "Let's do this. Although I'll admit it's unfortunate Sheriff McIntyre ended up on your list of potential dads."

"All I know is that he wrote a little poem in Mom's yearbook that rhymed 'hot stuff' with 'bold enough.' "

"Wow." Josh looked impressed despite himself. "It takes a confident guy to put something like that in writing."

"No kidding!" Missy said. "But hey, if it turns out the sheriff is Kristen's dad, think of the benefits."

Josh brightened. "We'll never get a speeding ticket!"

"That too. But I was thinking that of all the dad candidates, he'd best know how to deal with Kristen's grandma. He's not a pushover."

That was true, Kristen supposed. She wiped her hands on her jeans and tried to calm herself. "We all remember what to say, right?"

"Good Lord, yes," Missy said. "We've practiced it about a hundred times now."

They'd needed that practice, too, Kristen thought, remembering their stumbling efforts with Mr. Stevens at the hardware store. "We'll have to be at our best with the sheriff."

"Absolutely."

"Let's do this." Josh grabbed his notebook, opened the door, and climbed out of the car, Missy and Kristen following.

Soon all three of them were walking into the sheriff's office, looking around curiously. A huge bulletin board met their gaze. It was filled with announcements and notifications about lost cats, missing dogs, and small posters advertising the Dove Pond Spring Fling. Josh paused to stare at the most wanted list. "Holy cow, doesn't that look like Preacher Johnson? I —"

"Come on!" Missy hissed and grabbed his arm, pulling him with her.

They walked around the corner to find Sheriff McIntyre seated at his desk, stacks of paper all around him. He eyed them with a faint flicker of surprise. "Well, well, well." He closed the folder he was working on and dropped his ink pen on top of it. "Missy Robinson, Kristen Foster, and Josh Perez. Can I help you?"

Missy stepped forward. "We have a favor to ask."

"Ask away, but if you've come to sell me Girl Scout cookies, I already bought ten boxes from some racket-level little angel who wouldn't let me inside the Piggly Wiggly without buying every last box she had."

"It's not cookies. We just have a question to ask. A few questions, actually, although not that many." With each word, Missy's voice crept up an octave. For all her brassy talk and their hours of practice, it was obviously she was beginning to panic. "Just five questions, or six. I can't remember our list, but there weren't many and —"

"Missy!" Josh cut her off before casting a brittle smile at the sheriff. "Sorry. She's a little nervous. Some people get that way when they talk to an authority figure. We just wanted to do the interview for the yearbook."

The sheriff crossed his arms over his chest and leaned back in his chair, his gaze flickering over each of them. "Oh yeah, that's what you all were doing when I saw you at the hardware store. You had just interviewed Nate Stevens, if I recall correctly."

Kristen wet her dry lips. "We're going to interview several men —"

"People," Josh corrected. "Several people. Old students."

"I see." The sheriff stood and came around to the front of his desk. His gaze narrowed as he sat on the edge and recrossed his arms over his chest. "I can't imagine an alumni section would be a very popular feature."

"Really?" Josh looked surprised, although Kristen knew this was one of the things they'd expected the sheriff to say. "People like to see themselves in print. It'll be great for ad sales."

"I suppose that's true." The sheriff shrugged. "What do you all want to know?"

Kristen realized that both Josh and Missy were holding notebooks while she had nothing. Her empty hands suddenly seemed awkward, so she stuffed them into her pockets.

Josh opened his notebook and flipped through several pages as if looking for the sheriff's name. "Let's see. Sheriff McIntyre . . . Here you are." He squinted through the list of questions they'd written up. "What is your most fun memory of your time at Dove Pond High?"

"The usual. The football games. Pep rallies. Fire drills."

Josh, who'd been scribbling the sheriff's answers, paused at this. "Fire drills?"

The sheriff grinned. "They can be fun if you and your friends use the opportunity to shoot bottle rockets into the dumpster."

Josh couldn't have looked more impressed. "Did you get in trouble?"

"Once. I was suspended for a week. My dad was furious, and I lost the use of my pickup for a month, which sucked because I had to take the bus. But it was worth it."

"Wow." Josh was so swamped in admiration that he just stared happily at the sheriff.

Missy sent Josh an impatient look and clicked her pen, drawing the sheriff's gaze. She blurted out, "What was your favorite class?"

"Chemistry. I was good at it, too, although I never took another chem class after that."

Missy scribbled his answer in her notebook.

Josh took over once again, asking for the sheriff's favorite teacher, what sports he played, and if he approved of the changes that had been made to the field house over the years.

"This is so interesting." Missy took a deep breath and then blurted out, "You dated Kristen's mom for a while, didn't you?"

Kristen winced, as Missy's voice had gone from "slightly weird" to "super weird."

The faint smile on the sheriff's face stayed the same, but his gaze narrowed yet again. "That's an interesting question."

"And?" Josh's pen hovered over the paper.

He and Missy leaned forward, obviously hanging on the sheriff's every word. Kristen sent them a warning glare, but they didn't notice.

The sheriff's gaze moved from them to Kristen, a considering look on his face.

Her face, already hot, heated yet more.

"No," he said. "I never dated Kristen's mother. Julie was a good bit older than I was."

"How old are you?" Missy asked.

Amused, the sheriff raised his eyebrows. "What do you think?"

"I don't know." Missy shrugged. "Forty?"

His smile disappeared. *Forty?*

Missy bit her lip. "Thirty . . . seven?"

He frowned. "Good God."

Kristen cut a warning glance at Missy and hurriedly stepped in. "If you didn't go to high school with my mom, why did you sign her yearbook?"

He cut her a hard look. "I didn't."

"You did! You wrote a poem. I saw it."

"And I signed it, too? Blake McIntyre?"

Kristen frowned, trying to remember. She'd paid more attention to the poem than the signature. "I think . . . I think it just said Blake."

"That was probably Blake Reed. They were about the same age. You wouldn't know him. He went to college and never came back."

*Oh no.* Kristen could feel the weight of Missy's and Josh's accusing gazes. She shot them a self-conscious look. "I saw Blake and I only knew one, so —" She winced and mumbled, "Sorry."

Missy's shoulders dropped. "How about later? Maybe you dated Kristen's mom after you graduated?"

"Nope."

Missy frowned impatiently. "You're *sure* about that?"

*Oh boy . . .*

"I'm very sure," he said with a hint of impatience. "Julie moved away, and I didn't see her again until she came back years later. Kristen, you were what then? Six? Seven?"

"Six," Kristen said, trying to maintain her

smile and knowing she was failing miserably.

That was that, then. Sheriff McIntyre wasn't her father, and their only hope was Jack Lind, a man Kristen didn't know at all. Until that moment, she hadn't realized how much she'd been hoping she'd know the man who was her dad at least a little.

The sheriff's dark green gaze stayed on Kristen. "I'm looking forward to seeing this new section in the yearbook. I usually get my copy the week after it comes out."

*Oh no.*

"*You* get a copy?" Josh's voice cracked on the last word.

The sheriff cut a hard look at Josh. "The town always orders three of them. One goes into the library for the town archives. Another one ends up in the mayor's office. It's left out in the waiting room as reading material for people waiting to pay their tax bills. The last one ends up here. It's a useful tool for identifying juveniles when we get a complaint."

Missy stiffened. "You use the yearbook to identify us for *crimes*?"

The sheriff grinned. "It's public record, so why not. I'm just following standard police practice. They did it for years before I got here."

"That's just wrong," Josh said, obviously infuriated. "That's the last time I let them put my picture in the yearbook."

Sheriff McIntyre laughed. "Just don't commit a crime, and it'll be a nonissue."

"I think we've asked all our questions now." Dragging her disappointment with her, Kristen backed a step toward the door. "Thank you for your time, Sheriff. But we'd better get going."

"Yeah," Missy said. "We've got homework and stuff."

The sheriff pushed himself from the desk. "Sure. But before you all leave, I have a few questions for you."

*Oh no.* Kristen exchanged looks with Missy and Josh.

Josh squared his shoulders. "Sure. What do you want to know?"

The sheriff's gaze slid from Josh to Kristen. "What does Kristen's mom have to do with the yearbook?"

Kristen opened her mouth, her mind racing to think of an answer, but she couldn't think of a thing to say. Of all the questions they'd expected the sheriff to ask, this wasn't one of them.

Josh muttered something under his breath, but apparently he was just as trapped by surprise as she was, because he never said anything out loud.

"Wait! I know!" Missy gave an excited hop. "Kristen's mom is sort of famous, so we thought we might mention her, too. Did you know she's had pictures in museums and . . . and other places?"

"Just like every other person in this town, I did know that," the sheriff said in a flat tone. "But that doesn't explain why you all asked if we'd ever dated. Nor does it explain why you asked that exact same question of Nate Stevens when you interviewed him. So . . . what does Julie Foster's dating history have to do with the yearbook?"

Missy's smile faltered.

"It's just for me." Kristen struggled to keep her voice even. "I . . . I was looking at my mother's old yearbooks and noticed some of the signatures. The things Nate, the other Blake, and some others wrote seemed sort of romantic, so . . ." She shrugged. "I was just curious. I guess I'm trying to collect as many memories of Mom as I can before Grandma Ellen makes me move to Raleigh." Kristen hated pulling the sympathy card, but tough times called for tough moves.

The sheriff's gaze remained on her face as he absently rubbed his chin. "That makes sense, I guess." He dropped his hand back to his side. "What was in this poem Blake Reed wrote to your mom that got you guys so curious?"

Josh answered. "He called her 'Hot Stuff.' "

"Ah." The sheriff chuckled. "That doesn't mean what you think it does. When Julie was a freshman, she and some girls were joking around in chemistry class and some beakers got knocked over. I don't know what was in those things, but there was an explosion."

"No way!" Josh said.

"Oh yeah. There was a fire and everything. They closed the lab for a whole semester. Everyone in Dove Pond called her 'Hot Stuff' after that."

Well, that explained that.

Josh shook his head. "You guys had a lot more fun than we do."

"We didn't have nearly the number of rules. Which is why we lost more fingers and have more scars." Sheriff McIntyre's gaze moved back to Kristen. "You know your mom was the one who painted the mural in the gym?"

Kristen blinked. "The big one? Over the bleachers?"

He nodded.

Missy's eyes had gone wide. "No one ever

told us that. We see that mural almost every day."

Kristen couldn't stop a sudden, instant smile. It wasn't the Wonder Kristen mural, but it was something, and it was her mother's. Kristen wondered why Mom hadn't mentioned she'd painted the mural in the gym. *Mom must have decided it wasn't up to her standards. She was way too critical of her own work.* The next time Kristen went to school, she'd take a closer look at it. "Thank you, Sheriff. I appreciate you taking the time for this."

"No problem." The sheriff went back to his chair behind the desk, although he didn't sit. "If you think of any more questions, stop back by. I'm right here."

Missy grabbed her book bag and shoved her notepad into a pocket. "Thanks for your help."

Josh closed his notebook. "When you have the time, I'd like to hear more about those fire drills."

"Sure. By the way, tell your dad I said hello."

"Will do." Josh and Missy headed for the door.

Kristen followed.

She was almost there when the sheriff's

voice rang out behind her. "Just a minute, Foster."

*Uh-oh.* She watched with longing eyes as the door swung shut behind Josh before she turned back to the sheriff.

He'd crossed his arms again and now he rocked back on his heels, his gaze laser sharp. "What's going on? And I mean, what's *really* going on."

"Nothing. It's just like we said. We're doing a section for the yearbook."

He shot her an exasperated look. "It's pretty obvious this has nothing to do with the yearbook." He waited, but when she didn't speak, he sighed. "Fine. Let me tell you what I think you guys are doing. Ready?"

She didn't answer.

He seemed to take that as a yes. "You're trying to find your dad."

*Oh no.* Kristen cast another longing look at the door, but it seemed much too far away. *Great. Just great.* She forced herself to face him. "Maybe."

"There's no maybe. There's yes or no. Which is it?"

That sounded so much like something Grandma Ellen would say that Kristen had to fight a scowl.

He sighed. "Do you want to talk about it?"

She shook her head.

"Fine." He eyed her for a long minute. "Look, I'm not going to tell you what to do. I'm sure you have enough people doing that right now, and trust me, lately I've grown to understand how horrible that can be."

She wondered if he was talking about the situation with Ava and Sarah, but before Kristen could ask, he continued, "Just promise you'll exercise some caution."

What did that mean? "Caution?"

He nodded grimly. "I don't know why your mom didn't include your dad in your life, but it's possible she had a good reason."

Kristen had already thought of that. *What if he's mean? Or an alcoholic? Or* — She halted her spinning thoughts. She could think of so many bad things.

Aware the sheriff was still watching, Kristen said, "I'll take that into consideration."

"Good. And if you ever want to talk about things, or — and this is just hypothetical, you understand — but if you need to find out if someone is safe, let me know. I might be able to find out if they have, say, a long rap sheet or a history of violence or anything like that. So long as we stay within the letter of the law, I'm here for you." His deep green gaze locked on her. "You understand what I'm saying?"

"Yes, sir."

"Good."

That was more than she'd hoped for. A lot more. She wondered how much she could trust him. *Do I really have a choice?*

She took a calming breath. "There's only one man left on my list. Do you know Jack Lind? He does property management or something like that."

The sheriff smiled. "I know him well. His family and mine are close."

"And?"

"He's a good one. And yes, he was close to your mom at some point. I don't know their timeline, but I suppose anything is possible."

*That has to be it, then. Jack Lind is my dad.* She waited to see how she felt about it, but other than an odd flicker of dread, she had no reaction. *Shouldn't I be excited? At least a little?*

"Are you going to talk to him soon?" Sheriff McIntyre asked.

She nodded.

"That's going to be some conversation. If you want someone to go with you, call me. Like I said, I know him and I'm here if you need me."

"Thanks. I think I've got it, though." The sheriff was being kind, which she appreciated, but she was stretched so thin that she feared that if she tried to smile one more time, her face would crack.

Still, she felt as if she should reciprocate in some way. So before she left, she said, "Can I tell you something?"

His gaze narrowed, some of his smile disappearing. "About?"

"Ava."

His mouth hardened. "I don't want to talk about that."

"I understand. And look, I don't know what happened. The rumors are . . . well, they're stupid." She shrugged. "I haven't seen Sarah, so I don't know about her. But I see Ava every day, and I can tell that whatever happened, she regrets it."

"Kristen, don't —"

"Please. You did me a favor. So now I owe you one. I know Ava really well. I've worked for her for over two whole years. People are canceling tea and landscaping orders, and she's devastated. I doubt anyone will come to the tearoom when it opens now. She's not sleeping and hasn't been for a while. She was talking on the phone today, and her voice was shaking so bad that I worried she might . . ." Kristen stopped, out of breath from talking so fast. "I'm worried about her."

As she spoke, the sheriff's gaze had dropped to the top of his shoes. He was quiet for a long time. Finally, he sighed. "Fine. I'll talk to Dylan and see what's up. He's there most days, so he'll know."

"He's worried too."

"Great." The sheriff raked a hand through his hair. "She still shouldn't have done what she did."

"Whatever it was, I'll bet it was an accident or a mistake or something like that." Kristen shrugged. "I'd hate to be judged just on my mistakes."

He managed a smile. "It's not that easy."

"Nothing is," she replied honestly. "Life sucks."

He laughed and threw his hands up. "Okay, okay! That's dark, but I know where you're coming from. Thanks for telling me about Ava. I'm not sure what I'm going to do with the information, but I appreciate your honesty."

"You're welcome." She waved and, feeling as if she were escaping an interrogation, she left. As she walked out into the cold, she was suddenly so exhausted that she felt as if she could sleep for a hundred days.

She found Josh and Missy waiting beside the car.

"What did he want?" Missy asked.

Josh's gaze searched her face. "Is everything okay?"

"Yeah." Kristen rubbed her face with both hands. "He was just checking on me."

Josh muttered, "He blew our cover. I hate that."

Missy cut a hard glance at Kristen. "You never mentioned that signature didn't have a last name."

Kristen's face grew hot. "He's the only Blake I know."

"I would have done the same thing," Josh said staunchly.

Missy shrugged. "I guess I might have, too. Just to be clear, though . . . Mr. Lind *did* sign his last name, right?"

Kristen had to swallow a sharp retort. She couldn't blame her friends for being upset. *What a stupid mistake.* "It was definitely him. I remember because he looped his *L* like crazy. By the way, Sheriff McIntyre knows Mr. Lind and says he and Mom had a relationship of some sort."

Missy brightened. "That's good news."

Missy could pretend all she wanted; Kristen knew better. There was no good news.

Her dismal thoughts must have shown,

because Josh sent her a worried look. "You're sure you're okay?"

"I'm tired. I hadn't realized how much. Everything's happening so fast and . . . it's hard."

Missy slipped an arm around Kristen's shoulders. "Why don't you come spend the night? Mom and Dad would love to see you."

Kristen would love to see them, too. She longed for some normalcy, and Missy's home had lots of that. "That would be nice. We can study for the physics quiz tomorrow, too."

Missy rolled her eyes. "I was thinking we could watch a movie, but if you need to study, we can."

Kristen wasn't the one who needed to study, but she said, "I'll run home and grab my things and meet you there. I can drive us to school in the morning, too, if you'd like."

"Perfect. We can —" Missy's phone buzzed. "That's Mom now." Her thumbs flew as she texted. "I'm telling her you're coming over. She'll be happy to hear that. She worries about —" Missy's phone buzzed again, and she smiled. "She says you're always welcome."

"Great. I'll see you there. Bye, Josh." Kristen headed to her car, surprised when Josh fell into step beside her.

He slanted a glance her way. "So."

"So?"

"So this Lind dude is likely to be your dad."

"Maybe. We could have been wrong about the whole thing, too." Was that better? *Maybe. Maybe not. I don't know anything right now.*

Josh's dark gaze flickered over Kristen's face. "You think the sheriff will blab to your grandmother about what we're doing?"

"I hope not, but there's no guarantee." She sighed. "I guess we'll have to talk to Mr. Lind as soon as he's back."

"Sure. And listen, if it's not Mr. Lind, we'll keep looking. We won't stop until we find your dad."

Josh seemed so determined that she managed a real, if thin, smile. "Thanks. That means a lot."

He flushed, looking so pleased that her fake smile softened into a real one. "You and Missy have been great," she said.

He shrugged. "You'd do the same for us."

That was true. "Still, I really appreciate you all. See you tomorrow?"

He nodded, and so with a wave, she

climbed in her car and drove away, leaving Josh on the sidewalk, watching her go.

# CHAPTER 16
## ELLEN

Her Noir Epi agenda tucked under one arm, Ellen stood in the doorway of Julie's bedroom and eyed the colorful madness within. As of late this afternoon, she'd met all her benchmarks for freshening up the downstairs. She'd cleaned out a large portion of the endless fribble Julie had kept on every available surface and packed it away. She'd also thinned out the excessive number of rugs, tchotchkes, and art that had been stuffed into almost every corner and had it ready to be hauled off to a storage facility.

All that was left were these three upstairs rooms — Julie's studio, which Ellen had begun but had barely made a dent in, and Julie's and Kristen's bedrooms.

Ellen stepped over the threshold, instantly enveloped in the smell of the lavender-scented candles that lined the windowsill. It was painful, walking into Julie's bedroom without her there. It felt wrong, somehow.

Invasive. But for Kristen's sake, what had to be done had to be done.

Ellen's gaze moved over the room, taking in the large purple bed; two fat, overstuffed chairs; the huge dresser that had been painted to resemble a Harlequin mask; a pair of boldly pink, beaded, ruffled, bejeweled, fringed lamps on the nightstands on either side of the deep purple tufted headboard. She couldn't imagine anything more opposite in taste and color choice to her own home, which was clean, modern, gray, white, and cream. *I'm going to need more boxes. All of this has to go.*

And yet, she hated moving a thing. Julie had died here, in this room. Ellen walked to the bed, where she ran her hand over the colorful, slightly askew quilt. The design almost hurt to look at. Unicorns jumped over bright rainbows while busty green mermaids grinned at the large starfish floating past.

She put her hand on the pillow where Julie had slept her last. Ellen's heart tightened, and she closed her eyes. Grief poured over her in waves. *Stop this,* she told herself. *You're making it worse!*

Instantly angry at herself, she pulled a tissue from her sweater pocket, dabbed away her tears, and turned away from the bed.

"That won't help anyone," she announced to the empty room. Instead of indulging in her emotions, she should be cataloguing the furniture for the estate-sale company. At least that would be productive.

She made her way to the bilious yellow chair by the bed, but before she could sit, she had to move a tasseled footstool and set aside so many beribboned pillows that she doubted anyone had ever sat here before. No one would ever guess this had been the bedroom of a grown woman, not even her own mother.

Finally seated, Ellen rested the agenda on her knee and started writing, reading aloud as she went. "Purple-upholstered bed, yellow chair, red chair, huge dresser, large purple wardrobe —" Her gaze fell on the footstool she'd moved out of the way. It was covered in a cow print and decorated with ornate hot-pink fringe. It was hideous, yet she had to smile. *You did love chaos, didn't you, Julie?*

A wheezing sound made Ellen look toward the door. Yoda-like Chuffy stood just inside the room, staring at her, his tongue hanging out of the side of his mouth, a tuft of thin hair drooping limply over his head and covering one of his bulging eyes. She'd never seen an uglier Chihuahua, although she had to admit, this one had a lot of personality. For the past week, for reasons she had yet to fathom, he'd decided she was an okay person and had started following her wherever she went.

He wagged his tiny tail now, shivering under his yellow sweater. The poor animal was almost bald, his pink skin visible through his thin white hair. If it weren't for the knitted sweaters Kristen dressed him in every morning, Ellen was pretty sure he would have frozen to death long ago.

"What do you think?" she asked him. "Should I bother to catalogue the things in here for the estate sale, or just write it all off as a donation?"

His tail wagged harder, and he came to stand in front of her. Once there, he looked up at her, over his shoulder at the bed, and then back at her.

She couldn't say no to those soulful brown eyes. "You want up, do you?" She set aside her agenda and picked him up, surprised when he snuggled against her. He was so tiny that she felt as if she should handle him like a piece of valuable china, and when he leaned his head on her chest, she couldn't help but return the hug ever so carefully.

She placed him in the center of the bed, adjusting his little sweater so it covered him as much as possible. He wagged his tail gratefully, then curled up against a small pillow covered in orange faux fur. As he settled in, he beamed at Ellen as if he expected her to join him, his thin tail beating against the colorful quilt.

She didn't approve of having animals in the house, especially on the furniture, but this poor creature, with his hair loss and skin issues, his oddly crooked teeth (the few he had left), and those ridiculously long-lashed and pleading brown eyes, deserved a modicum of comfort, at least. "Poor baby." She patted him until he gave a contented sigh and settled down, closing his eyes for a much-needed nap.

She went to collect her agenda, her gaze moving to the window. Large elm and oak trees danced in the winter wind, the sky a weird bright gray. A dream catcher hung from the window latch, the red crystals on the bottom fringe sparkling where they caught the light from the lamps.

Ellen unhooked the dream catcher and held it up, admiring the glittering gems. *If only they could really stop disturbing dreams.*

She grimaced and returned the dream catcher to its spot. Try as she might, she couldn't stop thinking about her dream of Julie. *It was just a dream, nothing more,* Ellen told herself yet again. It was sad she had to keep reminding herself of that, but it helped, so she continued doing it. *Real or not, at least I got to say some things I've been wanting to say for a long, long time.*

She turned away from the window and wandered around the room, trailing her fingers over the remnants of Julie's last few weeks — a book about auras left open on a nightstand, a half-empty box of tissues, a pair of tennis shoes kicked aside beside a chair.

So many things of Julie's, all left to Kristen. *But nothing for me. I just wanted a letter — something I could hold. A sign you'd thought about me too.*

Her throat tightened, and she turned away from the bed. She hadn't found one written note or card with her name on it. *And no red cube, either.*

She almost rolled her eyes at the way she'd held on to the idea of that silly red cube. And yet her mind stubbornly lingered on her dream, replaying that conversation over and over in a seemingly endless loop. Even now, if she closed her eyes, she could see Julie's face as she —

Ellen opened her eyes and frowned. "Stop that," she muttered to herself. "It was just a dream."

Chuffy, who'd fallen asleep snuggled against the small pillow, jerked awake at her sharp words and was now staring at her in confusion.

"Go back to sleep," she told him. "I was just trying to keep myself from indulging in Dove Pond ridiculousness."

He obediently laid his head back on the pillow but watched her anxiously, as if afraid of another outburst.

"Don't worry. I'm not going crazy." Yet. But if she did, it was because she'd tried one of Ava Dove's ridiculous teas to begin with.

Besides, if local rumors were to be believed, Ava had played fast and loose with her "abilities" and had caused her sister Sarah some sort of harm. Ellen didn't know exactly what had happened, because she wasn't looped into the town gossip chain, thank goodness. What little she did know, she'd overheard in bits and pieces while standing in line at the post office this morning, but it seemed that everyone was in an uproar.

Which wasn't surprising, of course. People who believed in talking books and magical teas were destined to live with disappointment and crushed hopes. Shrugging, Ellen glanced at her wristwatch and then frowned.

Kristen should have come home by now. Ellen pulled her phone from her pocket, her thumb hovering. But after a moment, she set it on the bed. For a glorious while, she and Kristen had been getting to know each other, which had been deeply rewarding. But since the mural incident, Kristen had given Ellen nothing but frosty silence, barely answering when she spoke, which had left Ellen feeling equal parts lonely and guilty.

*We need to get away from here and start over.* The sooner they put this house on the market and got out of this weird little town, the better. Who knew? Maybe Ava's latest mistake, whatever it was, would finally peel the blinders from Kristen's eyes and she'd see the Doves and this strange town for what — and who — they really were.

Restless, Ellen opened the wardrobe and began to sort items into piles for boxing — trash, donate, store. A half hour later, she had just started to work on the nightstand drawers when the front door slammed. Chuffy sat up expectantly, wagging his tail, his gaze locked on the bedroom door as he waited for Kristen.

Ellen straightened and smoothed her hands over her face. She could hear Kristen talking to the dogs who'd been sleeping near the doorway, waiting on her. Seconds later, there was a low rumble as Kristen dashed up the stairs to the landing, the fluffy herd following.

Ellen stepped into the hallway and forced herself to smile. "There you are! I was hoping you'd be home soon."

Kristen's gaze moved past Ellen to the door she'd just come through. "What are you doing in Mom's room?" Her voice couldn't be colder.

Ellen kept her smile in place. "I'm packing things away. I've asked Mrs. Carter to come by later next week and do a walk-through. She's going to pull some comps so we can set a price for the house. Would you like to be here to —"

"No." Kristen pushed past Ellen and went into her own bedroom, the dogs following.

Ellen stifled a sigh and went to the doorway. In trying to respect Kristen's boundaries, Ellen hadn't crossed the threshold except to place washed and folded clothes on the bed. It was a pretty room and, unlike the rest of the house, was neat as a pin. Ellen liked the cool gray walls, which were the perfect background for the navy, dark gray, and red patterned duvet cover and throw pillows that decorated the bed. In one corner was a desk neatly lined with reference books, the desk chair painted a bright red. She had a very classic style, which Ellen appreciated. Not what one expected from a purple-haired, diamond-nose-stud-wearing, slouchily dressed teenager who scowled more than she smiled.

Kristen reached under her bed and pulled out a duffel bag.

"What are you doing?"

"I'm spending the night at Missy's."

"Tonight? It's a school night."

"We're going to study. We have a physics quiz tomorrow." Kristen paused, her gaze moving past Ellen to the hallway. "Where's Chuffy?"

"He's on your mother's bed."

Surprise flickered over Kristen's face, although she didn't say anything else.

"Do you want some dinner before you leave? We can heat up some of the lasagna I made yesterday. You barely touched it, so there's a lot —"

"No, thank you."

Ellen watched as Kristen added a T-shirt and a pair of blue jeans to her bag, then zipped it closed.

Floofy, Dangus, and Luffy jumped up as Kristen picked up her duffel bag. Her face softened as she looked down at them. "You guys can't come with me this time. Sorry."

They wagged their tails, looking at her

hopefully, as if they believed that if they were good enough, cute enough, she might take them with her.

It irked Ellen that she felt as if she was doing the same thing, hoping that if she was pleasant enough, nice enough, sweet enough, Kristen might give her a little pat too.

Kristen's phone jangled, and she pulled it out of her back pocket and glanced at it. "That's Missy. I've got to go." Kristen brushed past her and hurried down the hallway.

Ellen followed, trailing behind the dogs. It was all so frustrating. Would she ever have a relationship with her granddaughter? *I wish there really was a red cube.* "Kristen, wait."

Kristen paused at the top of the stairs, one hand on the railing. "What?"

Ellen came closer. She was going to ask if Kristen wanted to help go through Julie's room, but when Ellen opened her mouth, other words tumbled out. She listened, shocked, as she asked in a voice that wasn't quite her own, "I'd like to see the red cube."

Kristen froze in place, her gaze locking with Ellen's.

*She thinks I've lost my mind. Oh God, why did I ask that?* "Never mind. It's ridiculous. I just —"

"Who told you about that?"

*What?* Ellen blinked. "It's . . . it's real?"

"You haven't spoken to Mom in years, so she couldn't have told you. And I know I've never mentioned it either." Kristen's gaze narrowed with suspicion. "Who told you?"

*Oh God. I can't believe this.* Ellen spread her hands, which were as empty as her mind was full. "It's . . . I don't know what . . ." She took a steadying breath. "Someone told me about it. I — What is it?"

Kristen grimaced. "Years ago, Mom and I had a fight and . . . sheesh. I might as well show you. It'll be faster." She walked past Ellen back to her bedroom, the dogs following.

Ellen trailed behind, her heart thudding wildly.

Kristen threw her duffel bag on the bed, opened her closet, and pulled out a brightly colored cardboard box. She carried it to the bed and set it down.

Trying to calm her ragged breath, Ellen eyed the box. It was painted with roses and rainbows, and someone had glued a set of red glitter alien antennae to the lid. "I sense your mother's touch."

"One hundred percent Julie Foster." A smile flicked over Kristen's face and then disappeared as she opened the box and set the lid to one side. "This is my Life After box."

"Life after?"

"That's what Mom called it. 'Life After' just means 'life after Mom's gone.' "

"Oh. A memory box." She was astonished to see that it was filled almost to the top.

"I guess. We made it together. She put a lot of thought into it."

A sudden pang of envy pinched Ellen's heart, quickly followed by guilt. *How can I be jealous of Kristen's relationship with Julie? What is wrong with me?* Ellen pushed her negative thoughts away and moved closer to the bed. Inside the box were scrapbooks, a wadded-up T-shirt, a painted ceramic dog, several photos in frames, small plastic boxes of mementos, five or six thumb drives on gaudy key chains, and a number of other items.

Kristen dug into one corner and pulled out a handcrafted tissue box cover made of cheap plastic decorated with yarn. Each of the four sides was covered with a Christmas image — holly, a tree, a star, and a stocking.

Kristen handed it to Ellen.

"This is the red cube?" She turned it this way and that. "It's not even red."

"Parts of it are." Kristen shrugged. "Mom

called it the red cube, so it's the red cube."

How was this box supposed to help Ellen understand her granddaughter? Ellen looked at each of the decorations, trying to see some meaning in the pictures, some —

Kristen made an exasperated sound and took the cube. She turned it over, and there on the bottom, in a duct-tape pocket, was a piece of folded notebook paper. Kristen pulled it out. "These were the rules Mom and I set for each other."

*Oh my God. Julie said I needed to read this. And here it is.* It was suddenly hard to swallow. Aware that Kristen was watching her, Ellen forced a weak smile. "Not many kids get to set rules for their parents to follow."

"We didn't set rules for each other." Kristen handed the paper to Ellen. "We set rules for ourselves."

Ellen took the notepaper. It was slightly dirty and very wrinkled, like something a parent might find at the bottom of a child's backpack. She unfolded the notepaper.

I, Julie Foster, do hereby promise to do the following:

I will take my medication and continue my therapy. It's better to have a medicated mother than an unmedicated one.

I will make the most of my strengths

and lessen my weaknesses.

I will listen to Kristen when she makes suggestions on how to better my life even if those suggestions are annoying things like eating, sleeping more, or taking vitamins.

I will encourage Kristen to fly free and become who she is meant to be.

I will never, ever, ever, ever question Kristen's decisions unless I perceive something to be dangerous.

I will make sure Kristen knows without question that I love her and accept her for who she is, as she is.

"These are pretty big things." Ellen wondered why she felt every one of them said more about her relationship with Julie than about Julie's relationship with Kristen.

"My rules are on the other side." Kristen's phone went off again and she pulled it back out and began texting.

Ellen turned the paper over.

I, Kristen Foster, do hereby promise to do the following:

I will never lie to Mom.

I will try to keep from being too teen when Mom asks legitimate questions about where I am or what I'm going to do.

I will admit there are legitimate questions.

I will help around the house without being asked, especially when Mom's dealing with her down cycles.

I will make sure Mom knows I love her and accept her for who she is, as she is.

Ellen stared at the paper. When she looked at the things Julie and Kristen had promised, it explained exactly what they wanted and needed from each other. Acceptance, love, and trust. *Wasn't I giving those things to Kristen already?* Somehow, Ellen doubted Julie would think so.

She folded the paper back into its square and returned it to Kristen. "Thank you for sharing that."

Kristen returned it to its pocket and dropped the cube back into her memory box. "No problem. Now, if you don't mind, I've got to go."

She returned the box to the closet, grabbed her duffel bag, and left, Ellen following, already feeling lonelier even as her mind buzzed over the realization that the red cube existed.

Kristen stopped on the top step and

looked at the dogs standing at her feet, their tails all wagging hopefully. "The dogs sleep in my room at night. Since I'll be gone —" She stopped, obviously concerned.

"I'll take them out one last time and then let them in your room to sleep. I'll also make sure they get their breakfast in the morning. I've seen you do it enough that I'm pretty sure I can figure it out."

A ghost of a smile touched Kristen's mouth, gratitude flickering in her hazel eyes before she headed downstairs. "Thank you."

"We'll talk when you get back," Ellen called, her words drowned out by the thunder of Kristen's tennis shoes on the old wooden stairs and the click-clack of the dog herd.

Ellen stayed at the head of the stairs, listening as Kristen told the dogs to be good and then shut the front door loudly behind her.

A moment later, her car pulled out of the driveway.

Ellen realized she was holding her breath, and she let it out in a long sigh. Her gaze turned back to Kristen's bedroom.

There really was a red cube.

And it had provided exactly what Julie had said it would. *It wasn't a dream at all. I really and truly talked to Julie.*

Ellen was so excited, she didn't know what to do. She wanted to jump and yell and scream and cry and laugh — all of them at once. How had something as simple as a cup of tea allowed her to speak to Julie? Ellen couldn't begin to understand it, although she supposed she didn't need to. It had happened and that was that.

*Oh my God, I have more tea. I can see Julie again.*

The thought stole Ellen's breath.

Heart pounding wildly, she hurried down the stairs, little Chuffy joining her as if he knew something exciting was about to happen. The other dogs jumped up as she and Chuffy came spinning around the steps and hurried toward the kitchen.

Seconds later, she was standing at the counter, holding the small tin, the dogs watching her from the doorway as if they expected her to burst into flames.

She tugged off the lid, the soft aroma of peppermint, chamomile, and something else wafting out. She stared inside, her heart pounding. It was a small canister, so there wasn't much left, enough for maybe two cups. But that was okay. She'd get Ava to make her some more.

Ellen's heart fluttered at the thought. *I can see Julie as often as I want. Really see her. I can talk to her and get her help with Kristen, too.*

Ellen closed the lid and then hugged the canister to her chest, the dogs staring at her as if she'd lost her mind. Grinning, she bent and patted each one, giving Chuffy an especially gentle ear rub. "After dinner, I'm going to make myself a cup of very special tea, and then we'll all go to bed."

Soon, Ellen would be talking to Julie. Too excited to stand still, she gave an excited, very un-Ellen-like hop and spun in a dizzying circle. *Julie, I'm coming!*

# CHAPTER 17
## ELLEN

Ellen had warmed up soup for dinner but had been too excited to eat more than a few spoonfuls. She toyed with the idea of going to bed immediately but worried she was too awake for the tea to work as well as it should. So instead, she took her time rinsing the dishes and putting them in the dishwasher. Then she fed the dogs and settled in to watch a documentary on the building of the Golden Gate Bridge, although she was way too excited to pay attention.

She kept one eye on the clock, and the second it hit 9 p.m., she sprung off the couch, turned off the TV, took the dogs out one last time, and then — oddly inclined to giggle — made herself a cup of her precious tea. Remembering how much-too-short her last visit with Julie had been, she used far more tea leaves this time, hoping a stronger dose would give them ample time for a real talk.

As soon as her tea was ready, she carried it upstairs, careful not to spill a drop. She put the cup on her bedside table, then settled the dogs into Kristen's room for the night. Ellen was a little concerned about Chuffy, who seemed even more shivery than usual, so she made sure to tuck a blanket around him before closing the door.

She put on her best nightgown, sat on the edge of her bed, and drank the tea, using her finger to capture the last few drops that clung to the sides of the cup. That done, she slipped under the covers and turned off the light.

And now, here she was, in bed and staring at the ceiling, waiting impatiently to fall asleep at a ridiculously early time. She snuggled down, closed her eyes, and waited, rehearsing what she'd say when she saw Julie again. She had to fight the urge to crack open her eyes every few minutes to check the clock on the corner table as it ticked away the minutes.

The minutes turned into a half hour, and Ellen tried to still her jittery thoughts, stirring restlessly. *Why hasn't the tea kicked in yet?*

*I'm too excited. I need to calm down.*

The minutes ticked by. Another five.

Another ten.

She sighed and turned on her side, tugging the blankets around her. *Maybe if I breathe deep and slow, I'll fall asleep.*

She took a long, slow breath in. Then one out.

Then another. And another.

But when she next peeked at the clock, she was chagrined to see that only seven minutes had crept by and she was every bit awake as before. *Oh dear. What if I stay awake and the tea wears off?*

She flipped onto her back, hoping a new position might help. *There. I'll empty my mind and imagine I'm floating on a cloud.*

But emptying her mind proved impossible. Thoughts and hopes fought for attention. She couldn't believe she was going to get to see Julie. Talk to her, *really* talk to her this time. *If I can fall asleep. If I don't, then —*

"Oh, stop it!" she told herself, frustrated. She tossed off the covers and stared at the ceiling. *I need more tea.* She sat up and reached for the light switch —

"It's about time you got here."

Startled, Ellen looked over her shoulder.

Just as before, Julie sat in one of the chairs by the window, a pool of blue light encircling her. This time she was barefoot and wore a pair of paint-splattered coveralls and

408

a faded red Mickey Mouse T-shirt. Her purple-dyed hair was more mussed than ever, and a paintbrush was tucked over one ear.

Ellen pressed a trembling hand to her mouth. *Oh my God. It worked.*

Julie cocked an eyebrow. "What took you so long?"

*It's her. It's really, really her.*

Julie chuckled. "Yes, it's me. Ava's tea does the trick. It would have worked a half hour ago if you'd let it. You've been fighting it for a while now."

"Sorry. I couldn't fall asleep. I was thinking too much." Heart thumping, Ellen rose and automatically grabbed her robe, her slippers forgotten as she hurried to join Julie. It was hard not to run, which was so unlike herself that Ellen had to smile. She just wanted to be as close to her daughter as possible.

She stopped just short of Julie. "I want to hug you."

Julie's expression softened. She held up her hand so Ellen could see how the moon gleamed through it. "I wish we could."

"Me too." Ellen pulled her robe closer and tried to knot it, but her hands just fumbled with the long ties. Giving up, she sunk into the chair across from Julie, unable to look away, devouring the sight of her daughter. "I can't believe it's really you."

Julie held her arms wide. "Here am I."

Yes, here she was. "I'm so glad we can talk. The last time we were here, I —" Ellen winced. "I didn't think it was really you. I thought it was some sort of a dream."

"I'm here, and so are you." Julie smiled as her gaze flickered over Ellen's robe. "You and that robe." She shook her head. "You always had the fanciest pajamas." Julie leaned back in her chair. "How's Kristen?"

"You already know."

Julie sighed, her breath faintly visible, as if she were sitting in a pool of icy air. "I do. I just wanted to hear your side of it."

Ellen shifted in her chair. "There are no sides."

"It looks as if there are, and you and Kristen are on opposite ones."

Ellen grimaced, and she suddenly realized her shoulders ached. She rubbed one of them. In Raleigh, she got a massage every week to get rid of the tension she carried in her shoulders. What she'd give for a massage now.

"Call Lisa Tilden," Julie said. "She lives in Dove Pond and is a masseuse at Heaven Day Spa outside of Asheville. Her number is on the fridge."

Ellen dropped her hand from her shoulder. "It's disconcerting you can read my mind. It makes me wonder why we're even talking."

"If you could read my mind, too, then we'd just sit here and think at each other, but you can't, so we're going to have to talk. Which, I might add, was never one of your strong points." Julie tilted her head to one side, her gaze locked on Ellen. "So. What's going on with you and Kristen? I'd like to hear your side of it."

"You already know, but —" Ellen shrugged. "For a week or so, we were doing well — better than well. We were getting to know each other a little here and there. Having some nice talks. Not many, but enough. But then I . . ." Ellen's voice quavered, which surprised her. She really hated that she'd messed up her relationship with her granddaughter. "I made a horrible mistake."

"The mural."

"It has to be removed; I stand by that decision. But I should have spoken to her about it first. I didn't realize what it meant to her, and now she's furious with me."

"She told you she loved it. I heard her."

"I know, I know. I just didn't understand how much and I . . ." Ellen looked down at her hands, which were tight around the

411

arms of her chair. She released the arms and tucked her hands in her lap. "I made a mistake. There. Now I've admitted as much to you both. I had no idea you'd painted her into that mural as Wonder Woman. It never dawned on me to look."

"She's my Wonder Kristen." Julie's tender smile gleamed as brightly as the light around her.

"I know that now," Ellen said sharply, wincing at her own tone. Her time with Julie was too precious to waste arguing. Ellen's shoulders slumped. "I have to find a way to make it up to her."

"She's tough. When she makes up her mind about something, it can be difficult to get her to change it."

Ellen sighed. "Why didn't you paint that mural on a canvas rather than a wall so we could take it with us?"

"Because when I painted it, I was in the 'hey, I'm going to live forever' stage of my too-short life."

Ellen had to admit she understood that. "I think about death a lot more now than I did when I was your age. We never see our mortality coming when we're young, do we?" She absently braided her robe ties. "Kristen and I barely know each other. That makes everything difficult because we've got

412

some massive decisions to make." Which was totally Julie's fault, although Ellen hated to say it out loud.

"You might as well," Julie said into the silence. "I heard you think it."

Ellen's face heated. "Will you stop that! It's unnerving."

Julie gave her a sheepish grin. "Sorry."

Ellen had once seen a movie where aliens had taken over the bodies of young children. The father of one of those children had imagined a brick wall in an effort to keep them from reading his mind. *If I could just —*

"Mom!" Julie laughed again, the delightful, boisterous laugh that was uniquely hers. "Stop that! It won't work." Still smiling, she shifted her gaze from Ellen to the window where the trees were waving in the moonlight.

Ellen looked at her daughter's profile, trying to memorize it as best she could. Every moment felt precious, and Ellen wanted to soak them all in and keep them forever. *Which isn't true. I can get more tea.*

"Maybe," Julie murmured as if to herself. *Maybe what?*

Julie turned to Ellen. "I was going to call you on your birthday last year."

Ellen's heart lurched.

"I had the phone in my hand and everything. I don't know why I didn't." Julie's sigh made the blue light around her shimmer. "I've always felt there was a huge divide between us, and that the bridge over it was cracked and weak. I worried it might come crashing down if one of us tried to cross it, and we'd lose that last connection, bad as it was. It felt safer to just leave it alone."

"That's an interesting way to put it. And accurate too."

Julie's eyes glimmered softly. "You never called me either."

Ellen slowly nodded. "I almost called you hundreds of times. But I was afraid, too . . . although I don't know of what exactly. Being rejected, I suppose. Of the 'bridge,' as you called it, breaking while I was trying to cross it. It all seems stupid now. I should have called."

"We were both stupid." Julie leaned her head against the chair cushion. "I thought I had time. I'd always planned on us making up. I just kept putting it off."

"I told myself I was giving you space to figure things out. That one day you'd wake up and realize how sad it was that we weren't on speaking terms, and you'd reach out. I was waiting for that moment, and my pride kept whispering that it would be sweeter if you called me rather than the other way around, so . . ." Ellen's voice caught in her throat, and she swiped away a tear. "I wish with all my heart I hadn't waited. I love you, Julie. I always have."

"I know." Julie's eyes looked shiny, as if she was also fighting tears. "I love you too," she whispered. "I never stopped."

"Who knew that love can be just as stubborn as anger?"

"Maybe more so." Julie pulled her feet into her chair and wrapped her arms around her knees. "You found the red cube, so you know what she wants from you — acceptance, respect, and trust."

"I trust her. Or I do as much as anyone would trust a teenager." When Julie rolled her eyes, Ellen said impatiently, "I can't just stand by and let her decide every last facet of her life. She's too young and inexperienced to know what she's doing. She'll just get hurt."

"She might. But it's unlikely. Mom, if you wrap her in gauze, you'll just smother her."

Ellen frowned. "You think that's what I did to you."

"And still would, if you could reach me." Julie's eyes twinkled. "Stop looking so upset. I'm glad you came back to visit, but we have a lot of ground to cover this time.

There are some things you need to know. Do you remember when I told you Kristen isn't like me? She doesn't enjoy adventures and excitement and raw emotion. She likes schedules, hugs, comfort, home — all the things I ran away from." Julie's smile flickered back into place. "Despite my best efforts to convince her otherwise, she's all common sense and tradition."

Ellen gave a wry laugh. "She doesn't look very traditional, what with that purple hair and that nose piercing."

"She only dyed her hair because I dyed mine. It's something we did together. Mom, Kristen isn't me, but she's still a teenager. She's still figuring out who and what she is."

"I know a few things about teenagers. You fought growing up every step of the way."

Julie wrinkled her nose. "I was the worst teenager ever."

"Nonsense," Ellen said. "I'm sure there were worse. I can think of a few dozen, right off the top of my head." She smiled. "Although most of them are from TV."

Julie chuckled. "You have a sense of humor. Why didn't I notice that before?"

"Because I never showed it. I was too busy trying to be right during every argument." It wasn't easy to admit her flaws, but she knew that now was the time. "Even when you were young, you were so confident. You thought you knew everything and that I was the stupidest woman alive."

"I didn't think you were stupid. You were usually right, irritatingly so." Julie eyed Ellen for a moment. "But I never felt like I knew you. You're sort of a mystery woman, even now."

"Me?" Ellen couldn't hide her surprise.

"Every therapist I've ever had has asked about you. About your childhood, why you are who you are. And I could never answer their questions."

"You know enough." Ellen untangled her plaited robe ties and draped them over one knee.

"I know your dad left when you were young and that you and your mom suffered financially, but you've never really said more than that."

"There wasn't anything more to tell." Ellen moved restlessly. That was the last thing she wanted to talk about. "Can we talk about Kristen? Since our fight, she's been distant and —"

"Not yet." Julie's gaze was locked on Ellen. "I want to know about you. About your childhood. About what made you."

"There's nothing to tell." When Julie

417

didn't reply, Ellen sighed sharply. "Fine. Your grandmother died when you were three, but until then, we had Christmas dinner every year at her house. I know you don't remember, but she always burned the turkey." It had been a long time since Ellen had thought of her mother. If she closed her eyes, she could see her mother's thin face, always folded in worry, deep lines between her eyes. *She earned those lines, too. The hard way.*

"You loved her."

"Of course I did. She worked two jobs to help me pay for my first year of college. I managed to do it on my own after that." Ellen shrugged. "I'm sure I've mentioned that before."

"No, you didn't." Julie tilted her head to one side. "What about your dad? You rarely talk about him."

"Why should I?" Ellen asked impatiently. "He left. There's nothing more to say. Julie, we're on borrowed time here. Can we focus on Kristen?"

"It's almost as if he never existed."

"My father was what he was, and then he left. We did very well without him. Better, even."

"Better without him? What did he do to deserve that?"

Deserve? Ellen dropped her gaze to her robe ties. She slowly smoothed them over her knee, which kept her from tracing the faint line of a scar that ran across the bottom of her chin, out of sight but always present. There were so many things she could say about what her father "deserved."

She could explain how he would go through horrible mood swings, exacerbated by a steady stream of vodka. There were times, few and far between, when he was funny and charming and oh, how she'd loved him when he was like that. Too much, maybe, because of the giddy relief she and her mother had felt whenever he wasn't in a bad mood.

But most nights, he'd drink, sinking into a black hole that made him violent and unstable. His actions became progressively worse as he aged. Over the years, he'd destroyed more family dinners than she could count. He'd scream at her mother, who was too afraid of him to speak back and would always answer his demands in a soothing, begging-for-forgiveness tone of voice, *David, please don't* . . . Ellen's jaw tightened.

She would never, ever beg for anything. Not even if —

"Oh, Mom . . ."

Ellen looked up and realized that Julie's eyes had grown wide. *Oh God, she heard all of that.* Ellen flushed. "It's nothing."

"That's not nothing. You never told me any of that."

Guilt, deep and acidic, raced through Ellen. "It's in the past, all of it."

Julie eyed Ellen with wonder and sympathy. "I never knew. And I never asked, either."

"You had other things on your mind," Ellen said sharply. "Like what a horrible parent I was."

Julie winced. "You weren't horrible. But you weren't easy, either. It would have helped if you'd communicated more."

"I did my best." No one knew better than she that some things were safer kept inside where they couldn't hurt anyone.

"Wow. That's bleak." Julie tucked her hair behind her ear. "Everyone has a reason for being the way they are, don't they? I knew that, but it never dawned on me that you had a past. You were just my mother. I should have looked beyond that."

Ellen didn't know what to say. Her instincts urged her to slam the lid closed on this conversation, but her heart, which felt painfully exposed, warned her not to give in to her usual reactions. *Share,* it whispered.

*Stop being so harsh.*

It took a bit of a struggle, but Ellen managed to say, "I was taught not to be overemotional and to leave the past in the past."

"Oh, Mom. Your past isn't a memento you can store in a box. You carry it with you, everywhere you go. It's there, Mom. It's in your irritation with anything you consider disorderly, in your determination to never fail, and your need to control everything and everyone."

"I sound like quite the prize," Ellen said drily.

Julie's smile flashed. "You're not bad. But it makes you seem stern and abrupt, which, to a teenager, feels heavy and judgmental."

"I try not to be either of those things. But, for the record, I'd like to point out that I'm not the only one who hid a difficult part of my life. It must have been terrifying when you found out you were bipolar. You were alone then. I wish you'd told me."

"I was stupidly stubborn, too. I still am, I've been told." Julie leaned back in her chair, unfolding herself and stretching her legs out so they rested on the ottoman. "But I did okay. Once you and Kristen understand each other, you'll do okay too."

"You really believe that?"

"I do. But you've got to be more open.

Instead of acting like you've got all the answers, let Kristen know that you've got worries and fears, too, just like she does."

Ellen swallowed. "I'm not used to talking about my feelings. But I'll try."

"Don't try, Mom. Do."

*If it were only that easy.* "Right. Now, about Kristen. I get the feeling that something is off, and it's more than the mural incident." Ellen noticed that Julie didn't look surprised. "You know something."

"I do, and you'd better be prepared."

Ellen's chest tightened. "She's going to run away." Ellen couldn't think of the days after Julie had run off without her chest aching as if her heart had been newly ripped out. She was deeply relieved when Julie shook her head.

"I've already told you that Kristen will never run away. She's not an adventurer. But she *will* fight to get her own way. She has a plan, Mom. One that will keep her here in Dove Pond."

Which was exactly what Ellen had feared. "Will it work?"

"It might."

*Oh no.* Ellen wet her dry lips. "I see. And if it doesn't?"

"Then she'll have no option but to go to Raleigh with you."

"Then I need to block this plan of hers."

Julie flicked an impatient look at Ellen. "Do you? If Kristen's plan fails and she ends up in Raleigh, she's going to be miserable."

"At first, I'm sure. But she'll make friends, and then things will be okay."

"She doesn't make friends easily. She never has. She's like you in that respect."

"I have friends. Not many, but enough."

"Name one."

"Oh, Julie, for the love of heaven. There's . . ." Ellen shifted in her chair. "I — Oh! Denise Radcliffe. She and I've been friends ever since we worked together at Porter, Porter, and Turner years ago."

"Exchanging Christmas cards is not friendship. It's acquaintanceship."

"We're still friends."

"When's the last time you called her?"

Ellen shrugged. "I don't have time for such things. I've been very busy."

"Right," Julie said in a flat tone. "Kristen takes great pride in her independence. She loves order, calmness, organization, and control — does that sound like anyone you know?"

"That sounds like . . . me?"

"It is a wonderful thing," Julie said. "She has all your best qualities, but they're balanced out with a few of mine. In many ways, she's the best of both of us."

Deeply touched, Ellen didn't know what to say. She and Julie had never been able to talk like this, and it felt awkwardly new and totally wonderful. "She is a remarkable child. You were doing a fantastic job of raising her."

Julie's gaze rested on her mother's face. "Thank you. And thank you for putting up with me all those years ago. I didn't make it easy. Now I have Kristen, I understand that."

They smiled at each other, and it was only the pressing knowledge that time was running out that made Ellen break the moment. "So. What's Kristen's big plan?"

"Oh yes. That." Julie splayed her hands on her knees. "She is looking for her father."

Ellen's mouth dropped open. Good Lord, she hadn't thought of that. She instantly traversed a line of scenarios, none of them good. "Where is he? I assumed he was off . . . Lord knows where, out of touch, as usual."

"He's here in Dove Pond. Kristen wants to find him so she can convince him to let her live with him."

Good God. This was far more serious than Ellen had expected. "You said she wants to find him. Dove Pond isn't that big of a place."

"He's here, but . . ." Julie waved a hand. "It's complicated."

Ellen knew that hand wave, a rather dramatic "let the world sort it out."

Her unease grew. "Explain 'complicated'?"

Julie looked away, newly interested in the tree swaying outside the window. "It's possible — likely — she doesn't know who he is."

*What?* "You never told Kristen who her father is? And he lived here, in town?"

"There was no reason to. We didn't need him."

"I see." Ellen pressed her fingertips to her left temple, trying to work her way through this maze of Julie's making. "How long has she been working on this plan of hers?"

"Several weeks. Missy and Josh are helping her. Kristen thinks she's found a clue, but she's on the wrong track." Julie stuck her feet out in front of her and wiggled her bare toes. "There's a lot she doesn't know."

Which explained the increased flurry of text messages, as well as Kristen's distracted state. As much as Ellen hated hearing it, this was useful information. "You never told her his name?"

"No. I didn't introduce them because . . ."

Julie glanced at Ellen from under her lashes. "He doesn't know about her."

"Doesn't know? Julie, that's — Good God!" Ellen dropped back in her seat, too shocked to think clearly.

"I did it to protect Kristen. And me too."

"But . . . don't you think she deserves to know her own father?"

"Under normal circumstances, I'd say yes."

"What do you mean, 'under normal circumstances'?" Ellen asked, alarmed. "He's not violent, is he?"

"Mom, no! Not at all."

"That's a relief." A great relief. Ellen pressed a hand to her heart, where it had thudded hard against her chest. "What sort of person is he, then?"

"He's nice. Really nice." Julie pulled her feet back into her chair and hugged her knees once more. "I just didn't want the bother. Kristen and I didn't need anyone else. We're a family, the two of us."

"So you kept Kristen and her father apart all these years for no other reason than that you wanted her for yourself. Julie, that's rather selfish."

Julie's eyebrows lowered. "It sounds really bad when you say it that way, but I only wanted what was best for Kristen."

"Did you?"

Julie frowned sharply. "I was trying to protect her. I wasn't sure he'd welcome her into his life, and I didn't want her to have to face rejection."

"Julie! You could have told him without Kristen even knowing. Then, if he wasn't willing to take on the responsibility of having a child, you'd have reason not to tell her. You never gave him that option."

"I suppose." Julie's gaze dropped to where her hands were clasped together. "Like I said, it's complicated."

That was an understatement. Ellen's thoughts traveled from one what-if to another. What a horrible set of circumstances. *And poor Kristen! What she must be going through.* "Julie, Kristen deserves to know her father."

"What if he doesn't want to be her father? She'd be hurt."

"It's possible. But, if he does accept her, then . . ." *Oh no.* She pressed her hand to her mouth.

Julie nodded. "You see?"

Ellen saw all too well. "If he chose to, he could challenge the will and cut me out of her life." Oh, she would still see Kristen. But Ellen would only see her granddaughter here and there, and they'd never have a chance to develop a real relationship. *This is horrible.*

"Now you get it. It's not worth the risk." Julie said it as if that justified her decisions.

But did it? Ellen thought about her own father, about how mean he could be and how relieved she'd been when he'd finally left and hadn't come back. But some days, at odd times, she also remembered the sweetness of his laugh and how charming he could be when he was sober. Those days were still priceless.

She wondered if she'd have traded the good days away just to be spared the bad ones, and her fingers found their way to the half-moon scar under her chin. "You're sure this man is a good person?"

"He's wonderful," Julie said simply. "But Kristen doesn't need a father. She needs you, Mom. But you two have to come to some sort of agreement, or it's not going to work."

"It's not that easy, sweetheart, and you know it." Ellen wished she had her agenda nearby. Writing things down always helped her think. "Where is Kristen in this plan of hers?"

"She found three potential candidates. So far, she's eliminated two. That's left a guy by the name of Jack Lind who does property management."

"Is he her father?"

Julie shook her head. "I dated him years and years ago, but it was way before I had Kristen."

"So who *is* the father?"

"What are you going to do if I tell you?"

That was the question, wasn't it? Ellen leaned back in her chair, her heart aching anew. It was funny, but she already knew what she was going to do, and she hated it. "Kristen's adrift without you, Julie. She needs every anchor I can give her. If her father's a great guy, like you say he is, then I'm going to do what's right for her. I'm going to tell him the truth."

"And if he invites her to live with him?"

Ellen blinked back tears. "I'll worry about that if and when it happens."

Julie's eyes never left her mother's face. "You could lose her."

"You think I don't know that?" Ellen asked sharply. "Kristen's already lost you. If, in any way, I can make life easier for her, then I owe it to her to do it."

Julie stared at Ellen. "Wow. That's . . . that's not what I thought you'd say."

Every bone in Ellen's body ached. "Believe me, it's not easy. But you said I had to trust her to make her own decisions. I guess . . . I can't believe I'm saying this, but that's what I'm going to do."

Julie scrunched up her nose. "I should tell you who he is, then. I have to say, you're much stronger than I was. You're doing what I should have done, but couldn't."

"Yes, well, don't think I'm just going to hand her over. No matter what happens, I'm going to keep an eye on her. I may have to find another job and give up my home in Raleigh, but I'll make sure she's safe."

"Pinkie promise?" Julie held out her pinkie.

When Julie had been in elementary school, she'd made Ellen pinkie promise to everything. As worried as she was, Ellen had to smile. "I'd forgotten how you used to do that."

Julie's answering smile was worth millions. "A pinkie promise is a solemn vow."

Ellen held out her pinkie. "Pinkie promise, then." She dropped her hand back into her lap, wishing they could actually touch. It was with a thickened voice that she managed to say, "So. Who is he?"

Julie leaned back in her chair, clasping her hands behind her head. "He's going to be shocked when he finds out about this."

"Surely he knows it's a possibility."

"Mmmm. Maybe. Like I said, it's complicated."

*Uh-oh.* "There's that word again." Ellen frowned. "Julie?"

She shrugged. "Fine. He doesn't know he's Kristen's father because he and I never . . . "Julie waved her hand.

"That's — Julie, explain yourself. I don't understand."

"Fine. I ordered Kristen's father the way you might order a pizza. 'I'll have a double pepperoni, thin crust, hold the anchovies.' "

"What does that m—" Ellen sat up straight. "You used a *sperm donor?*"

Even bathed in blue light, Julie's cheeks were obviously flushed. "I wanted a kid, but I didn't want to put up with a father. And geez, don't look so shocked. Lots of women do it that way."

"Oh, Julie. How could you?"

"It wasn't hard. And I was careful. When I decided to have Kristen, I took my time. For three years, I lived on the cheap and saved every penny from my bartending job. I investigated the sperm route, but I hated how random it felt. There are profiles, and you just . . . click, click, click until you find one you like. They have childhood pictures and family health screenings and all sorts of things. None of them seemed . . . right, know what I mean?"

Ellen had no idea, but still stunned, she nodded anyway.

"Then I ran into this guy I used to know, and in the middle of a conversation about how we'd been broke at various times in our lives, we mentioned the crazy things we'd done to make money. That's when he told me about how much cash he'd made donating sperm to a place in Atlanta where he was going to college." Julie chuckled. "It was perfect. Like the heavens had led me to him. I thought it would be both safer and more personal if my baby's father was someone I knew at least a little. So I went to the company I'd spoken to before and went through their files. I already knew his eye and hair color, his height, his family, his college and major —" She shrugged. "All said, I knew a lot of stuff. It took a while, but I eventually figured out which donor he was, and the audio confirmed it — the donors answer survey questions like, 'Where do you want to be in ten years?' and 'How would you describe your personality?' I think they want women to feel like they know the potential donor personally, which is ironic, when you think about it." The light around Julie flared and then dimmed for a second.

"Julie!" Ellen slid forward in her seat. "You have to tell me who he is."

Julie looked at her hands, which were paler now. "You have more tea."

"Enough for another visit. I'll have Ava make more. But please, I need a name. If Kristen figures out who he is and confronts him, it could go badly."

"She . . ." Julie flickered in and out of sight, the blue light around her pulsing wildly. ". . . you know him . . . Ava . . . so be careful."

Ellen leaned forward. *"Who is he?"*

Julie opened her mouth just as the light around her flared wildly.

Ellen closed her eyes to shield them from the brightness. When she opened them, the room was dark.

Julie was gone.

"No!" Ellen stood and stared at the empty chair. *"Julie! I have to know!"*

In the growing darkness, as if from a long distance away, came a faint whisper. . . .

# CHAPTER 18
## AVA

A cold March rain pitter-pattered through the trees and tapped against the windows of the front parlor. Ava sat in a window seat, leaning against a bank of tasseled pillows, a red wool blanket tucked over her legs. When she was growing up, Momma had kept the parlor off-limits, saying it was for guests only. But Ava and Sarah had never understood this formal way of thinking, and once the house was theirs, they'd moved the stiff, antique furniture to other rooms and had invested in two well-cushioned chairs, a huge TV, a comfy couch, and a coffee table big enough for board games. After that, they spent most evenings in this room, Sarah reading her books while Ava worked on paperwork for her businesses or watched TV.

Now Ava sat here alone. She didn't think she'd ever get used to it.

*Sarah will never forgive me.* Ava tugged

the wool blanket higher, her gaze drifting over the front yard. Here and there in the garden that meandered down the sides of the front lawn, dark brown shrubs waited for the warmth of spring. It was barely six in the evening, yet Ava was already wearing her pajamas, her slippers on the floor beside the window seat. In the days since her fight with Sarah, Ava had found herself longing to go to bed and forget the world even existed.

It had been exactly two weeks and two days since Sarah had stormed out, but it felt more like a month. Ava was achingly lonely, and the house, which had always felt like home, now seemed as empty as she was.

She sighed and tugged the blanket a little closer. She'd called Sarah hundreds of times but to no avail. Sarah refused to answer. Ava had been forced to leave numerous rather rambling messages, none of which had said anything she wanted them to say.

Just saying "I'm sorry" wasn't going to be enough. But what else could she do? There had to be some way to repair their torn relationship. Some way she could earn back Sarah's trust. *But what if I can't? What if Sarah never speaks to me again?*

Ava was thoroughly battered and bruised. Seeking comfort and perhaps sympathy, over the past week she'd made the mistake of calling her other sisters, who'd staunchly supported Sarah. Even Ella, who was closest in age to Ava and was usually sympathetic, hadn't offered much in the way of comfort. Ava couldn't blame them; there was no excuse for breaking Momma's rules.

Sighing, Ava slid her toes under the pile of pillows near her feet. It had been a horrible, awful few weeks. Not only was Sarah gone, but Ava's professional reputation had been shot to heck, too. From Sofia's somber demeanor this morning, the number of canceled tea orders must be even more appalling than Ava knew. Her lawn service was normally dormant this time of the year, but people were calling to cancel their annual contracts there as well, as if Ava wasn't getting enough kicks in the shins. It felt as if the whole world was now against her.

Last night Kat and Aunt Jo had brought her dinner — a pan of Aunt Jo's famous heirloom tomato pie, some fresh-baked rolls, and a large salad. Ava had appreciated it, though she couldn't eat much of anything. It wasn't until they were leaving that Aunt Jo had turned to Ava and asked in her usual direct way, "Why on earth did you think it was a good idea to keep a secret from your own sister? You knew better than that."

Kat, looking embarrassed, had quickly interceded, hustling the older woman out the door and to her car, but the disappointment in Aunt Jo's deep brown eyes had already cut Ava to the quick.

She rested her forehead against the cool glass, looking out into the rain. Somehow, some way, she had to make things right with Sarah. *I just wish I knew h—*

Sarah's blue truck pulled into the driveway next door, the big tires splashing through puddles.

Ava sat up straighter, the blanket dropping away.

Sarah got out of her truck, rain pattering down on her raincoat. Ava could see she was wearing a bright yellow shirt and her favorite pair of leggings, which featured the covers of famous books. Water glistened on Sarah's raincoat as she reached across her seat to gather a book from the passenger side.

Ava watched wistfully as her sister went onto the porch, pausing beside a box that had her name written across it.

Sarah stood for a while, staring at the box. "Open it," Ava whispered. *"Please."*

Sarah's shoulders lifted and then dropped

with her sigh. She set her book on a porch chair and opened the box.

Inside the box were some clothes Ava had thought Sarah might need; her first copy of *Pride and Prejudice,* which Ava had bought for her from the annual library sale when she was still in middle school; a holograph bookmark of an eagle that Ava had won for Sarah at the local fair when she was thirteen; a small bottle of wheat pennies they had collected over the years and now used as a paperweight; and, most important, a long letter Ava had spent the past two days writing. Ava had poured her heart into the letter, saying everything Sarah wouldn't let her.

*Please read it. Please, please, please?*

Sarah, digging through the items, pulled out the envelope. She stared at it for a long time and then looked over to the window where Ava sat.

Ava untangled her hand from the blanket and waved. *Remember, Sarah. Don't just think of my mistakes. Remember all the good things, too.*

Sarah dropped the letter back into the box. She removed the clothes, grabbed the books, and then went inside, leaving the open box and the rest of the contents alone in the damp.

The door banged closed behind her.

Ava's disappointment pressed down on her shoulders. She closed her eyes and wondered what else she could do.

The grandfather clock in the hallway ticked away the minutes. The silence grew, and Ava, weary to the bottom of her soul, finally shoved off the blanket and wandered through the house, absently touching various pieces of furniture before ending up in the kitchen. She supposed she should make herself something to eat, but after staring into the depths of the fridge, she decided to make herself a cup of hot chocolate instead.

Outside, the skies opened up, and the heavy thrum of rain echoed off the porch roof. Ava had just pulled out the milk with a pan when a brisk knock sounded on her front door.

Ava's heart leapt. Had Sarah read the letter after all? Ava had already taken a swift step toward the door when she realized she was still holding both the milk and the pan. Muttering to herself, she set them on the counter, then hurried to the foyer.

Heart pounding, Ava threw open the door, the sound of the pouring rain rushing in.

Blake stood on the porch, dressed in his uniform, his coat and hat sparkling with rain.

His gaze flickered over her. "You're already in your pajamas."

She looked down and realized how she must look. Not only was she in her favorite two-sizes-too-big pajamas, but her hair was in a messy braid, her feet were bare, and she was sure her eyes were circled and red. "I finished work early today, so . . ." She shrugged. "What's up?"

"We need to talk."

*Just what I need, a stern lecture from a furious law enforcement officer.* But she supposed she deserved it, and so she stepped aside. "Come on in."

He walked past her, shrugged out of his wet coat and hat, and hung them on the rack. "I hope I didn't catch you at a bad time."

"Not at all. I was making some hot chocolate. Would you like some?"

"Do you have marshmallows?"

"Do I look like a novice?" She led the way from the foyer to the kitchen. "Have a seat." She nodded to the tall chairs that lined the island.

He adjusted his gun belt as he sat down, his gaze sweeping the kitchen. "I remember this kitchen from back when your mom was alive, and it looked nothing like this."

"Those dark cabinets, dark flooring, dark

440

paneled walls . . ." Ava shuddered. "I appreciate the quality of woodwork in this house, but the kitchen had disappeared under the weight of it. Sarah and I left as much of the original details in the other rooms as we could, but we declared the kitchen a free zone and never looked back." She pulled a can of powdered hot chocolate from a cabinet and set it on the countertop. "So. What's up?" She poured the milk into the pan and set it on the stove.

"I've been asked to check on you. People are worried."

Her throat tightened. She felt so alone that it hurt to accept even a kind thought. She had to swallow twice before she could speak. "I'm fine. I appreciate the concern, though."

He nodded. "I'm glad to hear it."

She pulled a spoon from a drawer and stirred the milk. "Is this one of those wellness checks I've read about?"

"Actually, no. I knew you'd be fine. I just thought you could use some cheering up."

"That's very kind of you, especially since" — she waved the spoon, a drop of milk falling to the counter — "you know."

He grinned, a lopsided smile Ava was glad Sarah wasn't nearby to witness. "Don't anoint me a saint yet. I have an ulterior motive."

"Oh?"

"I need a favor."

"Let me guess." Steam curled off the milk, so she stirred it a little more. "You want me to move to another country. That's how most people in this town feel about me right now."

"Give them some time. They'll remember all you've done for them. Right now, they're just being protective of Sarah. I'm sure you wouldn't have it any other way."

When he put it like that, Ava had to agree.

"Speaking of people behaving badly . . . I owe you an apology. I was angry and I shouldn't have said some of the things I did." He gave her a faintly sheepish grin. "We McIntyres have a temper."

"I've noticed that."

"It's not a secret. I could have handled that moment better. I know you love Sarah and would never purposefully do anything to harm her, or anyone else, for that matter. I'm sorry I blew up."

Wow. She hadn't expected that. "Thank you. But you were well within your rights to be angry. I shouldn't have given either of you that stupid tea."

He shrugged. "Fortunately for us both, I

don't have the energy to carry a grudge. When I was twenty, maybe. But not anymore."

She could relate to that. A surprisingly comfortable silence fell between them, one broken by the quiet clink of her spoon as she stirred the heating milk.

Blake crossed his arms over his chest and leaned back in his seat. "I spoke to Dylan yesterday."

"Why?"

"I figured he'd know how you were holding up. He reminded me how young you were when you made the choices you did, and what you were facing, raising Sarah. He had a lot to say." Blake flinched. "I'll save you the details, but he was brutal. He straight up called me an ass."

"That's surprising. Dylan's usually pretty mild mannered."

Blake's gaze met hers. "Not when it comes to you."

Ava flushed and busied herself, turning down the heat on the milk.

"The worst part is that he was right," Blake continued. "It's just that I have strong feelings where Sarah is concerned."

"She would say the same thing about you."

Blake shrugged. "That's the tea talking."

"Is it?" Ava put her spoon down and collected two mugs from a cabinet, stopping by the pantry for a bag of marshmallows. She returned to the stove and placed everything on the counter next to the canister of hot chocolate mix.

She stirred the gently steaming milk one more time, then filled the mugs and added the chocolate. "I'm assuming you really want marshmallows and weren't just being polite when you asked about them earlier."

"Of course. I'm not a heathen."

She smiled and added a generous pile to his mug, then slid it across the counter. "About that favor you requested. You know I'm going to say yes. I owe you and Sarah both a few hundred favors or more."

"I'm counting on it." He picked up the mug and took a sip. "Oh wow. That's good."

"That's Momma's hot chocolate recipe. She began with whole milk, then added powdered milk to make it creamier, dark chocolate to give it some depth, sugar to make it richer, and cinnamon and nutmeg to enhance the flavor."

"I hope you're selling this in your tearoom." He took another drink, then put his mug back on the counter. "At some time here in the next few days, I'm going to ask your sister out on a date."

Ava had just lifted her mug to her lips,

but at that, she froze. Slowly, she lowered her mug. "Are you serious?"

"As a heartbeat."

*Oh wow.* "That's . . . Does she know?"

"No one knows but you and me. I'm trusting you won't say anything to her or anyone else." He gave her a wry smile. "I feel confident you won't tell. If there's one thing you know how to do, it's keep a secret."

She flushed. "I won't say a word. I promise."

Blake took another sip of his hot chocolate, which left a faint band of melted marshmallow on his upper lip.

He didn't seem aware of his new mustache, which made Ava smile. "Blake, I don't know what to say. I'm happy — relieved even — that you want to give your relationship with Sarah another shot. But I don't know if she can —"

"Whoa! Stay in your lane, Ava. Whatever happens between me and Sarah, you're not to get involved. You can consider that an order."

"Message received. But if you don't want me involved, then why tell me?"

He put his mug down and reached for a napkin. "Because I need some advice." He neatly wiped away his marshmallow mus-

445

tache. "No one knows Sarah better than you."

"I hope you're not going to ask me how to reverse the effects of that darn tea. I spent years trying to figure that out and couldn't —"

"No, of course not. You made it clear you've done everything you could about that. Ava, I don't want magic teas, talking books, or any other kind of voodoo. But despite everything, I still can't get your sister out of my mind." He gave a frustrated laugh. "And oh, how I've tried. I've tried since I was seven years old, and it's not possible. She's special."

Ava nodded. She missed Sarah so much. "She's the most positive, happy, loving person I've ever known."

"Agreed. Which is why I've decided it's time Sarah and I approach our situation in the one way we haven't tried — the old-fashioned way."

Ava sent Blake a confused look. "What's the old-fashioned way?"

"We're going to talk it out. You know, like a normal couple."

*Oh dear.*

He didn't seem to notice her concern. "From here on out, whatever problems we face, whether it's a bad-tea hangover or a fight over who gets to hold the TV remote, Sarah and I are going to confront it together, as a team."

"Ah." Ava dropped her gaze to her mug so he wouldn't see her doubts. She took a slow sip of her hot chocolate. "You seem very determined about this."

"It's worth a shot." He hesitated and then added, "*She's* worth a shot. A million shots, in fact."

Wow. Ava didn't know what to say. Whenever Blake was around, Sarah was either silent, too tangled up in her own thoughts to say a word, or babbling incoherently in a way that made conversation impossible. How could they establish a relationship under those circumstances? Ava started to say as much, but the intensity of Blake's gaze gave her pause. Heck, she didn't know what would or wouldn't work. Why not try the old-fashioned way?

She put her mug down. "Count me in. What can I do to help?"

"I want to take her on a date. What things does Sarah like to do besides read? We need something we can do together that's active enough to bridge awkward silences, but quiet enough to let us talk."

"That's a tall order." Ava considered it for a moment. "I wouldn't suggest a movie. If even a portion of it is based on a book, she's bound to hate it. According to Sarah, movies never do justice to a book."

Blake nodded thoughtfully. "What else?"

"She likes casual more than dressy. She loves all sorts of food but hates buffets of any type."

"Noted."

"Every time we go out, I'll suggest she bring a sweater because she's always cold, but she never does and then she shivers and complains of the temperature."

"Good to know. Anything else?"

Ava bit her lip, thinking through the things she'd heard Sarah say about other dates she'd had over the years, although there hadn't been many. Very few, in fact. "She's not a bowler, but she enjoys Putt-Putt, although it's too cold for that right now." Ava grimaced. "I'm afraid I haven't been much help."

"You've given me a good start. But I need one more thing." His steady gaze locked with hers. "Whatever happens between me and Sarah — good, bad, doesn't matter — I want your promise that you and your teas will stay out of it. Sarah and I need to figure this out by ourselves. If we can, great. And if we can't . . ." He shrugged. "At least we tried."

She could see from his expression that he was as serious as a heartbeat. "You didn't have to ask; I've learned my lesson. And Blake, I'm really, truly sorry for what I did."

"I know." He gave her a ghost of a smile and then glanced at his wristwatch. "As nice as this has been, I'd better get going. I'm doing night checks at the middle school. We have a vandal who thinks he's hi-*lar*-ious spray-painting pictures of a dancing hot dog on the wall behind the cafeteria."

"Why would anyone do that?"

"I have no idea. You'll have to ask a bored twelve-year-old and see what he says."

She had to laugh as she followed Blake to the front door. "It sounds like you know who it is."

"I have my suspicions." He gathered his coat and hat and had reached for the door, when he stopped and turned to look at her. "I've been wondering about something. The tea you used on Sarah has lasted for years. None of your other teas seem to last like that."

"I got the recipe from my great-great-great-aunt Mildred's book. Some of her teas are brutally strong. I didn't realize that until after I'd made that one."

"I think I'd avoid that book from now on."

"I never want to see it again." Ava had to

fight the urge to shiver. "When I was a kid, I used to think that the fact that my teas didn't last long was a weakness. Now I realize it gives the people who drink them more control."

"Kids never understand power." Blake hesitated. "Speaking of kids, Kristen was one of the people who asked me to check on you."

"That was nice of her. She's probably noticed how distracted I've been."

"It's hard to miss. But I'd suggest you keep an eye on her, too. She's got a lot going on, that one."

Ava wondered if she was imagining the flash of worry that crossed Blake's face. Before she could ask, he said, "I'd better be going." He stepped out onto the porch and shrugged into his coat.

The rain from earlier had stopped, leaving a chilly dampness in its wake. He adjusted his hat, which shaded his eyes from the porch light. "By the way, I visited my mother earlier today, and she mentioned she was having trouble sleeping. Would you mind making her some tea? I think she'd like that."

Not a single person had placed a new order in the past few weeks. *No one but Blake.* Her voice was thick as she said, "I'd be more than happy to."

"Great. Let me know when it's ready, and I'll pick it up. Or, better yet, I'll grab it at the soft opening for your tearoom. Friday the eleventh, right?"

She nodded. "From five to eight. The soft opening is more of a party. We want to introduce everyone to the space and the menu. We'll open the café for real that Tuesday."

"You'll be open for lunches, right?"

"Breakfasts and lunches, six days a week, Tuesday through Sunday, from 7 a.m. to 4 p.m."

"Good. I love the Moonlight, but it'll be nice to have some options. Thanks for the hot chocolate and the much-needed advice. You've given me a lot to think about. See you around." With a wave, he headed down the walkway to his car. A moment later, the cruiser backed out of Ava's driveway and disappeared.

She rubbed her arms at the chilly evening air, breathing in the fresh smell of rain as she glanced down the length of the porch at Trav and Grace's house. She didn't know which room was Sarah's, but Ava would bet money her sister was already in bed, curled up with a book.

Sighing, Ava turned away and slowly went back inside her empty house.

# CHAPTER 19
## KRISTEN

Missy cupped her hands around her eyes and peered through the window of Josh's van. "We're on a real stakeout. I feel like we're on an episode of *NCIS.*"

Josh frowned at her from where he was slouched low in the seat in front of hers. "Stop pressing your face against the window. They aren't tinted. Everyone can see you."

Missy dropped her hands and glared at him. "So? If I saw this rusty old van sitting on the side of the street, I'd think it was abandoned and never give it a second look."

"Even if some girl had her whole face smashed against the glass?"

Missy gave a snide answer, and the argument was on.

Kristen ignored them both. Josh's van was parked across the street from a tall, three-story, pale green house, the intricate scroll-work highlighted in cream, the target of

453

their "stakeout." And inside sat the man Kristen was pretty sure was her dad.

Missy, who announced she was no longer speaking to Josh, changed seats so she was beside Kristen. "The houses in this area are so pretty."

Kristen's house was only a block over, so she couldn't help but agree. "Most of them were built in the 1800s." A few had been built earlier, but she wasn't sure which ones.

Josh eyed the house with a frown. "I don't know if I'd call that house pretty. It sort of looks like a horror-movie house."

Kristen eyed it, squinting a little as she imagined how it would look in a thunderstorm, with its square turrets and gargoyle rainspouts.

"It does sort of look like a horror-movie house, doesn't it?" Missy said, losing a little of her enthusiasm.

Horror-movie style or not, Kristen thought it was beautiful. It was obvious, too, that Mr. Lind was a customer of Ava Dove's Landscaping. Even though it was early March, there were signs of life in the flower beds, and the lawn — still damp from yesterday's heavy rain — was such a vivid green that it seemed as if Kristen were looking at it through a filter.

Josh leaned forward so he could see down

the long driveway. "His car's still here, so he hasn't left."

Kristen cut a hard look at Josh. "We watched him pull in not five minutes ago. Why would you think he'd left?"

Josh flushed. "I don't know. He's got that huge house and that fancy car and he comes and goes at weird hours. The whole thing seems slippery to me."

"I'm glad he finally came back to town," Missy said in a grumpy tone. "Where do you think he was all that time?"

Kristen shrugged. "I asked Ava about him. She said his property management company oversees a bunch of apartments on the west side of Asheville. He probably stayed at one of those."

"Yeah, well, we've been waiting forever."

"I needed that time to practice," Kristen said. After Sheriff McIntyre blew their cover, she'd announced to Missy and Josh that she'd be doing the next interview alone to save them from having to coordinate their stories. She'd expected them to argue, but they'd just looked relieved.

That was fine. This was something she should have been doing for herself, anyway. They didn't know it, but she was done using their cover story. It was time for some boldness. *Rip off the Band-Aid, and the faster the better.* All too soon, Kristen would be on Mr. Lind's doorstep asking, "Are you my dad?" just like Sophie did in *Mamma Mia!,* only this time there would be no banging soundtrack.

Josh sent her a worried look. "When are you going in?"

"He just got home. I figure I should give him a few minutes to breathe before I knock on his door." *And change his life forever.*

"Good thinking. Did you bring a notebook so you can pretend to take notes?"

"No."

"Here." Missy grabbed her book bag, fished out her pink notebook, and handed it to Kristen.

"Thanks." Kristen set it on the seat beside her. They waited a bit longer, Missy and Josh arguing over whether the house had a "turret" or a "torrent," Missy settling the disagreement with a sharp spite-Google.

It was all Kristen could do not to scream. Her friends had been annoying her so much lately. When they weren't arguing, they were breathlessly excited about what they were doing, as if they were in some sort of fun spy game.

This wasn't fun, and it wasn't a game.

*I need to get this over with.* She wiped her damp palms on her jeans. "It's time."

Missy bounced on her seat. "This is it! I'm so excited for you!"

"Maybe we should go with you." Josh's forehead had a deep crease.

"No, I'm good. I know what to say. But thanks." Kristen took a deep breath and climbed out.

Missy leaned between the seats, her curly brown hair wildly out of control because of the humidity after last night's rain. "While you're in there, look around and see if there are any mementos that might point toward your mom, like pictures of the two of them together or some of her paintings, anything like that."

"That's a good idea," Josh agreed eagerly. "And remember, if you need us, just stand in front of one of those windows. We'll be watching. If we see you there, we'll run up and knock on the door and distract him so you can get away."

Kristen frowned. "How would you distract him?"

Josh reached under his seat and pulled out a box of Girl Scout cookies. "I brought these from home. Missy will pretend she's selling Thin Mints."

"I love those!" Missy grabbed the box from his hand. "Why is this so cold?"

"They've been in our freezer. It keeps

them fresh."

Kristen didn't think much of their rescue plan, but the last thing she felt like doing was getting into an argument. She was out of arguments. She was almost out of caring. "Great plan. Save me some cookies." Before they could reply, she left, slamming the door closed behind her.

She made her way across the street to Mr. Lind's front lawn. She'd rehearsed what she was going to say so many times that she was pretty sure she wouldn't falter. *Be quick,* she told herself. *Don't overthink.*

She'd just stepped onto the sidewalk when someone behind her called, "Kristen?"

*Mom?* The voice, the intonation, the accent, were all the same. Too startled to think straight, her hopes soared, and she spun around.

Grandma Ellen stood just down the sidewalk. She wore a pale blue coat and cream-colored slacks, her pearls gleaming against her wrinkled neck. She looked as if she belonged in a New York boardroom instead of standing on a crooked sidewalk in a small town in the North Carolina mountains. With her, on a red leash, was tiny, wall-eyed, near toothless Chuffy, sporting a new red sweater that Kristen had never seen before.

*She sounded so like Mom.* Disappointment

458

fell onto Kristen's narrow shoulders. Sadness morphed into irritation that made her snap, "What are *you* doing here?"

A noise made Kristen glance back at Josh's van. He and Missy were each pressed against a window, their mouths hanging open, their eyes wide. They looked so much like hungry fish waiting for their daily food flakes that Kristen surprised herself with a laugh.

Grandma Ellen joined in. She shook her head. "Your friends are something else."

"They're idiots," Kristen said.

"From what I've seen, they're the best friends a girl could have. They're always there for you, aren't they?"

Kristen didn't know what to say to that. She agreed, but why would Grandma Ellen say something so positive? "Grandma, what are you doing here?"

"Me?" Grandma Ellen threaded the dog's slack leash through her fingers. "I could pretend I accidentally happened by while taking your dog for a walk, but you wouldn't believe that."

"You had to have carried him here. He can't walk a whole block."

"I did, and I'm not out here walking the dog. I wanted to speak to you, and I wanted to do it before you saw Mr. Lind."

Kristen's heart sunk. "You've been talking to Sheriff McIntyre."

"What? No." Grandma Ellen's frown sharpened. "Does he know about this?"

*Oops.* Kristen hid a grimace. "If you came here to tell me I can't speak to Mr. Lind, then I —"

"No, no. I came to tell you something else. Good luck."

Kristen blinked. "Good luck?"

"With Mr. Lind. Or, more importantly, with finding your father."

*How did she find out?* "If the sheriff didn't rat me out, then who told you I've been trying to find my dad?"

Grandma's smile turned bittersweet. "It's a long story. When you're ready, I'll tell you. But right now, it appears you're on a mission."

Kristen looked over her shoulder at the towering green house and then turned back to her grandmother. "Do you know why I want to find my dad?"

"You've had one goal since I got here, and that is to stay in Dove Pond. I think I can safely assume this search for your father is connected to that."

Kristen hunched her shoulders. "Maybe."

"In some ways, it's a terrific plan. It covers all the issues: location, the need for adult

460

supervision, the legal question of who has a right to decide your living situation. As plans go, I'm impressed."

It was a good plan on paper, true, but in real life, it wasn't working out at all the way Kristen had wanted it to. But stubbornness made her say, "I'm going to do it. I'm going to find my dad."

"Yes, well, when you're done here today, no matter the outcome, come home for dinner. I found your mom's recipe for chicken and dumplings and I want to give it a try."

The wind rustled, tugging at Kristen's coat. She should be knocking on Mr. Lind's door right now, but instead, she stayed where she was. "You're not mad I'm trying to find my father?"

"Not mad, no." Grandma pursed her lips thoughtfully. "I just wish we could find another way to resolve our differences. But" — she shrugged — "you're free to do as you see fit. I'm — Chuffy! What in the world is on your sweater?" Grandma Ellen bent down to pull a half dozen burrs from the pompom that hung under the dog's thin neck.

Over the past few weeks, the dogs had warmed even more to Grandma Ellen. *Dogs are good judges of character, aren't they? Maybe I'm wrong about her.* A wave of uncertainty hit Kristen, and she looked back at Mr. Lind's house. It really did look like the set of a horror movie.

*It doesn't matter. It has to be him. He's our last suspect.* She turned back to Grandma. "I should go."

"Of course." Grandma Ellen straightened back up, dusting her hands. "I'll start dinner, and we'll watch a movie or something. And I promise I won't ask any questions about this." She tilted her head toward Mr. Lind's house, although her gaze never left Kristen's face. "How's that for a relaxing evening? Wonderful food, a movie, and no questions asked. Unless you *want* to talk, that is. In which case, I'm there for you."

Kristen tried to remember the last time she'd relaxed — really relaxed — but couldn't. She had to admit that Grandma Ellen's understanding gaze had a calming effect, which was just what she needed. Her chest eased a little, and her breath, which had felt strangled all day, settled into a slower rhythm. "I love chicken and dumplings. But I'm not ready to talk about any of this. Not yet."

"Sure." Grandma Ellen scooped up the dog and tucked him under her arm. She turned to go, but stopped. "I believe your friends are about to send out a rescue party."

Kristen glanced over and had to smile when she saw Josh and Missy now standing outside the rusty van, Missy clutching the box of Thin Mints with both hands as if afraid it might get away. "Yeah, I think I'm covered." She waved at Missy and Josh and yelled across the street, "Everything's fine! You can put the cookies away. She's going home now."

They gave her grandmother a suspicious stare and then reluctantly climbed back into the van.

Grandma Ellen's smile widened. "I'm glad they're looking out for you. See you at home." She turned and walked along the sidewalk, cuddling the little dog as if it belonged to her.

Kristen watched her grandmother until she disappeared out of sight. *What was that all about?* Kristen had no idea, but this new thing her grandmother was doing — acting as if she was okay with Kristen's decisions and not pressing her to explain herself — was far preferable to the suspicious, worried air her grandmother usually projected.

*It doesn't matter. I don't have time to figure her out.* Kristen turned and looked at Mr. Lind's house where it loomed overhead.

Straightening her shoulders, she started down the walkway toward the door.

# CHAPTER 20
## SARAH

Sarah picked up a book from the cart, glanced at its call number, and carried it to the correct shelf. "Here you are," she told the book as she slipped it into place, making sure the spine was even and that the books weren't too tightly crowded.

*Thank you.*

She patted the book. "You're very welcome."

It had been three long, lingering weeks since she'd moved out of her home and away from Ava, and it felt like forever. Sarah glanced at the clock over the door and stifled a sigh. In about an hour, she was going to meet Kat to look at another apartment that would soon be available.

According to Kat, this particular apartment was "a too-cute little charmer" over a liquor store, of all places. Kat had gushed about the place, but then, she'd gushed about the last four, too, none of which had been even close to acceptable.

Sarah wondered if Kat was showing her subpar apartments on purpose, hoping Sarah might change her mind about never returning home. It was possible, Sarah supposed, especially since Kat and Ava were friends.

Well, Sarah was about to throw a wrench into that particular scheme, if it even existed, because she'd already decided that if this apartment was close to acceptable, she'd take it. Although Grace and Trav had been great, Sarah missed having her own space, and she was sure they were beginning to feel the same way.

Sighing, she started to push the cart down the aisle when she saw the book she'd just replaced scoot forward, sliding so that its spine was ahead of those of its brethren. "Stop that!" She pushed it back into line so the spines were once again even. "That's not going to help you get noticed."

Which was a little bit of a lie. Sometimes, when Sarah wanted something to read but had no idea what, she'd walk the book stacks and trail her fingers over the spines until one caught her attention. A book that was out of place like that might, just might, have made her pause to look.

But surely she was the only person in the

world who did such a thing. Still, in the interest of order, and to keep the other books from bumping forward and backward, jockeying for position and perhaps hurting themselves, she said, "If you do that again, I'll put you in the reserve section."

Every book in earshot gave a horrified gasp.

The book she'd just placed on the shelf slowly slid even farther back.

A book on the bottom of the cart said in a smug voice, *You won't put me in the reserve section.*

She bent down and there, on top of the books that needed reshelved, was the book about ballroom dancing. Sarah frowned. "How did you get there? I reshelved you yesterday."

The book smirked but didn't answer.

Sarah picked it up and put it on top of the cart. "You're going back."

*No. You need me.*

"I already read you."

*You have to read me again and —*

"I'm reading two other books right now, and they're long ones. I have no desire to begin a thir —"

"Sarah?"

She stiffened. She knew that deep, golden-toned voice. She knew it because she'd dreamed about it every night for more years than she could count. Slowly, carefully, she turned around.

Blake stood at the end of the aisle, dressed in a pair of jeans, his jacket open to reveal a faded red Henley, looking like the hero from every Hallmark movie she'd ever seen.

He looked past her, frowning. "Were you talking to someone?"

"No." She choked out the word, then had to step on her own foot to keep from blurting out a long, unnecessary explanation. The pain refocused her on Blake, although the words struggled for release, piling up like rocks waiting for an avalanche. She wanted to tell him about the conversations she'd just had with the books, the reason she kept the shelves straight and how it was a constant struggle, the way books never left her lonely, and a thousand more things. She wanted to share every inch of herself, every thought she had, and it was killing her to keep it all inside.

His gaze moved over her face. "Ah. You were just talking to the books."

She nodded mutely, clutching the book cart with both hands for support.

"Sarah, don't look so self-conscious." He smiled, which made her heart pound like crazy. "I've seen you talking to books since first grade."

The urge to explain herself, to share her thoughts, to blurt out every secret she'd ever had, grew yet more. She stepped on her foot a little harder, her eyes watering.

"I'm glad I caught you alone. I wanted to talk to you. And if you don't mind, I don't want you to say anything until I've said what I came to say and have explained myself."

Oh dear. She could only hope she could keep quiet.

"I need to tell you something and I . . ." He gave an unsteady laugh, and she was glad to see that he was laughing at himself and not her.

He moved a little closer, just a few steps, but close enough that she noticed his dark hair was getting longer and now curled over his collar.

She liked that, she decided. She liked it a lot. *Dontsayanythingdontsayanythingdontsayanything.*

He spread his hands. "I don't know exactly how to put this or where to begin, but . . . Sarah, I want us to have another go at this."

*What?* Her eyes widened. He couldn't mean —

He moved closer still, and now only the cart stood between them. Sarah was suddenly aware that this morning, after a sleepless night, she'd whipped her hair into a messy braid and hadn't put on any makeup at all. She looked down at her clothes to see what she was wearing and almost winced at the bright orange tunic top printed with a large purple cat reading a book and the leggings featuring three different unicorns burping up rainbows.

The outfit was a lot of things — comfortable, stretchy, well loved by the kids during Children's Hours — but it wasn't at all sexy. And oh God, how she wished she looked sexy right now.

"So." He took a deep breath and raked a hand through his hair, looking unusually uncomfortable. "We've both been through a lot lately. I don't like what Ava did. But I want us to move past that, if we can." His gaze locked on Sarah, a question in it. "We should, don't you think?"

A million thoughts gurgled into her throat, all of them fighting for release.

He stepped to the side of the cart.

Sarah's hands tightened around the cart handle. What was he doing? Was he —

He reached down and tried to capture one of her hands, but it was locked firmly in place and she couldn't seem to unwind her fingers and release the handle.

He tugged again, sending her a surprised look.

*Oh God. This is so embarrassing.* She tried to loosen her fingers, but they were frozen in place.

He reached over and pried her fingers loose, one at a time, until her hand was free. "There." He lifted her hand and pressed a kiss to her fingers.

A deep tingle ran up her arm, through her shoulder, and into her heart. All she could do was stare up at him, a million words fighting for release. She bit her lip and ground her heel into her other foot. *Please don't let me spoil this moment! PLEASE-PLEASEPLEASE.* And yet she could feel her control slipping away.

Unaware he was about to be drowned in a flood of words, Blake continued, "I've thought and thought about it — about Ava and her tea and you and — Sarah, I think the only way for us to break this curse or spell or whatever it is, is to beat it at its own game."

He tightened his hold on her hand. "Sarah Dove, will you go out with me?"

Sarah's mouth dropped open, and all the pent-up words disappeared, blown to dust by sheer shock.

The books around her whispered their

excitement. *Do it! Do it! Do it!*

*Finally!* 475 said one of her favorite young-adult books.

The other books murmured along in approval.

Her silence rang louder.

Blake gave an awkward laugh. "Just to be clear, I'd like us to go on a real date, away from Dove Pond. Maybe in Asheville, safe from prying eyes, where we can just be ourselves. What do you think?"

She closed her mouth and, blinking furiously, struggling to believe this moment was real, managed one short nod.

Blake smiled, a charming half smile that made Sarah think of happiness and ice cream and secret kisses. "I heard from a good source that you don't like buffets or movies made from books."

That was true. Very true.

"So I'm not yet sure what we should do for our first date, but I'll think of something. Maybe we can do one of those paint-and-sip classes, if you're into that sort of thing, or —"

*Thunk.* A book landed on the floor in front of Blake. He released Sarah's hand, bent down, and picked it up.

Sarah's gaze dropped to the book. She

could hear it laughing as it settled into his hands.

"Ballroom dancing?" he said in a thoughtful tone. "I hadn't thought of that. I've seen ads for classes in Asheville." He placed the book back on the cart and looked at Sarah. "What do you think of that? I can call this afternoon and see if I can find us a class."

She nodded again, her mind going in a million directions. Blake McIntyre was asking her out on a date.

A real date.

To learn ballroom dancing, of all things.

But it was more than that. He knew she had a tough time saying what she thought in a way that didn't bowl them both over. And instead of running away, he was trying to find a way to make things work.

Her heart danced with a violent happiness, and she had to press her fingers to her mouth to keep from burbling out a string of excited thoughts.

"Are we set, then? Want to see how we do?"

*Yesyesyesyesyeswecangoonadateandmaybedanceandyourhandswillbe* —

She took a gulping breath and moved her fingers aside just long enough to whisper, "Yes." The second she said the word, she covered her mouth once more.

"It's a date, then." He grinned, his eyes crinkling.

Sarah took a deep breath. She had to say something. Just one sentence. That was all she needed to do. She swallowed, closed her eyes, and lowered her hand from her mouth. "I'd love that." Her voice was breathless.

There. That wasn't bad.

But other words edged forward. They sifted into her thoughts and tumbled toward her mouth.

She swallowed, trying to hold them back. "I've never taken a dance class before." The words piled higher still, and another sentence slipped through. "I wanted to take ballet when I was younger, but we didn't have the money. So I didn't." Before she could stop it, another sentence joined the last. "I wonder if we'll learn the tango? I've always wanted to learn that. It looks so romantic. Or maybe we can learn how to waltz. I've never done it, but it seems simple enough. Have you ever taken a dance class before? I wonder if it'll be hard or if we shouldn't practice —" The floodgates opened, and on and on she went, the words tumbling out faster and faster until she could barely breathe, and she was helpless to stop.

To give Blake credit, he didn't flinch.

Indeed, he watched her with a warm half smile, unsurprised by her rattling.

God, but she hated this. She stepped hard on her big toe, but her mind seemed disconnected from her body and the pain did nothing but make her wince. "I read a book once about how the tango first developed in the 1880s around the Rio de la Plata, which is the natural boundary between Argentina and Uru—"

He kissed her.

Shocked, she froze in place. *Oh, wow.*

That was it. That was all she could think. Just that one, solid *Oh, wow.*

He slipped his arms around her and deepened the kiss, teasing her lips apart.

She melted against him, and the heat he'd created burned away all the words in her head like a piece of paper in a roaring fire. Oh, what a delicious, delightful kiss it was.

She didn't know how long they kissed, but the sound of the door opening a few aisles away made him lift his head.

Sarah burrowed her face against his chest, listening to the sound of footsteps moving away and the low murmur of two voices, one of them a child's wondering aloud where her mother and sister had gone.

Sarah realized she was holding him tightly, so she released him and stepped back a little. Her voice hoarse, she choked out, "They went to the children's section. Other side of the library."

"Good." He put his finger under her chin, tilted her face up, and dropped his forehead to hers, his green eyes twinkling. "About that kiss. That was a good start, if I say so myself."

"It was," she said, her face heating, shyness quivering through her. Oddly enough, no other words crowded into her mind. Not one.

"I didn't plan on doing that," he said. "But I'm glad I did. It seemed to help."

She nodded, unable to look away from his green, green eyes.

"I've spent years wondering what a kiss with you would be like." He slowly released her, stepping back with obvious reluctance. "It was even better than my imagination led me to believe." He flashed a delighted grin. "Sarah Dove, I have the feeling we're going to make our own charms, you and I."

She returned his smile, her heart fluttering wildly. She couldn't believe this was happening.

His phone buzzed, and he glanced at it and then winced. "I've got to go, but before I do, I should mention something. I spoke to Ava a few days ago."

Sarah looked at him in surprise.

"I wanted to apologize to her. I was so angry when I found out about that stupid tea. . . ." He slid his hands into his pockets. "Anger is toxic. I just didn't want that to be me."

Sarah could understand that. She wasn't used to being angry either, and she'd discovered it was as soul-wearying as grief.

"I'm worried about your sister. She seemed really down. The people in this town love you, and you should know that some of them have been pretty hard on her."

The thought of Ava hurting gave Sarah pause. She might be mad at her sister, but that was between the two of them and no one else.

His phone buzzed again, and he made an impatient sound. "Darn it, I'm late. I've got to go, but if you don't mind" — he picked up the book on ballroom dancing — "I'll keep this for a while. I'm going to need all the help I can get."

The book chuckled and told Sarah gleefully, *I bet you wish you'd read me a second time.*

Sarah ignored it, although she had to admit she did wish that very thing. She smiled at Blake, frustrated when a fresh batch of words began to bubble up. She focused on controlling them and said, "I look forward to it."

"Great. We're going to have fun." He was backing away, but slowly, obviously reluctant to go. "I'll book the class. I . . ." He stopped at the end of the aisle, his gaze as serious as his voice. "We can do this. I know it. Thank you for taking another chance on us."

As if she would have ever said no. She wanted to tell him she was excited about their date, that she thought they'd both enjoy dance lessons, and so many more things. But the words were building again, so instead, she settled for a simple smile.

It was enough. With a wink and a very pleased look, Blake left, the book tucked under his arm.

Sarah waited, holding her breath until she heard the door swing closed, and then she sagged against the shelves, her knees as wobbly as jelly, her heart dancing inside her chest. It had happened. It had finally happened. Blake McIntyre had asked her out.

All around her, the books whispered in excitement, some humming, some offering hints and suggestions.

She wanted to hop up and down. She wanted to dance through the aisles and kiss every book along the way. She wanted to laugh and cry, both at the same time.

But more than anything, she wanted to tell Ava.

Sarah had missed her sister so, so much. Maybe . . . maybe Blake was right, and it was time to let her anger go.

It was time for Sarah to move on, too. Besides, Ava's tearoom was set to open in just a few days. She couldn't leave Ava to face that alone. If what Blake had said was true, that people were taking out their anger on Ava, the tearoom opening might be in danger.

And it was then, while standing alone in the aisle with the return cart, that it dawned on Sarah just how she'd heal the breach between herself and her sister. She'd do it with a gift. One perfect, simple gift.

She turned back to the cart and hurried to shelve the rest of the books. She had a lot of work to do between now and Ava's opening.

# CHAPTER 21
## AVA

Dylan placed the last stack of extra tiles in the box by the front door and straightened. He put his hands on his hips and looked around the tearoom. "You did it." He grinned at Ava. "The Pink Magnolia Tearoom is officially ready for business."

Ava, who'd been giving the prep area a final cleaning, dropped her sponge into the small bucket and looked around the tearoom. He was right. Everything was ready for the big launch tomorrow, and it couldn't be lovelier. The wrought-iron tables were perfectly placed, the wood floors gleamed from the fresh coating of polyurethane, and the colorful paintings Julie had given Ava were neatly hung on the back wall. Overhead, the tin ceiling tiles shone with silver finish, while below them the long mahogany bar gleamed from a recent polish. Glass bakery cases at the end of the bar were ready to be filled with the cakes, scones, and pastries that were to be delivered tomorrow afternoon. On the reclaimed-wood wall were shelves where canister after canister of her teas sat in neat rows. Near the door sat two stands of tea-related items — cups, saucers, teapots, sampler boxes, infusers, tea-themed dish towels and aprons, strainers, and more, all neatly priced.

It was perfect. All of it. She should have been beyond thrilled with it all. And yet here she was, lower than low. What did she care about opening her tearoom when her own sister wouldn't even speak to her?

"You don't look happy."

She realized Dylan was watching her from across the room. "I was thinking about Sarah. I really wanted her to come to the opening."

"She's still not answering her phone?"

"I haven't called her in a few days. I figured she needed some time without me pestering her." The only bright spot in the past few weeks had been Blake sharing that he was going to ask Sarah out. Ava wasn't sure what she'd thought that might change, but the days had flown by without a word from either him or Sarah. And so, the one ray of hope Ava'd had that maybe, just maybe, things might change for the better had vanished.

Sighing, Ava picked up a dish towel and dried her hands. "I should reschedule the opening. Maybe move it to this fall."

Dylan looked genuinely shocked. "Why would you do that? Everything's ready."

She shrugged.

He eyed her a long moment. "You think no one will come tomorrow."

"People have been pretty clear whose side they're on. Not that I think there are sides, but . . ." She shrugged again.

"You're wrong. They'll be here. Everyone is talking about it."

She threw the dish towel onto the counter. "They're talking about how I made my own sister hate me so much that she moved out. *That's* what they're talking about, not the tearoom." She crossed her arms and leaned against the counter. "The tearoom won't succeed without customers. None of my businesses will." Her shoulders felt weighted. "Maybe I should just sell this place and move."

It wasn't the first time she'd had the thought. She'd sign the house over to Sarah and then get out of the way. The thought was depressing, and Ava had to swipe a tear from her cheek with the back of her hand.

Dylan muttered a curse and came to stand at the counter near her. "You're a Dove.

You belong here."

She used to think that, too. "I don't know anymore. Except for Sarah, all my sisters have moved away."

"Where would you go?"

"My sister Ella invited me to stay with her in Paris for a while. She's feeling the urge to move on too, though. She goes where the wind takes her. I used to think that was a horrible way to live, but right now, starting over fresh seems like a good idea." It would be a relief to go somewhere people didn't know her.

"Ava, this place is your dream. You can't give up on it."

"It used to seem so important." Ava picked up the dish towel and folded it. "I don't know how to get Sarah to listen to me. And even if I could, I don't know what I'd say. I can't explain away what I did. It was wrong and I knew it."

"Come here." Dylan sat down on one of the barstools and patted the one beside him. "We need to talk. That stupid shoebox has been gone for weeks, but you still look exhausted."

That was true. Even with no secret thumping under her bed, Ava had found herself staring at the ceiling all night, her troubled thoughts too noisy to quiet. "You can tell, huh?"

He patted the seat again.

Too tired to argue, she went around the counter and sat beside him.

He eyed her for a moment. "I know you're feeling down, but things are going to get better. Just give it some time. Besides, there's a part of this story that people are missing."

"What part?"

"The level of skill it took to keep a book from talking to your sister." He gave a silent whistle. "That's some hefty lifting there. I once saw her talk to the church bulletin, and it's just a pamphlet. She said it was complaining because the church secretary kept spelling the word *communion* as *communism*."

Ava had to smile. "If it has pages and a binding, it's a book. Growing up, she never had to read her textbooks. She'd just fix a cup of tea, curl up on the couch, and sit with her hand on the cover and they'd read themselves to her. Some would even explain the harder sections. I used to be so —"

The door opened, and Ellen entered. "Ava! There you are." Ellen took a few steps inside and then came to a sudden halt. "Oh. Dylan. I forgot you might be here."

He looked surprised that she'd remembered his name, but he lifted his hand in greeting. "Good afternoon, Ms. Foster. How are you?"

"I'm fine." She eyed him narrowly, then said in a pointed tone, "I hope you don't mind, but I need to talk to Ava." She set her purse on a chair, removed her long wool coat, and hung it beside the door.

He sent Ava a droll look and then climbed off the stool. "I should get my tools together." He headed across the room to where he'd been packing his things away.

Ava slid off her stool. "Hi, Ellen. What can I do for you?"

"I need some more tea." Ellen reached into her huge purse, pulled out a canister, and handed it to Ava.

Ava glanced at the label and gasped in surprise. "Where did you get this?"

"Kristen brought it home with her. She said it would help me sleep." Ellen frowned. "Why are you looking at me like that? You said you'd been encouraging her to try your diffusion teas."

"Ellen, this isn't from the diffusion line. It's Erma Tingle's misbehaving tea. I should have destroyed it along with the other two, but I forgot they were in the storage cabinet."

"Whatever it is, I want more."

"No. I've got to destroy the rest of this. It's unstable, and I can't let you —"

*"No!"* Ellen snatched the tea back, cradling it against her, looking genuinely horrified. "You're not destroying this tea! It works perfectly."

Ava's gaze moved from Ellen's face to the canister, then back. What she saw there made her eyes widen. "Oh my God . . . you spoke to Julie."

Dylan, who'd been wrapping up a long orange extension cord, shot a surprised look at them.

Ellen flushed. "Maybe."

Ava pointed at the canister. "This tea let Erma talk to her dead uncle."

"Wow," Dylan said. "That's —"

"I need more," Ellen said sharply, ignoring Dylan completely. "I'll take two — no, make it a half dozen canisters." When Ava didn't answer, Ellen added, "Of course, I'll pay you for them. Whatever you want, too."

Ava shook her head slowly. "Ellen . . . I can't."

"Of course you can!" Ellen's voice grew shrill. "You make teas. I want some of your tea. *This* tea." She dropped the canister inside her purse, then pulled out her check-book and a pen. "How much? A thousand?

Two thousand? Ten? Just name your price."

"Ellen, it's not that I won't. It's that I can't. That tea was made from a very special plant that was suffering. It's healthy now. If I made tea from it, it wouldn't be the same."

"Whatever you have to do, make it happen."

"I'm sorry, but I can't."

"You have to!" Tears were visible in the older woman's brown eyes. "I only have enough for one more cup and then —" Her voice broke. She dropped her pen and checkbook on the counter and pressed her hand to her trembling mouth as two fat tears rolled down her cheeks. After an agonized moment, she reached past Ava and pulled a napkin from a holder. "Please," she said in a desperate tone as she dried her eyes. "Don't tell me you can't do it. Please don't tell me that."

Ava's heart ached. "If I could, I would."

Ellen looked drained. She sunk onto the barstool and wiped a final tear from her eyes. "You're sure you can't make more?"

"I'm positive. There's no way."

Ellen picked up her purse and hugged it to her chest. "One more visit. That's all I'll get."

Dylan sent Ava a sympathetic look, and then he started folding the last tarp, turning his back to the two women to give them some privacy.

Ava pulled some more napkins from the holder and handed them to Ellen. "I'm so sorry."

Keeping her purse close, Ellen took the napkins and dabbed at her eyes. "I was so foolish. I thought you'd make me some more, and then I could see Julie whenever I wanted . . ." Ellen gave a deep sigh, her shoulders sinking. "I don't know what I'm going to do."

"When Kristen comes in, I'll ask her why she took that tea home with her. She shouldn't have."

"No, please, don't say anything. She's got a lot going on right now. I'll ask her later. I'm sure she was just trying to help."

Ava remembered what Blake had told her about Kristen. "What's going on with Kristen? She's been super preoccupied. Yesterday, I caught her filling the saltshakers with sugar. That's not like her."

"She's looking for her father. He lives here in Dove Pond, but she doesn't know who he is. Julie never told her. Kristen won't discuss it with me, but until a few days ago, she thought Mr. Lind might be her father. He's not, of course."

Wow! That explained a lot. "No wonder

she's been so distracted."

Ellen nodded absently. "She's hoping that if she can locate him, he'll let her live with him until she graduates."

"Will he?"

"If she finds him, it's possible she might be able to talk him into it."

Ava narrowed her gaze. "You know who her father is."

Ellen nodded.

"Oh wow. That's — Are you going to tell her?"

"If she asks, yes." Ellen hugged her purse a little tighter, her gaze moving restlessly past Ava to the tearoom. "I see you got everything finished on time."

Ava decided to ignore the surprise in the older woman's voice. "Yes, although I'm not even sure why I'm opening the tearoom right now. I'm a bit of a pariah here in Dove Pond."

Ellen's gaze softened. "Publicly scorned, are you?"

"And also publicly pitied, which is worse."

"It there's one thing I've learned, it's that time forgives, or it does once you make amends."

"I don't think I can fix this one."

"I didn't say you had to," Ellen said with a sharp glance. "We can't always fix what we break. Sometimes we just have to accept the consequences and let time heal things as well as it can." Ellen sighed and gave her purse another wistful look. "I should speak to Kristen's father. It would be better if he had a little time to handle his own emotional reaction to discovering he has a daughter before he has to face her."

"He doesn't know?" Ava asked.

"Not yet." Ellen put her purse on the bar and walked toward Julie's paintings.

Ava followed.

"He is going to be surprised," Ellen said over her shoulder. "He never had a relationship with Julie, not a physical one, anyway."

That was odd. Ava, still following, almost ran into Ellen when, instead of continuing to the paintings, she came to a halt beside Dylan.

Ellen looked at the contractor.

He was taking off his tool belt, but he stopped when he realized she was standing there, looking at him. "Ms. Foster?"

Ellen folded her hands in front of her. "How do you feel about having a child?"

"What?" His eyes widened, and he took a step back. "Are you kidding?"

"I don't kid," Ellen said flatly.

Ava stared at Ellen. "Wait. I'm — You're suggesting that Dylan is Kristen's father?"

"That's not possible," he said firmly. "I barely knew Julie, and we never — No. I only saw her once after you all moved away, and we only talked."

Ellen didn't seem the least bit perturbed by his denial. "What did you talk about?"

He shrugged. "Nothing important. Dove Pond and how much we missed it, how hard it was to go to college when you didn't know for sure what you wanted to be — that sort of stuff."

"During that talk, you mentioned to her all the crazy things you'd done to make money to get through college."

"I guess so. I don't remember exactly what we talked about, but . . . Oh my God." Dylan flushed. "She didn't."

Ellen nodded.

"I don't understand," Ava said.

Ellen's gaze never left Dylan's face. "To pay his way through college, Dylan was a frequent donor to a local sperm bank in Atlanta."

His flush deepened, and he sent a self-conscious glance at Ava. "I wouldn't say frequent."

Ellen continued, "He told Julie about it, and when she decided she wanted to have a child, she went to a well-known sperm bank and, using the character sketches they provided, she located him and requested his donation."

"Good God. I —" Dylan blindly groped for a chair, sinking into it as if his knees wouldn't hold him up. "Kristen is my daughter?"

Ellen nodded. "She's been looking for you. She wants to stay in Dove Pond, and she believes you're her ticket."

"I can't . . ." He raked a hand through his hair. "I can't believe this. I never — Look, I'm working six, seven days a week and I don't have time for a cat, much less a kid. I can't —"

"You won't have to," Kristen said.

Ava gasped, and they all turned to find Kristen standing in the door, her mouth a stubborn line in her pale face.

Dylan stood, the chair scraping the floor. "Kristen! No, I didn't mean —"

"I heard exactly what you said." Her gaze was locked on Dylan, her lips trembling. "You don't want a kid. Fine. I don't want you for a father. I don't need you, anyway."

"Kristen, please." Ellen held out a hand and stepped forward. "You're not giving Dylan a chance to —"

"A chance to what? Lie? A chance to *pretend* he wants me when he doesn't? No, thank you."

"Hold on," Ava said. "Listen to your grandmother. Don't —"

"Grandma Ellen." Kristen lifted her chin, her eyes shiny with anger and tears. "You win."

"No, no, no. I don't want to 'win.' I just want you to be —"

"I'll go to Raleigh. I'll go to whatever school you want me to. There's nothing for me here in Dove Pond. There's nothing for me anywhere."

Ava could feel the despair coming from the teenager's stiff form. "Kristen, Dylan wasn't saying —"

"I want to leave right away. Tonight, if we can. I don't want to stay in this town anymore. Not one second. I'll — I'll pack my things and give the dogs away —" Kristen's voice broke. She whirled on her heel and ran out, the door closing behind her.

"Oh dear!" Ellen ran to the counter and grabbed her purse. "I've got to go after her. This is exactly what I wanted to prevent."

"Lord help us . . ." Dylan rubbed his face as if he'd just woken up. "I've got a daughter. And look, I already pissed her off."

Ellen pulled on her coat, sending him an impatient look. "I have to catch her. She shouldn't drive while she's so upset." Ellen hurried out of the tearoom.

As soon as the door closed behind her, Dylan sunk back into his chair. "I can't believe this. What was Julie thinking?"

"I don't know," Ava said. "Julie was her own person. She did things her way or not at all."

The door flew open, and Ellen returned, looking deeply worried.

"You couldn't catch her?" Ava asked.

Ellen shook her head. "I saw her face as she drove past, and she is so upset. She shouldn't be alone. I'll head home. Maybe she's there. I'll —"

"That's not where she'll be," Ava said. "When her mother died, Kristen went to the greenhouse. She loves that place. It makes her feel safe. I'll get my coat, and we can —"

"No."

Ellen's quiet voice made Ava pause.

"I need to talk to her alone. There are things I need to tell her."

Ava couldn't argue with the sincerity she saw on Ellen's face. "Of course. You'll call me if I can help, right?"

"I'll let you know how things go." Ellen headed for the door.

"Ms. Foster?" Dylan called.

She stopped and looked back.

He straightened his shoulders. "I'm coming with you."

"Nonsense. She's —"

"— my daughter." He said it firmly, without hesitation.

Ellen didn't look pleased, but her gaze flickered over his face as if measuring his intent. Whatever she saw must have reassured her, because she waved her hand. "Come along, then. But I'm driving."

Dylan grabbed his coat and hurried toward the door Ellen had already disappeared out of, giving Ava a quick smile and a hurried thumbs-up as he left.

Ava watched as the door closed. *Wow. Just wow. I never thought of Dylan as a dad sort of guy, but he was pretty determined to go after Kristen. That's promising.*

Still, Ava couldn't help but remember Kristen's expression. *Poor Kristen. She's had it rough.* But maybe . . . maybe it wasn't poor Kristen at all. Kristen didn't yet know it, but two adults, both determined to make sure she was okay, were hurrying her way right now. Julie would be glad to know that.

As impulsive as Julie had been, when it came to Kristen, she'd always seemed to have a plan. Although Ellen and Dylan were complete opposites in some ways, they both had the same work ethic, believed in things being "done right," and were good, decent people capable of caring deeply. Ava had seen Dylan's compassionate side firsthand after her falling-out with Sarah. No one had been kinder to her. As for Ellen, Ava couldn't question her capacity for love after watching her struggle to reach her grand-daughter over the past few months.

If it came to pass that Ellen and Dylan teamed up to raise Kristen, they'd be a force to be reckoned with — one softer and more understanding, the other stricter but stronger. *A perfect combination.*

Whether Julie had planned it that way or not was a question for another day, but right now, Ava couldn't help but be encouraged.

# CHAPTER 22
## ELLEN

Ellen pulled into the long drive that led to Ava's greenhouses, relieved to see Kristen's car far up ahead, parked near the front door.

It was a good thing Ellen had brought Dylan with her. She'd only had the faintest idea where Ava's greenhouses were, and his directions had saved her many precious minutes. Even though she was deeply distracted, she'd used the drive over to get to know him.

Although he seemed nice enough, Ellen thought Dylan was far from a perfect candidate for a father. He'd admitted without embarrassment that in college he'd changed his major seven times — seven! — before getting a general studies degree just so he could graduate. Ellen couldn't fathom that level of indecisiveness.

Still, he seemed content in his current job, which he was quite skilled at, and she had to admit that his determination to apologize to Kristen was touching. Ellen wondered if perhaps she was being too picky and realized that was exactly what Julie would tell her.

Ellen parked near Kristen's car. Dylan hopped out while Ellen gathered her purse. She tucked it under her elbow, the feel of the canister through the pebbled leather reassuring. She only had enough tea for one more, very short visit with Julie.

Ellen's throat tightened. *It's so unfair. There are so many things I need to tell her.*

Dylan opened the greenhouse door and stood back to let Ellen enter.

She took several steps inside, then slowed to a surprised stop. She'd found the Garden of Eden. Row upon row of fragrant greenery met her astonished gaze. A heavy line of herbs, all clearly marked with small black signs bloomed green and fragrant down one aisle while in another, flowers grew among shiny green leaves, and in yet another, thick vines climbed up short trellises. The air was heavy with a mixture of rich, sweet, earthy scents.

A short, slender, dark-haired woman stood several rows over, a clipboard in her hand.

"Hi, Sofia," Dylan said from where he'd stopped behind Ellen. "We're looking for

Kristen."

"She's with the peppermint plants. She looked pretty upset when she came in, so I left her alone." Sofia's dark eyes gleamed with sympathy. "Is she okay?"

Dylan's cheeks grew faintly pink, but he said without flinching, "She found out who her father is in the worst way possible."

Ellen waved her hand. "I wouldn't say it was the worst way. Not one of the best, yes. But definitely not the worst."

"It sure felt like it," he said glumly.

Sofia eyed them curiously, and Ellen was glad Ava's assistant didn't ask more questions. "Could you point us in the right direction? I'm not sure where these peppermint plants are."

"She's right through there." Sofia nodded toward a door in the back of the greenhouse. "Row two."

Ellen thanked her and headed for the door, Dylan following.

She stepped over the threshold into an even larger greenhouse with yet more rows of steel tables, tall, thick greenery on each, making the greenhouse feel more like a jungle. Ellen called out, "Kristen?"

A faint sniff answered her.

Dylan pointed to the right, and he and Ellen walked around the end of the row.

There, about halfway up, sitting on the floor with her back against a table, her arm around a leafy plant, sat Kristen.

The teenager's eyes were dry, although a definite tremor showed her struggle to keep the tears at bay. She glared at them now. "Go away!"

"I know you'd like to have a little time to yourself right now," Ellen said. "I would want to be alone, too, if I'd overheard what you did, but I owe it to you and your mother to clarify some things."

Kristen turned away. "There is nothing to clarify."

"There's a lot to clarify. A whole, whole lot."

Dylan cleared his throat. "Kristen, I wasn't saying I didn't want you for a kid. I was saying I didn't think I was ready. And I guess I'm not, seeing as how I've already hurt your feelings, which I never meant to do."

Kristen kept her gaze locked on the plant.

Shifting from one foot to the other, he shoved his hands into his pockets, looking lost. "I'm sorry for saying what I did. I was just surprised, that's all."

Kristen's lips thinned, but she didn't speak.

Ellen sighed. "Dylan, would you give us a

few minutes?"

He looked miserable, as if he both wanted to stay and also longed to leave.

"Please?" Ellen asked again, a little more impatiently this time.

He nodded. "I'll be in the other room." He started to turn away, but then stopped, his gaze on Kristen. "I don't know much about being a parent, but I do know that you don't walk out on your responsibilities." He took a deep breath. "From now on, I'm here for you. I hope you know that."

Kristen didn't look up.

Dylan sighed and, with a grimace at Ellen, he left.

As soon as the sound of his footsteps faded, Ellen looked around the concrete floor for a clean place to sit. She finally gave up and accepted that her slacks would need dry cleaning and sat down on the concrete floor beside Kristen. "I hope this isn't damp." Settled, she tucked her purse in her lap and crossed her legs at the ankles.

Kristen scooched away a few inches.

"I don't bite." Ellen tentatively leaned back against the table leg behind her, glad it stayed firmly in place. When Kristen didn't answer, Ellen let the quiet linger, giving her a little more time to calm down.

She looked around at the bright greenery

and listened to the quiet hum of the irrigation system in the background. "It's very peaceful here."

Kristen lifted a leaf to her nose and sniffed it. "Mom loved peppermint."

Ellen took a deep breath and could just make out the peppermint scent over the others. "She did."

Kristen's mulish expression softened.

Ellen reached across Kristen, picked up a peppermint leaf that had fallen to the ground, and sniffed it, the scent stirring so many memories. "When your mom was little, I could never keep candy canes on the Christmas tree."

"I know. She told me she'd sneak in at night and steal them."

"Every last one." Ellen smiled. "Later, I'd find them under her pillow, some of them half-eaten and stuck to her pillowcase. Once, she got two of them stuck in her hair. I thought we were going to have to cut them out."

Kristen gave her the smallest of smiles.

Ellen chuckled. "I used to fuss at her about it, but honestly, I didn't care."

Kristen tilted her head to one side. "Then why did you fuss at her?"

"I don't know. I guess I thought that was what I was supposed to do. They don't give you a manual on parenting. You have to figure things out for yourself, and I'm not afraid to admit there were some things I could have done better." She looked up at the ceiling. "Sorry, Julie."

Kristen's eyebrows rose. "You talk to Mom?"

"I do now."

"I do too." Kristen hung her head, a strand of her hair falling across her cheek and partially hiding her face. "She can't hear me, but —"

"Nonsense. She can hear every word."

"You really believe that?"

"I don't just believe. I *know* it." Ellen reached over and tucked the strand of purple hair behind Kristen's ear.

Flushing, Kristen jerked her head away. "Don't."

Ellen sighed, adjusting her purse on her lap. "I'm sorry about the way you found out Dylan is your dad. But please don't judge him too quickly. He'd just gotten a huge shock. I understand why you'd be mad —"

"I'm not mad," Kristen said sharply. "Not at him, anyway."

"Oh. You're mad at me, then?"

"I'm mad at myself." Kristen pulled up her legs and clasped her arms around her knees. "When I first started looking for my dad, I thought I'd tell him who I was, and we'd live together happily ever after. Like a movie, you know." She made a face. "That was stupid."

"I wouldn't call it stupid."

"It feels stupid now. I know Dylan. I know him better than the other men I thought could be my dad, anyway. We've worked at Ava's for the past few months, so we've talked here and there. And while he's a nice enough guy, I couldn't live with him. It would be weird."

Ellen nodded slowly. Hmm. This was progress of a sort. "Can I tell you something?"

Kristen shrugged.

"I feel sorry for him. He never dated your mom, you know. Not even once."

"He had to have."

"I thought that myself at first. But the truth is this." Ellen turned so she was facing Kristen. "Your mom picked your father from a listing at a sperm bank. Dylan had no idea he was your father."

Kristen's eyes widened. "Are you *serious*?"

"You weren't an accident. In her own way, your mom planned everything out. She decided she wanted to have you, but she didn't want the complication of a partner, so she went to a sperm bank. She knew he'd been a donor and knew enough about him to pick him out of their book or computer listing or whatever it is." Ellen shook her head. "I don't know exactly how that works."

Kristen's hazel eyes, which Ellen now realized were the exact color of Dylan's, had darkened. "He didn't have any idea?"

"None. *If* he gave it any thought at all, which I doubt he bothered to do. He was quite young at the time, barely in college. I suppose he knows it's possible he has children out there somewhere, but none here, in his own backyard, as it were."

Kristen was silent a moment and then, to Ellen's surprise, she chuckled. "Mom was something else, wasn't she? When she wanted to do something, she just did it. I could never be as brave as she was."

"Your mom was an original. I think she'd like being called brave."

"She'd love it. She used to say she could never say no to an idea, even a bad one." Kristen rested her chin on her knee. "I don't think she believed that was a good thing, though."

"No. But you're right, in many ways, your mother was as brave as they come." Ellen looked at Kristen. "You really believe you'll be miserable in Raleigh?"

"I'll try to make it work. I'm going to miss Missy and Josh. They've been good friends, as annoying as they sometimes are." She swallowed as if her throat had tightened. "I hate leaving them. I feel like I've lost so much lately, and I don't want to lose them, too."

It was frustrating because just as Kristen was agreeing to do what Ellen had been praying she'd do — willingly move to Raleigh — Ellen was beginning to believe that would be a mistake. *I guess it's not just Dylan who has to face an uncomfortable truth today.*

Ellen sighed. "Fine. We should go ahead and just say it."

"Say what?"

"That you'll be miserable in Raleigh."

Kristen looked guilty. "I said I'd try and make it work."

"You could try, but we both know it won't work. Meanwhile, you feel safe and are happy here in Dove Pond. You have a job and friends and a home you love." Ellen leaned her head against the leg of the metal table. "I don't know what the solution is, but there has to be one. We just have to figure out what it is. And, Kristen, we have to figure it out together. That means we have to talk things through, you and I, even if it's sometimes uncomfortable."

Kristen's eyes had widened. "You think there's a way that I can stay here?"

"There has to be. We're both smart. Maybe if we put our heads together, we'll find a compromise that leaves us both, if not perfectly happy, at least satisfied."

"You'd compromise?"

"I will. Will you?"

She nodded.

"Pinkie promise?" Ellen held out her pinkie.

Surprise flickered across Kristen's face, but after a moment, she smiled and linked her pinkie with Ellen's. "Pinkie promise."

Kristen dropped her hand back into her lap.

"Feel better?"

"A little." Kristen shot her a curious look. "I have a question. How did you know I'd be at Mr. Lind's the other day?"

Ellen's gaze dropped to her purse, where the canister rested. She owed Kristen the truth. "You're going to laugh at this, but —" Ellen opened her purse and pulled out the canister.

Kristen flushed. "I can explain that."

"Good, because I can't."

"I brought it home hoping you'd sleep so

I could search Mom's bedroom for clues as to who my dad might be."

"Ah. I see. You knew this was Erma Tingle's bad tea?"

Kristen shrugged. "It didn't hurt her. She just had weird dreams."

"It did a little more than that. It let Erma speak to her dead uncle."

"It just made her *think* she'd talked to her uncle."

Ellen smoothed her thumb over the torn label. "Kristen, this tea let me talk to someone who'd passed away, someone I loved dearly. Someone who needed to tell me something."

Kristen's mouth dropped open, and her gaze locked on the canister. "Mom?"

"She's the one who told me you were searching for your father. That's how I knew about Mr. Lind."

"Oh my God." Kristen's gaze lifted back to Ellen's face. "You saw Mom. You *really* saw her?"

"More than once. The first time, I thought it was a dream, but she told me about the red cube, which you showed me."

"That's . . ." Kristen swallowed noisily. "How was she?"

"When she wasn't arguing with me? She was great."

Kristen gave a short laugh. "You two went at it?"

"A little." Ellen added with a wry smile, "It was good that we had a limited amount of time. She looks the same way she always has — wild clothing, too full of opinions and emotions. She was happy, too. She likes where she is, wherever it is."

"I'm glad she hasn't changed." Kristen twisted a strand of her hair around her finger, her gaze pensive. "I worry that I'll forget her voice. She made some videos for me, but I can't look at them yet. They're too much to handle right now."

"They'll be there when you are ready." Ellen sighed and, her mind filled with memories of her daughter, she hugged the canister. "I never understood your mother. She and I were too different in many ways. But talking to her has made me realize that perhaps I didn't need to understand her. I just needed to accept her and love her as she is." *I wish I'd figured that out years ago.* Ellen blinked back tears, and she was so blurry-eyed that she didn't see Kristen lean closer and envelop her in a hug.

Ellen slipped her arms around her granddaughter and hugged her back. For a long while, they sat there, leaning against each other, soaking in the warmth of the hug and the faint scent of peppermint.

Ellen rested her cheek against her grand-daughter's soft hair and closed her eyes. She would have missed this if she'd approached this moment the way she usually did, pouring out unwanted advice right and left, stamping out the quiet required to listen, *really* listen, to another person.

This time, she'd been honest and had shared her true thoughts and feelings, and had done her best to take Kristen's into account as well. Julie was right yet again. Ellen's "helpful hints" were neither helpful nor hints. They came across as cold, hard criticism that could maim if not kill fragile spirits. *Oh, Julie, that was never my intention.*

Kristen gave Ellen a final hug, then pulled back, looking a little embarrassed. "I'm sorry I've made this so difficult. I haven't been myself since Mom died."

"You haven't done anything wrong. You were just trying to be heard." Kristen nodded. "We'll figure something out."

"We have to, now that I told your mom we would."

Kristen smiled. "Thanks. Can . . . can I ask you to do something for me?"

"Anything."

Kristen's clear gaze met Ellen's. "Will you tell Mom I miss her but that everything is going to be okay?"

Ellen looked down at the canister. *Only one more visit. That's all I have left.*

*No. It's all I* had *left.* She hugged the canister one last time. *For you, Julie.*

Her eyes so blurry she could barely see, Ellen took a deep breath and handed the canister to Kristen. "Tell her yourself."

Kristen's hands closed over the canister. She raised her startled gaze to Ellen. "Are you sure?"

"There's not much left. Just enough for one short visit. But long enough." Ellen slipped her arm around Kristen and kissed her forehead. "Long enough to remind you what your mom's voice sounds like. Just don't do what I did, and waste your time arguing."

Kristen choked back a sob as she hugged the canister, smiling through her tears. "Thank you! I don't know what to say."

"Save your words for your mom." Ellen gathered her purse and stood, stopping to brush the dust from her slacks. "I'll leave you to your peppermint plants, but before you go home, I think you should talk to Dylan."

Kristen's smile dimmed. "Right now?"

"He came all the way here to see you. He

deserves a few minutes of your time, at least."

Kristen held the canister tightly, seeming to struggle with her answer. "I guess I'm going to have to talk to him sometime. It might as well be now."

"I'll tell him you're ready, then. I'll see you at home for dinner, right? We have a lot to talk about, you and I."

Kristen nodded.

"Good." Ellen smiled and headed for the door. She'd just gotten there when Kristen called out, "Grandma Ellen?"

Ellen looked back. "Yes?"

"I'll tell her you love her."

Ellen's lips quivered as she tried to smile. "Please do." With that, she left.

Dylan was leaning against a table, watching Sofia pot some basil plants, but on seeing Ellen, he stood up straight.

"She's waiting for you," Ellen said. "I'll be outside when you're done."

She watched him head for the back room and then, struggling to contain her tears, she murmured a goodbye to Sofia and went outside.

The refreshingly cool breeze rose up over the field below the greenhouse and wafted over the parking lot, bringing with it the smell of damp earth as it dried Ellen's eyes.

She lifted her chin and let the breeze blow over her, strands of hair coming loose and tickling her cheek.

She wasn't sure why, but she felt lighter than she had since the day she'd heard of Julie's death. And younger, too, as if the weight of her past mistakes had lifted a little.

Ellen sighed, her breath mingling with the breeze, then disappearing from sight. And somewhere in the distance, she thought she heard the unmistakable sound of Julie's unique laugh.

# CHAPTER 23
## AVA

Ava nervously straightened her apron as she looked at the clock that hung over the kitchen door. The Pink Magnolia Tearoom's soft opening had started a full twenty-two minutes ago, and they had only three customers — Grace, Trav, and Daisy. The three of them were all seated at a table near the door, sipping cups of hot chocolate and sharing a piece of chocolate silk pie from Ava's supplier, the Moonlight Café.

The tearoom was off to a sad, sickly start. Ava, trying not to stare at her only customers, was dying to ask Grace about Sarah, but she refrained, as she didn't want to put any of them in an awkward position. So instead, she pretended to be cleaning the already scrubbed bar while casting furtive glances their way.

Kristen brought out a tray of muffins from the kitchen. Dressed in a cheery blue apron with a pink magnolia embroidered on the pocket, she placed the tray beside the bakery case and used the tongs to arrange the muffins beside a long line of cream scones, blueberry bars, and bear claws.

Ava had resisted questioning Kristen about what had happened yesterday, but the teenager seemed fine, if a little quiet. *When Dylan gets here, I'll ask him.*

She watched as Kristen put another muffin into the case. "Leave the rest in the back. We're not going to need more food."

"Grandma Ellen is coming."

Ava sighed. "I hope she brings a few people with her."

Grace got up from her table and brought two empty cups to the bar. "I've requests for more of your delicious hot chocolate."

Ava took the cups and refilled them. "How was the pie?"

"Divine." Grace idly picked up a menu from the stack on the bar. "I see you're doing both breakfast and lunch. The list of quiches is making my mouth water." She dropped the menu back in place and watched as Ava added whipped cream to the cups. "How are things?"

"With the tearoom? You can see for yourself."

Grace glanced around. "People will come. I'm sure of it."

"I hope so." Ava placed the cups of hot chocolate on the bar and asked as casually as she could, "So . . . how's Sarah?"

"You'll see."

Hope flared. "What does that mean?"

Grace grinned. "You'll see that, too." She winked, took the cups, and carried them back to her table.

Maybe . . . maybe Sarah was coming? *Please, yes!* Despite the noshow at her opening, Ava was suddenly happier than she had been in the past three weeks. She'd give up every one of her businesses just to see her sister smile.

Kristen closed the back of the baked-goods display, set the tray in the sink, and came to stand with Ava. "It's okay to jump up and down if you feel like it."

Ava laughed. "Is it that obvious?" At Kristen's nod, Ava said, "It may not mean anything. Sarah could come here just to tell me off."

"At least she'd be talking to you," Kristen pointed out.

"That's true." Ava caught the teenager trying not to yawn. "Still not sleeping?"

"Oh, no." Kristen cut Ava a wide grin. "I slept like a baby."

There was something in the way she said it that made Ava eye her a bit closer. There was a softness to Kristen that hadn't been there in a long, long time. "You seem different today."

"Last night, Grandma and I had a long talk."

"And?"

"We haven't reached an agreement yet, but we have some ideas. She's going to talk to you about one of them when she comes."

Ava could have told Kristen that her grandmother didn't think enough of Ava to "run ideas" by her but decided against it. Instead, she asked, "And Dylan?"

Kristen made a face. "It's weird thinking of him as my dad. But I guess he's okay. Not everyone can say that about a parent."

"Did you ask if you could live with him?"

"No!" Kristen flushed. "I don't want to, either. It would be awkward." She shook her head. "That was a stupid idea."

"It wasn't stupid. It was hopeful. And sometimes hope works. You never know until you try." Ava's gaze moved around her tearoom. "Not that hope works *every* time."

"Things will turn out fine. Call it a hunch or a —"

The door opened, and Ava turned. She'd just opened her mouth, ready to welcome her next customer, but instead she came to a surprising halt. "Dylan?"

She'd expected to see him, but not in a well-tailored suit. Not only that, but some-time between yesterday and today, he'd gotten his hair cut and his beard trimmed.

He looked good.

Better than good, in fact.

Her staring must have made him uncomfortable because he awkwardly touched his hair and then shrugged as if telling himself to stop it.

Kristen waved at Dylan, and he waved back. "Hi, Kristen. Are we still on for Saturday?"

She nodded.

When Ava sent her a curious look, Kristen said in a casual tone, "We're going bowling." She rolled her eyes. "Dylan thinks it'll be a 'fun' way to get to know each other." She air-quoted *fun* as if her sarcasm wasn't enough.

"I didn't say it would be fun." Dylan made a show of cracking his knuckles. "I said I'm going to beat you soundly at bowling. Then I'm going to take you out for Putt-Putt. Once I've destroyed you with my master windmill Putt-Putt-one-stroke-genius, I'm going to plan a tennis outing where I'll dazzle you with my Venus Williams–like backhand."

"He's getting uppity," Ava announced.

"Kristen, I hope the bowling gods shine their blessings on you."

"*Getting* uppity? He's always been that way. You've just never noticed."

Dylan adjusted his tie. "At least one of you should tell me I clean up good."

Ava pretended to suddenly see a spot on the bar that needed scrubbing while Kristen collected the tray from the sink and disappeared into the kitchen.

He sighed and took a seat at the bar. "May I have a cup of hot tea and one of those scones, please?"

"No manly coffee for you, eh?"

"Nope. I'm going full *Bridgerton.*"

"How about Earl Grey? That's a manly sounding tea." At his nod, Ava dropped the rag. "Do you want the scone warm? With butter?"

"Is there any other way?"

Ava put a scone in the toaster oven, then fixed him a cup of tea. "There you go. It'll be another minute or so for the scone."

"Thanks." He picked up his cup and blew in it.

"So . . . it's been a big twenty-four hours for you, hasn't it?"

He put the cup down. "I'm a father. A dad. A pop. I've said it about a hundred times and I still can't believe it."

She leaned against the counter across from him. "You don't seem old enough."

"I know, right? I haven't told anyone yet, because I felt that should be Kristen's decision. But to be honest, it's sort of wonderful." He shook his head, surprise lighting his eyes. "I wish Julie had told me. I missed out on so many things. I —"

The door opened, and Ed and Maggie Mayhew came in. The owners of the local pet shop, Paw Printz, Ed and Maggie were Dove Pond movers and shakers. He was a short, wiry-haired man with a rotund figure, while Maggie was even shorter, more wiry-haired, and even rounder in size. "Hi, Ava!" Maggie called.

Ava's heart warmed. Not everyone would come, but at least a few of her closer friends would be here. That would be more than enough.

"I hope we're not late," Maggie said. "Ed overbooked us for grooming." She rolled her eyes. "Again."

"It's only five thirty," Ed pointed out. "We made it in plenty of time. The opening is from five to eight, right, Ava?"

"Right."

Kristen came out of the kitchen and, seeing the new customers, sent a quick I-told-you-so glance Ava's way.

"Are those scones?" Ed said in a hopeful voice.

"Strawberry, raspberry, chocolate, and pecan," Ava said.

Kristen added, "We have muffins, too. Lemon, poppy seed, oatmeal, and blueberry."

Ed beamed. "You're singing my song. I'll have a raspberry scone and a decaf, please. Maggie, what about you?"

"A pecan scone and a cup of . . ." Maggie's gaze went to the board behind the bar. "How about some Lady Grey?"

Kristen set about filling their order. Ava had just started chatting with them about the coming Spring Fling, one of two big Dove Pond events, when the door opened and Kat Carter and her mother walked in. Kat wore a bright red dress, but she was outshone by her mom, who wore a tight suit that showed off her figure. Even at sixty-seven and while standing beside her gorgeous daughter, Mrs. Carter still managed to be the most beautiful woman in the room.

She looked around and gave a theatrical gasp. "Why, Ava Dove, you've performed magic on this place! I wouldn't have even recognized it."

Kat smiled. "Ava's tearoom will be the perfect place to bring our real estate customers to let them experience the flavor of Dove Pond, won't it?"

"Indeed it will. Why, this place is darling! I love the tables, the chairs, and the —"

The door opened again, and Aunt Jo strolled in wearing her Sunday finest, a deep purple suit with a bright pink, floppy-brimmed hat. She made her way to the bar, clasped her hands together, and cast her gaze heavenward. "Lord love us, but it's finally here." She dropped her hands. "Do you know how long I've been waiting for this day? For years, I —" She gasped. "Is that hummingbird cake I see?"

"Ella sent me the recipe last week." Ava peeked over the bar. "Where's Moon Pie?"

"I left him at home. He twisted his hip hopping off the couch after he saw a cat wandering across the yard. He's laid out in his bed, enjoying the painkillers the vet gave him."

"Oh dear. I hope he's okay."

"He'll be good as gold in no time. Meanwhile, I'll have a slice of that cake and a cup of dandelion tea."

"Aunt Jo!" From where he and Maggie now sat at a small table across the room, Ed Mayhew held up what was left of his scone. "Did you make these?"

Aunt Jo beamed. "I am proud to announce that I am indeed the sole scone supplier of the Pink Magnolia Tearoom. The rest of this stuff is from the Moonlight and not near as good."

"I knew it," he said. "They're delicious."

Aunt Jo went to sit with Ed and Maggie while Ava fixed her cake and tea.

Moments later, Sofia arrived with her son, Noah, and husband, Jake, at almost the same time as Erma Tingle came with her partner, Christine. All of them asked for hot chocolate, saying Kristen and Missy had told just about everyone in town how good it was.

The next hour was a blur as, one after the other, the people of Dove Pond came to Ava's tearoom and ordered food and teas, hot chocolates and coffees, and more. They sat, talked, and laughed.

Ava's heart filled. Not just because her friends and neighbors had showed up in support of her tearoom, but because one after another, almost everyone who'd canceled their long-standing orders quietly and sheepishly reordered. Several even apologized, although Ava quickly let them know it wasn't necessary.

A while later, Missy and her parents arrived and clustered around Kristen, ordering lattes and bear claws. Kristen, peeking over their heads at Ava, had smiled, looking so happy and at ease that Ava had to force herself not to give a happy jump.

The minutes blurred by as they grew busier and busier. And yet Ava kept looking past the crowd toward the door, hoping to see Sarah.

A little before seven Blake came in, dressed in slacks and a turtleneck. He ordered a cup of plain coffee and was immediately joined by Wilmer Spankle, who wanted to complain about his neighbor's son's tendency to set off fireworks.

Ava was dying to ask Blake if he'd asked Sarah out yet, but other than giving her a quick smile, he stayed away from where she was pinned behind the bar. *Thanks, McIntyre. And after I gave you all that helpful advice, too.*

A few minutes later, Zoe Bell, looking stunning as ever in a peachcolored sheath dress, came in with new-to-town Jessica Cho Graham.

Jessica owned the Last Chance Motel at the edge of town and was refurbishing it into a fancy boutique sort of place. While waiting on her turn to order, she looked around with delight. "What a crowd," she told Ava. "I'm impressed."

Zoe agreed. "This might be my new

favorite place." She crossed her arms and leaned them on the bar. "I'll take a lavender tea and some lemon shortbread cookies."

"Same," Jessica said.

"Coming right up." Ava went to the bakery case and placed the cookies on small dishes.

Jessica added, "I'm not even sure what lavender tea is, but it sounds good."

Ava set the cookies in front of them and went to make the teas. "Thank you all for coming."

Zoe snorted. "Like we had a choice."

Jessica nibbled on a cookie. "We were ordered here. Like troops in a war."

Ava, about to pour hot water into two teacups, looked over her shoulder at them. "Ordered?"

"Not that I wasn't coming anyway," Zoe said quickly. "But when you're threatened to never again get a book you'll love from the only library in town, you do what you're told."

Ava's eyes widened. "Sarah?"

Jessica nodded. "We've *all* been told that if we didn't come here today, we'd be cut off cold."

"She meant it, too," Zoe said. "She spent all day going up and down the street and all through town telling everyone that she expected us to be here."

Ava's heart swelled.

"Most of us were coming, anyway, though," Zoe added. "Well, except my dad, but he's a stubborn fool, so there's that."

Ava finished making the teas, her throat too tight for her to speak.

Zoe must have seen Ava's struggle because she reached across the counter and patted Ava's hand. "You had to know she'd forgive you. She just had to do it in her own time."

Ava grasped Zoe's hand and gave it a squeeze. "Thank you."

"Hey, like I said, Jess and I were coming anyway, Sarah's threats or no."

Jess tried her tea, her eyes widening. "Oh my! I love this!"

"See?" Zoe said, picking up her cup. She looked back at Ava. "By the way, my dad said he'd canceled his tea order."

"And his yard work, too." Ava shrugged. "But that's fine. I understand."

"I don't. He had no reason to get involved in this disagreement. None of us have. And I'm sorry I didn't make that clearer, not just to him, but to everyone else I know. But Dad needs your tea. His knee aches without it."

Jess grimaced. "Arthritis?"

"He's had it since I was a kid, and it's just gotten worse. But at least he can walk when he has Ava's tea. Without it, his knee swells up like a football, and he's as grumpy as a hungry bear."

"I'll make some more if you think he'll use it."

"Please do. I'll make sure he does." Zoe turned to Jess. "Let's go look at those teapots we saw in the window. I may need one or two of those."

They left, and Ava — so happy she could almost have floated — turned to the next customer. "Ellen!"

The older woman was dressed in a cream-colored sweater over a silk shirt and a pair of tailored slacks. She slid onto a seat at the counter and looked around. "I'd call this a success."

"Sarah did it." At Ellen's surprised look, Ava nodded. "I was surprised, too. I think she's forgiven me, at least a little."

"You haven't spoken to her?"

"I haven't seen her yet." From across the room, Ava caught Dylan's gaze where he stood talking to Josh's dad, Tony Perez, who was there with Josh's three little sisters. Dylan glanced at Ellen and then back at Ava and winked. *What does that mean?*

"I'm glad your sister has come to see reason." Ellen picked up the menu. "What do you suggest in the way of tea?"

"How about a honey mint tea? It's delicate but strong."

Ellen put the menu back on the counter. "Sold."

Ava got a teacup and saucer, filled the cup with hot water, dropped in a tea bag, and slid it in front of Ellen. "I'd let it steep for three to five minutes to get the full flavor."

"Thank you." Ellen's cool, clear gaze rested on Ava. "Did Kristen mention I wanted to talk to you?"

Ava looked down the bar to where Kristen was fixing huge cups of hot chocolate for Missy and Josh, who were laughing at her exaggerated attempts, which made her look more like a bartender than a barista. "She mentioned something, yes."

"We were up late last night, trying to come up with a compromise, and we may have finally found one. But it depends on you."

"On me?" Ava wasn't sure what she should say to that. "How so?"

"I have a project starting April first and I have to be in Raleigh to oversee it. Kristen, meanwhile, has school through late May. I can't let her stay alone, and Dylan and she aren't yet well enough acquainted for her to feel comfortable staying with him. To be honest, I'm not sure I know him well enough to agree to that. However, I do know you, and so does Kristen."

Oh wow. "You want Kristen to stay with me?"

"Just Monday through Thursday for the next few months. I'll be here on weekends, of course."

"I — Ellen! Of course she can! We have so many empty bedrooms, and I . . . I promise I'll keep an eye on her. I'll make sure she does her homework and lets me know where she is at all times and . . ." Ava didn't know what else to say. "This is very generous of you."

"Before you agree, you should know that she'd like to bring her dogs. Well, three of them. I'm going to take little Chuffy with me. The poor thing isn't well."

Three dogs. That was a lot. Ava glanced down the bar again, to where Kristen was now fixing a cup of tea for Marian Freely. Kristen was laughing at something the older woman was saying, her smile lighting her whole face.

"The dogs are welcome," Ava said. "We'll meet up tomorrow and work out the details."

"Thank you. The dogs are very good, to be honest. Kristen is already giving up a lot of things, but I won't ask her to give up her pets."

"Of course. It sounds like you and Kristen worked everything out."

"Not everything, but we're getting there. During the rest of this school year, she'll spend at least one weekend a month in Raleigh with me and get to know the town a little. We haven't made plans for the summer yet."

"And after that?"

"After that, we'll see." Her gaze locked with Ava's. "You're a good person, Ava. Thank you for all you've done for Julie, Kristen, and me."

"I'm glad I can help."

Ellen pulled her teacup closer. "I gave Kristen the rest of Erma's tea."

Ava blinked. She couldn't imagine how much that had cost Ellen. "That was generous of you."

"Kristen needed to see her mother."

"That couldn't have been easy."

Ellen's smile quavered, but only for a second. She used a spoon to remove the tea bag and carefully set it on the edge of her saucer. "It was the hardest thing I've ever done, but also the easiest. Kristen needed to see her mother one last time. I couldn't get in the way of that."

Ava could see the pain in Ellen's eyes. "You're a good mom, Ellen Foster. One of the best."

Ellen laughed then, a genuine, soft laugh. "I'm better at it now than I used to be. That's all I can say." She collected her tea. "If you'll excuse me, I think I'll have a chat with Kristen's dad. It would be in all our best interests if he and I got to know each other a little better."

Ava watched her make her way to where Dylan stood. He looked over Ellen's head and smiled at Ava.

Ava smiled back. He was a nice guy. Really nice. And wow, he looked good in his suit.

The door opened, and Doc Bolton came in with Tom Moore, the ex-mayor-turned-fishing-guide. Doc and Tom had recently become fishing buddies. They were talking striped bass as they made a beeline to the cupcakes.

Over the next half hour, more and more people wandered in, chatting and laughing and excitedly selecting scones and muffins and various hot drinks. By the time the clock hit seven thirty, Ava's Pink Magnolia Tearoom was packed.

The last person to arrive was Sarah. Ava, who'd been moving from group to group, grateful to her toes for the smiles that greeted her, immediately went to greet her sister.

Sarah watched as Ava approached, no welcoming smile on her face.

Ava's heart sunk. *She's still mad. I should have expected that.* Ava took a deep breath and plunged in. "Sarah, I'm so, so sorry —"

"Shush." Sarah grabbed Ava's hand and held it between her own. "I already know you're sorry. So am I. I'm sorry I got so angry. But it hurt, Ava. That's all I can say."

Ava blinked back tears. "I know, I know. I was so wrong. I'll never again keep a secret from you. And I'll never, *ever* give anyone a tea they didn't ask for, you or anyone else. And I'll —"

"Sheesh, Ava! That's enough!" Sarah laughed, a low, wry laugh that warmed her gray-green eyes. "We need to move on, but this is going to take some time. Months, maybe longer."

That hurt, but Ava nodded. "We'll work on it, you and I. And I'll do whatever I can to make things right again."

Sarah pursed her lips. "Well . . . I could use some help right now."

"Name it, and I'll do it."

Sarah leaned in closer and whispered, "I have a date with Blake and I need to find something to wear."

"*Sarah!* That's —"

Sarah squeezed Ava's hand so hard it hurt.

"Shhh! Keep your voice down!"

Ava swallowed the rest of her sentence. "It's a secret, then." She glanced across the room at Blake, who, catching her eye, lifted his coffee cup in a silent toast.

*He should have told me, the wretch.*

Sarah looked around to make sure no one was close enough to hear and said in a low voice, "Blake and I want to try things out without everyone in town being involved. I haven't told anyone but you."

"I won't tell a soul."

"Oh, I'm sure you won't. You're good at secrets."

Ava grimaced. "Most secrets are horrible. It'll be nice to have one that's wonderful."

Sarah flushed, looking pleased. "You think it's wonderful?"

"Very."

"So do I." Sarah's smile bloomed. "Blake and I haven't figured everything out yet, and who knows if it'll work, but I think trying might be very . . . rewarding."

Ava laughed. "I'm not even going to ask what that means. Oh, Sarah, it's going to be wonderful having you back home! Did you already leave your things, or . . ." Her words faded when Sarah shook her head.

"Ava, I'm not moving back home."

*"What?"*

"I signed a lease for an apartment today."

"But — Sarah, why? You've never lived anywhere else."

"It wasn't an easy decision to make. But I've been thinking a lot these past few weeks. When Mom died, you stepped in. And you were wonderful. I couldn't have asked for a better caretaker."

Ava winced. "Except for —" She waved her hand.

"The tea. That was a mistake. But you had good intentions, and I know how difficult that time must have been for you. You were grieving just as much as I was, and you had a ton of new additional responsibilities — me, the house, our finances." Sarah added in a thoughtful tone, "You did all of that and you were barely more than a kid yourself."

"If our situations were reversed, you'd have done the same for me."

"I wouldn't have done it half as well. I've come to realize that over the years, I've taken you for granted. I think just about everyone in this town has."

Ava's face grew warm. "I enjoy taking care of you."

"You do it well, maybe too well. And that's not always a good thing. Right now, we both need some space to live our own lives."

Ava wanted to argue. She missed having her sister around. But she couldn't help but realize that Sarah had changed over these past few weeks. She had a new air of confidence and maturity. Maybe, just maybe, she was right. Ava sighed. "I'm going to miss you."

"How? I plan on having lunch in your tearoom every single day. Which reminds me, is there a friends-and-family discount?"

Ava had to laugh. "I hadn't thought about it, but I'm sure we can work something out."

"Good. I'm on a budget now, and it's not pretty." Sarah's eyes twinkled as she reached over and gave Ava a huge hug. "I'm going to miss you, too. But I don't mean for this to last forever. I'll be moving back eventually."

Ava only hoped that was true. "You have to do what's best for you. And don't worry about me. It appears that I'm going to have a roommate, at least for a while. Starting in April, Kristen is going to be staying with me during the week."

"Wow! A teenager. It'll be just like old times. I'm sure you'll keep an eye on her."

"Like a hawk. I'm surprised Ellen's trusting me, but it's nice. I'd like Kristen to be happy."

"She will be." Sarah glanced toward Kristen. "Uh-oh. People are starting to line up, and poor Kristen looks overwhelmed."

Ava glanced at the bar. "Oof! You're right. I'd better go help her. Catch you later?"

Sarah nodded. "You know it!"

Ava watched her sister join Zoe and Jess where they stood near the window, admiring the teapots on display. They welcomed Sarah with a loud, boisterous greeting, hugging her as if they hadn't just seen her hours before.

Smiling, Ava slipped behind the counter and was soon helping Kristen serve tea, coffee, and desserts to an ever-changing line of friends and customers.

It had been a long, tiring day, but Ava didn't want it to end. She wasn't quite convinced that Sarah would ever move back home. After all, that was Sarah's decision and not hers. But Ava knew one thing: they were sisters now, and forever.

That was the thing about love, Ava decided. Even when damaged by life's uncertainties, if given enough care, effort, and sunlight, it could bloom again.

# EPILOGUE

In an elegant apartment off Rue Saint-Rustique in the heart of the sophisticated Montmartre district of Paris, Ella Dove woke up, her legs tangled in the silk sheets of her massive, gilded, king-size bed. The large doors to the terrace off her bedroom were open, a sharp, unusually strong breeze billowing through the sheer white drapes and carrying in the marvelous scents and quiet chatter from the bakery below.

Ella sat up, her thick blond hair, darker than that of any of her sisters, tangled over one shoulder. Beside her on the pillow, sleeping deeply, was her current "friend." Gabriel was a tall, handsome French chef and an expert lover. Sadly, he had the unfortunate tendency to use the word *I* far too often, which had doomed him to temporary status in Ella's bed. He was not yet aware of this fact, but he soon would be.

For now, Ella closed her eyes and breathed

in the smell of buttery croissants, sweet macarons, rich mille-feuilles, and fruit-laden tarte tatins. Her bakery was located below the apartment, and she'd made every tempting morsel now being served and on display in the glass windows. She shivered at the delicious smells and then slipped out of the bed, her bare feet whisper quiet on the thick rug as, draped in her silk sheet, she walked to the open balcony doors.

She paused there, closed her eyes, and let the breeze whip around her, teasing her hair and tugging at her sheet as if trying to persuade her to follow it outside, over the railing, and into the morning sun. The breeze grew stronger, and a murmur of protest came from the diners sitting at the tables in the little square below as their tablecloths danced around them.

Ella pulled her sheet over her shoulders, holding it like a great cloak, and stepped onto the balcony just as a gust, bigger than the last, swept through. Napkins flew from the diners' laps, and shopping bags were blown over, while a newspaper, ripped from the top of a stack at the newsstand on the corner, tumbled across the cobblestones. The wind carried the newspaper through the maze of tables, going right, then left, then right again until it fell open right below

Ella's balcony.

The wind ceased with the same sudden- ness that it had started. Ella, standing at the edge of her balcony, looked down at the tumbled newspaper, which had opened to the "Monde" section. A picture of a hand- some older man at the bottom left page made her gasp.

She bent down, trying to read the words in the article even though she was too far away.

Not that it mattered, because the second she saw it, she knew the time had come.

Ella Dove was going home.

# ACKNOWLEDGMENTS

A big thanks to my agent, Nancy Yost, my light in the dark. Thank you for taking a chance on me and Dove Pond.

A special shout-out to fabulous editor Lauren McKenna, who started me on this magical venture. You were an inspiration from day one and continue to be so today.

And an equally big shout-out to my new editors, Sara Quaranta and Abby Zidle, for their exquisite patience when the uncertainty and stress of the pandemic affected my writing schedule. Thank you for being thorough, optimistic, and clear as a bell. My bruised soul needed exactly that.

# A CUP OF SILVER LININGS
## KAREN HAWKINS
## A BOOK CLUB GUIDE

1. When Ellen Foster is first introduced in chapter 1 at her daughter's funeral, she isn't the most likable character. What life circumstances make her this way? As the story progressed, did your opinion of her change? Why?

2. Ava Dove's secret is determined to break free from its enchanted prison. Whose good opinion was Ava unwilling to risk by revealing her own mistakes? How does the revelation affect Ava's relationship with that person? With herself?

3. Julie Foster calls her bipolar disorder "bipolar lite." What benefits does it bring to her life? What frustrations? How does her condition affect her relationships with the people of Dove Pond? With her daughter, Kristen?

4. While growing up, Kristen asks to meet her dad only once, when she wants him to take her to a father-daughter dance at school, but she changes her mind when she realizes it would upset her mother. After her mother's death, Kristen realizes that finding her dad could potentially make her life more complicated, not less. In what way was that so?

5. Sarah and Blake have a long, uncomfortable history mainly due to Sarah's inability to simply be herself whenever he's around. Have you ever known people who were unable to "be themselves" around someone they might be interested in romantically? Did they ever overcome it? How?

6. Much of *A Cup of Silver Linings* deals with grief and the different ways people navigate sorrow. How does Ellen handle her grief compared with the way Kristen manages hers? How does this difference affect their relationship with each other?

7. Because of Ava's tea, Ellen gets the chance to speak with her daughter again and say the things she should have said when Julie was alive. During these conversations, Ellen has to face some uncomfort-

able self-truths about her decisions as a parent. What does she learn that helps her become a better parent to her granddaughter?

8. Grief can be caused by more than death. Grief can also be caused by a betrayal. Once Ava's secret breaks free, Sarah has a very good reason to be angry with Ava, as Ava well knows. We see in the final chapter that Sarah has found the strength to forgive Ava, although Sarah warns that it will take time for their relationship to return to normal. They both also realize that their relationship will be forever changed by it. Have you ever been betrayed? Did you experience a sort of grief, too? How did you overcome it?

# ABOUT THE AUTHOR

*New York Times* and *USA Today* bestselling author **Karen Hawkins** writes novels that have been praised as touching, witty, charming, and heartwarming. A native Southerner who grew up in the mountains of East Tennessee where storytelling is a way of life, Karen recently moved to frosty New England with her beloved husband and multiple foster dogs. The Dove Pond series is a nod to the thousands of books that opened doors for her to more adventures, places, and discoveries than she ever imagined possible. To find out more about Karen, check in with her at Facebook.com/Karen HawkinsWriter, @KarenHawkinsAuthor on Instagram, and at her website, KarenHawkins .com.